THE GLORIES

I am a local author. If you enjoyed this book, please spread the word!

7/4/26

Richard Milne

The Glories

First published in 2025 by Richard Milne.

Copyright © Richard Milne in 2025.

All Rights Reserved. No part of this publication may be reproduced, stored in a retrieval system, or transmitted, in any form or by any means, electronic, mechanical, photocopying, recording, or otherwise, without the prior written permission of the author, nor be otherwise circulated in any form of binding or cover other than that in which it is published, and without a similar condition being imposed on the subsequent publisher.

All characters in this publication are fictitious, other than a handful of real politicians and TV personalities who are mentioned or make cameo appearances. Other than these, any resemblance to real persons, living or dead, is purely coincidental.

By the same author:

Misjudgement Day (Novel).

Rhododendron (factual; Reaktion Books).

Bojo's Woe Show book 1: A Cabinet of Horrors (Cartoon anthology).

Bojo's Woe Show book 2: A Plague of Idiots (Cartoon anthology).

Bojo's Woe Show book 3: The Fall of Chaos (Cartoon anthology).

Countless scientific papers about things to do with plant evolution.

DR RICHARD MILNE is an evolutionary plant biologist who writes cartoons and novels in his (currently very limited) spare time. His eclectic CV includes a lot of research on plant biogeography and hybridisation, the curate's egg of publications listed above, a few articles for Bylines Scotland, and four awards from students for his off-beat teaching style. You can experience this yourself by searching for "*Can nettles swim? The riddle of how plants cross oceans*" on Youtube. His first love is wild flowers, which he has been hunting in the British countryside since he was about 7, and for the past four years he has been systematically photographing the entire British flora to build an identification resource for the public. This is now available at namethatplant.org.

@milneorchid.bsky.social

Acknowledgements.

Sincere thanks are due to my very good friends Elena Brebner and Mike Long, and my lovely wife Nenya, for carefully reading this story, meticulously picking up errors, and suggesting improvements. I am grateful to the six first year students who posed for the cover image of the book. I also thank Regina Spector, whose song "*The Genius Next Door*" inspired the central idea of this book.

For Lawrence, who is magnificent.

PART ONE

"Some said the local lake had been enchanted, others said it must have been the weather."

Regina Spektor, "The Genius Next Door"

Chapter 1: The lake

Antony

On the day I saw a Glory, everything changed. I'd got up that morning, bored as hell, stuck at home like everybody else, as we tried to hide from this new 'Corona' virus that had swept across the world. Spring 2020, I'm sure you remember. That world is gone now, at least for me.

My name is Antony Blake, and I lived at 21 Hawk Street in Swinton, when it all started. Not Swindon, Swinton. It was a boringly ordinary street, neither rich nor poor. Small gardens, if you could call them that, since mostly they were grass and not much else. Our house was the one with the massive perfect rainbow for the NHS on it. Gran made it a 'project' for me, so I had to use string and protractors to get the curves exactly right across two dozen sellotaped-together sheets of paper in a rainbow shape. Then I had to colour them all in, even though I'm 16 and not six. It had to be the best rainbow on our street. She's like that. I'm not complaining, because I'd had nothing much better to do. It's odd to think how bored I was, before the Glory.

I'd heard the rumours about Glories, of course. There was nothing about them on the telly, which Father said proved they were just some silly invention, a fever-dream from people stuck at home with nothing to do except make up stories. I thought he was probably right – how could a massive patch of bright colour just simply appear somewhere for a few hours, and then vanish again? Jay from our Dungeons and Dragons club was obsessed with them though, scanning the internet for any descriptions and then regaling us with them during our now virtual game sessions. He went out searching for them every day in the hills near our town, stretching the rules about daily exercise as far as they would go. But he'd never yet seen one. Only a handful had ever been recorded, by that point.

After breakfast, I'd been standing in the back garden, playing Swingball with myself, batting the ball on the string one way, and then the other. Part of my new routine of pointless things to fill up the day. Other than the odd grudging chess match, Father doesn't do games. He's never seen the point of them, especially since Mum died. Everything needs to have a purpose, with him. Gran once told me that that is why there's no 'h' in my name, and I've never been sure if she was joking. He used to be different before Mum died, and I can just about remember there being more light and more laughs in the house. Anyway, you can't imagine Gran playing Swingball, so I played it with myself, counting how many hits I could rack up before I missed one. And then, as often happened, Daniel's face popped up from the alley behind the fence. Bright eyes full of mischief, framed in golden-blonde hair. He was my cousin, two years younger than me, and he lived a few streets away.

"Jeebus, Cuz!" he said. "Only you could lose a one-man tennis game against yourself!"

"Actually, I held myself to a draw," I replied.

"Whatever. You gonna come and do something more interesting, or what?"

What he meant was, time for me and him to break the rules by going for a walk together. Daniel loved breaking rules, and always had done. He had a

Chapter 1: The Lake

round face that my Gran called 'cherubic'. He could make eyes at you like a puppy that wanted to be loved, and grown-ups totally fell for it all the time. Especially Gran. It didn't work on me, so he would just tell me I was boring, instead, if I didn't agree to do things with him. Before the lockdown he did all this stuff with kids from school, and whenever he got in trouble someone else always got the blame, because they couldn't do the puppy eyes. Other boys, teachers, or somehow even me, but never Daniel. But now, it seemed he couldn't get the other boys to come out of their houses and join him, so boring old Antony would have to do instead. The last resort. I never knew how Daniel got out of the house on his own, but he did.

Apparently Daniel's mum was scared that some horror would befall him, out on his own, so Gran had said I should go with him, whenever he turned up. The ideas of trying to stop him sneaking out, or marching him back home, were never even mentioned. So I did what I always did, tapped on the window to tell Gran he had appeared, then left the house for my 'daily exercise', then meet Daniel in a nearby alley. After that we'd walk together and say we were brothers if anyone asked, or scare them away with a faked coughing fit. We'd walk, and find places to trespass that were empty because of the lockdown. We started with a swanky private golf course, but when we saw an old lady walking her dog across one of the greens, I'd said to Daniel that perhaps this particular idea wasn't as 'badass' as we'd thought. He'd responded with one of those withering, icy stares that he sometimes does, and we'd walked off the course without another word. After that we'd got into a couple of temporarily abandoned building sites, and even our old primary school. This time, Daniel announced to me that I was to choose the day's location. I thought for a moment and said, "Swynn Hill."

"Jeebus, Cuz! I've done Swynn Hill already!"

Swynn Hill is right on the edge of our town. It's part of some posh estate and there are signs telling everyone to get lost. There didn't use to be – I can just about remember Mum taking us here when she was alive. She used to enjoy just walking, and showing us things. Flowers she didn't know the name of, or the cows in a field that's now been turned into houses. But when she died, Father stopped being interested in walking. He wasn't really interested in anything back then, and that's why Gran eventually came here to 'sort him out.' Family walks did resume, but they became serious missions – route marches with no space for frivolity.

We had tried to go to Swynn Hill right after the funeral, because Mum had wanted her ashes scattered there, only to find that the estate had changed hands, and visitors were no longer welcome. I don't know what happened to her ashes after that, Father and Gran never told me.

"What, you went there on your own?" I asked Daniel, now.

"No, you dimwit. Me and some mates, last year."

There was nowhere else I could think of that I wanted to go, so I said, "But now we'll be breaking two rules at a time, won't we?"

"Yeah well, your call, Cuz." He didn't sound impressed, but I was buoyed by the chance to finally return to this place that my mother had loved so much. Daniel explained that the open path up the hill was a no-go, with signs claiming video surveillance, even though he reckoned that was a lie, but it was also plainly visible from several house windows. But the slope of the hill facing our town was clothed in dense woodland, and we could get to the top through that.

Chapter 1: The Lake

At the bottom of the slope was a high brick wall, with a lane running parallel to it on the town side. In one place, the lane curved around a small group of trees that were on the town side of the wall, and that would give us the cover we needed to climb over. "We can get almost to the top inside the woods," he said, grinning, as he used one of the small trees to scramble up to the top of the wall. "And we have to sign a tree at the top!"

"Sign a tree?"

"Yeah, otherwise they won't know we've been there, stupid."

"We didn't do that in the other places."

"That's because they're not owned by rich arseholes."

"OK, fair point," I said, starting my own climb up while he grinned from the top of the wall.

After scrambling through all manner of low shrubs, thorns and God knows what else, Daniel showed me a tree that he and his mates had signed, by cutting into its bark a series of names I didn't recognise. "You gotta choose a name," Daniel said. "I'm *Crux*."

"Uh, I'll be Calleth," I said, recalling a character I'd been in a role-playing game.

"If that's the best you can do," he said, with a weary expression.

"So do I sign here?" I asked.

"No, stupid. I *said*. We're going right up to the top. We're gonna sign a tree where the rich bastard will see it."

At that moment, he was glaring at me with his 'why is my cousin such a square' expression, while I was turning to start moving up the wooded slope again. And that's why I saw it first.

"Uh, what's that?" I said, pointing.

"Jeebus Twist!" he replied.

It was a beautiful blue lake, lying ten, maybe twenty metres up the slope from us, visible as a shimmering patch of deep, clear blue through the trees. We walked on up to its edge, saying nothing. Normally ponds have some sort of border. I didn't really realise that until I saw this one, which didn't. There were no tall grasses or rushes, no patches of wet sand, no mud. Just the forest floor stopping and the blue water starting. And my, how that water was blue. I had never seen water so blue. I wasn't sure I'd ever seen anything so blue. I stared and stared at it. Maybe I was avoiding looking at the thing about it that was so obviously impossible. Eventually, I remember, I made myself look up. I got so dizzy I almost fell over. The far side was definitely a whole lot higher than the near side. The entire lake was on a slope, as steep as the sides of the hill it was sitting on. To make things worse, it didn't have an even surface; some bits bulged up, and some down, and the water in these just stayed where it was, even though the ripples happily passed across them. I remember looking at the trees at the side for perspective, but they all stood defiantly upright, proving that the lake was sloping. There was an odd rhododendron bush on the left-hand side, looking like part of it had been cut away to make room for the lake, like one of those pictures of the Earth that you get in text books, sliced open like a cake so you can see the inside.

With a trembling hand, I brought out my mobile phone with its cracked screen and buttons that Daniel said makes it older than him. But it had a camera. I texted one word to Jay, the guy who'd told me all that incredible stuff

Chapter 1: The Lake

he'd read off the internet, which I now knew had to be at least partly true. And who'd told me the name of what I was looking at.

'*Glory.*'

Then I took a photo. Only, the image in the camera did not have any blue in it. The Glory wasn't there. Just trees, bare ground and bluebell leaves, and the same rhododendron bush, only in the picture, it didn't have any part of it missing. I lowered the camera; the Glory was still there, just as before. I recalled how someone had asked Jay if he'd seen any photos of Glories online, and Jay had replied, 'you can't photograph them, idiot!' I would draw it when I got home, I decided. No, I'd paint it. I was pretty sure there were oil paints in our cellar, sitting there unused since Mum died. So now, I just stared at the Glory, running my eyes over every part of it, taking it in. At some point, I think I saw a face in its centre, somehow both above and below the ripples. A beautiful woman's face, and I started to think that maybe it might be my mother. But then I blinked, and the face was gone. My heart started beating very fast, but I recall allowing myself to calm down, and realising there was no need to be afraid.

A little later, I knelt down and scooped up some water in my hand, surprised to find that this was possible. The water in my hand was blue, and it continued to ripple as if connected still to the rest of the lake. Feeling that it might bite me, I let it drop back to where it came from. It re-entered the rest without a splash, or even a ripple, like a damp snowflake being swallowed up by wet pavement.

I turned my head upward again, to take in the whole thing. I had never seen anything so beautiful, and I felt I could stay there and stare at it for ever. Maybe I would have done, but something, I think it was maybe a bird taking flight, made me snap out of it. I felt like I'd woken from a dream. "Daniel?" I said, looking left, but he wasn't there. I looked right, and he wasn't there either. He was gone.

Chapter 2: One last walk

Julia

So that was it, then. The last, tiny chance, snuffed out.

My eyes ran along the swirling lines of the little wooden table as I put the phone down. I stood up, but everything tilted sideways, so I sat down again. "It was nice of him to call me in person," I said to myself gently. "He sounded so upset." I stood up again, more carefully this time.

"Looks like you won, Bernard," I said, leaning on the wall as I made my way to the window. Yes, I call my cancer Bernard. Bernard the Third, to be precise, after his two predecessors were zapped by the NHS, but like all wise despots, they each left behind a son and heir. Bernard the Third is more prolific, he's the Boris Johnson of cancers, with children all over my body that he's never even met. Early on, during the reign of Bernard the First, I'd found this woman on an online support forum, all crystals and chanting and healing energy probably, telling everyone that all you needed to do to beat cancer was talk to it. Goodness me, I'd typed in reply, why hadn't anyone thought of that before? I was in the angry phase back then. But I'd caught myself doing it less than a day later, and you can't talk to something without giving it a name. Well I can't, anyway.

I made it to the window. A pigeon flew past, banking hard as it passed close by. There was no human life to observe, though, as whole minutes ticked past without a single car or pedestrian coming along the road. I turned to the little orchid in a pot that was gazing out of the window with me. "Looks like you'll be getting a new owner soon, Jenny. You're not going to flower again, are you? I mean, not in time for me to see it. That's OK. I love you anyway."

Sixty-one isn't old. Seventy is a bit old, eighty and ninety are properly old. Sixty-one is the sort of age that you thought was old, when you were a kid and you couldn't believe you'd ever get there. Well I did get there, but it looked like I wouldn't be going any further. "I'm going to die here, Jenny," I declared softly. "The hospitals are full of people with that horrible virus. No space for a hopeless case like me, with a one in God-knows-how-small chance of survival. Did you hear that doctor's voice? He was almost crying, poor man, and I don't think it was over me. It must be utterly awful there. So I'll be staying right here, with you."

I moved slowly through my house, somehow feeling like I'd already become a ghost, ahead of time. Was it better, I wondered, to have certainty, instead of riding that nauseating emotional rollercoaster of flickering hope? There'd be no more moments when I woke from a nap feeling refreshed, and briefly thinking that I might survive. Now, I had to accept what was coming, and make the best of the days that remained to me. The last, dwindling scraps from the table of life. I gazed at the painting on the wall, the one my mother did. It had been there for fifteen years, ever since we'd sold my childhood home after she died. She was there, somehow, in every brush stroke, every detail. What was I going to leave for Nick? I never learned to paint.

Chapter 2: one last walk

In the bedroom, I came to the picture of Nick, Gina and baby Tabitha. Instantly I was carried back to a month before the lockdown, and Tabby was running down the path to cuddle "Gabba," as she calls me. And then they were leaving, and she was cuddling me again, "Don't want to leave Gabba," she'd cried as they prized us apart. But for her it was a game, she didn't understand that she'd never get to cuddle me again. They hadn't told her anything, of course, about Bernard or the lockdown that we all thought was coming. But children sense things, don't they? I was sitting on the bed now, eyes swimming with tears. It was only the thought of her that gave me the strength to go through with the new round of treatments. Dr Singh had, as always, been brutally honest. Quantity of life versus quality of life. Tabby didn't want to leave Gabba. Well, Gabba didn't want to leave either, but sometimes we don't get a choice. The thought that I would never get to hold her again was almost unbearable.

After a while I gathered up all the soggy tissues from the bed and dumped them in the bin, then tottered into the kitchen. Tea would make it better. Tabby's pencil drawings were scattered over the walls, real ones and print-outs of scans that Nick had emailed me. She was good, for her age. A few days earlier, I'd rearranged them all in chronological order, so you could see the stick people with huge heads gradually morphing into more realistic figurines. My mother's skill had skipped two generations. Maybe Tabby would be an artist when she grew up. I'd never know. The tea tasted lovely. For some reason I'd started to like it with extra sugar.

I actually felt quite good today. The sun was shining outside. I hadn't left the house all week. Nick had reeled off a long list of things I wasn't to do, with going into shops near the top of it. What he'd meant of course was that if I caught the virus in my frail condition, then it would finish me off faster than Bernard. Funnily enough I'd worked that out myself, but I hadn't said so. One can put up with being patronised when it comes from a place of love.

Nick didn't even want me to leave the house, but the empty streets outside felt safe enough. Plus the sun was out, and I had strength in my legs that might not be there the next day, or perhaps any day after that. Today might be the last walk I ever took.

I slipped off the long, pale nightgown that I'd been wearing non-stop for the past two days, or was it three? I got dressed. It was hard work, and I had to stop for a little rest halfway through, but I wanted to look smart, like a healthy person. I even put on a little blusher, to reduce the deathliness of my pallor. I brushed my hair, still miraculously curly, brown and attached. I'd never go grey now. Next, I dug out my mother's walking stick from the stygian depths of the understair cupboard. Finally, I tottered to the front door. Was it really a good idea to go out in this state? Probably not. But staying in felt pointless. "Mind the house for me, Ethel," I told the Kentia palm in the hallway.

I remembered how, when we'd first moved here, Geoffrey and I used to walk on the downs two or three times a week. It was why we'd chosen this house. Just five minutes' walk, and you were into the countryside. But he was gone now, had been gone a decade, and today the hills loomed ahead of me like a distant mountain, a daunting and impossible challenge. A tingle ran down my

Chapter 2: one last walk

spine. It was one of those perfect spring days where the air was crisp and cool, but the warm sun stroked my skin like a lover's touch. There was no need to reach the top. There were woods on the lower slopes, where I could sit and look at spring flowers. That would do, for me. One last little day in the sun.

I reached the small crossroads, about twelve houses up from mine. Already I felt tired. Crossing the little road felt like a challenge, but I made it. The upper half of my own road continued on for at least another thirty houses' worth. Two and a half times what I'd managed so far. At the far end, there would be a main road to cross, after which it became the little country lane that eventually mounted the hill. A young man was walking along in the other direction. He saw me, nodded, and walked into the road to give me space.

I made it to nine houses past the crossroads. Yes, I was counting them. I soldiered on, but by the sixteenth house, halfway to the main road, tiredness had come up on me like a surging tide, a personalised form of gravity pulling down on every part of my body. I didn't know if I could go any further. I wasn't even sure if I could make it back home. A crazy notion flitted through me, to keep going, climb the hillside and find a quiet spot and just … stay there. No, no, I was being silly. I could outlast this lockdown, and then there might be a tiny chance I'd see Tabby again. I guessed that this would be as close as I was going to get to the hills. I took one last long, lingering look at the unattainable hilltop.

And then I saw it.

It was as if it had appeared out of thin air.

A swirl of bright colours had winked into existence on top of the hill. It was a perfect circle, containing a spiral of liquid colours a bit like one of those huge lollipops you used to get at fairgrounds. Judging from a patch of trees on the slope, the thing was at least twenty metres in diameter.

"Are you in my brain now, Bernard?" I muttered. I screwed my eyes shut, counted to three and opened them again, expecting it to be gone. But it was resolutely still there. All the colours of the rainbow, only brighter. The red was as vivid as a field of poppies in the sunlight.

"Come on, woman, think now. If I'm making this thing up, then it'll move if I turn my head, won't it?" So I did. Moved my eyeline one way, and then the other. The luminous lollipop remained stubbornly fixed to the top of the hill. Slowly I found myself accepting that it was actually there. I'd heard of rare clouds that take on pastel rainbow shades, but this was no cloud. Clouds were not perfectly circular.

A young man was jogging along the pavement towards me. He was about four metres away before he even noticed I was there, and made a sharp turn towards the road.

"Please!" I called. "Could you help me a moment?"

He stopped between two parked cars and looked at me gormlessly, as if he hadn't known till now that other people could talk. Cautiously he pulled the headphones from his ears and stepped back onto the pavement, eyeing me warily.

"I'm really sorry," I stuttered, "but I think I may be seeing things. Could you … could you have a quick look at the hill behind you and tell me if you see anything odd?"

Chapter 2: one last walk

He looked at me condescendingly for a moment, then shrugged and turned his head for a quick glance behind him. His head wobbled comically, and then he turned his whole body towards the hill and stood, motionless.

"You can see it, can't you?" I called. "Can you tell me what you see?"

He didn't respond, just stood stock still for long moments, then brought up his phone to photograph the scene ahead of him. Then he brought it up to his face and gazed at the screen. Why do young people do that? Why pore over photos when the real thing is right in front of them?

"They're real," he said, still facing away from me. "Oh my God, they're real."

"What are real?" I asked, closing the gap between us to the legal 2 metre range.

"Glories!" he said, his voice full of wonder. "It's a Glory!"

"What are Glories?" I asked, feeling unaccountably stupid.

"That is," he said, pointing at the thing on the hill. "You're not on social media, are you, love?"

"Well, no," I said, tartly.

"Government's been trying to hush it up, haven't they? People reckon it's 'cos of the lockdown. TBH I thought it was just some wacko conspiracy myself, till just now! My God, it's beautiful! I'm gonna get closer!"

"Please!" I said. "What are they? What are these 'Glories'?"

"No-one knows, do they? Or if they do, they ain't tellin'. Story goes, they just appear out of nowhere, usually away from towns, big and weird and beautiful. Hang in the air for a few hours then … *pouff*! They're gone. Did you see this one appear? Out of nowhere?"

"I think so, yes," I croaked. "Just before I called to you."

"Then it'll probably hang around two, three, or four hours more. But I've heard that some are gone much faster, so I'm going up there, right now! You should too, if you can! They're supposed to be really rare!" And before I could reply, he was off, running down the pavement away from me, towards the Glory.

I tried to process what he'd said. They appeared from nowhere, then vanished again, no-one knew why, and the government were trying to hush them up. It sounded utterly preposterous. And yet there it was, on the hill in front of me. I found myself staring at it, and it seemed to enlarge as I watched, the spiral of colours rotating yet staying still. A family of four came bundling out of a house across the road, all wearing masks, the children pointing right at the Glory. "Magic," said the little girl. The father ushered them into the car with promises that they were going to get closer.

I wanted to get closer, too. I'd started walking again, though I didn't recall deciding to. I pushed away my exhaustion and background nausea, as far as I could. The walk felt like a mission now. I passed ten houses then had to lean on a lamp post, gasping for breath. Other people were emerging from various houses as I passed, some alone, some in family groups. A few seemed content to gaze from their front gardens, while others headed off towards the hill by foot, bike or car. One woman asked me if I was OK.

"I'd give you a hand if I could," she said, "but we're not supposed to …"

"I know," I told her with a weak smile. "I'm fine, just a little out of breath."

Chapter 2: one last walk

She probably thought I was about ninety.

How long did the man say these things hung around for? Two or three hours? Had I any hope of reaching the hilltop within that time? I wasn't even sure I could do it by nightfall. I started walking again, pushing back the industrial-grade tiredness inside me. After this I was going to have to sleep for a week, at least. I made it to, and across, the main road, and started along the little lane. People overtook me from time to time, swinging out into the middle of the road to give me distance. Many were on the phone as they walked. "I dunno what the fuck it is," said one, "but it's on top of the hill, like a giant glowing beachball, and it's fucking huge! You need to get up there and see it, man!"

The road bent to the right (another milestone!) and beyond this point, a strip of trees began on the left-hand side. I saw a patch of deep purple violets, and a single plant with delightful papery blue flowers but pinkish red buds, and big white spots on its leaves. I lowered myself awkwardly into a kneeling position to admire them. There was a patch of tiny daffodils nearby, almost gone over. Daffodils. All the ones in my garden were over, and all in the other gardens I'd seen, too. This was very probably the last daffodil flower I would ever clap eyes upon. I touched it with a shaking finger and then raised my head, taking a breath. Things were spinning again, the world tipping sideways and then repeatedly righting itself. How far was it to the top? The road hadn't even started climbing yet. I felt like I was at the base camp of Everest without any oxygen. Maybe I should just stop where I was for a bit. Maybe seeing these flowers was accomplishment enough.

"Mrs Barnes! Are you alright?"

A little delivery van had stopped, and I recognised the young man who had carried food to my door a few times recently.

"I'm ... well ... a bit tired," I said.

"Are you trying to get to the Glory?"

"I was ..." I croaked. "Stupid woman that I am, I'm nowhere near strong enough."

"Do you wanna get in the back? Van's almost empty, don't think it breaks any rules."

"Bless you, but ... there's no way I could climb in."

Behind the van a car hooted angrily, and then squeezed past the van on the other side. Two more followed. The van driver jumped out, ran round to the back, and pulled out six plastic crates, with which he built a set of three steps at the back. "There you go, Mrs Barnes, can you climb up that? Use the inside of the door as a bannister, I'll hold it firm from the other side."

The crates looked unsteady but they took my weight and didn't wobble much, and I made it into the van on all fours. What must I have looked like, doing that? The driver put the crates back in via the side door. "Lie flat, Mrs Barnes, and put your arms out so you don't roll. I'll go slow and steady." He closed the side and back doors, then it was almost dark. What if he was kidnapping me? The thought was almost funny, like stealing a rusted old car that would fall apart after half a mile. The engine started, and true to his word, he drove slowly and carefully. The floor was hard, but the vibrations were soothing, and almost restful.

Chapter 2: one last walk

Some minutes later, we stopped moving, and horns started hooting. The back doors were pulled open. "I'm sorry, Mrs Barnes, there's nowhere to park. I should have thought of this. We're as close as we can get to the top. Your best bet is to get out here. I'll have to drive on and look for somewhere." Behind us a mum and three kids disgorged from a car while the father stayed at the wheel. "I'll get the crates," said my driver.

"No need," I said. I might have had the fitness of a sprightly hundred-and-four-year-old, but my legs were only sixty-one. I shuffled backwards, and managed to exit by hanging my legs out and dangling them to the ground. "Thank you," I said. "I don't even know your name!"

"Robert."

"Thank you, Robert."

I tottered out of the road, between clumsily parked cars, and joined the socially distanced queue to go through the kissing gate, beyond which lay the footpath going to the top. Young and agile people were just climbing over the fence, some more adeptly than others. I tottered through the gate and started walking. The mother of three was leading her eager children up the path, with other walkers ahead of them. And beyond lay the technicolour disc. Focussed so much on the journey, I'd almost forgotten it was there. Now, close up, it was mind-blowing. Bigger than I'd thought before, about as wide as three or four houses, and hanging just above the ground on the hilltop. I couldn't decide at first if it was spherical or flat, but realised that it had to be a sphere, because I was looking at it from a different direction to when I first saw it, and it still looked perfectly round.

The colours were not just bright. They were beyond bright, beyond vivid. The grass by my feet was the fresh green of spring, and the sky above me a clear blue, yet both looked like the washed-out pastel shades of a long-faded photograph, when viewed beside the Glory. I had to get closer. One foot forward, then the next.

Two men were arguing in the middle of the path, their eyes fixed on the Glory. "I tell you, it's aliens!"

"No such thing as aliens!"

"Well, what the hell else can it be?"

"How would I know? Some government science thing gone wrong, probably!"

People were overtaking me, spreading out either side of the path to keep their distance. The effort cost them nothing. But to poor little me, the extra few metres required to swerve around the arguing duo felt too much. "Please," I croaked. "Could you move two metres to the side for me?"

They looked at me for a moment as if I, too, must have come from another planet, then nodded meekly and took a few steps sideways before continuing their argument.

"Thanks," I gasped. And on I struggled, another ten, then twenty metres. The thing seemed to fill half of the sky now. Many watchers had decided this was close enough, and were fanning out left and right, to find a socially distanced spot from which to gaze up at it. One or two of them were kneeling and praying.

Chapter 2: one last walk

Others were paying homage in a more modern way, by trying to film it on their phones, yet they kept pulling their phones down and looking oddly at them.

"What the hell is wrong with this thing?" said a young female voice close behind me.

"Glories can't be photographed," replied a deep, booming male voice that sounded vaguely familiar.

"*What*?" said the young woman.

"It is called a Glory," boomed the man, "and from everything I've heard, they don't show up on any kind of manmade image. Nothing but the human retina can perceive them."

"So you're saying my phone won't work? Shit. No-one's gonna believe me."

By now I'd turned to watch them. The young woman, somewhat ungraciously I thought, shoved her phone into her pocket and moved off from the path to find a spot to watch from. The man was about seventy, and very tall with silver hair. "Julia?" he said. "Is that you?"

"Errr ... yes," I replied, desperately trying to place him.

"Malcolm Phillips," he said. "From the book group!"

"Oh, of course! I should have recognised you, I'm afraid I'm a little unwell. Nothing you can catch, don't worry ..."

I'd only been a member for a few months, before Bernard had taken control of my life. "You look ..." he began, then paused. "You look like it took a lot of determination to get up here."

"You have no idea," I managed a weak smile. "You know about these things? These Glories?"

"I had to learn to do Twitter, they're all over social media. General consensus is the government has leant on the BBC and papers to keep it quiet, and they're pushing the line that it's some lunatic conspiracy, like 5G masts, etcetera. I wouldn't have believed it myself, except that a friend of my granddaughter saw one. It measured perhaps ten metres across, and was shaped like a perfect cube, and everything within that area was colourless, as if it were a black and white print. Even their clothes if they walked into it, but not their skin. She described how there were leaves right on the edge that were grey inside the borderline, but green outside it, and when they moved in the wind, the colours would switch on and off as they moved. Of course, it all came out in normal colours when they photographed it. Which reminds me, it's time for an experiment."

He pulled out a hulking great camera from his rucksack, seemingly unconcerned by the weight. "Dug this out from the loft," he said. "Polaroid! Still got a few shots left. Won't come out well, but I still want to see." He pointed it at the Glory and clicked. The camera spewed forth a square print and he waved it in the air. Then he flipped it over and looked. "Nope, chemically formed images don't record them either." He held the print towards me and I could just about make out the little image of a clear sky over the hilltop, with the odd cloud in it.

"It's ... incredible," I said. "Thank you for explaining."

Chapter 2: one last walk

"My pleasure. Would you like to approach it more closely?" he asked with a smile.

Well, he was an attractive man, and I distinctly recalled wondering if he was married, before Bernard pushed all thoughts of romance from my mind, and then stamped them all into a bloody mush. Still, some tiny seed of it remained, and the absurd thought of one last crazy, illegal fling gave me pleasure.

"Some people at the top are touching it," he added. "I'd like to know what it feels like. Want to come along?"

Thanks to Bernard, I probably didn't have enough blood left in me to blush, which at that moment was just as well.

I wished, so badly, that I could lean on his arm. Yes, it'd be romantic, but mostly I just really, really wanted the physical support. But he remained obediently two metres away from me, on my right side, as I slowly plodded upwards. More than once I told him I'd catch him up, but he insisted on staying with me. The Glory was now above us, obscuring the sun. "Look," he observed. "We've still got shadows. The sun will be about there," he said, pointing to a bright orange curving strip. You'll feel your eyes hurt if you look at it. Don't, I believe that the sun would burn your retina if you do."

"So you can't see the sun, but it can see you," I croaked.

"A nice way of putting it."

Just metres ahead, a tall man was reaching up and touching the Glory. Or was he? His hand was wobbling a bit. Beyond him a few others were doing the same. Some seemed to have forgotten the Two Metre Rule. I followed Malcolm as he veered to the side, around the tall man. "Let's see," he said, pushing his own hand up. "It pushes back," he said excitedly. "Like two magnets repelling each other! It pushes back!"

"Shortarse here will need to get a bit higher," I told him. His company seemed to have given me back a little of my lost energy. Though my legs still felt leaden, I tottered on upwards a bit faster than I'd gone before. Less than a foot over my head now was the confluence of the circling colours. "The middle," I said. "The middle of the spiral. It's over my head. Is it over yours?"

"Yes!" he replied. "Do you know, I never thought of that! Wherever I've viewed it from, I'm always looking at the centre of the spirals! It must be the same for everyone! How delightfully impossible!"

Gingerly I raised my hand, aiming for the centre point. The expected feeling of resistance didn't come. My finger reached the surface of the Glory, and made contact. Moments later, the lines of swirling colour began to run along my finger, across my hand, and up my arm. With it came a glorious tingling, somewhere between an orgasm and an electric shock, moving through my arm to my shoulder, my chest, and the rest of me. Now I was burning, but the flames were of sparkling pleasure, and the world around me dissolved into a maelstrom of swirling rainbow hues.

Chapter 3: The search

Antony

  I shouted Daniel's name. I told myself not to panic, that he was bound to be hiding nearby, waiting to jump out and surprise me. He didn't. So I ran around looking, checking inside bushes and looking up into the more climbable trees. After about twenty minutes of this, I started to worry. Daniel loved a prank, but he got bored very easily. It would be very unlike him indeed to wait this long to get to the punchline. A joke isn't funny if there's no-one about to laugh at. So I went back to the edge of the sloping lake, shouted his name in the most desperate voice I could manage, and pretended to cry. If he was playing a joke on me, there'd be no way he could resist jumping out and gloating if he saw me like that. But he didn't. Could he have somehow gone into the lake? Walked into it and drowned? I put forward a tentative foot and tried to step into the water, but I couldn't. The foot hovered just over the water, as if some invisible force was pushing it back. In desperation I took a few steps back, ran forward and jumped onto the lake. I landed on it, fell over, and then slid fast and helplessly back to the edge. So he couldn't have gone into it. Then I left the Glory and searched the woods again, going much further this time, but there was no sign of him, no clue where he'd gone.

  Don't panic, I told myself again. *He's probably gone off back home. He'll be sat there on the sofa now, pissing himself laughing.* Except that Daniel would not have gone home. Before the lockdown, when we went out doing stuff together, a parent would tell us a time to be back by. I would always be trying to get us home by the appointed time, while Daniel called me boring and square and a daddy's boy. I'd have to badger him, repeatedly, to go back, telling him they might not let us out next time, before he'd grudgingly concede. Typically I'd get him to his door about half an hour late, sometimes more. So the only way he'd have gone home was if someone had made him.

  I also knew that Daniel didn't like going off on his own. He let our parents think he did, but he didn't. However 'boring' I was, however 'lame' or 'annoying', he always stuck with me, unless we bumped into his cooler friends from school. Me, I was different, I quite liked walking on my own, but he seemed to hate it. He would always be out of breath from running, when he appeared at the garden fence. He couldn't have gone to a friend's house, because they wouldn't have let him in. So I couldn't see where he could be, at all. If I went to his house and he wasn't there, I'd get in all sorts of trouble for losing him. The only other thing I could think of was that he'd sneaked off to hide then got lost, so I decided to go back to the Glory and wait.

  I had a fairly good sense of direction, so I thought I'd find the Glory quite easily, but I didn't. I came out on the east side of the woods, where there's an open path, then doubled back and got all the way to the west side, marked by a wire fence. Somehow, I didn't pass the Glory, either time. In desperation I picked my way down to the bottom, found the place where we'd climbed over, and followed what I thought was the route we'd taken, recognising the odd snapped branch. But then I came to a patch of bluebell flowers that I didn't recall seeing before, and started to doubt myself. It was only when I came upon

Chapter 3: The search

the signed tree, with 'Crux' and the other names, that I knew where I was. So the Glory would have to be just up above me.

Except that it wasn't.

I walked up, slowly. There was no blue lake, only trees, just the same as everywhere else. There, too, was the rhododendron bush, intact again. And there were tree trunks, one large and several small, growing exactly where the lake had been. Where had they gone to? How had they come back?

I remember pinching myself, even hitting myself. Trying to wake myself up, because if it didn't make sense – and it certainly didn't – then it had to be a nightmare. Yet everything around me remained stubbornly real. I shouted Daniel's name, repeatedly, pointlessly. If I went to his house and he was there, the nightmare would end. If he wasn't … it didn't bear thinking about.

I had an idea. It was crazy dumb, but I couldn't think of anything better. I'd call their house, pretend to be one of his schoolmates, and ask to speak to Daniel. Simple! I reached for my phone, and found that it wasn't there. I searched the ground where I thought I'd been standing, just in case, but it wasn't anywhere to be seen. Okay, okay, I thought. Daniel must have nicked my phone. He was probably going around using it for prank calls, or to order stupid stuff to come to my house.

There wasn't much point hanging around the wood anymore, so I went down the slope, over the wall and onto the street. I spent the next fifteen minutes wandering the side streets of west Swinton, hoping to see Daniel, and also looking for a phone box. When I finally found one, I realised that I didn't have any coins on me, so that was a bust. I walked to the other places he and I have been. First the primary school, though I didn't go in, only circled around the edge. Then the two building sites. On the way, I caught sight of a woman pointing at me and saying something to her husband in a furtive way, on the other side of the road. I saw him nod, and reach for his phone. I guessed I'd been out of the house for a lot longer than I was supposed to be for my 'daily exercise', but how did the two of them know that? I hurried along and turned a corner.

I was out of ideas. It had to be an hour, more likely two, since I'd realised Daniel was gone. I could go back to my own house, but then I'd have no way of knowing if Daniel was safe without alerting Father and Gran to the fact that I'd lost him. No, I would have to bite the bullet, go to his house, and pray for the relief of his smug cheesy grin, pointing at me from the window and laughing his head off. If I was lucky, I'd see him there without even having to ring on the doorbell, and I'd be able to turn and go home. But if he wasn't there, then what? The real nightmare would begin, because then it wouldn't be one of Daniel's jokes. Something would actually have happened to him, and it would be my fault. So I walked to his house by the most absurdly indirect route, telling myself that I might as well check as many possible streets as I could before getting there, as if he might just be sitting on one of them, waiting to be found.

It was still strange to me, how there were hardly any cars on the road. I walked along the middle of the streets, looking alternately to one side, then the other. At one point, a police car went across a junction in front of me, and I hoped that perhaps they'd caught Daniel, or maybe they were going to extricate him from the clutches of the Swynn Hill owner. But I didn't dare call them. I turned onto the main street, where there were lots of closed shops and a greengrocer who was open, with a small but spaced-out queue of people

Chapter 3: The search

waiting to go in. One of them turned to the man behind her, said something, and then pointed at me. Spooked, I turned around and went the other way. That made me see the town's curiously small clock tower, and the clock face reading quarter to five.

Quarter to FIVE?

I'd left the house about ten fifteen, and we'd walked more or less directly to Swynn Hill. We could not have encountered the Glory much later than eleven. My fruitless searching since I'd noticed Daniel was gone could not have lasted more than two or three hours, though it had felt like forever. I had to have spent four hours or more, just staring at that Glory! It wasn't just Daniel's parents who'd be worried, Father and Gran would be, too. Worried for him, and cross with me. Daniel could have just given up waiting for me to move, and gone home, thinking it funny to just leave me there. There was a chance, a real chance, that this was what had happened. I changed direction, and headed straight towards his house.

I knew it was a small chance. I knew that most likely I'd find two very worried parents, no Daniel, and my last best hope snuffed out. Yet that tiny chance drove me on, for it was all I had. I wanted to be bored at home again, wanted it so very badly. I plodded on, oblivious to all around me. It was as if I were walking along a tunnel, with invisible sides, from Swynn Hill to Daniel's house. No-one could get in or out, except through the ends. I was alone in it, moving inexorably forward. From outside the tunnel, Daniel grinned in at me like a Cheshire version of Schroedinger's cat: lost, but also safe at home. When I came out of the tunnel, he'd settle as one or the other.

The tunnel ended, as it had to, with me walking up his street, heart pounding. *Let him be there, let him be there.* The curtains of his window were drawn, and no cheeky face looked out at me. I gulped, steeled myself, walked up to the door and pushed the bell. At least, I tried to, the doorbell didn't seem to work. I wouldn't have put it past Daniel to disconnect it for a laugh. So I walked round to the living room window, whose curtain was not drawn, and looked through. His parents were there, watching telly. His dad had his back to me, but his mum didn't, and she had a haunted look about her. Daniel wasn't there, I could see that in her eyes. A terrible chill began creeping down my spine.

Then his mother jumped up, shouting something and pointing at me. Her husband spun around, eyes wide, then he ran to the door. I moved back towards the main path, but the door flew open before I got there.

"Where is he? What have you done with him?" His eyes were wild as he shouted at me.

"I – I don't know!" I stammered. "Didn't he come home?"

"No, of course he didn't! Where is he?"

"I said I don't know! I haven't seen him since this morning!"

"Oh, so he WAS with you. Where have you been?"

"We were ... we went to Swynn Hill. There was a Glory."

For a moment he almost smiled. "Ohhh, well that's alright then. It was a **Glory**, was it? Opened up and swallowed him, did it?"

"I don't know what happened. I was looking at it for ages, and first he was with me, and then he wasn't."

"He just vanished, did he?"

Chapter 3: The search

I started to reply, but he quickly added, "Was that before or after the little green men all jumped out and started dancing around?"

I stared at him gormlessly, not knowing how to reply. He glared back, eyes full of venom. Long, painful moments ticked by, before he said, "how about you stop making up fairy stories, and tell me where he actually is?"

"I told you everything I know."

"Bull*SHIT*. There's no such thing as Glories. Oh, I've seen all the made-up crap on fucking Twitter, and it's no surprise that you're trying that line. But it doesn't work on me, see, because I know it ain't true. So I'm going to ask you nicely, one last time. Where. Is. My. SON?"

Whether he believed me or not, I had nothing to respond with but the truth. "We went to Swynn Hill, and saw a Glory in the woods there, and – "

Without warning he leapt forward, trapping my neck in his hairy arm, and forcing me up against the wall."

"Terry, no!" Daniel's mother was now standing in the doorway. "Please, Antony, just tell us where you've been! Is he still there? Just tell him to come home!"

"I'm sorry!" I gasped. "I'm so sorry, I don't know! We were on Swynn hill, we really were, and we saw a Glory, this sloping blue lake ..." The arm around my neck tightened.

"Listen to me very carefully," he hissed into my ear. "I am going to ask you the question one final time, and you are going to give me an honest answer, one that does not in any way involve invented nonsense or the word 'Glory'. And if I don't like what I hear, I am going to drag you inside and teach you what happens to kids who lie to me."

My heart pounded with raw fear. I had no idea what to do.

"Let him go, Terry." I looked up, and relief flooded through me as I saw my Father striding down the road towards us. The arm around my neck loosened, and I pushed free.

Terry, Daniel's father, looked furiously at his wife. "Did you call him?" he asked her, angrily.

"Of course I did," she said, voice just about holding firm. "His son's been missing too!"

"Where have you been, Antony?" asked Father in a calm and reasonable tone.

"He's been spinning me some bullshit about a Glory," said Terry.

"I want to hear it from him," said Father.

So I described the events of the morning as honestly as I could, including as clear an account as I could manage of the Glory itself. When I'd finished, a strange silence followed. I stood there, on the grass, with Father still standing at the gate with his arms folded, Terry leaning on the wall looking murderous, and Daniel's mother by the front door, eyes red with tears.

Then Father said, "Son, I made it very clear to you what would happen if I ever caught you taking drugs."

"What?" I said. "I've never touched anything."

"Your story does not make sense, and there is no such thing as Glories. I have read the accounts, and they are patently absurd, an invention. Therefore, I can only conclude that you are lying to cover up something bad. If not drugs, then something worse. Was there an accident? Did something happen to Daniel? This is your last chance to tell me the truth."

Chapter 3: The search

He didn't believe me, any more than Terry did. Yet Father's quiet fury scared me far more. There was no lie I could tell that would satisfy either of them. I cast around in my head for an escape. "Alright," I said in a quiet voice. "I'll show you exactly what happened. Follow me."

I slunk, slowly with head down, towards the side passage. Father and Terry had some sort of dispute about who should follow me first into the passage, given that they were supposed to stay two metres apart. It was all I needed – I broke into a run, through the wooden door to the back garden, slamming it shut behind me. Then I threw a bucket of tools onto the ground right in front of it. I was halfway across the back lawn as they shoved the door open, swearing and then squeezing through. I ran at the back fence and vaulted it into the garden beyond, squashing some flowers as I landed. I ran across the garden, making for their side passage. Father roared at me to stop, but I didn't look back.

I ran down street after street, taking left and right turns at random, in case they were following me. After a few blocks, I realised that they weren't, but I kept running anyway. As long as I was running, I didn't have to think. Eventually, in a cluster of trees by a meagre stream near the edge of town, I stopped running.

They don't believe me. No-one believes me. My own Father doesn't believe me.

And I couldn't go home. Not until I'd found Daniel.

Chapter 4: My little nap

Julia

I opened my eyes slowly. I felt warm, and fuzzy, like I'd had a blissfully long sleep in a sumptuous bed. It was very bright. There was blue sky above me, which was odd. And a face was looking down at me, which was even odder. I wasn't in a bed, I seemed to be lying on the ground. Wait, not all of me was. My top half was tipped upwards, and was resting on ... was it someone's thighs? That would explain the man's face looking worriedly down towards me.

"You're back, thank goodness. Are you alright?" That booming voice. His name was Malcolm.

Other voices floated in from further away.

"... like she was paralysed..."

"... dare touch her because ..."

"... just standing there with her hand up."

"... drugs or something ..."

"Yeah, since I got here ..."

"... police down there, we'd better go!"

I could see, hear and feel just fine, but was having real trouble putting any two things together. So I went with the only solid fact I had available to me. "I seem to be on your lap," I told Malcolm.

"Well, someone had to catch you," he said gently.

"Catch me?"

"Come on, man, we'd better go," said a young voice. I tipped my head sideways. There were people milling about, most of them making their way downwards, away from me. We were on a hilltop, I remembered now. Yet something was different from before. The sun in the sky – had it been there before?

"How are you feeling?" asked Malcolm.

"Uhhh, dizzy," I said.

"There are two policemen coming up the hill towards us. I suggest we tell them you're my live-in girlfriend."

"Oh!" I said. "Alright then." I decided that I'd very much like to be his live-in girlfriend. With this thought came a quite ridiculous urge to giggle like a schoolgirl, which I just about swallowed down with a little cough.

"You sure you're OK?" asked Malcolm.

"Yes," I said brightly. "Why wouldn't I be?" I sat up, finding it a lot easier than I expected, and looked down the slope. It was a beautiful day. People were hurrying down the slope in ones, twos and family groups, all in different directions, some into the scrub on the town side, or the woods on the other side. No-one was using the path to go down, because the police officers were on it, walking up. For some reason I found it quite funny to watch.

"Will we get in trouble?" I said. "For being part of a group?"

"I hope not," he replied. "I shall try to talk them round."

The police reached us. We were the only ones still there.

Chapter 4: My little nap

"You do realise that being a part of this impromptu gathering is against the rules?" the female officer said. I suddenly felt vulnerable sitting on the ground, and quickly scrambled to my feet.

"There was a Glory," said Malcolm. "Did you see it? That's why all these people were here. But it did something very unorthodox to my partner. It paralysed her when she touched it."

As he said this, the memory came rushing back, of that strange, electric sensation running down my arm, and enveloping my body.

"You can't touch a Glory," said the male officer. "Not this type, at least. It pushes you away."

"So they do officially exist then, after all?" said Malcolm, with a smile and a raised eyebrow.

"You can't touch a Glory," the policeman repeated. "Perhaps she was just acting hypnotised or something foolish like that?"

"She was motionless for fifty-five minutes," Malcolm said simply. "Unresponsive. The colours from the Glory were playing across her body and clothes, like she was connected to it. I tried to touch her, to pull her away, but her body repelled me as though she was part of it. She collapsed the moment the Glory disappeared."

Fifty-five minutes? I nearly fell over again, with the shock.

"Did anyone else attempt to touch her?" said the woman.

"Of course not!" said Malcolm. "It would have been against the rules."

The two police officers walked a little distance away from us, and conferred. "We'll let you off with a warning this time," they concluded, before turning away and proceeding down the hill away from us.

"That was big of them," Malcolm said, and I sniggered. "How are you feeling?" He asked me.

"Okay," I said. "Fifty-five minutes? Was I really out that long?"

"Yes. Everything I told them was true. Just as well the Glories don't photograph, or you'd be all over social media. As it is, I'm not sure images like this would attract much attention."

He handed me a polaroid. There I was, eyes closed and with a stupid smile on my face, standing with my hand in the air touching nothing. Further back were other people, in varying degrees of focus, some looking up, others at me. "Keep it," he said. "I only took it because I thought it might tell me something about what was happening. Can you remember anything? From after you touched it, I mean?"

"There was this nice feeling running up my arm, and I saw colours flowing with it and then ... it's like I fell asleep." For a brief moment I had an image of me floating in some sort of warm darkness, but it fell away before I could capture it clearly.

"Well, I guess we'd better get you home," he said, gently.

"Yes, quite," I said. "Hey, now that I'm your 'live-in girlfriend', perhaps you could give me a lift?"

"I would, but I walked all the way up here. Did you walk as well?"

"Oh, I ..." and my voice trailed off. Incredibly, I'd only just remembered that I had terminal cancer.

Chapter 4: My little nap

"Julia?" asked Malcolm, looking concerned.

I didn't feel nauseous. I didn't feel weak. I didn't feel sore, stiff, or weird, anywhere. "Let's walk down," I said.

We started descending. He began very slowly, but I found that I was able to go at a fairly brisk pace. By the time we reached the road, we were holding hands. Just to keep up appearances, of course. I felt like I was nineteen again, awash with emotions, and an indecent tsunami of lust. When we got back to my house, I was all for pulling him inside and ripping his trousers off, but for some reason he limited himself to a socially distanced farewell, and promising to phone me in the evening. It wasn't until I got back inside that I began to remember clearly how very, very sick I'd been feeling for the past month. Because I didn't, not anymore.

* * * * *

I cooked. Not the plain steamed vegetables I've been forcing down of late, but actual pasta sauce with herbs in it. I wolfed it down, too, then sung an aria from *Carmen* as I washed up. Nick called and I'm sorry to say I dissembled, telling him I felt a bit better and had managed a nice little walk, but needed to get to bed now. I held on for a quick exchange of "I love you"s with little Tabby, but otherwise was keen to end the call. There was no point telling him the truth, he'd assume I was delirious, and who would blame him? He'd probably decide that I'd swallowed my entire supply of morphine, and call 999 to have someone come and pump my stomach. I flopped onto my sofa, laughing at the idea. But the laughter soon drained out of me. What if that was what had actually happened? Not morphine itself, but something similar, from touching the Glory? Would I wake up the next morning, sick as I'd been before, only with the added cruelty of hope having been snatched away?

I hadn't taken morphine, not yet. It had sat there on the shelf, and as long as it remained unopened, I'd been able to tell myself I was not yet in the final decline into oblivion. But today I hadn't even needed the anti-nausea pills that were my usual pudding. Still, the feeling that this extraordinary remission might be temporary would not let me go. I felt utterly amazing, but what if this was my last evening on Earth? Should I spend it on my own, talking to my plants? The Rules, of course, stated that I had to. But then, Malcolm and I had already been in close contact, so what point was there to staying apart now? Also, the police now believed that we were almost married.

Half an hour later, I turned up at his door, an impressive house on the edge of town, set back along a private lane and with trees over his own front path. No prying neighbours. I was panting as I rang the bell; I'd actually run part of the way. He opened it, and the look on his face was utterly priceless. I should have photographed and framed it.

"Much as I'd like to let you in …" he began, but I cut him off.

"I think I may be dead by tomorrow," I said.

"Oh."

"So I'd really like to enjoy tonight."

"Oh."

Chapter 4: My little nap

"I have very terminal cancer, you see."

"Oh," he said, for the third time. "I'm most terribly sorry. But you must understand, I have never broken the law in my life."

This was ridiculous. So I did a pretend faint forward into his arms. "Oh my goodness," he said, but he finally let me inside.

We sat together on his sofa, and I told him the full story. He'd seen how ill I'd been on the way up, and how sprightly on the way down, so to his credit he was sceptical but not dismissive, asking occasional questions that I answered as best I could. "There's no way I could be cured," I said. "That's obviously impossible."

"Everything about Glories is impossible," he observed.

"I suppose. The thing is, I think it's much more likely that it's some kind of brief remission. Like a massive dose of morphine. I think I may well drop dead tomorrow, when it runs out."

"The function of morphine is to anaesthetise pain, but it could not give you all this extra energy," he said thoughtfully. His manner was very like that of a doctor dealing with an unruly patient. I found it rather funny.

"Yes, that's true," I agreed. "So not exactly the same. But imagine maybe some drug that makes you use up all the energy you've got in one go."

"There's no drug that can do that," he said.

"Everything about Glories is impossible," I reminded him.

"Touché," he replied with a smile.

"So this may well be my last evening on Earth," I concluded, "and there are quite a few things I'd like to do with it, all of them involving a handsome man like you."

Again he threw an absolutely priceless expression. "Umm ... well ... I think perhaps some drinks are called for," he said. "I have some excellent single malt."

It took him quite a while to adjust to the fact that he had a wanton woman in the house here with him, and a little longer to accept the fact that her willpower was stronger than his, but we got there in the end. As he led me up to bed, I felt like I was going to explode with happiness.

And the next morning I woke beside him, feeling as healthy and strong as I had in my twenties. And happier.

* * * * *

I got up and made him breakfast. He looked both pleased and bewildered when he came down to find bacon and eggs waiting for him (another expression for my collection).

"Do you want to stay?" he asked, rather awkwardly. "I mean you are welcome, of course, it's just that this was all a bit ..."

"Illegal?"

"Unplanned."

I nodded. What if I really was cured? Yesterday I was nearly dead, today I was having illegal carnal relations with a man I barely knew. "I'm sorry," I said. "You're an honest man, and I've barged in and made you break the law. I shouldn't have done that."

Chapter 4: My little nap

"There were extenuating circumstances," he replied. "I cannot deny that I would have preferred a more gentle and formal courtship" (*goodness me, he's a bit pompous*, I thought), "but I also cannot deny that it was extremely pleasant, not to say rather exciting, to be forcefully seduced by a beautiful younger woman."

I beamed at him. A man could be as pompous as he liked if he called me beautiful. "I think …" I began, that lovely word still echoing around my head, "I think I need to go for a little walk on my own. I need to make sense of what has happened to me. Then I'll come back here. Is that OK?"

"Yes, it's fine. How long, do you think?"

"I'll see you for lunch," I said. His expression implied that he didn't completely believe me. "I promise," I added. And then I was off, striding along that footpath we'd walked down by, crossing a field, then up through a wood, enjoying the violets, bluebells and primroses speckled among the trees. With every step, the conviction that somehow, inexplicably, the cancer had gone from my body grew stronger. *Are you still there, Bernard?* I asked inside my mind. *Did the Glory eat you all up?* I emerged from the wood and crested the now deserted hilltop where the Glory had been.

In time, two things became clear to me. First, I'd been given my health back, in what could very literally be called a miracle. And second, there was no way of telling how long it would last. The Glory might have sucked all the poisons out of my body but left the cancer cells themselves intact. All of which meant, I should enjoy every moment that life had to offer me, here and now.

Yesterday morning, I'd felt ninety, but yesterday evening I'd felt nineteen. Now, I felt sixty-one, for what was actually the first time in my life. That rush of giddy and undignified energy had largely faded away now. I would speak to Malcolm and suggest that we reset our courtship to the more sedate pace that he would have preferred, and which would befit our age and experience. Yes, we'd be breaking the rules, but that was spilt milk now, there was no point separating again at this point, since we'd already been in contact. Pretty close contact, in fact. He'd told the police we were a couple, so perhaps that would be enough. If not, well, we'd pay the fines and move on. I called Nick, and spun him a line about some experimental drug the doctors had posted to me, not formally approved but I was part of a clinical trial. He was predictably alarmed, but then I told him I felt better than I had in over a year, and was currently striding across the hills above the town. He didn't believe me so I stuck my phone upwards and let him hear the birdsong. He was clearly confused and uncertain, not wanting to hope. But there was no way he'd believe what actually happened. The drug story was my way of easing him into the idea that I might not be on the way out, that I had leapt out of the coffin just as the lid was about to clang shut. Life, glorious and unexpected, stretched out in front of me like the first new shoots of spring.

* * * * *

For eight happy days, we fell into a routine. We'd spend the nights in our own homes, take our lunches early, and then go for our 'exercise walks'. We'd meet in a quiet spot near his house, then walk as a couple, exploring the hills and

Chapter 4: My little nap

some more woods further on. I'd tell him the names of the flowers and birds that I knew, and he'd tell me what he'd learned about the virus and the Glories. He seemed to spend half his life glued to his computer – luckily the half when I wasn't there. There were a few other stories floating around social media of people who'd reacted in unusual ways to Glories, but none the same as mine. You had to search hard to find them, he said, because according to him the government was desperate to maintain a news blackout on the Glories, in order to keep people in their homes. He reckoned they were paying obscene sums to Twitter, Facebook and the rest to take down posts about Glories as soon as they went up.

He told me that the most prevalent (and yes, he used that exact word) personal stories were those in which someone's personality was completely changed by the encounter. Some for the better, some for the worse – and the account never seemed to come from the person themselves. Finding religion, losing it, becoming obsessed with aliens or terrified of an impending apocalypse, becoming a hermit, vanishing for a month and blaming a Glory, briefly regressing to childhood, becoming utterly fixated on apologising for a lifetime of ordinary behaviour. One man apparently spent 24 hours convinced he was an octopus.

"Becoming excessively horny is another," I contributed.

"Well, yes," he said, with gently reddening cheeks and another delightful expression for my collection. Our first night together has become a source of both joy and gentle embarrassment to both of us. But we were both teenagers once, so we'd had half a lifetime to learn how to deal with embarrassing pasts.

"Some of those Glory accounts are bound to be false," he said knowledgeably. "Cover for misdeeds or simple lockdown-breaking. But others are a lot more convincing. There are several different accounts of people who've seen one Glory becoming compulsively obsessive about wanting to see another. If these things keep appearing, they're going to start having a wide impact on society."

Each day after the walk, we went back to his house as if we'd both always lived there, and took it in turns to cook for the other. Then I would head home, varying my route, hoping there weren't too many twitching curtains. Sooner or later though, I felt sure that there would be.

On the ninth day, he asked me to move in and I said yes immediately, as long as Jenny, Ethel and Gilbert could come with me.

"You didn't say you had pets! They are pets, aren't they?" He produced yet another priceless facial expression.

"They're plants," I replied.

"Oh. Good."

Getting the plants and some of my stuff to his house involved a comical clandestine night-time operation involving his car and the alley behind my back garden. I slept alone at my house that night, then moved in with him after our daily walk.

On the eleventh day, a woman with a badge turned up on our doorstep, and asked for me by name.

* * * * *

Chapter 4: My little nap  24

I'd been in the living room when Malcolm answered the door. "I would like to speak to Julia Barnes please," said a female voice that sounded unaccustomed to being disobeyed.

She was also, I thought, unaccustomed to being wrong, so I walked from the room to stand beside Malcolm before he had a chance to dissemble. The woman at the door was short, perhaps five foot two, mid-thirties, denim clad, with shoulder-length straight brown hair and an expression that matched her voice. She was standing exactly two metres back from the door. I found myself wondering if she'd checked the distance with a tape measure before ringing the bell.

She cocked her head to one side. "Would you like to explain why you are not at your home address, Ms Barnes?"

"I was taken ill while out on a walk. Fainted, I'm afraid. Malcolm caught me. After that there seemed to be no practical value in staying apart. It's really no different from how it would have been had we been sharing a house before the lockdown began. We are both willing to pay the appropriate fines if necessary."

"How very noble," said the woman drily. "How's the cancer?"

"Do you mind if we ask who you are?" asked Malcolm.

"My name is Locksley, and I work for the government."

"Which branch?"

"One you won't have heard of."

"Then how are we to know that you're not some crank?" asked Malcolm.

"Do I look like a crank?"

"No, you more closely resemble a school teacher," he replied.

I stifled a snigger. The woman's eyes flashed with anger, but only for a moment. Yet that was enough to convince me she was genuine. You don't get angry at being called a teacher if you're playing a con.

"I'm willing to hear you out, and answer your questions up to a point," I said. "But we shall need some proof of your credentials if you require us to do anything."

"Right," she replied tersely. "Then could you tell me please how your health has been for the past eleven days?"

"Why is a government agency interested in Julia's health?" asked Malcolm, sharply. But I thought I knew the answer.

"It has been very good," I said. "Ever since I touched the Glory. You know, those things the rest of the government says do not exist? That is why you're here, isn't it?"

"Clearly your mind is in good condition, too," said Locksley. "Now tell me about your health before the Glory?"

"You already know I had cancer. I was very sick indeed." I gave her a full account of how ill I'd been before the Glory, and how healthy and fit I'd felt afterwards. "The cancer's either gone, or producing no detectable symptoms. I've no way of knowing which, what with the NHS overwhelmed."

"Thank you for being so straight with me, so I will be straight with you," she said. "Yours is the only verifiable account we have of a Glory curing a disease of this severity. Any physical disease, in fact. Mr Phillips, when Ms

Barnes touched the Glory, was anyone else able to touch it? And can you tell me how many people you saw try to do so?"

"Between thirty and forty, over the full time I was there. None were able to, before or after Julia did so."

"And yet statistically, several of those would have had illnesses of some sort, perhaps not serious. The implications are clear."

"Are they?" I said. "You mean they can only cure the very ill?"

"No," said Malcolm, who was ahead of me this time. "She means it's not this particular Glory that was special …"

Locksley looked at me pointedly.

"It's … me?" I gasped.

"That is our conclusion, yes. You would appear to be one of a very small set of people we have learned of, who are capable of interacting with the Glories in an exceptional fashion."

"What can the others do?" I asked.

"I'll let you ask them yourself," she said. "You see, I'm here to recruit you."

Chapter 5: The fugitive

Antony

I tried to call Gran. I had no idea if she'd believe me, but hers was the only voice left to me that might still be friendly. If I did it right away, then there was a chance that I'd get her before Father got home. I backtracked one block to where I'd seen a phone booth, a thing I'd never used in my life. I had no coins on me, but dimly recalled some safety talk at school, when they'd told us about 'reversing the charges' by asking for the operator or something. But as I reached for the phone, fear hit me that Gran would reject me too, and I couldn't pick up the phone. I just stood there like an idiot, hand wobbling all over the receiver, before finally giving up and slinking away.

I walked along the alley behind the closed cinema, round through the too small and empty car park, along the little road leading into the car park, around the cinema front and back into the alley. Having completed one circuit, I started another. I had no home to go to, no idea how to find Daniel, no clue what to do. So I walked down the alley, through the car park, up the little lane, and past the cinema front, again and again. In the alley, I counted the bricks. In the car park, I traced routes along the cracks in the ageing tarmac. Occasionally I pinched myself hard, pretending this might be a nightmare I could wake up from, but knowing it wasn't.

Eventually, I found myself climbing over the wall into the Swynn Hill woods, again. Enough time had passed for me to think there was some tiny chance that Daniel might be there. He wasn't, of course. I searched for my phone, crawling on my hands and knees, and found nothing. Nothing, nothing, nothing.

The wood was getting darker, as the sun moved lower in the sky. I needed to find a place to sleep outside. I thought of those poor people who sat on the street, not even asking for money, just silently staring downwards with a foam cup beside them, hoping for spare coins. Was I one of them now? I didn't even have a sleeping bag or blanket. I couldn't go to anyone's house, not with the lockdown.

Perhaps I could just shelter on the wood side of the big wall. That wouldn't be too bad. I meandered down to the wall, and miserably progressed along it. Then a strange sort of distant clanking and rattling filled the air, coming from beyond the wall. My first thought was that this was something else supernatural, like a Glory made of sound instead of colour, or whatever the hell that blue lake had been made of. Then I lifted my head to look over the wall, and saw people standing on their doorsteps, clapping their hands and rattling pots and pans. I almost laughed – they were clapping for the NHS, of course they were. Except that today was a Wednesday, or at least it had been when I'd woken up, and the clapping only happened on Thursdays. My head started spinning again, and the clapping and clanking sound became muted, distant, separated from me. Because now I finally understood why Daniel's parents had been so angry and distressed when I'd come to their house. Why Father had said that my story made no sense. He hadn't just been missing for a few hours, he'd been missing for one whole day. And so had I.

Chapter 5: The fugitive

* * * * *

I had lost a whole day. I didn't understand how that was possible. Had I been somehow frozen in time? I closed my eyes, tried to remember everything that had happened after I'd seen the Glory. I recalled the rippling surface, the cut-away rhododendron bush, my failed attempt to photograph it. Could Daniel have my phone? Unlikely – he'd have used it by now, for some sort of prank, and his parents or Father would have mentioned it. Had something scared him, so much that he'd simply run away? He always said that nothing could scare him, ever, but sometimes I wasn't at all sure that was true. Like I said, he doesn't like going off on his own. What else, what else? Slowly I dragged forth two other memories. The first was that face I'd seen in the Glory, indistinct at first, and then changing to someone beautiful, who might have been my mum. It could have been a dream, I decided, and gave me no clues about Daniel. The second was that I'd picked some of it up. I'd actually held a blue, rippling portion of the Glory in my left hand. Looking at that hand now, I felt an odd sort of tingling in my fingers and palm.

I'd never been anything special at school, quite good at science and maths, but pretty much average at everything else. Picked neither first nor last for sports teams. A constant mid-leaguer. But I loved logic puzzles. Occam's razor. *Never look for a complicated explanation, when a simple one will do.* I'd learned that one from an old comic book about some future war. What was the simple explanation, here? Glories were impossible, Father had been right about that. For me to be standing there, for a whole day, like I was frozen in time, was impossible too. Two impossible things had happened together, so clearly the first must have caused the second. And then a third thing that I couldn't explain – Daniel's disappearance. Occam's razor told me that the Glory must have somehow caused that, too. Daniel was not hiding out, was not playing an elaborate prank, had not been accidentally killed in a way that had hidden his body, and had not been kidnapped by person or persons unknown. He'd disappeared because of the Glory. And at last, I had something to cling on to. I had to find more Glories. I had to learn everything I could about them. And if Daniel had somehow got inside of one of them, then that would be what I would have to do, too.

* * * * *

A fragile flame of hope had lit within me. At least I knew *what* I had to do, even if I had no idea how. I could come up with no better plan than to walk around until I found another Glory. I was trying to decide whether to rest or even sleep here, when I noticed the leaves on the trees above me flashing blue and red. The light was coming from beyond the wall. I lifted my head up to look, and saw a police car, lights flashing, coming to a stop maybe forty metres along the road by the wall from where I was. Two policemen got out, and one gave the other a boost up onto the wall, then passed up a torch. They were after me! One of the parents must have called them.

I dropped back down, and ran along by the wall in the direction away from them, veering upwards after a while, eventually reaching a barbed wire fence, which I scrambled over into the grassy field beyond. By now the sun was down,

Chapter 5: The fugitive

just a faint orange glow on the horizon, and the world around me was a sort of yellow-tinted monochrome lit by streetlamps via the clouds above. When I'd been very little, our car had broken down, after dark, on our way back from somewhere, maybe Gran and Grandad's house. Father had used some strange angry words and Mum had told him off for it. Then she'd led me out of the car and said something about how Father needed to cool down. We'd walked some way along the lane, and it had been a little bit magical, being outside after dark. We'd reached a gate and looked into a field, which had these big rectangular things in it, like small trucks on stilts, with steam coming out of them.

"Mummy, are those alien spaceships?" I'd asked her (I only remember this clearly because Mum had told Gran, and Gran told it back to me later).

"No, silly! They're cows!"

I dimly recall not understanding how they could be asleep and yet standing up at the same time. The cows in my field, now, were doing the same thing, standing still. Some might have been asleep, others not, but I walked right between them and none of them moved. I could see no torchlights behind me, so I reckoned I'd given the police the slip. I decided that the direction I was going in was probably as good as any, so I resolved to keep walking until I got too tired, or too hungry. When had I last eaten? I didn't feel hungry now, and that was odd. Maybe it was the adrenaline. Maybe I wouldn't feel hungry again until I got somewhere that was safe. A mile or two later I picked up a farm track that took me right through a yard with farm buildings on both sides, and found a tap on the outside of a building. I thought I could drink from it, but the damned thing was stuck. Twenty minutes later I came upon a little mossy waterfall by a woodland path, and stuck my mouth into that, instead.

By this point the path was climbing again, alternating between woods and grassland, with occasional chunks of chalk glowing weakly in the dull yellow light. In the wooded bits, I had to almost guess where the path was, by looking at the silhouettes of trees and placing my feet where they weren't. I knew there was a thin line of chalk hills to the north of Swinton, and another to the southwest, and I reckoned I was on the latter. I reckoned if I went along the top, it would keep me away from streetlights and searching police cars. On I went, sometimes following paths, at other times blundering through woodland. Then I happened upon a tall mesh fence on my right, with a slight gap in the trees beside it, so I worked my way along that. There seemed to be a huge garden beyond it, I could see a big house and a pond, reflecting the dim orange clouds. And further on, what looked like a large shed.

There was a place where the fence had come apart a little, and on impulse I managed to squeeze through. I headed for the shed. It seemed a better place to sleep than any other I'd found, and I reckoned I'd be up and away again before anyone in the distant big house got up. Coming closer, I realised it wasn't a shed, as such, but some sort of summer house, with only three walls, with the open side facing back up towards the house and garden. There was a table, two spindly chairs, and a long bench behind it with a thin cushion all along it. So I lay down on that, and let myself sleep.

* * * * *

Chapter 5: The fugitive

"So where is it?"

For a moment I thought it was Father, come into my room to shout at me about some transgression he'd noticed. Then it all came back to me – Daniel, the Glory, my own exile from home. The sun was just coming up, and I'd been sleeping on a hard bench in some giant garden, and now six people were standing on the grass nearby.

"Don't shout," said an old lady. "If we wake them up, we'll *all* get in trouble!" She pointed at the big house.

"There is something here, I can feel it," said a third voice. This one came from a thin woman in a long red floaty dress, the hem of which was wet from the dew. Her voice was quiet and sort of wobbly, and her blonde slightly scraggly hair almost reached her waist.

"But there's nothing here," said the man whose voice had woken me. He was dressed like one of those big-headed morons who go on *The Apprentice* ('*I think our team should be called Nuclear, because we're all about power and energy!*'), and had neat short hair to go with it.

"It's not like the others," said the red dress. "Maybe it's invisible. There's no reason why we'd be able to see all of them."

"Could be a Type Two," said another young woman, in a serious voice like a teacher. She had a round face, not very pretty to my eyes, and pale brown hair cut short like a boy. "We could be standing in it."

The other man, who was fat, balding and about Father's age, said nothing. He looked slightly bored.

"Let's try Calling again," said another old lady. She was tall, taller than either of the men, and something about her reminded me of a heron. Her thin grey hair was swept backwards, and her long thin legs wore canvas trousers.

"Oh, because it worked so well last time," said the *Apprentice* candidate.

"You don't have to join in, Mister Greene," said the other old lady. She had a gravelly voice, and a spark of mischief about her. She was the shortest of the group, but made up for it with a mass of curly grey hair. Mister Greene rolled his eyes, and then the six of them joined hands in a circle.

"I'm cold," said the balding man.

"We must clear our minds of distractions, then focus upon our collective needs," said the heron-like woman. "The cold will help you, if you let it! Bring your minds back to the moment you met your Glory. Bring forth the feelings that came to you at that moment. Visualise the Glory! Tell it we are Ready!" I expected them to start chanting, but they just stood there, eyes closed, faces turned upwards. The bald man kept fidgeting with his legs to keep warm.

"Oy!! What the hell are you doing here?" A large man wearing a barbour jacket over his striped pyjamas was storming across the lawn towards them, with a very large dog straining at the lead, beside him. His deep voice resonated with the self-importance of the rich.

The red-dress woman detached from the circle and turned towards him. "A Glory is coming. They are coming for all of us, soon. Join the circle, and be ready!" She held out her hands towards him.

"Listen, you bloody nutters, this is private land! I don't know how many laws you're breaking, but I want you off my land, NOW!"

The dog barked its agreement.

"Listen, Sir," said Mr Greene, gently pushing the red dress to one side. "I appreciate that my colleagues may seem a bit, well, mad to you. They are a bit

Chapter 5: The fugitive

eccentric. But I've seen a Glory with my own eyes. I work in the City, so you can trust me. These things are real, and if we could just find a way to monetise them …"

"I am going to count to five, then release my dog!" shouted the rich man. "ONE …"

"We're going," said the heron woman. She grasped the red dress woman's arm. "Come on, Linda!" The six of them began hurrying away. I looked at the dog, and made a snap decision. I jumped up from my bench, and hurried along after the group of six. The rich man saw me, of course, but made no response, assuming as I'd hoped that I was just a seventh member of the group.

They walked towards the left side of the house, where grass gave way to gravel, and Mr Greene grumbled about how the whole outing had been a total farce.

"Give it a rest, Frank," said the round-faced young woman.

None of them seemed to have noticed me walking behind them. I tried to process what I'd heard. The red-dress woman, Linda, seemed to think she could detect Glories, maybe even predict where they'd be. Frank, Mr Greene, worked in the city, which was not at all surprising from his outfit and manner, but he had seen a Glory, and clearly wanted to see another. Wanted it a lot, I decided, because what else could make him hang out with these people who he clearly had so little time for? And judging from the tall heron-like woman's pronouncements as they'd all joined hands, they had each seen a Glory at least once. So they'd joined together as a group to try and see another one.

I had to join them. They were by far my best chance. But what if they knew who I was? What if they knew I was the missing boy who'd caused his cousin's disappearance? I thought that the short old lady would be sympathetic, and maybe some of the others too. They knew Glories were real. But I couldn't help thinking that Frank was the type who'd dob me in, first chance he got.

I was hoping they'd come here on foot, which would mean I could follow them to base, and maybe talk to them one by one. The group of them passed between two grand pillars then along a little track until it met a road, where two cars were parked awkwardly on the verge. I had to decide, and I had to decide now.

Chapter 6: My second life

Julia

We went walking in the woods with Locksley, still keeping a 2m distance. She didn't seem to want to come into the house, and there was only so long I was willing to stand in the doorway talking. So we compromised. I had hoped that the setting would loosen Locksley up a bit, and it seemed to have worked. If I was going to let her "recruit me", I wanted to get a sense of who she was as a person. She'd admitted that her people were all over social media, gathering information about Glories and people's encounters with them. But when Malcolm asked if they had agents making false online profiles to ask people questions, she had said "No comment," instead of denying it. And though she didn't admit it outright, we got the impression that the government had no other way of detecting Glories.

"So what do you think is causing them?" I asked her.

"Not my job to speculate," she replied tersely. (When I said she'd loosened up, you have to remember that everything is relative).

"But you must have seen more evidence than most people. You said you'd been scouring social media accounts of them to find oddities like me."

"Not me personally. We have a guy for that."

"Just one?" I asked

"We're a small operation. There's a pandemic to deal with, remember?"

"No, I'd forgotten," I said. "But come on, you must have had a thought or two."

"Nope."

"I believe that the secret service screening process automatically rejects candidates who show any sign of imagination," observed Malcolm, who was plodding along behind us.

"Malcolm thinks it's aliens," I said cheerfully.

"What I said was, there is no technology on Earth that could produce a Glory, nor do they seem to be a natural phenomenon, which leaves only one logical conclusion."

"No *known* technology," countered Locksley.

"Hah!" I said. "So you *have* thought about it!"

"It has been discussed."

"And presumably, at least some of the discussion has centred on the Pertwee Paradox," said Malcolm.

"Pertwee Paradox??" chorused Locksley and myself, in unlikely unison.

"The fact that Glory occurrences now appear to be strongly if not wholly concentrated in the British Isles," explained Malcolm. "Mainly England, in fact. Like the alien invasions from 1970s *Doctor Who*, which conveniently always happened to occur in England, where the Doctor was based. But that, of course, was down to BBC budgets. So why is it happening with the Glories, hmmm? It implies some connection to someone or something on this landmass, does it not?"

"You seem very well informed, Mr Phillips," replied Locksley.

Chapter 6: My second life

"He spends his mornings glued to the computer," I told her. "He's become quite adept at trawling the internet for information about the Glories."

"So do you know?" persisted Malcolm. "Do you know why they are now appearing almost exclusively in Britain?"

"Not at this time, no," replied Locksley.

"Malcolm's very good at finding out things," I said. "Perhaps you should recruit him, as well as me?"

She took some time to reply. "Let us talk about what I am going to ask from you, Ms Barnes."

"Call me Julia, please. If we are going to be working together."

"Okay … Julia." She pronounced my first name as though it were unnatural to her, and did not offer up her own. "What we are hoping to achieve is to bring yourself, and a small group of others, into contact with further Glories. It is possible to detect them via social media and, at least sometimes, to reach them before they vanish. Through yourself and those others, our goal is to learn more about their properties, and hence their origin."

"Malcolm, what do you think?" I asked, turning back to him.

"Firstly, I would place a substantial bet on her being what she says she is. There's no way an imposter could fake that level of stiffness." Locksley's face offered not even a flicker of response to his comment, but I wondered if she took it as a complement. "So, it depends on what you want, Julia. There's a chance that this group could get some real insights into the Glories, maybe even learn how other cancer sufferers could find a miracle cure. But also, there's a question you've been wanting an answer to, isn't there?"

"Me?" I said. I couldn't work out what he meant.

"About what precisely has happened to you?" he said carefully.

"Oh. Yes. If I joined your little band, Ms Locksley, would someone be able to check if my cancer has actually properly gone?"

"You'll appreciate that the country's doctors are all extremely busy at present."

"That may be so," Malcolm interjected, "but it would seem to me to be rather futile, going to all this trouble to try and put Julia in contact with another Glory, when you don't even know what the first one actually did."

Locksley thought for a moment. Two brown butterflies flitted past, having a silent quarrel. "You make a good point, so I will see what I can do, but I cannot promise. You will of course be paid for participation, one thousand pounds per week, tax free."

"Oooh," I said, before I could stop myself. I wasn't poor, I had a tidy nest egg, but since Bernard had put paid to my job, it had been steadily dwindling. "I'd like it if Malcolm could come too. He is very good at net surfing."

"I would do it free of charge," he added.

"The offer is appreciated but I cannot accept," said Locksley stiffly.

I felt a little stab of disappointment, but it made me realise that I'd already made up my mind to go with her. I'd been given my life back, and felt a certain obligation to do something in return. What, and for whom, I wasn't quite sure. "Okay, Ms Locksley, I'm in."

"I will need a blood sample," said Locksley, which I translated from Locksley language as 'thank you'. "We'll do it when I get back to my car."

"For a Coronavirus test?" I asked her. "Seriously? You're doing one on me when there's not enough for all the nurses?"

"Listen Ms Barnes – "

"Julia."

"You may not think it, but the Glories constitute potentially a greater threat to this country than the virus. They defy scientific explanation, they have the potential to kill, and they are increasing in frequency at what may be an exponential rate."

"To kill?" I asked.

"We have two fatalities in Britain that were almost certainly caused by a Glory, and a not insignificant number of disappearances that are suspect, including at least one child. We have absolutely no idea what they are, what is causing them, or what intention, if any, lies behind them. Consequently, unlike the virus, we have absolutely no plan in place to bring the situation under control. There can be no plan, without information. And Mr Phillips, you will not repeat any of this to anyone."

"How have you managed to keep it out of the papers?" Malcolm replied. "They've never been this compliant since before Profumo."

"They understand the need to save lives. Now will you …"

"You have my word," he said calmly. "But it's not the danger from the Glories that's behind the secrecy, is it? It's the lockdown. They don't want everyone haring off Glory-hunting."

"I am not party to top-level thinking on this, but what you suggest is plausible," said Locksley. "Now, Ms Barnes, you will be collected in around 48 hours' time. It would be useful if you would prepare a suitcase in advance with everything you would need for a four-night stay. Meals will be provided, but any snacks you wish to have you must bring yourself. I would also advise bringing several books, as there may be a lot of waiting. That is all."

We walked the last ten minutes in thoughtful silence, with Malcolm holding my hand.

* * * * *

The next two days passed in a blur. My imminent departure had changed things again, and now Malcolm and I were like young lovers on a holiday romance, spending every moment we could together. He almost managed a day without opening his computer! We listened to his vinyl LPs and watched favourite movies cuddled up on the sofa, cooked each other our favourite dishes, and did one long walk together each day.

I called Nick, gave him another chapter in my miraculous recovery, and had a lovely chat with Tabby. I could never get my head around Zoom and why you don't have to pay for it, talking to people on the other side of the world. I didn't tell them about Locksley and my looming mission, they don't even know about the Glories. I kept it that way because they would worry. Nick was a world class worrier. I supposed that me getting cancer, and his father dying ten years back

made him a justified worrier, but still. I knew he felt terribly guilty about moving to New Zealand, but it had been a superb, once in a lifetime opportunity for him. Frankly, there'd also been a small part of me that was relieved about not being fussed over twice a week. Of course, none of us had known that Gina was about two weeks pregnant when they decided to go. I'd only met Tabby in the flesh three times. The first one she didn't remember, but the second was my four weeks in New Zealand, during the interregnum between Bernards I and II, and that visit lit the flame of burning love between us. Then their visit in February, which Nick and I both thought at the time would probably be the last time any of them saw me in person, for the virus was already spreading its tentacles by the time they flew home.

On the second morning after Locksley's visit, Malcolm took me through what he knew about the Glories. It seemed they could be any shape, any size, any colour or texture. Dedicated websites sprung up regularly, collating tales and even trying to map their occurrences, but they tended to vanish within a few days, presumably shut down by the government. "I reckon they're paying some hackers a fortune to find and attack them," he said, "because they're mostly not hosted in the UK. Anyway, here's my potted summary of what seems to be known for certain." He printed it out for me.

Shape: either a geometric shape from simple (sphere, cube) to complex (dodecahedron), or a natural object (cloud, pond, rock, one report of a tree).

Size: longest dimension from 1 m to around 50 m. May be similar lengths in all three dimensions, or with one or two dimensions much longer than the other(s).

The Two Types: TYPE 1 Glories have a boundary that humans cannot pass through, or even (with rare exceptions) touch. Effect is like a forcefield, or strong magnetic repulsion. Animals and objects pass through this barrier as if it isn't there, and often part of the Glory is underground. TYPE 2 Glories have no physical effect on humans or anything else, just a very precise boundary between objects changed and not changed.

Visibility: only visible to humans, not visible to animals or cameras of any kind. TYPE 2s are completely undetectable with eyes closed.

Appearance: may be one colour, many colours, or have the appearance of a natural texture (water, ice, sky, rock, etc). For a TYPE 1, this is the appearance of its edges, and regardless of size, it is always completely opaque. For a TYPE 2, every object inside it, including plants and animals but not people, takes on this colour/texture on every surface. Some have a fluid surface that appears to ripple.

Movement: all Glories so far are completely stationary, though some appear to rotate. Many have lines or shapes of different colour(s) to the background moving across them.

Duration: Shortest time from appearance (when witnessed) and disappearance is 81 minutes. Longest recorded duration 5 hours and 52 minutes.

Range: Almost exclusively Great Britain, mostly southern England ('Pertwee Paradox'). Very few reports from other countries during winter 2020.

Chapter 6: My second life

Effects on people: most people appear unaffected by seeing or touching a Glory, but there are some reports of memory loss, memories regained, religious experiences, or a powerful desire to see another Glory.

"I noticed you didn't include 'miraculous recovery from cancer' in the last category," I said.

"I know it's probably silly, but I worry about hackers," he replied. "But of course they found out about you anyway."

"Locksley said there were others with special abilities of some sort. Did you find any of those?"

"Nothing convincing. But then, posts about Glories don't stay up very long, so I'm sure I miss most of them. It's not just hackers, either. They're trying a more sinister tactic on Twitter, just the last few days. Using an army of bots to make anyone who posts about a Glory look ridiculous, callous, and often like a crazed attention seeker. They attack in a coordinated manner, each taking a subtly different line," Malcolm explained, as he typed in a few search terms. "Many people didn't even know they were called Glories, only learning the term if someone else who saw it with them shared the name. I've found that 'weird colourful' is quite good for finding new posts," he said. Within a few minutes he'd found one.

```
Incredible weird thing appeared hanging over river near
home.  Triangular pyramid with water flowing through.
Thought it was mirrors but when looked at through phone it
wasn't there.  Other people saw it too, tho.  One boy threw
a stick at it, went right through.  Watched for half hour
then it was gone.  Anyone know what it is?
```

Malcolm showed me the replies.

```
Heard a lot of stories of increased drug use since the
lockdown.  Guess it's true.
```

```
What are you trying to do, get people killed?  This sort
of nonsense is going to spread the virus.  People will die
because of you.  Happy?
```

```
It's called a Glory.  They are real.  My friend saw one,
looked like a flat mass of yellow balls hanging in the air.
Like yours it didn't come out in photos.
```

```
Believe it, sister.  You've seen it, don't listen to the
haters.  You are one of us now.  The Glories are real but
the virus is a hoax, they are going round killing old people
to make it look real.  Don't eat bananas, the government is
putting nanobots into them to take control of your brain.
```

```
I saw one too!!  Mine was a pink elephant running along
the rooftops with pigs flying after it.  But then I was
ripped to the tits on vodka, heroin and funky pills at the
time.  Come to think of it, you probably were, too.
```

Chapter 6: My second life

> I've seen some sick, evil posts since the pandemic started, but yours is the worst. People are supposed to stay inside, you selfish bitch.

"Vile," I said

"But effective," replied Malcolm. "Often the poster is someone who normally posts bland stuff, and not very often. 'Look, I'm in the pub!' 'Here's what I had for dinner,' that sort of thing. Then suddenly they get a pile-on. They get upset, and delete the post. Which is the idea, of course. That, and to make others doubt it was real in the first place."

Malcolm calmly copied the post, and the reply about the yellow balls, and pasted them into a spreadsheet he'd created, containing dozens of reports of Glories he'd pulled from the net. And, being Malcolm, he was doing it very systematically, with a whole series of columns to categorise the reports. Was it floating or on/in the ground? Solid or walk-in? Did other people see it? The date. The location if stated, with latitude and longitude, if possible. Time of day. Colour(s) or texture. Duration of time it was seen for. Size, if stated. Shape. Distance from nearest town, if known. Any responses from animals. Other notes.

I pored over the list, fascinated. Some were all one pure colour, some a mix of colours. Some had texture, usually something natural like rock, water or the ground nearby. Two accounts, separated by a week and hundreds of miles, each described what one called a 'sky window', a patch of blue sky with scattered clouds sitting flat on the ground like a pool. One had people jumping on to it and sliding, frictionless, to the other side.

The first account marked "Walk-in" was the one he'd told me about when we first met, with leaves all turned to black, white and grey. Another account said this:

> "The oilseed rape plants swayed in the wind just like the normal ones, but they all looked like they were made of ice. Felt like plants, though. It was like a circular track, I followed it round to the hedge, and that was ice too, and so was the grass in the next field. And even a cow that was standing there. But not me, not even my clothes. And it all looked normal in photos."

I could feel the nerves rising slowly inside me. Locksley hadn't said what time she'd come, so I couldn't go out for a walk. I read through Malcolm's list of Glory accounts three times, then got up and paced about. After a few minutes of this he looked at me like he was trying not to get annoyed, and suggested I go in the back garden.

Then the doorbell rang.

* * * * *

Chapter 6: My second life

A policeman was standing at the door, looking stern. For a moment I thought he'd come to arrest me for breaking lockdown, and that Locksley would have to come barging into the local police station to extract me. But then he said,
"Ms Barnes? It's time to go."
"I'll get my things."
"Be quick."
This guy made Locksley look positively loquacious! Malcolm had already brought my suitcase to the door, so it only remained to say – or rather kiss – our farewells. "I'll miss you," he said, his eyes going just a little bit watery. "Be safe."
"You too." We kissed again, and now my eyes were going, too. I turned away from him, holding onto his hand. Locksley had said it would be fours days, then back here for a bit, but I felt a strange certainty that I'd be away for rather longer than that. I reached for the suitcase with my other hand, but the policeman had already carried it to a grey van parked by the garden. There was nothing to do but walk after him. But as I stepped into the doorway, fingers just about holding onto Malcolm's, I turned to him once more. "I wish we'd had longer," I said.
"Me too."
And that was that. I turned and walked down his lovely little front path and got into the van.

Chapter 7: The allies

Antony

"Can I come with you?" I walked towards the six of them as they were opening the car doors.

"Where did you come from?" asked the round-faced young woman.

"I was there, in that big garden with you. I'd felt something, that maybe there'd be a Glory there, so I found my way in through the fence," I said, making it up on the spot. "You're hunting Glories too, aren't you?"

Five pairs of eyes appraised me (the fat balding man was watching a butterfly). Linda walked towards me, completely oblivious of any social distancing regs, tilting her head and looking at me like I was some kind of rare animal in a zoo. "He's been Touched," she said.

"I've touched a Glory, yes," I told her. "I picked a bit of it up in my hand."

"Seriously?" said the tall heron-like woman. "That shouldn't be possible!"

"Nothing about the Glories ought to be possible, Thelma," said the short old woman, cheerfully.

"What I mean is, Martha, there do seem to be certain rules that normally apply to Glories, and one is that you can't pick them up," said the tall woman, Thelma.

"Describe the Glory," said the round-faced woman.

So I did, leaving out anything about Daniel, and also the face in the middle. I figured one strange occurrence they might accept, but more would make them start to doubt. "You could have got all that from reading about someone else's encounter," said Thelma.

"If he had, would he have made up the bit about picking it up? Of course he wouldn't," replied Martha.

"It was this hand, wasn't it?" asked Linda, pointing at my left hand.

"Yes it was," I said.

"I think he's for real," said the round-faced woman.

Frank Greene had been scrolling on his phone during most of this conversation. Then he looked up at me triumphantly. "I knew it! It's him!"

Everyone turned to him, seeking an explanation. "Oh, I forgot that none of you bother with *real* news, these days. The missing kids! This one's Antony Blake! Look at the photo, here!" he waved his phone at them. "Disappears with his cousin after sending some random text to a mate about a Glory, then pops up yesterday claiming the Glory must have gobbled up his cousin, before running away again!"

"Is this true?" asked Thelma.

"Yes. I was with my cousin when we found the Glory. Then he wasn't there, anymore. I've been searching for him ever since. No-one else believes me. No-one." I realised I was fighting off tears.

"You should be with your parents, not running loose in the woods," said the round-faced woman. "They'll be worried."

"They're not!" I said, almost shouting. "Mum's dead, and Father, he didn't believe me. Said I was doing drugs when I wasn't. So I'm not going home. I'd rather be in a police cell."

Chapter 7: The allies

"It's alright, love," said Martha. She held out her arms towards me. "Come here."

"Martha, you can't just – there are rules," said Thelma.

"Rules be damned," said Martha, looking right into my eyes. I stumbled forward and accepted her embrace. For long, precious moments, I remembered what it was to feel safe, and cared for. "I say we vote," said Martha. "But you should be aware that if it comes out as a no, then I will leave the group and look after this boy for as long as he needs me."

"That's blackmail," said Frank angrily.

"It's not," said Martha calmly. "Merely a statement of what will happen. Anyway, I vote yes."

"He belongs with us," said Linda.

"I do believe the young lad should be given a chance," said Thelma. "And I would like to know more about what led him to where we were, just now."

"Ginnie, Frank, what about you?" asked Martha, unwrapping her arms from me gently.

"What does it matter what I think," asked Frank angrily. "We all know Croyde's going to abstain, like he does from everything," he said, indicating the bald man, who had indeed shown no inclination to make any contribution. "We're outvoted. But don't blame me when the police come and charge us all with kidnapping."

"The police really aren't important anymore," said Linda, dreamily.

"They are if they stop us getting to any more Glories," said Frank.

"We should get moving," said Thelma. "Frank's right about one thing, and if that gentleman's called the police, then we need to be away from here, and quickly."

"Frank, would you take Ginnie and Croyde in your car?" asked Martha, cheerfully.

Ginnie made a show of protesting, but Frank gruffly acquiesced, and the three of them got into the Merc. Thelma got into the driver's seat of the battered Renault in front of it, with Linda beside her, and me in the back with Martha. Clearly, they felt that lockdown rules were for other people. Soon we were under way.

"You've probably got quite a few questions," said Martha to me, gently.

"How much do you know about the Glories?" I asked. "And can you really find them?"

"I'd like to ask you the same thing," said Thelma from the front. "Can *you* find them."

"Well, I found that blue lake," I said, which was true, of course, but pure chance. It gave me a few moments to think, and I invented a story, inspired by how Linda had indicated my left hand. "Then when I woke this morning, my left hand sort of tingled a bit, and it was like it was telling me where to go. What about you, err, Linda, is it?"

"I can feel their light. Their warmth, like another sun. I can feel it now. But sometimes it gets stronger, and that's when I think there may be one close by. I don't think we can see them all, not yet. But we will. We have to learn better how to look."

"Frank's not behind us," said Thelma.

"Oh bugger," said Martha. "Stupid, I should have gone with him to make sure."

Chapter 7: The allies

"You don't think he's calling the police?" I asked.
"Wouldn't put it past him," said Martha.
"But Ginnie will stop him, surely?" asked Thelma
"Ginnie will do what he asks her to," said Martha. "Haven't you heard the creaking bedsprings? And they actually think we don't know about them!"
"Well, I didn't," said Thelma.
"That's because you're a deep sleeper," chuckled Martha.
"Oh, look, I can see them now," said Linda, pointing at the mirror.
"Phew," said Martha. "They probably just stopped for a snog or something."
"So you've all seen a Glory?" I asked.
"More than that," said Thelma. "We've been touched by them. Changed, you might say."
"Even Frank?"
"Francis more than any of us," said Martha. "I suppose you would say 'affected', rather than changed, though."
"There's another one!" said Linda, suddenly. "It's close! I can feel it, much stronger this time!"
"Which way?" asked Thelma. Linda pointed, sort of ahead and to the right. "Martha, call the others then look at routes, would you?"
Martha pulled out a her mobile, made a quick call, and said "Ginnie? She thinks she's got another one. Follow us, OK? And call me if you lose us." She quickly ended the call and opened a map on the screen. Linda evidently wasn't sure how close it was, so Martha navigated us onto a motorway, where we were almost the only vehicle on it. I asked them how their odd little group had got together.
"Well, Ginnie is my niece, and we had been sharing my big old house since my husband passed away," said Martha. "Now, now, don't fuss, he had a good life. So we were the starting point. When the lockdown started, I'd taken to doing daily walks, then one day, this was just after lunch, you understand, everything started sparkling. Like when there's a lot of dew on a cold sunny morning, you know? Except the sun was high, and the grass was dry. But it sparkled anyway. And not just the grass, the tree stumps, the fence posts, even my clothes. Tiny spots of brilliant light, never dazzling, always beautiful. I had no idea what was happening and I didn't care. I just sat down and drank it in. And I started to have this most wonderful feeling, as though everything was right, and it all made sense. Everything that had ever happened to me, and everything I'd ever done, had been the right thing, both for me and for the world, and I knew exactly why. Can you imagine how good that felt?"
"I think I can," I said.
"And then it was gone, and all the good feelings with it. And all that lovely certainty, that was gone too, and I couldn't even remember the reasons I'd had behind any of it. I felt utterly lost. I sat there alone till it got dark. Of course, when I got home, Ginnie was having kittens!"
"It cured your habit too," said Thelma.
"Yup! I smoked like a chimney most of my life, despite all Ginnie's heroic efforts to make me stop. But since that Glory, not a single one. I just haven't felt the need. There's a goodness about these things, I swear to you, Antony. I honestly believe that they come from God."

"I had a very different experience," said Thelma. "When I touched mine, I felt myself floating in something, air or water, space, I've no idea, but there were thousands of souls in there with me. All waiting to ascend, waiting to be let into Heaven. For a lifelong atheist, a woman who has spent the greater part of her life teaching science to unwilling children, it came as a profound shock, I can tell you. But if there's one rule of science that must remain immutable, it is to accept the evidence that is placed before you."

"How can you be sure it wasn't a dream?" I asked her.

"The same way you're sure you're sitting in this car, right now," she replied simply.

"We all met because of Ginnie," said Martha happily. "She didn't believe me about the Glory, of course – I mean, there'd been nothing on the news about them, had there? I think she got a bit worried that I was going loopy. We had plenty of free time, so she went into overdrive scanning social media, looking for other people who'd claimed to have seen these things, and she found plenty. Then she started to sort of believe me. But the posts kept disappearing."

"It wasn't just social media," said Thelma. "I'd had the local radio on, a few weeks after the Lockdown started, and there was this caller going on about this magic illusion he'd seen, like a rainbow lying on the ground and stretching over a river. The DJ said oh, someone had just drawn that, but the caller insisted that no, it couldn't be, because the water itself had turned those different colours. The DJ made a mean joke about magic mushrooms and cut him off. Then ten minutes later they had another caller saying she and her husband had both seen something that looked like a giant upside-down spotted toadstool hanging over a field. The DJ gave in at this point and decided to make a feature of what other crazy optical illusions listeners claimed to have seen. Someone else called in who'd seen the mushroom, too. And then a lady, who lives alone out in the sticks, called in to say everything at the bottom of her garden had turned to granite, even the spiders and their webs. But after that day, there was nothing. Not a mention, on that or any other station. The government had told them to black it out, they must have."

"Well, it backfired on Ginnie," said Martha proudly, "Because as soon as she got a whiff that someone might be trying to cover it up, she was totally convinced I was telling the truth. So she changed tack, looking for stories of people being affected by them. She came across quite some tales, I can tell you! But it just so happened that Thelma and Frank were the ones who lived locally. Thelma she connected with on social media. Of course Linda was the real find, her predictions really are quite accurate, most of the time."

"But not all?" I said.

"No forecaster gets it right all the time," smiled Martha. "Ask Michael Fish."

"Is that some kids' cartoon character?" I asked.

Linda pointed again, a bit to the left this time, and Martha checked the map. "Take the exit after next," she told Thelma.

Thelma said, "Frank was scathing at first, but when he heard what Linda could do, he was very, very keen to join us. Though it sounds like it might just have been about Ginnie."

"Trust me, it wasn't only about Ginnie," replied Martha.

"So have you found more Glories, working together?" I asked.

"Just the one, so far, plus a few near misses," said Thelma. "One winked out just as we were arriving. The one we got to properly was a Type Two –

that's where there's no physical object that appears, but everything within a defined area changes colour, or texture. Or sparkles, like Martha's first one. This one was maybe the size of a house, and everything in it was an exact colour negative of its normal colour."

"The leaves were red, the celandines purple. The tree trunks dark blue," said Martha.

"And did you feel anything? Like before," I asked.

"Not the same," said Martha. "I felt good, sure, but not euphoric. So I wonder now, if the first one was a one-off."

"Or if certain Glories are more powerful," concluded Thelma. "Which is my hypothesis. I cannot conceive of so profound a message not having a continuation."

"Anyway, that's where we found Croyde," said Martha. "He was just wandering around there, lost, not really saying anything much. He talks like a small child, does what he's told. Don't even know his real name, but he had this unwritten postcard in his pocket, from Croyde in Devon. So we called him that. I think maybe the Glory took his memories, like it took your cousin. We're going to ask the next one to give them back."

* * * * *

We could tell we were getting close because Linda's directions kept changing. More than once we had to turn the car around ("I bet Frank's *loving* this," said Martha the second time). But eventually we worked out where it more or less had to be, and parked by a nondescript bit of road, with Frank's car pulling up behind us.

"So where is it?" said Frank angrily (though I thought I could feel the worry in his voice).

"I think we're early," said Linda.

"How early? A year? Twenty?" said Frank, grumpily.

"I don't know, a few minutes, maybe more."

"I'm glad you can be so precise about it," he said sarcastically.

"Give it a rest," said Ginnie.

"We think it's that way," said Martha, pointing to a footpath that crossed the road, with styles in the hedges either side. Soon we were standing in a large, very dull grassy field, sloping gently downwards away from the hedge by the road, towards some trees. Sheep were grazing in a distant corner, and the field had scattered patches of thistle.

"Well it was worth the trip for the view," said Frank.

Then a Glory winked into existence right in front of us.

Chapter 8: Julia Barnes, special agent

Julia

There was one other passenger in the van. A lad barely out of school, clad in leather with jet black hair to match. He had a thin face and would probably be handsome in a few years' time; right now he looked sullen and reeked of late male adolescence. Nick had been a relatively scentless teenager, but one or two of his friends had brought with them their own special miasma whenever they'd come to the house, and it had usually taken half a day to dissipate. I reached down and gently opened the window by my seat. It was clear he wasn't going to introduce himself so I said "Hello, I'm Julia."

"Lucasz."

"You're Polish?" I'd caught the accent.

"Lived here all my life," he said, looking me right in the eye, defiantly.

I nearly panicked – the last thing I needed was to be thought xenophobic. "My niece is engaged to a Polish guy," I lied. "He's a sweetheart." I didn't have a niece.

"Oh," he said.

For some minutes we were silent as scenery whizzed past the window. Then I remembered the provisions Malcolm had assembled for me, about enough to get me to the South Pole and back, I reckoned.

"Are you hungry?" I asked.

"A bit," he said noncommitally.

I tried offering crispbreads and hummus, but he seemed unwilling to believe that they were food. Biscuits, however, were readily accepted.

"So what's your story?" I ventured. "Did you have a weird close encounter with a Glory?"

"That's why we're here," he said.

"But I'd like to know," I said gently. "We're going to be working together, aren't we? We ought to know a bit about each other, and especially what Glory-related … I dunno, … superpowers we've got. I suppose we're a sort of Happy Shopper version of, what's it called, '*Avengers Assembly*?'"

"It's *Avengers AssemBLE*," he said, knowledgeably.

"Ah. I suppose '*Avengers Assembly*' is the sequel where they all buy a cupboard from Ikea and try to put it together," I said.

He looked at me blankly for a moment, then gave me a detailed account of what actually happened in the second *Avengers* film, which went right over my head. Then, warming to his topic, he told me that there had been a lot more films in the series, twenty-six in fact, and looked like he was going to spend the whole journey describing them all, so I said, "You were going to tell me how you saw a Glory, and how something odd happened that landed you on this little ride with me."

"Was I? Oh." Removed from the Marvel universe, his loquacity had vanished again.

"You were," I said, even though he wasn't.

Chapter 8: Julia Barnes, special agent

"Well, I was working in a hospital," he began, unenthusiastically.

"A hospital? You're a nurse?" My eyes probably half popped out with surprise and respect.

"Floor cleaner."

A moment's pause, before I said, "Still an essential worker."

"Volunteer. Wanted to get away from home, and they were asking. They had people for all the more important stuff. I said was there anything else, and the woman said no, but another man said the cleaner was off with the Virus, so could I clean floors until she came back. But she didn't come back."

"You're probably helping more than you realise," I said, encouragingly.

"Only soon I wasn't only cleaning floors," he continued, as if he hadn't heard me. "Soon there were other jobs, bathrooms, toilet pans, even gaffer-taping bin bags together with two porters and a senior surgeon. Then it starts to be like, '*we need you to wheel these trolleys up to the ward, because everyone else is busy,*' and first there's just stuff on the trolleys, but then suddenly it's dead people, and I'm taking them to the bloody morgue. And first I'm leaving them outside but next day it's '*just wheel them in, find a space and roll them onto the table there.*' Some days there's eight or ten black bags in there, it's like a bloody disaster movie."

Now the words were spilling out of him like a torrent.

"And then it's, '*look I'm sorry to ask this but the nurses are too busy and a load of them are off with the Virus, so we need you to do a few jobs on the ward,*' and I'm asking what kind of jobs, only I'm pretty sure I know, and it's putting people who've just died into body bags. Then wheeling them off to the morgue, of course. I'm meant to be cleaning floors! And then last week they started running out of body bags, and now they've got me wrapping the poor buggers up in the sheets they died in. With gaffer tape. It's somebody's grandpa, and I'm rolling the poor sod up in sheets and fucking duct tape, as if I'd murdered the poor bastard and I'm gonna dump him in the river.

"And one morning I've done three of those already and I swear it wasn't eleven yet, and I'm just trying to stay out of sight so I can just clean floors for a bit like I'm meant to be doing, it's not like they're paying me, though I don't care about the money, and anyway this man finds me. And he's not the boss or a nurse or a doctor so at first I'm thinking, '*thank God, he can't be asking me to wrap any more dead people*', but it turns out it's worse, because his wife is dying in one of the wards and they won't let him see her. He's only about thirty, you know? And he's crying like a fucking baby. And I'm thinking I'm going to be wrapping her up soon, and she's probably thirty too, and then I'm thinking thank God so far I've only had to wrap up the old ones."

Lucasz' eyes were starting to water, but there was no stopping his story now.

"So I ask the man if he's had the virus and he says yes, it was him that gave it to her, and now he's crying even more, and I think, fuck it, if he's had the virus and got better like I did, then he's immune like me, that's why I volunteered to help there in the first place, that and to get away from my parents, anyway so he's immune and I think, fuck the rules, I'm going to let him see his wife. So I grab a mop and tell him to walk behind me, like he's my apprentice or something, and

Chapter 8: Julia Barnes, special agent

everyone will be so busy they won't ask us, and they didn't, so we found his wife's ward, and in he went.

"I didn't stay, just buggered off downstairs to find some out-of-the-way floors to mop again. I hadn't been there an hour when my bloody boss came down. Said she '*wanted a word,*' and I went off at her about how the poor bloke wanted to see his wife and what was the bloody harm in it, and if I was just cleaning floors like I was supposed to be then maybe I wouldn't have to be dealing with stuff like that, only it turns out she hadn't heard anything about the bloke and his wife, only now I'd just bloody told her. I thought she'd fire me, even though she couldn't because I'm only a bloody volunteer! But she'd come to talk to me because she was worried and said she felt bad that I'd had to wrap up all the dead people, but of course now she was even more worried, and probably angry, but she didn't say, and she basically said I had to go home and I said no, I'm not fucking going home, because my mum and dad argue all the time and mum was just about to fuck off back to Poland when she got ill, then he got ill, and then there was the lockdown so they're stuck in the same house together and yes, it's bloody hell in there, and why does she think I keep volunteering for twelve hour shifts and wrapping up bloody dead people, it's because that's still better than hearing them shout at each other and if she bloody sends me home, then she can't possibly be as bloody short-staffed as she keeps telling me she is.

"And she says look, I'm not firing you, but you're not right in the head, it's all the stress and I say it's not the stress, I'm just not doing the job I volunteered to be doing, and she says she's sorry, it's not her fault and she's not blaming me either, but I need to take a break, and I don't want a break, I just want to clean floors and she says but people will keep asking me to do other stuff so I need to get out for a while, but I don't want to go home, so she says go for a walk."

He paused, for the first time in quite a while, gasping for breath. I got the feeling he hadn't told this to anyone else, at least not in that kind of detail. It sounded like he didn't have anyone else that he could tell.

"So I went for a walk," he said.

"Go on."

"There's this great big wood right by the hospital, I see it out the window all the time, but I'd never been in it. I had to go somewhere, not home and not the hospital, so I went there. Into the wood. The bluebells were just coming out, and the leaves on the trees were pale and new. I'd forgotten what spring looks like, you know? The birds were singing. Then there was a fence and I just hopped over it, kept going through a field, the soil was bare. Then more fields, but they were planted so I went along the edge. Didn't know where I was going, didn't care, thought maybe I'd just keep walking till it was night, and maybe I wouldn't even stop then.

"And then I got into this other wood. There was this wide trackway going through it, I saw two other people walk into the wood that way, so I went that way too. And then it was there. It was … it was just … I thought maybe I'd died. That I'd got the virus and just dropped dead, and all my walk had been some sort of … I dunno. But it was there."

"A Glory?" I asked.

Chapter 8: Julia Barnes, special agent

"Didn't know the word back then, but yeah. A huge wall, with smears of green and brown, moving slowly around, like someone had pained the forest but then the paint was running."

"How big? What shape?" I asked.

"Don't really know. Big. Bigger than a house, maybe lots of houses. Curvy edges. The tips of the trees were sticking out of the top. It wobbled a bit, well I thought it did, but Lockey said maybe it was the trees swaying and the Glory thing was still. I don't know. People were trying to touch it and photograph it. I just walked up to it to touch it too, only I didn't. There was nothing to touch. My hand just went right inside, like it was some sort of mirage or something. There were two people looking at me, and first I thought they were taking the piss, pretending it was solid, but they looked really surprised, even scared. One of them, the woman, tried to push hard at it, but it was like it pushed back and she fell on her bum. Then I just took a step forward and walked right inside it."

"In*side??*"

"Inside."

"What was it like?"

"Like I was … inside the night. Black starry skies all around me, even below. I should've been scared but I wasn't, I felt safe. I walked a bit and just sat down."

"You said there were trees sticking out of it. So their trunks must have been inside it?"

"Yeah. But I didn't bump into any. I couldn't see them. Just sat on what must have been the ground, and looked at the stars. It was like I was floating alone in space. Could've stayed there all night. Dunno how long I did, maybe half an hour, maybe three. Then the light came back on."

"It vanished?"

"Yeah, in one moment. Then there was this ring of confused people, and lots of them were pointing at me and looking at their phones."

"Glories can't be photographed," I said. "Even old polaroid cameras don't see them. So anyone who tried to take a picture of your Glory would have got nothing but an image of you sitting there among the trees."

"I guess that must be how Lockey found me. Someone posted me on social media. I didn't talk about it to anyone. Just went home and into bed, then back to the hospital next day. Four days later Lockey turns up with a picture and asks if it's me. I say yes, and she says, do I want a better job than cleaning floors and wrapping up dead people, and also I don't have to live at home."

"She does her homework" I said. "And her name's Lock*sley*."

"Oh. Yeah. I call her Lockey. Cos she's so stiff and there's this guy called Loki in the Marvel films and he's like totally the opposite and …"

"I think we're going to get on, you know," I interrupted, partly because I meant it, but mostly because I really didn't want to let him get back onto the Marvel Universe. Honestly, twenty-seven films? Dear God, where did anyone find the time? So I started on my story. He looked genuinely upset when I told him about the cancer, and I was touched.

* * * * *

Chapter 8: Julia Barnes, special agent

Some time later, we pulled into a motorway service station car park. It was almost empty, and I wondered if the facilities were even open. A couple of trucks were parked across where cars would normally be, but we drove straight past them to the far end of the car park, where a white minibus was waiting, with two figures standing nearby, one of them waving. His skin tone, accent and cheery manner all suggested Caribbean descent, and consequently the drab, grey clothes he was wearing didn't suit him at all. We got out, and he broke into a broad smile. "Julia Barnes? Lucasz Kowalski? It's a pleasure to meet you both. Call me Bart. I'll be your driver today. Every day, in fact."

An engine started behind us and the car we were in drove away, leaving our stuff there on the ground. Bart picked up my luggage with ridiculous ease, lifting with one hand the case that I could barely manage with two, and hoicked it into the back of the minibus. Lucasz tried to copy him with his own, and I had to suppress the urge to laugh as he staggered toward the minibus carrying his pack with an outstretched arm, while trying to look nonchalant.

I knew exactly why he was doing it. The second person standing by the minibus was a young woman of about his age. She was slim and very pretty, though that was partly because she'd gone all out with make-up – eyeliner, blusher, lipstick, the works. Her hair was smooth, dark blonde and shoulder-length, she had enviable cheekbones, and was dressed in somewhat impractical shoes, a tight blouse and a smooth beige skirt that ended above her knees. Well, no wonder poor Lucasz was trying to show off. But she seemed utterly uninterested in us, her attention being wholly focused on the phone in her hand.

"This is Lara," said Bart. She looked up at last, said a cursory hello, and then went back to her phone.

I said quietly to Lucasz, "Are all girls your age obsessed with their phones?" It was a rhetorical question, because I had taught for years in a secondary school.

"Most of them, yeah."

"My condolences."

Bart invited us into the minibus, telling us merrily to sit together in the back and get to know each other. He put on some jaunty music, not too loud, and we were away.

Perhaps I was being too harsh on Lara. For me this was an adventure, and for Lucasz an escape, but what of a young woman who had been perfectly comfortable and happy at home? To be whisked away by the secret services with people she'd never met, in the middle of a global crisis? Perhaps I would be hiding in my phone as well. And though the fancy shoes, make-up and skirt all seemed extremely silly to me, she'd probably been sat at home in her pyjamas for weeks. And for some young women, make-up was armour, according to our old school counsellor. I've never really understood that myself.

"Lara?" I said. "May I call you Lara?"

"It's my name."

"I was just wondering – what's your story? Something happened to you with a Glory, yes? And that's how you ended up being recruited?"

She put her phone down on her lap, and turned to us. "I can move them."

"Move them?"

Chapter 8: Julia Barnes, special agent

"Yeah. Was out walking with my dad, and there was this mountain in front of us that shouldn't have been there. I mean, it's a field, a flat field, with some sort of crop in it just starting to come up. It's on one of the walks we've been doing for our exercise. Only that day it wasn't flat, it had grown into this steep pointy mountain, twenty metres high. The sides were all like rock, only you couldn't touch them, it sort of pushed people away. There were a few other people standing there. Thing is, when I tried to touch it, it sort of moved away from me. Slowly at first, then faster. It moved at least five metres. But it wouldn't for anyone else."

"Wow," I said. "No wonder they recruited you."

"Locksley, the woman that came to my house a few days later, said I was some sort of shaman. I didn't get what she meant at all. She said something about how shamans could move mountains."

Lucasz perked up. "It's a pop reference," he said. "*Move any Mountain*" was a song by a 1990s pop band called The Shaman."

"Oh," said Lara, dismissively.

It was her rudeness to Lucasz that made me do it. Some people just deserved to be needled. "Well, I don't believe you," I said.

Lara's eyes flared with anger. "Well, I don't bloody care what you think, Grandma! It happened, alright?"

"Oh, I don't mean the Glory-moving stuff," I added quickly, surprised by her vehemence. "I totally believe you on that. It's just the bit about Locksley having a sense of humour that I'm struggling with."

"She's got a point," added Lucasz, with a cheeky smile.

I'd expected Lara to find this at least a little bit funny, and maybe even build a little camaraderie among us, but it failed completely. "Yeah, well, she said it," was her only response.

"You must be her favourite," I told her. "She never even smiled at me."

"Same here," said Lucasz. But Lara had retreated back into the world of her phone. I smiled sympathetically at Lucasz.

"Do you want to hear our stories?" Lucasz asked her. "About Glories, I mean?"

"If you want to," she said, unenthusiastically.

"Well I was volunteering in this hospital," he began. "It started off that I was just cleaning floors, because the normal cleaner had coronavirus, but soon they were asking me to do more and more dangerous stuff. After a week they had me dealing with actual dead bodies …"

I listened with amusement as he stripped out all of the emotion and fragility from his story, and reinvented it as some sort of cut-price superhero origin tale, clearly believing that this would impress Lara. To be honest, I wasn't sure Clark Kent himself could have got a smile out of her, unless he turned up with a gift of a newer model of mobile phone. Still, she looked up from her phone occasionally as he talked, which was a minor triumph on his part. But she reacted exactly the same way to my story as well. But other than a few polite questions about our stories, she didn't say anything else for a while. Meanwhile we sped along the almost empty motorway, and it was an event every time we saw another vehicle.

Chapter 8: Julia Barnes, special agent

* * * * *

We pulled in, after over an hour, to a large cottage in a medium-sized town. It had the look of a dwelling that once sat alone and proud in the countryside, before being swallowed up by new development.

"Is this going to be our base?" I asked, as Bart got out.

"No, it's a pick-up!" He sauntered over to the front door, where I noticed a gleaming disabled ramp that contrasted with the old-style garden and brickwork. The door opened before he reached it – clearly we were expected. A wheelchair emerged with a frail looking woman in it, apparently asleep, pushed by a plump man with thick glasses – both about my age, I would guess. He had a round face with reddish cheeks, balding on top but with a wide moustache providing some compensation. He wore a checked jacket over two jumpers and a belly with thoughts of escape. Bart stood aside to let them pass, then went into the house and emerged with three huge suitcases, again carried with no apparent effort. Lucasz leapt out to help the new arrivals.

Bart explained apologetically that our minibus lacked a proper disabled ramp, and gently lifted the lady and her wheelchair into the back. The portly man got in with her. "Bluebell, my darling," he told her, in a rather loud voice, "we're going on a little trip now. Not sure how long for, but I'll be with you all the way. Now I've spoken to the driver, and he's a really lovely man, so if there's anything wrong, anything you need, just tell me and I'll pass it on. I'll be right here, see? Right here with you."

The woman didn't respond, she seemed to be asleep. Bart motioned us to take our seats. As the bus moved off again, I turned to introduce myself but the man got his in first. "Hector's the name! And my dear wife here is Bluebell!"

"We can hear you fine, you don't need to shout," said Lara grumpily.

"I'm Julia," I told him, before anyone could react further, "and this is Lara, and Lucasz. So they've recruited you too? Do you have some special thing you can do with Glories?"

"Not me, I'm as mundane as they come," he declared, a little less loudly. "Boringly normal, you might say! No, it's my good ladywife that they want!"

"Oh," said Lara. "So what happens to her, when she touches a Glory?"

"She wakes up."

Chapter 9: The vanishing

Antony

I gawped at the Glory. I think the others did too. It was stunningly beautiful. A rippling curtain of aquamarine blue, which had to be twenty-five metres across, and so tall I couldn't see where – or if – it ended. Down it fell petals – well, they looked like petals, of various sizes. They were pink, red, purple, yellow, azure blue, bright green, every colour you could name.

"I take it all back," said Frank, his voice quivering a little. "Well done, Linda"

Linda didn't respond, but those words seemed to break the spell that had held us all motionless. Linda ran forward, arms outstretched, and sort of hugged the Glory like a hippy trying to embrace an enormous tree. Croyde just sat down where he was, and looked at it. "I can see them," said Thelma, though I couldn't tell who she was talking to. "I can see them all!" Slowly, she stretched out her arms as far as they'd go.

Martha began walking forward towards the Glory, a beatific smile on her face. It was as if each of them had forgotten that anyone else was there. "You have to go to it," said Ginnie, just behind me. I looked around, but she was talking to Frank. His eyes were full of terror.

"But what if it's the same?" he said, voice breaking, as he gripped her shoulders. "Don't you see? Thelma's seeing what she saw before. Martha as well. That means *I* will, too!"

"You've come this far," she said. "You can't turn back now. You don't know what you'll see this time."

"Don't want to," he said, in the tone of a small child.

"If you turn away now, you'll be scared for the rest of your life. Those nightmares …"

"Oh, you mean the ones of me burning in Hell, while all those demons laugh at me? Those ones? And how do you think seeing it all for real a second time is going to make it any better!?"

"Because it isn't real! It was never real! It was like a bad trip, I keep trying to tell you, that was all it was! Look, I'll hold your hand, I'll touch it with you, we'll do it together."

Then he burst out crying, burying his head in her chest, and I turned away, realising rather too late that I was intruding on something private. Martha was touching the Glory now, with one outstretched hand. Thelma was walking towards it, one thin leg at a time, like a heron stalking a fish. Croyde was gazing at the Glory from his sitting position, smiling contentedly. Somehow, among all these people, I was still alone with this Glory.

I wondered, if I looked at it too long, would I wake up a day later, again? But this time, there were sensible adults around me, they would shake me awake if that happened, surely? The Glory had changed colour now, the curtain was dark green, but the falling petals were still every possible colour. I felt the urge to move closer, and took one step down towards it, then another.

"OH MY GOD, WHAT IS THAT?"

A sporty-looking woman was standing on the style behind me, with her mouth hanging open in wonder and shock. "Well, get out of the way and perhaps I'll tell you," said a man's voice from behind her. She stepped down

Chapter 9: The vanishing

from the style and he appeared behind it. "It's a Spectral Glory" he declared. "I told you they were real!"

"But it's impossible," she said.

"That it may be, but it's there! Jessie, come and see this!"

He helped a little girl with pigtails over the style. She yelped with delight at the Glory. "Pretty!" she said, letting go of her father's hand. She ran towards it.

"Jessie, stop!" yelled the mother. "We don't know if it's safe!"

"Wait!" agreed the father.

I tried to block the girl's way, putting my arms out wide, forcing her to dodge around me. Then her father ran past me and caught her, just metres from the Glory. "That's close enough," he said. "We're just going to look, okay?"

"Those other ladies are touching the Pretty," she said.

Martha was still touching the Glory with one hand, her face drenched in ecstacy. Thelma was leaning against it, her hands moving around as if to massage it, as she mouthed what might have been a prayer. Linda was still in hug mode, her expression that of a child cuddling its favourite pet.

"Yes, but we don't know what it's doing to them," said Jessie's father.

"It looks like it feels nice," said Jessie.

"Things that feel nice aren't always good for you," he replied.

"What will I do?" It was Frank's trembling voice, coming from behind me. "What'll I do if it's the same thing again?"

"*We*," (she emphasised the word) "will deal with it together. If it's the Christian Hell, then we'll have to try Christian solutions, won't we? Priests, Confession, Baptism, that sort of thing. You see? There's always a way."

"I'm scared."

"There's no need. I'll be with you."

"Oh God, oh God, oh God," he said, screwing up his eyes and stretching out his hand. He was almost touching the Glory, but his hand seemed to hover a few centimetres away from it.

"Frank?" said Ginnie. "What are you feeling?"

Frank opened his eyes fully, and pushed his other hand firmly against the Glory. "Nothing!" he said. "It's like pushing a wall. There's nothing! I've come all this way, and there's *nothing*!!!"

"Frankie," said Ginnie, her hand on his shoulder.

Frank began pounding his fists against the Glory. "Show me!! Show me something!! I need to know! *I need to know*!!!!"

Ginnie tried to soothe him with words about having overcome his fear, and that was what made me realise, suddenly, that I was standing there like an idiot watching everybody else, instead of facing my own situation. A dog was barking merrily, which meant more people were arriving. I needed to walk forward, and touch the Glory, and somehow – I was far from clear on that bit – search for some sign of Daniel. I stepped closer, ignoring the voices from behind me that told me more onlookers were arriving. The falling coloured petals seemed to get smaller as I approached, or rather, they looked the same size however close or far away you were, in exactly the way that real objects don't. By this point I was close enough to touch the Glory, and I could see nothing else but falling colours and rippling dark brown, as if it were enclosing me. I had to make contact. I stretched out my hand towards it, expecting resistance like Frank's hand had been met with, but finding none. My hand passed straight into it, my

Chapter 9: The vanishing

fingertips vanishing behind the rippling surface. I could feel nothing, as if my fingers were wiggling in mid-air. Then I curled my fingers, and plucked out a piece of the Glory. It came like jelly in a spoon, wobbling and rippling in my palm, the coloured petals appearing from one side, moving quickly across the surface and vanishing from the other, as if it were a mini computer screen. Keeping it there, I closed my eyes and thought of Daniel.

I began with his face, then his voice, and the sort of things he said. *'Don't be borrrring, Cuz!' 'Jeebus Twist! Look at that!' 'That's just hypertronic!'* Daniel could say things that would have sounded epically lame coming out of my mouth, and somehow make them utterly cool. I called forth more memories, of us playing at home, building complex structures with my Lego, sometimes playing games that he'd usually win, often by cheating. It was always in my house. I'd asked him, one time, why we never played in his house, and he'd snapped at me. *'It's just better here, OK? Now drop it!'*

None of this remembering seemed to do anything useful. I was still standing there, with the piece of Glory in my hand, same as before. I heard a gasp from my left, and saw two people I didn't know, pointing a mobile phone at me, and looking from the screen to each other in great confusion. I recalled my own phone, and how the Glory had simply not been there, on its screen, and felt profoundly grateful, as the last thing I needed was pictures of me with a hand full of Glory going viral on Instagram.

Even so, if they recognised me, they might be calling the police, in which case I was running out of time. Taking a piece of the Glory hadn't worked. But if I was right and the Glory had made Daniel disappear, then I wasn't going to find him by standing here doing what I'd done last time, was I? I'd have to do more. I'd have to go in after him.

I put my hand into the Glory once again, allowing the piece I was holding to flow back into the rest. Then I reached out with the other hand, and that went in too, but with some resistance. I stepped forward, pushing my arms further in, and now I felt something pushing back on both arms, steadily harder as I pushed further in, a bit like trying to force a balloon under the water. I closed my eyes, took a deep breath, and plunged my head into it. I felt myself swaying, not sure if I was being pushed one way or the other, and opened my eyes. I saw nothing – it was utterly black, then the sky reappeared, and I fell back onto my arse. The Glory had spat me out. I stood up and tried again, this time trying to keep my eyes open. The same thing happened, it pushed me out. I thought for a moment, then tried crawling into it, head first, with my fingers gripping the soil to resist the increasing push against me. Deeper I went – perhaps if I could get every part of me inside it, it'd stop pushing and accept me. I had no way of knowing how deep in I was, so all I could do was keep going. My fingers strained against the soil, muscles tight in my arms. I should have got someone to give me a shove from behind, but who could I have asked?

Keep going, keep going. I tried to dig my toes in, too, but the ground was dry and hard. Then I put my hand down straight onto a thistle. I yelped with pain, lost my grip, and was ejected from the Glory once more, like Incy Wincy bloody Spider being shot out of his drainpipe.

I shook my head in frustration, and readied myself for another try. Then the Glory disappeared. I swore, loudly. "Antony? Is that you?" said Martha.

Chapter 9: The vanishing

"Gone," said a male voice. The bald man was pointing at where the Glory had been.

"Yes, Croyde, it's gone," she replied.

"I don't think he means the Glory," said Ginnie, who was still cradling the distraught Frank.

"Oh," said Martha.

Thelma and Linda were nowhere to be seen.

* * * * *

I felt a horrible sense of déjà vu. This time, at least, I was not alone, and surely someone else would have seen what happened to the two women. I ran up the slope, looking for the girl called Jessie and her parents, the people other than us that I knew for certain had been there the longest. But they were gone, too. *They just walked off*, I told myself.

Ginnie was speaking to a young woman with a dog. The dog walker was holding out her phone at arms' length, while Ginnie squinted at the picture from a government-approved distance. I went over to look as well. "Could you text me the picture?" asked Ginnie, giving the woman her number, and the walker obliged. Now we could see the picture on Ginnie's phone. The dog-walker explained that she'd taken a series of photographs, and of course the Glory did not show up in any of them.

"Bouncer ran right through it, like it wasn't there, and didn't come back when I called" the walker said, indicating her dog. "I was terrified I'd lost him, but then I thought, hang on, I'd already tried to photograph it, the Glory, and it didn't show up. I mean, they don't, apparently. So I tried to see where Bouncer was by looking through the Glory with the camera on my phone, it sort of worked but it really hurt my eyes, so I just took wide angle photos and found him on those."

The walker pointed to the corner of one of the photos. "He was harassing the sheep, of course he was. But look, there's your friend in the red dress, and the tall lady." By now, Frank and Martha were standing with us too, and the walker showed all four of us the photo. Even from a back view, Linda and Thelma looked oddly like mime artists, pressing their bodies against nothing. There was Martha, hand outstretched, and Ginnie, back to us, cradling Frank. Jessie and her parents were there, too.

Ginnie thanked her, and went haring off up the slope to talk to other people, most of whom were waiting in a spaced-out line by the style to take their turn to cross it. A minute later she'd returned, having got one of them to text her another photo. She showed us. Ginnie, Frank and Martha were all there, but no Linda or Thelma.

"Oh, thank God," I said. The others looked at me, so I explained. "There was a family of three, and they weren't there at the end, either. I thought they might have disappeared, too. But look, you can see them, walking away from the Glory."

"The girl's being pulled away by her parents," said Martha. "The parents look scared, both of them."

"They weren't before," I said. "Cautious, yes, but not scared."

Chapter 9: The vanishing

"He's right," said Ginnie. "They're almost dragging the girl away, she wants to stay, but it's like they've seen something and they're scared for her. If we could catch up with them, ask what they'd seen?"

"Gone," said Croyde, standing behind us. 'Gone into the Glory."

"Croyde?" said Martha. "You saw what happened?"

"My name's Adam," said Croyde. "I was watching. One minute they were there, leaning on it, and the next it just opened up and accepted them."

"They fell into it?" asked Ginnie.

"That was what they wanted, wasn't it?" I asked. "I mean, Thelma was literally talking about it."

"That doesn't make it okay, if the bloody thing ate them!" said Ginnie, eyes blazing with teary fury.

"I don't think it would have eaten them, exactly," said Martha. "For all we know, they are doors to somewhere else. Perhaps one of them found the key."

I felt my insides contract as a wave of horror ran through me, as I remembered the piece of Glory in my hand. '*Key.*'

"Hang on," said Frank. "We're all missing something here. That guy – Blake" (he pointed at me) "he was there with a Glory when his cousin disappeared, and now here he is, with a Glory, and suddenly our friends are gone!"

"We don't know it's his fault!" countered Martha. "For all we know, this happens all the time! The government haven't exactly been forthcoming about it all, have they?"

"Anything that would scare people into staying clear, they'd be shouting from the rooftop!" countered Ginnie.

"But it didn't do anything to me," said Martha. "I was touching it too, the whole time!"

"But you weren't *leaning* on it," said Ginnie. "Look at the photo. You're reaching out and touching it. The other two are pressing themselves against it. Was there a moment when it seemed to go softer, against your hand?"

"Not that I remember. But I was, you know, out of it."

"Something made it go soft, and the obvious answer is him," said Frank, again pointing at me.

"My wife died. From that virus." We turned to look at Croyde/Adam, who was standing close by with tears rolling down his face. "I remember now. We'd only been married a year. Since then, I've just … walked."

"Do you remember us?" asked Martha. "We've been looking after you?"

"I'd like to go home now," he replied, and told us his address.

"I can take you," said Frank. "I'm going home myself. I'm done here, and I'm done with Glories. Ginnie, I think I have fallen in love with you, would you please come with me?"

Ginnie's face melted into a broad smile. "Of course I will. Martha, I'll call."

"You do that, love," said Martha. "Look after him, but don't take any crap." She turned to me, her aged face forming a warm smile. "Looks like it's you and me, kid."

I looked back at her, unable to speak, feeling quite incredibly grateful. She must have seen it in my eyes, because she nodded and said "Now, now, let's not get silly about it."

"No," said Frank.

"What?" said several people at once.

Chapter 9: The vanishing

"The two of you are not going off together. I won't have Ginnie worrying about her aunt disappearing next. Martha, I'll give you a lift back to the house. You, and only you. I'm sorry kid, nothing personal."

"Now just you hang on, young man!" Martha's voice was suddenly full of steel. "I have never taken orders from self-important young men, and I do not intend to start now!"

"Well, you could walk home, I suppose?" said Frank sarcastically. "Unless you happen to have the keys to Thelma's car, and are willing to risk being arrested for driving without insurance."

"We'll walk," she replied, but if I could hear the uncertainty behind her defiance, then he certainly could, as well.

"Alright then," said Frank, and he turned sharply, and started walking up the hill.

"Aunt Martha, please," said Ginnie. "Don't make me choose between you."

I thought of my lonely walk in the dark, the night before. I was young, Martha was not. "Go with them," I told her.

"But love, I can't leave you alone," Martha said to me, and I almost cried to see the care in her eyes, concern that I didn't deserve.

"And I can't let anyone else get hurt because of me," I said, my voice rising.

"I know, let's have a vote on it, shall we?" said Frank, with a note of triumph in his voice.

"Leave it," said Ginnie, slapping him hard on the hand.

"Your niece is going to need you, when she realises she's hitched herself to a TOTAL DICKHEAD," I told Martha, shouting the last two words. Then I dropped my voice, speaking to her alone. "I'm grateful to you for wanting to help me. More than I could ever say. But I won't see you hurt because of me. I couldn't bear it. Go with them."

"You're a good boy," Martha replied, her eyes welling up. "Don't ever let anyone tell you different. And you're going to find what you're looking for." We hugged. Then she slowly started up the slope after the others, turning to look at me again and again, as I stood where I was. Then, when she was about halfway up the slope, she suddenly turned and hurried back towards me. I walked up to meet her, puzzled.

"There's a young man," she told me. "Name of Jamie. I helped him out once and we stayed in touch. If you mention my name, he'll probably help you, at least give you a place to stay. He lives alone, cottage called Pulsar, on the west side of Merryvale, fifteen or twenty miles from here, can you walk that?"

"Easily," I said.

She gave me more details on how to find it. She did a sort of socially distanced hug, putting her arms around nothing as her eyes locked with mine, then she wiped away a tear, before hurrying after the others. Then they were over the style, and I was still standing in the field, alone once more.

Chapter 10: Adventures in the Glorybird

Julia

"Her name's Bluebell," announced Hector. "We've been together forty-one years, and when I met her, she was the most beautiful woman I'd ever clapped eyes on. Still is! But she doesn't know me anymore. Doesn't know anyone. Do you, love?" He almost shouted the last three words. "There was an accident, and she's never been the same since. So that's all. All that's left of my Bluebell. But she loves the countryside, so I take her out every day, three hours wheeling that squeaky chair, and she hears the birds and she smells the flowers and sometimes I almost hear her talking to me.

"Then we saw the Glory. It wasn't like the ones I'd read about. It was all red. I mean, everything was red. The trees, the grass, the flowers, the hedge and the fence, the birds flying through. The ants! The bees! And we went right in. There were other people there, I said hello but they didn't say it back. The red area was big, size of a Tennis court, or bigger! And when we were in it, the wheelchair was red and our clothes were red and her jewels were red, but not us. Not our skin. Not our hair, not our bodies. Same on the other people we could see. And then there's this little voice saying 'Hector, where am I?' and it's Bluebell. She's trying to stand up, can't understand why her legs won't support her, and then she's asking more and more questions, and slowly she's realising that she doesn't remember anything about all these lost years, and she keeps asking me and asking me what's happened to her, and the only question she isn't asking is, why is everything red?

"And I have to tell her that she's been ill but it's alright, she's better now, and she remembers everything from before the accident, she's right back how she was, cleverer than me, she was always cleverer than me, and I ask her what she can see around her, and she says she can see the whole world, and I don't understand and I ask her what she means, but then the red colour's all gone and so is she. Back in her chair with eyes glazed over, like she was before. So we're damned well going to find her another one, and hear what she has to say!"

* * * * *

We stopped for a late lunch at another motorway service station, trooping across a near-deserted car park into a restaurant where a masked woman told us we could have burgers, hot dogs or cold meat sandwiches. None of these appealed, so I said I'd have some of the sandwiches Malcolm had packed me. When everyone had got something, we went to sit down. Most tables were of course deserted, just the odd trucker sitting alone. One large table had a man in his thirties, who looked like he hadn't cut his hair since his teens. He looked rather thin, possibly because he was intently interacting with his computer instead of eating. A thin black leather jacket hung open over an equally black T-shirt

Chapter 10: Adventures in the Glorybird

advertising some obscure band, magazine or *Doctor Who* episode. A familiar woman strode up to his table.

"Got anything, Farron?" asked Locksley.

"Not like you to be late, boss," he replied, without looking up. "I think we may have a live one,"

"Within range?" asked Locksley. "You have corroboration?"

"Not yet. But it's eighty-six minutes' drive away, so I reckon our best bet is to launch the Glorybird and I'll track for mentions as we go. If it looks hoaxey we can easily turn round."

"OK, let's roll – hang on, where's Sharpe?" said Locksley.

"Having a dump."

Locksley rolled her eyes. "Right," she said. "We're going to have to eat on the move. Anyone needs the loo, go now, and if you see Sharpe in there, tell him I said 'hi'. Otherwise, back to the minibus."

"Oh, aren't we going in the Glorybird?" I asked, and got a fierce look.

The 'Glorybird' was of course the same minibus we'd been in before, only driven much faster. I took a seat behind Bart, the driver, and Farron clambered in beside me, holding a laptop attached by some puny wire to a mobile phone.

Within ten minutes, Farron said, "There's another one."

"What?" asked Locksley.

"Massive one. I'm talking way, WAY bigger than anything anyone's seen before. They're gonna have a job covering this up, unless it goes quickly."

"Where?"

"Too far away from us, I think. And it's some way above the ground, so there'd be no chance of touching it."

"Then we ignore it, focus on the original target," said Locksley.

"I agree, it's just … with the dark curtain one this morning, and two reports from further afield, we're already on five for the day. They're accelerating. A lot."

"Then we'd better do our job," she replied firmly.

As we drove, Farron filled us in on what he'd learned. The Glory we were heading for had been there for at least an hour, with a young woman live-tweeting about it. Two other apparently unconnected accounts gave consistent descriptions. It sounded even more impressive than my own one. I watched the others. Lucasz looked excited, holding a poised position, as if ready to spring into action. Hector was silent for once, holding tightly onto Bluebell's unresponsive hand, while Lara was buried in her mobile phone, seemingly as unconcerned by our mission as she was by travel sickness. I found myself wondering what I had to offer among this strange assemblage of sort-of superheroes. Lara could move a Glory, and Lucasz could enter one. Bluebell could see inside them, possibly even glimpse what was causing them. Whereas I had the power to pass out without falling over. On the bright side, I reasoned, people with the power to interact with Glories had to be extremely rare, if they'd considered me one of the four most useful people they could find.

Several people were posting accounts of the Glory we were heading for, and Farron used them to work out the location. It was in a grassy valley, much of it

Chapter 10: Adventures in the Glorybird

a nature reserve, and well over a mile from the nearest road. "Best bet's a farm track, from the North side," he said. "Try for Heston Farm with the Satnav."

The roads got smaller and wigglier, with Bart taking every corner fast and hooting to warn oncoming traffic we were coming. Lara looked terrified. Then eventually we were bumping along a farm track until a giant brown puddle that looked like a communal loo for cows blocked our way. "Everyone out!" barked Locksley, and soon there was running – Lara, Lucasz and Locksley haring off into the distance, followed by Hector, trundling Bluebell in her wheelchair through the grass at surprising speed.

Bluebell's head and arms bounced and lolled around. "Gonna make you just right again," shouted Hector, "you see if I don't! Vroom vroom! Just like Margate, eh? Remember Margate?"

I kept up with them for all of about ten paces, then ground to a halt, gasping. "My running days are over, I'm afraid," I told Farron, who was standing beside me.

"I try not to run, on principle," he replied with a smile. So we walked together, through one grassy field and then another, which ended in a barbed wire fence with a gap cut into it. "Oh Hector, you vandal," smirked Farron. "There it is! Down there, do you see it?"

Beyond the gap, Hector was now ploughing Bluebell's wheelchair along the edge of a field of oilseed rape, his determination aided by the downhill slope. Beyond that field was grass, levelling out into a snaking valley bottom with willow trees dotted along a stream. The valley went on calmly for perhaps a quarter mile, and then there it was, the Glory. I'd known roughly what to expect from Farron's descriptions, but they could not come close to capturing what it was like to look down on it.

I was looking at an enormous sky blue cylinder hanging in mid-air over a country valley. It was perhaps ten metres in diameter, and close to fifty metres long. Its surface looked smooth, but also like distant, immaculate sky, except that rings of deeper blue expanded from the centre of the disc at its end, then travelled down its length away from me, meeting others coming towards me. The near end was three metres above the ground, well out of reach of the dozen or so folk gathering there, but the far end was embedded in a grassy slope where the land rose. I understood at that moment precisely why some people were saying we'd been invaded by aliens, or at least were being talked to by them. It was unearthly.

"I sure as hell don't know what it is, but my God it's beautiful," said a rich voice beside me.

"You're right there, Bart," I said. We gazed at it together. In the valley, some were running, others sitting or standing like us. Only at the far end, where the ground was higher, could anyone touch the Glory. The running forms of Lucasz, Lara and Locksley were almost underneath the near end of the Glory now, but as I watched, Lara stumbled suddenly, and pitched forward onto the ground.

"That'll be the daft shoes she's got on," I said.

"Guess no-one told her there'd be running," chuckled Bart. "I'd better go help." And he hared off down the slope.

Chapter 10: Adventures in the Glorybird

In the valley, Lucasz was immediately beside Lara, helping her up, and Locksley was visibly remonstrating with them both. Farron, beside us, had dropped to one knee to do something with his laptop. "Are you live-twitting about the Glory?" I asked.

"Live-twEEting, and no," said Farron. "I'm using this software I built called Gloryfy. You know you can't photograph them, so what I've done is photographed the land without it, and now I'm using a simple graphics interface to try and draw it in, with animation for the moving colours."

"So you can show people what it's like to see one?" I asked

"If I'm ever allowed to. Locksley says I should do it deliberately badly and then claim it's a real photo, to give credence to the hoax theory."

"Hah," I said. "What do you think they are? The Glories, I mean."

"Me? I think we're all living in a complex computer simulation, and now it's glitching."

"Seriously?" I said. "You believe that?"

"Believe it?" he smiled. "No, not really. But it's the only explanation I've heard that makes even a tiny amount of sense. It has a certain logical elegance, does it not?"

"Could computers really create billions of conscious beings inside a single program?" I asked. Malcolm had not been impressed by the simulation theory.

"Not yet," said Farron. "But I think they will start to, in my lifetime, assuming Bart's driving doesn't cut that short. But if we are in a simulation, it's thousands of years ahead of our own technology."

"But if you're right … and the rules are breaking down … then anything could happen, couldn't it?" I said.

"Yup. The laws of physics could change in a heartbeat. Or we could, too, because we'd be simulations as well, like characters in a computer game. We could both suddenly wake up smarter than Einstein, or dumber than Trump. The barriers between past, present and future, or even reality and fiction could break down. We could see dinosaurs, Clangers, Bugs Bunny or an army of Orcs turning up. Trouble is, if the beings running all this are anything like us, then if it started going wrong, they'd probably just turn it off and on again."

"And that'd be bad, right?" I said.

"Game Over," he agreed. "So let's hope I'm wrong."

"Yes, let's."

By now I had got my breath back. "I suppose I should try and get closer," I said.

"They've cleared a track for you," replied Farron happily.

I half walked, half jogged down the slope, following the path Hector had created through squashed crops and cut fences. Apart from one comical faceplant, I made it to the bottom just fine, and settled for a brisk walk from there, entranced by the looming blue behemoth above me. Then it vanished.

When I caught up with the others, Hector was on his knees and shaking his fists furiously at the air, raging at himself and everyone else for not getting Bluebell to the Glory in time. If anyone came close and tried to console him, he angrily waved them away.

"You should have driven faster, you fool," he yelled at Bart.

Chapter 10: Adventures in the Glorybird

"He really shouldn't," muttered Lara.

"And YOU need better shoes," Locksley told her, sternly.

"Yeah right," the young woman replied coldly. "You gonna open a shop up specially? Make my shoes an *essential item*?"

"I'll make a few calls," replied Locksley, either missing or ignoring the sarcasm. "We'll get you kitted out tomorrow unless we get another live call."

"Well I can't fucking run now, even if you get me fucking running shoes," snarled Lara.

"I'll settle for just walking," said Locksley. "We'll get you strapped up."

Lara turned away with a disgusted expression, and began hobbling back towards the van, ignoring me as she passed by. Hector had run out of curses and was noisily weeping into Bluebell's lap.

"Waste of time," growled Locksley. "Total waste of time."

"I did get my hand inside it once, maybe twice," offered Lucasz, who'd just reached us at a run. "I had to jump. Is Lara OK?"

"And the other people there couldn't?" asked Locksley, ignoring his question.

"I don't think so."

"That's good, man" said Bart to Locksley. "Means he can do it in all of 'em, probably. Gotta be worth something, right?"

"I guess so," said Locksley. "Come on, let's go. How'd you get the wheelchair down here, by the way?"

"We've got a budget for compensating land-owners, haven't we?" replied Farron.

"We do now, I s'pose," growled Locksley.

"Is Lara OK?" persisted Lucasz.

"Why don't you carry her back, then you can ask her yourself," said Locksley curtly.

* * * * *

Hector remained downcast all the way back to the bus.

"There was no way you could have got her to it in time," I told him, gently. "Even Lucasz only just managed it. You did better than anyone could have expected."

"But I still *failed*," he said. "It doesn't matter how close I got, I still didn't do it. She's still ... she's still ... like this. And I was going to cure her! The Glories ... they can do amazing things, you know. There was a blind lady, got her sight back."

"Seriously?"

"Legally blind, but not totally," Hector explained. "Cataracts or something. Waiting for an operation, way I read it, cancelled of course, bloody virus! And she was out on her exercise with her husband on her arm, saw a Glory, and then – *thank you Lord, I can see again*!"

"I hadn't heard about this," I said.

"Well, they're trying to keep it all quiet, aren't they! Keep all the sheep indoors!"

Chapter 10: Adventures in the Glorybird

"Why did they recruit me and not her, though?" I asked.

"Locksley said she doesn't believe it! I think the term she used was, 'religious nutter'!"

"But you do. Believe it, I mean."

"Why wouldn't I?"

I shrugged. "Aren't you worried that, for Bluebell, the effect won't last?"

"What effect?"

"The cure."

"Why would I? Ah. Yes. I know it didn't before. But there's different kinds of Glory, aren't there?"

"I guess. Yours was a one you could walk into. Look, between Farron's computer wizzyness and Bart's crazy driving, we're bound to get another chance in a day or two."

"Yeah? Yeah, I guess we will." His pace quickened now, and he took over the wheelchair from Lucasz for the last part of the walk.

* * * * *

I felt strangely relaxed on the way back, finding entertainment in Locksley's prolonged bickering with Farron over whether five hundred pounds had been too much to offer the farmer for the damage done.

"We don't even know they were his fences!" said Locksley at one point.

Eventually the subject switched, to reports about the huge Glory that Farron had mentioned earlier. Apparently there had been a lot of car accidents from people trying to run away from it. When I got the chance, I asked Farron if he'd heard the story about the part-blind woman who got her sight back, after seeing a Glory.

"Oh yeah, *that* one. Maybe it's true, or maybe it isn't. But the boss didn't give it much credence, and anyway, she's after people who can do stuff to the Glories, not vice versa."

"I didn't," I said.

"How do you know?" he replied.

"Well … I was just sleep-standing under the thing."

"You touched it, when no-one else could. And how do you know you didn't affect it?"

"Well, nobody watching saw anything."

"They did. They saw it flow over your body. And you could have changed the duration of it, for all we know, made it stay longer than it would have done."

"How would we know that?"

"We wouldn't. But with your help, maybe we'll learn. Just imagine how useful it'd be for our research if you could force them to hang around for forty minutes or more, every time you touched one! Today might have gone a lot differently."

* * * * *

Chapter 10: Adventures in the Glorybird

I was expecting barbed wire fences and checkpoints as the Glorybird approached what was to be our base. But in fact it was simply a house, ordinary-looking except for its large size. Some time after we'd been shown our rooms and left there to freshen up, we were served a fantastic spread of Creole curry by a beaming Bart, bedecked in a colourful pinny.

Farron ate with his eyes glued to his computer screen. While waiting for Bart to serve him seconds, Farron said "There's a website I follow that the government keeps failing to shut down. A sort of pirate radio for Glory nuts. Anyway, they're concurring with my own analysis. Today has been by some margin the most active day for Glories yet. At least nine corroborated accounts – and of course the actual number is likely to be at least double that."

"Makes our job easier," said Locksley, through a mouth full of rice.

"Perhaps," said Farron. "But you'll recall, four days ago we'd never had more than three confirmed records in a day, and most days had one or two. The last three days, four, six, and now nine. And bigger, too, at least some of them. If they keep increasing at this rate, the country is going to be inundated in the space of a month."

Chapter 11: The girl

Antony

I walked. I went back over the style, noting Thelma's car, alone on the verge now, waiting for an owner who would probably never return. Then I crossed the style on the other side of the road and followed the footpath north, the direction Martha had told me to go. Would I be able to find this Jamie? It was good to have something to aim for, I supposed. On I walked, crossing fields, sometimes on footpaths, sometimes squeezing through hedgerows and vaulting fences. I got the odd feeling that there were things I should be doing, things I seemed to have forgotten about. But I kept my mind on Daniel. Two things worried me. The first, of course, was that I'd now sent three people to what might have been their deaths. So I clung, hard, to what both Martha and Thelma had said, about the Glories being good. Could Heaven actually be real? I'd believed for a long time that Mum had gone there, but in my teens, as I'd started to learn about science and logic and evolution, the ideas of Heaven and God had fallen apart in my mind. But now, the Glories had changed the rules. There was a chance, just a crazy, tiny, wonderful chance, that I'd sent Daniel and the others into Heaven. I recalled how Frank had seen the exact opposite when he'd touched a Glory: Hell. But he hadn't actually gone there. The guy was an arsehole, so maybe he'd seen where he expected to go when he died, maybe that was how it all worked. It was all guesswork, really. It made me wonder how all those priests and vicars and the like could be so certain, about anything. There was one thing I had in common with Frank though – I had to know. If I'd sent Daniel somewhere, I needed to know where it was. Good or bad, and regardless of the cost to me, I had to know. Somehow, I felt better for realising that. I wasn't out here on the hills because I'd been chased out of my family. I was here by my own choice, seeking answers.

The second worry was the age-old *how*. It seemed that I could send people into the Glories, but only other people. Worse, it was beginning to look like a one-way ticket. How, then, was I to learn Daniel's fate? I consoled myself that I knew more, now, than I had this morning, even if that knowledge had come at great cost. If I could find a third Glory, and this time approach it with more care, then perhaps I might get closer still to an answer.

I saw hardly anyone, just the odd walker in the distance. It was a beautiful day, and I tried to appreciate it. An hour passed, almost happily, then another. I followed a path up a hillside, hoping to catch sight of a landmark from the top. But it was an entirely different sight that greeted me as the track levelled out and farm buildings loomed in front of me.

A young woman was standing by the track, gazing in my direction, with an expression of delight on her face. She had thick, wavy blonde hair down to her shoulders. She was probably two or three years older than me, though not quite as tall. She wore mud-splattered denim dungarees, but somehow managed to make them look sexy. She was pretty as anything, and I fancied her immediately. Was she looking at me? As I came closer, it seemed that she wasn't.

"Can you see it?" she said, suddenly. "Isn't it the most wonderful thing, ever?"

Chapter 11: The girl

She wasn't looking at me. I turned around to look behind me. Far away in the distance, a huge blue-green globe was hanging in the air, some way above the ground, about as high as the lowest clouds. "I think it's the world," she said.

"It's a Glory," I said. "It has to be. But it's massive."

"I know what they are," she said. "I've seen one before, up close. They're wonderful, aren't they?"

I looked at it for a while, and could make out distinct patches of blue and green. The green patches did seem to be about the shape of the continents, and it was rotating slowly, too. There was no ice at the top or bottom, though, nor patches of yellow or brown where mountains or deserts should be. It was like a child's cartoon of the Earth. A cloud drifted towards it – a real one – and slowly disappeared into Africa.

"It doesn't have a shadow, look," I said to her. "That cloud does, on the ground, but not the Glory." But she just said 'mmh-hmm', or something like that, and kept on gazing. I used the cloud and its shadow to work out roughly where the thing was, and how big. "Got to be nearly a mile across," I said, and she didn't respond at all.

"Do you want to get closer?" I asked. "I could navigate?" This got her attention, and she actually looked at me.

"Closer ... yes I'd like to get closer," she said. She wobbled her head a little, as if trying to shake something out of it. "Well that's a good idea, but I'm not sure I need a navigator, do I? You can come though. Actually you can drive, I'll just sit and look at it."

"Sorry, I can't drive," I said.

"Hey, you're not much use, are you? Cute, though. I'll get the car." She walked, backwards, past the farmhouse, feeling her way with one hand so she could keep her eyes on the Glory. I did wonder whether she might not be the safest driver, but when a girl has called you 'cute' for the first time in your entire life, things like logic and self-preservation tend not to matter. She vanished round the corner briefly, started an engine, and reappeared driving a chunky car.

I jumped into the passenger seat. "Seatbelt's stuck," I said.

"It's an old car. Better just hang on as best you can!" she said happily. Then we were bombing along the farm track. Briefly I looked at the door I'd got in through – there was something odd about it, though I couldn't work out what, not with the car hurtling and bouncing along. I had to brace myself with both arms, as best as I could, while also fighting back the urge to say something like 'do you really think I'm cute?', which would have been hopelessly lame.

The farm lane ended in a T-junction, and she braked sharply, turning hard to the left, then going on down the lane, accelerating on every straight bit then braking sharply at the last minute whenever a bend approached. We got out onto a slightly more major road and she quickly hit sixty miles an hour. "Ohh, yeah, definitely getting closer," she said.

"Not like a rainbow then," I said.

"What?" she glanced at me briefly, like she'd almost forgotten I was there.

"Well, you could never find the pot of gold at the bottom of a rainbow, because they move whenever you do. It's all about refraction of the sunlight, you see."

Chapter 11: The girl

For a moment I heard Daniel's voice in my head, and almost saw his face. *"Jeebus, Cuz, try to be less of a nerd, for once?"*

She didn't answer, eyes back on the Glory and (I hoped) the road ahead.

"What's your name?" I asked her, hoping to distract from the rainbow debacle.

"Sally." She kept her eyes straight ahead.

"I'm Antony."

"Uh-huh."

"There's gonna be other people driving to see the Glory too," I said, "keep an eye out for other cars."

"Well, yeah, it's a road."

She was doing seventy now, and using both sides of the road to get round corners faster, like an F1 driver. The Glory hung in the sky ahead of us, impossibly big even at this distance. People must have seen this one from dozens of miles, in every direction. We'd passed a couple of cars, driving towards it, and a few delivery trucks going in either direction.

We rounded a corner. "Ahh, fuck, what's this?"

Several cars were queueing in front of us. Beyond them, a truck lay on its side, completely blocking the road. A line of cars were hooting on the other side of it, too. "Looks like an accident," I said, needlessly. The car we'd just overtaken trundled up behind us, slowing to a stop.

"Hell with this," she said. "Grab the road atlas. Back seat!" I reached round but was flung forward as she hit reverse at full pace, swung the car sideways, changed gear and completed the three-point turn. My hand flopped around the back seat but I couldn't find anything.

"Uhh, not sure it's there," I said.

"Fuck it, I'll just take the first turning and guess!" She swung the car into a small side road on the left, and dropped her speed down to fifty. We passed a small crossroads, and one of those old-fashioned white signposts with place names in different directions. Then dangerously fast down a narrow lane with hedges on each side, hooting occasionally in case anything was coming, with me catching glimpses of the giant Glory through gaps in the hedge. We came to a T-junction, and swung hard left onto a two-lane road. She kept to our side of the road on the bends this time, and her speed crept up to sixty-five.

"Up there, look!" She pointed suddenly at what looked like a fragment of blue glass hanging just above a hedge up ahead where the road bent. "Another Glory!" she said with delight in her voice. "Look how it's OH SHIT!!!"

A car shot round the bend coming towards us the other way, much too fast, skidding on the bend and sliding onto our side of the road. "HOLD ON!" Sally wrenched the steering wheel and thrust her body sideways into me, and our car pulled sideways too, then a crunch as the driver's side of our car glanced off the side of the other one. The world broke into pieces of glass and leaves flying at my face, and something shook me hard, before a final crunch.

Chapter 12: Ghosts and liars

Julia

I was sitting in a big garden somewhere, golden sun streaming over the river that ran past. My boy Nick walked up to me – said he'd been searching for me everywhere, and I joked that it couldn't have been everywhere or he'd have found me sooner. We were late, he said, and next thing I knew we were at a wedding, an outdoors reception in a lovely garden. I didn't know the bride or groom, but did recognise the newsreader Richard Baker, who was dancing with Kate Bush. The England Cricket team were there, too, though for some reason they all looked like former Prime Minister Harold Wilson. Blondie were providing the music, dressed for their *Parallel Lines* album cover. My husband Geoffrey was there, but all he would say was how lovely I looked, over and over, like a stuck record. A huge black cloud appeared in the sky, cutting off the sunlight, and I felt the chill as the wind got up, brown leaves dashing across the table. No-one else noticed, even as spots of rain began to fall. The cloud had come for me, I knew that. My own personal monster, here to exact its due.

There was a little twinkling stream running from a spring in the middle of the grass, snaking away through some beautiful flowering azaleas. I needed a pee and the only toilets here were open air bowls in the middle of the dance floor, which didn't appeal. So I followed the stream into the azaleas, but couldn't find a suitable spot there either, and very soon I was lost. I found myself running along a canal towpath, thinking that if I could only get back to the wedding, then I would be safe. But the black cloud was growing, darkening, and filling the sky. I ran through empty streets, and thunder flashed behind me. In front of me now was a hospital, its gleaming white walls in stark contrast to the jet-black clouds filling the sky. Black tornadoes snaked down from the sky and reached out to grab me, but I ran to the hospital entrance and flung open the door, only to find it completely blocked by a brick wall, with a message scrawled onto it: *You Belong With Us*. Rooted to the spot, I screamed.

I jumped, or possibly flew out of bed, landing in an upside down heap by the radiator in the bedroom of my house. Righting myself, I saw that I wasn't alone. An oily black figure was sitting on the chair by my dresser, playing with a hairbrush. He looked like he'd been put together clumsily from lumps of solidified crude oil.

"Bernard," I said. "I've just had another of your entertaining little dreams."

"Glad you enjoyed it," he gurgled, turning to face me, even though he didn't really have a face. "Final performance, I'm afraid, since you decided to murder me." He indicated a luminous multi-coloured shard, projecting from a gash in his stomach.

"Oh. Yes. Well, you were slowly killing me, you see."

"Kill or be killed," he croaked. "There is nothing else."

"For us, there never could be," I said. "But if you're dead, why are you here?"

"To tell you to wake up."

Chapter 12: Ghosts and liars  67

"Really?" I asked. "Why?"
"You need to wake up, NOW!"

I opened my eyes. The room was spinning above me. I felt sick, and couldn't remember how to move my limbs. Someone was standing over me, a woman with a surgical mask and some sort of goggles. "I've got the first sample," she said.

I wanted to ask what she was doing, but I couldn't recall how to speak.

The woman turned away from me and another, deeper voice said something about cutting in. "We need a few cells of the brain," the deep voice added.

The woman picked something up, a scalpel, and then her voice turned to panic. "Dammit, she's waking up! You got the dose wrong AGAIN!" Moments later something wet and chemical-smelling was placed hard over my mouth.

* * * * *

"There's a Glory! A big one!! Type two, close by!! We need to go right now!" Someone was banging on my door. My eyes seemed to have been welded shut, and I felt sick and groggy. A wave of dread broke across me as I forced myself to sit up. Bernard. Had he come back? I felt around my chest and belly, and found no pain there, no 'wrongness', as I'd always called the sensation to the doctors. There was a pain, but it was somewhere else.

"Come on Julia! We need to go!"

"All right, all right," I croaked, and staggered to the door. Behind it were Farron and a fully dressed Lucasz, though the latter had his rugby shirt on back to front. Lucasz' mouth curled into a smile. "Are you coming like that?"

I was still in my nightdress.

"Oh." It didn't seem fair to delay all the others while I got dressed properly, so I nipped to the loo, pulled on some leggings, and grabbed a toothbrush. Then I followed the others down the corridor brushing my teeth as I went, dripping bits of mouth foam down my front. By the minibus stood Locksley, immaculately dressed of course. Yet Lara looked distinctly rough, with jeans and top thrown on just about accurately, though her hair was a bushy mess, and I reckoned she'd probably shoot anyone who tried to take her photo this morning.

Bluebell was also in a nightdress, being wheeled along by a fully dressed Hector. Somehow, minutes later, we were all in the minibus and on our way. Also on the bus was a thick-set, heavily tattooed bald man whom Farron introduced as Jenks. He looked utterly bemused to be there.

Feeling a bit sorry for him, I asked him why he was with us.

"Ain't got no idea," he replied.

"He got moved," said Farron. "Physically displaced by a Glory, several hundred metres. We're not even sure how, but he woke up by an electricity substation, trapped by high wire fences all around."

"Buck naked, way I heard it," said Bart from the driver's seat.

"Dunno what the fuck happened," contributed Jenks. "Then they got me out, and offered me a wad of dosh to come along with you lot." He looked shell-shocked, poor thing. I imagined that he'd lived a life of beer, heavy work and

Chapter 12: Ghosts and liars

football fandom, and now he'd been wrenched a long way out of his comfort zone.

Farron handed round bananas, cereal bars and cartons of fruit juice. My mouth tasted horrible, and my lips felt parched. I sipped tiny drips of orange juice through a straw, and eventually graduated to a few bites of banana, but that was all I could manage. Tiny, pathetic breakfasts were a familiar routine to me, and a wet chill of horror ran through me. Was the cancer back? I'd eaten like a horse every morning since that Glory had cured me. *The cancer felt different*, I told myself. I repeated it in my head over and over, but the thought refused to stick. *Perhaps it's something else*, I thought, *like a cold or ... Oh.*

A very different chill ran through me.

Coronavirus.

I knew the symptoms varied wildly between people, but changes to taste and smell were the surest ones. If I had it, then even if I could be cured, what about the others? They'd tested me of course, said they'd tested all of us, but what if I'd caught it after, or the test had missed it? What if I'd infected all these people? I looked at them all. Jenks, the fish out of water. Lucasz and Farron were bursting with excitement, like schoolboys on a trip. Lara looked poorly, the impromptu breakfast items lying untouched on her lap, and her right hand rubbing her left shoulder. She'd still made no attempt to tidy her hair, which made me think that she must feel very out-of-sorts indeed. Could Lara have given it to me? Hector had not said a word since we set off, and that was out of character, too. He looked nervous and keyed-up. Well he would do, I supposed, if there was a chance that Bluebell would wake up again when they got inside the Glory. What would I say to my dear Geoffrey, if he somehow woke from the dead to speak to me, now?

"Hey, are you okay?"

I snapped out of my thoughts, ready to come clean about my virus fears, except that the question from Farron wasn't addressed to me. He and Lucasz were looking at Lara.

"I don't know," said Lara weakly. "I don't think it's the Coronavirus. My throat's not tickly or anything. "It's more like a hangover, but I didn't drink anything last night. And my shoulder hurts like fuck."

"It took three tries to wake you," said Farron.

"It wasn't till I started describing the Glory to you that you even replied," added Lucasz. "Hopefully it'll make you feel better." A thought seemed to strike him. "What if it's not just Julia and Bluebell? What if they can do that to anyone?"

"There'd have been more reports of it, surely?" replied Farron.

"But think about it," said Lucasz excitedly. "Anyone who's feeling even remotely poorly would be staying at home, wouldn't they? Either avoiding the virus or thinking they might already have it! Maybe Julia and Bluebell are the only really sick people who've ever been in contact with these things!"

"I really hope you're right," croaked Lara.

"I'm feeling a bit poorly as well," I admitted. "My shoulder hurts too." I hadn't even realised it until Lara had mentioned hers, but I had a sore patch in the exact spot that she was now rubbing on her own shoulder.

Chapter 12: Ghosts and liars

"Well why in God's name didn't you say so sooner," shouted Locksley, from the front seat.

"You never gave us a chance," chorused Lara and I, almost in unison. "I didn't even have a chance to get properly dressed," I added.

Locksley muttered a few profanities, and something about running school trips for toddlers. Then she made a phone call, telling someone that they'd be needing more virus tests. Then she turned back to us. "Well, it's too late to do anything about it now. If you've got it then we've probably all got it. Put masks on and open the windows, though, might as well try. Bloody virus tests probably don't even work. Well maybe this Glory will cure Julia, at least. Fuck me, if it is the Corona, that'd be a result."

Lara turned to look at me. "Did you say your shoulder was hurting?"

"Yes," I croaked back. "My left shoulder. Somewhere between a big bruise and a wasp sting."

"Same here," said Lara. "Does the Coronavirus normally do that?"

"I don't think so," said Farron. "Here let me check the known symptoms … no, nothing about localised pain away from the head and chest."

"I dunno, my head hurts too," said Lara. "A headache … but there's a sharp pain here," and she indicated the right side of her head, above the ear, a spot hidden by hair.

An image of a very sharp scalpel flashed through my mind, and I was suddenly aware of a sharp pain in exactly the same place on my head that Lara was pointing to on hers. I was about to say something, when another image flashed into my head, of a masked woman standing over me, saying something about sampling my brain. I felt like it was from a dream. It should have been from a dream. But that didn't explain why Lara and I were both hurting in precisely the same places, and both feeling like death warmed up, while everyone else felt right as rain. And how, I wondered, could we both have developed the exact same virus symptoms at exactly the same time, especially when we'd only met the previous day?

This was not the virus. Someone had done something to us in the night.

* * * * *

The first sign that we'd reached the Glory was the string of clumsily parked cars along the roadside. Ahead, people were milling about, and lines of colour seemed to be moving over them. I was finding it hard to focus. Locksley took charge, and told Jenks, Lucasz and Lara to get out with her. They obeyed, with an unsteady Lara leaning on a delighted Lucasz. The rest of us stayed on the bus as it moved forward, slowly overtaking them. Then a slice of pure purple colour moved through the bus, passing through everything, moving towards me. Seats, floor, clothes, Farron's laptop, everything except people turned that same exact shade of bright purple then back again, as it passed. Looking closely, it was a mass of bright purple spots. I just had time to see a golden yellow layer come in diagonally before the purple layer was upon me, and everything faded to black.

* * * * *

Chapter 12: Ghosts and liars

Something was tugging and shouting at me. For a moment I remembered seeing Bernard and his warning. Then I was back in the minibus, and Hector was tugging at my hand.

"Come on, please, you have to touch her, you have to make her better!"

"Let go of me!" I snapped. Chastened, Hector obeyed. Tears were streaming from his eyes.

"I'm sorry," he said. "I thought maybe if I got her to a Glory she might wake up. There's all these stories out there, but I could never do it on my own. Please, will you touch her? Because maybe you can do it, don't you see?"

I carefully rose from my seat, expecting to feel stiff and groggy, but my head felt gloriously clear, my limbs free of stiffness, and with no pain anywhere. I recalled the euphoria that had followed my first contact with a Glory. Waves of colour were still running through the bus and everything in it – green, pink, golden yellow. I felt fully restored, and strangely powerful, as I moved towards Bluebell, and placed my hands gently on the sides of her face. Layers of colour played over her nightgown, and I waited for her to respond, but she didn't. After a while, Hector sank into a chair and began to weep.

I stayed in position for a few more minutes, until I could take no more of Hector's despair, and quietly stepped out of the minibus. I wished I could help him, but I couldn't. Our bus was one of many vehicles parked on grass by the road, and the coloured layers were moving across everything, from all directions. A wood of loosely spaced trees with tussocky ferns among them sloped upwards from the road, and the colours of the Glory swept over these too. Within the wood were evenly spaced people, or groups thereof. The Glory colours swept across the ground below them, as if they were all standing in some giant outdoor woodland disco.

"So he was making it up?" asked Farron, who was leaning against the minibus, looking sympathetic.

"I guess so," I replied, not wanting to talk about it. "Where are the others?"

"Well, Lara and Lucasz can't interact with Type Twos, so they're just enjoying the show. And Locksley's got her hands full with Jenks," he replied, glancing meaningfully up the slope into the wood. "There. No, a bit higher. Look."

I could see something pale and moving, seemingly hanging in the air among the tree trunks, some way up the slope. "What is it?"

"Jenks," he replied simply. "Type One Glories move him physically. Type Twos apparently do the same visually. Spectrally, if you will. The real Jenks is currently invisible. Like Jack Griffin, you can only see his clothes. But his visible body is displaced about forty metres to the left, and again to the right. It happened gradually. It was quite terrifying at first, he thought he was disintegrating. Then when he realised what was happening he went a bit, well, crazy I guess. Like he was high on drugs. And he either hasn't twigged, or doesn't care, that the spectral versions of him are hanging in the air buck naked and flashing their bits at all the other Glory-watchers. It's attention we don't need. Locksley's trying to persuade him to go back to the bus but he's not having

Chapter 12: Ghosts and liars

it. She asked me to go get you, if you were awake, or the others if I could find them."

"You don't seem in too much of a hurry," I said.

"Between you and me, it'll do Locksley some good to lighten up a bit."

"Does she know about Bluebell?" I asked.

"She's acting as if the pair of them don't exist," replied Farron.

"Well, I'd better go use my charm on Jenks then, hadn't I?" I said. We went up through the wood, weaving apologetically between where people were standing.

"Hey you can't just barge through," said one man.

"We're here to deal with the flasher," I replied, trying to sound important.

It wasn't difficult to spot where the real Jenks was. A ring of people, perhaps ten metres across, had formed, and its members had clearly thrown aside social distancing in favour of the spectacle within. Farron and I joined the circle via a gap between two of its more cautious members. There before us was a pair of jeans with a t-shirt hanging above it, plus socks and shoes below its legs, doing a routine from *Saturday Night Fever*, while a furious Locksley shouted at it. The waves of colour passing along the ground and through the clothes were relegated to a sideshow. As we watched, the knees on the jeans bent briefly, then a stick rose up from the ground and whacked Locksley three times on the bottom before she grabbed it and snapped it. The watching circle found this hilarious. Until Locksley drew her gun.

"Right, you moron, that's enough. We are going back to the vehicle ***right now***!"

Several of the watching circle turned and ran. Others gasped and remained, rooted to the spot.

"You can't shoot me! I'm *invisible*!!" declared Jenks.

"You're endangering the public! The local police will have been called! You're going to spend lockdown in a police cell unless you come with me ***now***!" she yelled.

"So you're not going to shoot me then? *I'm the invisible man! I'm the invisible man! Incredible how you can … see right through me!*"

He resumed his dancing as he sung the old Queen hit, or at least the bits he could remember. I stifled a laugh at the thought of the naked spectral versions doing the same thing nearby. But there was nothing funny about Locksley's gun, so I caught her eye, and gestured to her to lower the gun. Reluctantly, she complied.

"Hey big boy, you're putting on a great show, but you do know that there are naked versions of you over there, copying your every move?" I said.

"Yeah? So what. It's not actually *me*, is it?"

"There were some very distressed mothers and children."

"They don't have to look. Hey I've lost my place in the song, now!"

Then, in an instant, Jenks reappeared inside his clothes. There were dramatic gasps from the onlookers, even a smattering of applause, but Farron was first to realise what had happened.

"The Glory's gone!"

Chapter 12: Ghosts and liars

I looked around, and saw that the dancing lines of colour were all gone. Watchers down the slope were already turning to head back to their cars. Then something further down caught my eye. "There's a police car!"

"Dammit," said Locksley.

"Maybe they're just here for the crowd," said Farron.

"Perhaps," said Locksley, "but if I'm a random Glory watcher and the cops start trying to give me a fine, I'm gonna be telling them straight off there was a flasher in the woods, to divert their attention. We need to get this guy back in the bus before anyone ID's him. I'm giving you one chance, Jenks," Locksley turned to him as she spoke. "You come to the bus now, head down, no fuss, and maybe we get you out of here and forget this ever happened. You do anything to annoy me, and yes I do mean anything, and I'll hand you to those bloody cops myself. Are we clear!?"

"Uhhh, yeah," he said, looking chastened. He began slouching down the hill, flanked by Farron and Locksley. Farron produced a woolly hat from his pocket and told Jenks to put it on, so he'd be less recognisable. Then I felt a tap on my shoulder, and turned to see Lucasz and Lara, both looking worried.

"We need to talk," said Lucasz.

Chapter 13: The moon

Antony

I opened my eyes. I was looking through a screen at a close-up of grass and rushes. No, it wasn't a screen, it was a buckled car windscreen with no glass in it. I felt pains all over, but I seemed to be able to move my arms and legs OK. My legs seemed to be inside some weird white blanket. Then I remembered what had happened. "Sally!"

She was in the driver's seat, with a floppy white thing on her lap, too. Her nose was bleeding. "Sally, can you hear me? Are you alright??"

"Ahh, fuck, Dad's gonna kill me. My fucking car!"

"Can you move your arms and legs OK?"

"Not sure. I think so. You?"

I managed to extract myself through the windscreen, which seemed easier than fighting with the door. I looked back behind us. Our car was in a shallow ditch that ran alongside the road, and from the looks of it, it had slid along this ditch for some distance, sheering off a layer of vegetation on the rim of the ditch nearer the road. Of the car that had bumped us, there was no sign beyond a broken wing mirror, lying on the road. "Hey, can you pull me out?" Sally asked me.

"Check you can feel your toes first," I said, remembering some first aid class they'd made us take at school. "In case you've hurt your back."

"Just get me the fuck OUT!"

They didn't cover angry women in the first aid class, so I grabbed her arms and pulled. She swore a few times, but then for a moment I was holding her clumsily in my arms, kneeling on the crumpled bonnet of her poor wrecked car.

"Owwww, that fucking maniac! What the fucking *fuck*?" She limped onto the roadside, surveying the wreck of her vehicle. "Fucking phone's knackered too," she added.

A car whizzed past. I tried to flag it down but it ignored me. It was going in the same direction as the one that had hit us, and nearly as fast. Then another whizzed past the same way. "Away," I said. "They're all going away from the Glory."

"Yes, of course they fucking are," said Sally. "Great big planet appears above your house, 'specially in the middle of a bloody plague, and what are you gonna think? You're gonna think it's the end of the fucking world, or some people are. So they'll jump in their fucking cars and run for the hills. Should have fucking thought of that, shouldn't we! Fucking stupid! And we'll never see the fucking Glory close-up now, will we?"

"Well we could still get close to that one," I said, pointing at the giant sliver of blue glass we'd glimpsed just before the accident. "Can you walk OK? I can help you."

"I'll manage," she said, but her tone had perked up a bit. She hobbled a dozen or so metres forward then accepted my arm for support. The Glory was another fifty metres or more ahead, and a little off to the left side of the road. I helped Sally through a gap in the hedge, and then we picked our way along the edge of a field planted with young maize. The Glory loomed closer. It was dizzying to look at. Only four or five metres from top to bottom and a little less

Chapter 13: The moon

wide, it was shaped like a very jagged diamond. And it looked like a window into somewhere else. We were looking up at it, but through it we were also looking down, at a rolling ocean far below us. Wispy clouds drifted by. We kept going till we were under it. It was just out of reach above us.

Sally was staring up at it with a dreamy smile on her face. "I think I'm in love," she said, and I couldn't tell if she was joking. We gazed up at it together for some minutes. "I want to touch it," she said. "Could you lift me up on your shoulders?"

I liked the thought of getting certain parts of her anatomy so close to my body, so of course I said yes. I crouched down and she lifted one dungareed leg over my back, then I wrapped my arms gingerly around her shins in front of my chest.

"Doesn't hurt?" I said.

"I'm fine, stop fussing. Ow! Can you lift me now?"

Slowly, methodically, I managed to rise to a kneeling position, then one bent knee, then a crouch, from which I wobbled to my feet. "I can touch it!" she said. Then a shock of fear ran through me and I took a step backwards, lost my footing and fell backwards. We landed with a thud on some maize.

"Clumsy idiot," she said. "I had it! I had a piece of it in my hand!"

"*What?*"

"I put my hand in, and it just came away. A tiny patch of distant sea, right in my palm, it was AMAZING! Then you go all Mister fucking Bean on me and dump me on my arse, and I've lost it. That hurt more than the fucking crash!"

"S-sorry."

"Okay maybe not quite as much as the crash. But that really hurt, you dickhead!" She eased herself into a sitting position, looking at the Glory above us. "Ahhh, that feels better" she said, gazing up at it.

"I'm sorry, I ... well the last two times I've been touching a Glory, the people I was with disappeared. I got scared it would happen to you, too," I said, feeling totally lame as I said it.

"Probably ran away before you could dump them on their arses," she said, cheerfully.

"No, I mean, really disappeared. Like, into the Glory."

"Well, you could have warned me."

"It only just occurred to me when you said you were touching it. I sort of panicked."

"I kinda like the idea of getting myself inside that," she said, still looking up at it.

"Even if you could never come out again?" I asked.

"I want to touch it again," she said.

"I don't think that's a good idea," I replied.

"Well, I wanna do it anyway."

"I'll help you!" The voice came from behind us. A man in paint-spattered overalls was lumbering towards us, gazing up at the Glory. I could see his eyes running up and down Sally's rather attractive body, and a faintly lecherous smile came onto his face. "Better mask up," he said, putting a somewhat weedy cloth mask over his face and nose. Otherwise he seemed utterly oblivious to social distancing, at least where Sally was concerned. He linked his fingers together to make a step, and Sally got up, climbing onto his shoulders in a matter of seconds. I pulled a face that they didn't see, then took a few steps backward.

Chapter 13: The moon

If my own presence was what made people fall into the Glories, then I needed to keep my distance. I didn't want to look at her sitting on his shoulders, but supposed I had to, in case the Glory swallowed her.

Sally was pressing her hands against the bottom slither of the Glory. "I can't do it," she muttered. Her hands were pressing against it, but she couldn't pull a piece of it away. Maybe she could only do it when she was touching me! My mood improved a bit. Then the Glory vanished, and Sally almost fell forwards, but the man took a step forward and steadied them both.

"Where'd it go?" said the man, as he set Sally down.

"It vanished," I said. "They do that."

"It's impossible," he said.

"We know," I replied.

"The big one's still there, look," said Sally, pointing. "We need to get closer."

"I thought it was a hot air balloon," said the man.

"Have you ever seen one that big?" I said scathingly.

The man gave a grumpy shrug and turned away from us. Sally called after him, "hey! Are you going that way?"

"Might be."

"Could we hitch a lift?"

"Only got room for one," he said without turning round.

We followed him, and I felt sure that within minutes I'd be left standing there by the road on my own. We passed through the hedge and saw a small pick-up truck parked on the grass on our side of the road. Cars were still speeding past from time to time, away from the Glory. I made sure I reached the truck just ahead of Sally, to remind her we were together. There was indeed only one passenger seat.

"We could both go in the back," she said.

"On there?" said the man. "I s'pose. Why not stick the boy back there and you can sit up front with me?"

"Well," said Sally uncertainly. I was pleased to see she did seem to feel some loyalty towards me. I, in turn, thought of her injured leg, and the sore bottom I'd given her when I fell over.

"I'll be OK in the back," I said, hopping up there. There were only a few paint pots and a thin lake of dried paint. Sally got in the front, the man started the engine and off we went. He drove quite a bit slower than Sally had, which was a relief, as cars continued to speed by in the opposite direction. Some of these had whole families in them. I hoped the driver wasn't coming on to Sally, but I thought she could probably fend him off easily enough. Assuming she wanted to. At one point I saw another Glory – a slab of dirty ice hanging between two trees and already receding fast away from us by the time I spotted it. How many were there, right now? Were these little ones connected to the big globe in some way?

The truck pulled over by a junction, and Sally got out. "Traffic's totally blocked up ahead," she told me. "He's not going any closer." As if to back this up, I could hear distant car horns tooting angrily. The globe was much closer now, about a 45 degree angle upwards from where we stood. I could make out the wiggling coastlines of Britain and Ireland, but it made me giddy to look at it. It was easy to see why people were fleeing from beneath it. A helicopter hung in the sky at its side.

Chapter 13: The moon

"Let's walk," said Sally. "Sounds like it'll be quicker anyway."

Within minutes we reached a mass of hooting, honking cars, queueing up towards a roundabout that was completely gridlocked. Some people had left their cars and were heading up the slope verge on the other side of the roundabout. "Look!" Sally cried. Beyond the roadside hedge was a huge pale grey mound, forming a perfect hemisphere. It was covered in craters, and seemed to be glowing slightly. "I think ... I think it's the moon," she said in a tone of wonderment.

"Come on!" she said, with a look of childlike delight, and she grabbed my hand, weaving through the cars and then dragging me willingly up the sloping verge, her limp now gone. At the top was a line of sickly bushes which we burst through easily, and there, ahead of us, was half of the moon, rising out of a field of corn. It was massive, forty metres across at the bottom. Much of the crop was trampled, because at least thirty people were milling about looking at the moon, with little concern for social distancing and none at all for the farmer. I imagined there were probably just as many round the other side (the dark side?) that we couldn't see. Sally and I ran forward, looking for a gap among the milling watchers.

Chapter 14: Time for a change

Julia

I watched Jenks, Locksley and Farron continue down through the wood towards the road, while the Glory-watchers around them did likewise. But Lucasz and Lara led me off to the side, past some holly bushes to a ditch at the edge of a field. Lucasz looked around, furtively. "I don't think anyone can see us here. We've got a minute or two before they start wondering where we are."

I was about to ask what on earth was going on, but Lara answered.

"Something happened to me in the night. At first I thought I was maybe getting ill and it was just a bad dream, but ... the memory came back clearer when I got out of the bus. Someone was standing over my bed in a mask. I think ... I think they injected me."

I felt a jolt of unease as my own memory of the night came rushing back.

"Julia?" asked Lucasz.

"I'm not sure, but ... I had something like that happen too. I felt like Hell this morning, didn't know why. Then the Glory came, and I've been fine since."

"Did you have a pain just under your ear?" asked Lucasz.

"Uhhh, somewhere around there, yes, I don't quite remember."

"Can I look?" His tone was urgent.

"Alright."

Gently, he reached up with a hand and pushed my hair away from my left ear. His fingertip brushed my skin for an instant, and an image of Malcolm flashed into my mind. "You've got a scab here," Lucasz declared. "It's tiny, but it's there. Exactly the same place as the one on Lara. Does it hurt now?"

"No, not since the Glory."

"Maybe it healed the damage but left the blood clot," said Lucasz. "Here, look at the one on Lara."

Lara moved her own hair aside, and there was a small scab, in exactly the same place. "Only mine hurts like fuck when I touch it," she said.

I felt a wave of dizziness as I tried to process the information. "What about you, Lucasz?" she asked.

"No sign that they did anything to me," he replied.

"Who's '*they*'?" I asked, with mounting alarm.

"Locksley, of course," said Lucasz.

"We don't know it's her," replied Lara.

"You said the person you saw was female!" said Lucasz.

"I thought it was but I can't be sure, and anyway it didn't look like Locksley. She had a mask on. But either Locksley knows about it and arranged it, or she doesn't, and someone else is doing it under her nose."

"Either way, the house isn't safe," said Lucasz.

"And we can't tell Locksley, or even Farron, in case they're in on it. If they know we're on to them, they might lock us up or strap us down to use as lab rats."

"Lab rats?" I was struggling to keep up.

Chapter 14: Time for a change

"What do you think they're doing it for?" asked Lucasz. "I don't think they were injecting you. I think they drugged you some other way, but maybe got the dose wrong or something, because Lara woke up for a moment. I think they were trying to sample your brains!"

"Sample our brains??" I said, a little too loudly.

"They'd need to search real hard!" replied a droll young man who was passing and had overheard.

"Keep your voice down," hissed Lara.

"I know it sounds absurd," said Lucasz in a loud whisper, "but think about it. Each of you has a power that could save lives. Julia, yours could stop the pandemic dead if they could harness it, not to mention every other disease. So of course they'd try to bottle it, and wave all ethics aside when they were doing it. Okay, it seems a really clumsy attempt, but what else could they try, short of major surgery? My guess is they took blood samples too, just in case that helps."

"Dear God," I said. "What do we do?"

"We have to get away," said Lucasz.

"I don't think we could do it now, though," said Lara. "We've missed the chance to slip away. We need to get back quickly or they'll start to wonder what we're talking about."

Lucasz nodded, and we started down the hill.

"We could tell the police?" I suggested. The other two both looked at me as if I'd gone mad. "Or not," I added.

"Next time we go after a Glory," said Lucasz. "We could try to slip away then."

"Just the three of us?" I asked.

"Jenks is too unpredictable," said Lucasz.

"And he makes a pretty good diversion, too," added Lara with a rare smile. "If you hadn't been out for the count we could have been gone by now."

"I'm sorry about that," I said. "You waited for me?"

"You looked groggy in the bus," said Lara. "I started to think maybe it had happened to you as well."

"Thank you," I said. "That was very kind. And yes, I think it did."

"We'll stick together," said Lucasz. "We'll deal with this together."

The Glory-watchers slunk down the hill, reminding me somehow of kids dispersing after some after-school fight had broken up. I slunk along with them, successfully avoiding the attention of policemen, who had the air of lions bemused by too many antelopes, not knowing which one to go after. Lara and Lucasz followed a minute later, their hands briefly touching and their clothes looking ruffled, she looking embarrassed and he with a beaming smile.

"Oh, for goodness' sake, that's all we need," said Locksley.

"He's a quick worker, I'll give him that," said Farron.

"Lucky bastard," growled Jenks.

Only I knew that it was a pre-arranged cover story to explain their absence, much as Lucasz might wish it to be otherwise. Soon, we were underway. "Where to?" asked Bart.

Chapter 14: Time for a change

"We'll drop the two frauds at the nearest motorway service station, and call a cab to take them home," said Locksley. "I'm sorry about their situation, but it's not our problem and there's nothing we can do about it, except get held up."

"There's another one!" shouted Farron. "Fifty miles away!" Bart broke a slew of traffic rules by doing a U-turn in the middle of an A-road, and for thirty minutes we were speeding onwards again. Lucasz and Lara were now sat together, whispering things in each others' ears, while Hector sat still and silent, seeming barely more responsive to the world than his wife was. How useless it felt, for me to be able to heal myself but no-one else. Then Jenks said,

"Bluddy 'eck!!"

Jenks pointed out of the window. A thin column was visible in the distance, poking up beyond the few clouds in the sky, and gradually becoming fainter with height until, some way above the clouds, it seemed to disappear. It was a deep, rich reddish-brown, but all manner of other objects or images were shooting upwards along its length, away from the ground and towards the sky.

"That's what we're heading for," said Farron.

"No way I'm touching that fucker," said Jenks.

"Oh. It's gone," said Lara, because the column had just vanished.

Locksley was unimpressed, and made this plain with a few choice words.

"Well, there's no call for that kind of language," I felt compelled to say.

"We win some, we lose some," said Farron.

"I'll tell the bastards again that we need a helicopter," hissed Locksley. "Might as well turn around, unless there's any other reports?"

"One in Scotland," said Farron. "A couple of unconfirmed ones further east."

"Turn around," said Locksley wearily. "Back to base. We need a rethink."

"Umm, can we stop at a bathroom on the way?" said Lara. "Like, really soon?"

"Yes please," said I. I'd been trying to ignore that particular issue, but I was bursting.

"Well there's some bushes up ahead," said Locksley brusquely.

"BUSHES?" wailed Lara.

Locksley sighed. "Farron, find us a service station or something that's somewhere on the way? We can drop Mr and Mrs Fraud while we're at it."

Farron replied softly, "Look, I know you're pissed off with them and you've a right to be, but we can afford a little compassion, can't we? People will do anything for the person they love. Hector, you live close by, don't you?"

"Fourteen Spindle Crescent, Salbury," he replied, with forced jollity.

"That's half an hour away," said Farron. "We could drop them off. One road's as good as another for Glory-hunting."

"Hmmphh. I s'pose so."

Ten minutes later we were in the services, where Locksley declared that we had ten minutes and not a second longer. I followed Lara into the building, but instead of the Ladies, she ushered me into the disabled cubicle and shut the door. "Now listen," she said, "whatever you do at the next one, don't touch the Glory. We need you awake. I'm going to feign injury from touching the Glory, you'll

Chapter 14: Time for a change

help me back to the minibus, and ask for the keys to get in. Lucasz will disappear into the Glory, loop round, jump in, and drive us off."

"We're stealing the bus?"

"How far do you think we'd get on foot? We'll not keep it long, just far enough to get us some distance, then we'll ditch it. They'll find it soon enough."

Back at the minibus, Locksley was talking to Lucasz. "The country's just about holding itself together for now," she said. "But if the Glories keep increasing, what then? How can we handle two crises at once?"

"Are the Glories a crisis?" I asked.

"You've seen how many idiots come out to see the Glories, even though they don't officially exist. And how many of them forget about social distancing, and absolutely *all* of them ignore the rules about gatherings," she replied. "The Glories are so far outside of anyone's lived experience, they make people do strange things. And they haven't even got organised, yet."

"Who haven't?"

"Anyone. There's anti-lockdown groups starting to form – not much traction yet, but give them time – but can you imagine what those selfish fools are going to do with this?"

It was a good question, but my mind was on other things. Could Locksley really be aware of whatever had been done to us in the night? For all of her hard-nosed exterior, she struck me as a rather honest person. And if it was being done without her knowledge or approval, then surely there'd be no better ally than she? But we couldn't be sure, and that was the problem. Her first duty was clearly to Queen and Country, and if she perceived the Glories as a threat to that, then would she consider violations against us to be a necessary evil?

* * * * *

We had entered the small town of Salbury, and couldn't have been more than a few minutes away from Hector and Bluebell's home, when Farron suddenly declared, "There's another one!"

"How far?" asked Locksley

"One hour seventeen, on the satnav," he replied.

"Go!"

We ran a red light, turning left and heading north out of the town.

"We're on track to have more than yesterday, aren't we?" asked Locksley.

"Looking like it," Farron replied.

"Let's hope this one hangs around."

Another eighty minutes of driving to look forward to. My legs and back were getting sore. Lara was sat behind Lucasz now, apparently texting, but in fact the message was for me, as she held it out so only I could see it.

    Be ready.

I nodded. Could we really steal the bus? How far would we get? We'd have Hector and Bluebell for passengers, too.

It was a relief when, over an hour later, Farron announced that we were ten minutes away. "There'll be quite a crowd," he said, "but at least this one's not

Chapter 14: Time for a change

visible from a distance. Couple of walkers found it, told friends, word spread quickly. Medium-sized town just four miles away. Of course, some didn't come because they think it's a hoax."

"What does it look like?" I asked.

"Spherical, twenty metres across, one third of it buried. Red strings with other colours inside – the descriptions I've read aren't very precise and they contradict each other."

Soon we started encountering cars, clumsily parked with two wheels on the thin verge. Two were coming towards us, the frustrated looking driver of the first one motioning to us to give way because the parked cars narrowed the road. "We might as well park here," said Farron. "Cars coming from both directions trying to park is gonna be a total nightmare." More cars appeared, and several horns tooted.

"Morons all expecting a car park, footpaths and signposts, probably," muttered Locksley. "You're right, grab the spot here while we can."

Bart reversed us into a gap between two parked cars, leaving the cars on the road to sort it out between themselves who gave way.

"As far as I can tell, it's up through that wood," said Farron.

"As far as you can tell?" growled Locksley, incredulously.

"No-one had the foresight to provide a six-figure grid reference, I'm afraid. I'm working off vague descriptions here."

"Well, we'd better start searching then. Everyone out!"

"What about us?" asked Hector.

"You do what you want," replied Locksley coldly. Hector got out with us, but there was a two metre drop to a gully in the trees by the road, then a feeble wire fence before an upward slope with young trees, brambles and thistles to fight through. Hector shook his head sadly and retreated inside the vehicle.

The rest of us surged onwards. Lucasz had already grabbed a stick and was bashing down the brambles to make us a semblance of a path up the slope. Higher up, we entered a beech hanger, and the going got easier. Ahead of us a man we didn't know was now striding off, looking at his phone.

"Let's follow him," said Lara the phone expert. "Reckon he's got an app showing where his friend's phone is, so he might lead us right to it."

"Good thinking," said Farron, and even Locksley gave a brief nod of approval. We had to walk fast, straining my poor old legs as we went. The route now switched to a descent through a young spruce plantation, and we squeezed between the trees, losing sight of our unwitting guide. Next, we had to jump or wade through a muddy stream, then ascend again under older spruces, reasoning that all we needed to do was keep in a straight line. But Lucasz had gone ahead, and now reappeared.

"It's just through here!" he said, looking excited.

We crossed a shady bridleway, forced an opening through a mass of hawthorns, and emerged onto a slope of chalk downland speckled with cowslips. Think of the reddest thing you can imagine – a poppy, or blood, perhaps, and then imagine it looking like faded paint beside the colour of the dome we could now see over the rise of the downland slope. We hurried towards it, with more of it

Chapter 14: Time for a change

becoming visible as we moved closer. There was a crowd around it, of course – moths to a flame – but we'd never have found it without them.

I stopped to drink it in. It was, as Farron had said, a sphere perhaps thirty metres across, with the bottom third buried. The outside layer was a lattice of red lines, each perhaps as thick as an arm, connecting into hexagons, and steadily rotating at an angle diagonal to the horizontal. Immediately inside this layer was another, similar but orange, rotating in a different, near vertical direction. Then a yellow layer, then green, blue and glimpses of a sixth purple layer when gaps in all the others aligned. All rotating in different directions. It was truly extraordinary.

"Come on, people," said Locksley, "we're not here to gawp. It's time to see what you can do. Put these on." She produced some small devices on wristbands.

"What are they?"

"They monitor heart rate and a few other things" said Farron. We obeyed.

"Lucasz, you go first, then Lara. Just walk straight into it, if you can. Try not to draw much attention."

"As you literally vanish into the impossible," I said. "Good luck with that."

As usual, social distancing had broken down around the Glory as people jostled to get close, and touch it. Lucasz found a gap and walked through. His head vanished first, then the rest of him as he simply strode into it. Remarkably, the people either side didn't seem to notice.

"Gotta admit, that's impressive," said Locksley.

"And the rest are all pushing against it like it's solid," said Farron.

"Lara, you next," said Locksley.

"Better wait till he's out though," she replied. I don't want to move it while he's in there."

"Actually, you'd need to be careful moving it at all," said Farron. "I imagine there's people all round it."

"Try pushing it upward," said Locksley. "And not a long way. Farron, get yourself into a spot where you can judge the movement against something behind it."

"Wilco!" he said, which I guessed meant 'yes' in normal person language.

"Oh fuck, that's all we need," said Locksley.

Two men in black hoodies with large white circles of linen inexpertly sown onto their chests had been walking around the crowd, handing things out, and they now approached us.

"Have you accepted the light?" said one, his eyes wide open in an idiotic smile.

"Well there's one in my bedroom," said Locksley. "Now piss off, we're busy."

"The time has come to ascend," said the other. "This is the work of the Lord. Surely you can see that?"

"I can see that it's beautiful," I said.

"Join us," said the first one, pressing a piece of paper into my hand. "Accept the light. Be among those who are brought forward." The other man tried to give a similar slip to Jenks, but Jenks shoved his boot into the man's midrib, and pushed him over."

Chapter 14: Time for a change

"Get lost, weirdo!!"

"The truth is here," said the first, leaving a few more slips for us on the ground as he helped his colleague to his feet. Then, unperturbed, they walked on to hassle someone else.

"How many fucking rules are those morons breaking?" fumed Jenks. "They're a fucking cult, aren't they? Walking up to strangers! They touched her hand! You'd better sanitise it, girl, quick! They should all be locked up! Look, they even gave us their address! Get the fucking police to arrest them all!"

Locksley offered an expression that was both pained and sympathetic. "The police have been told to pretend they don't exist. These sorts of nutters thrive on publicity, so they're best ignored."

Lucasz had emerged from the Glory. "It looks totally different inside," he said. Complete white-out, couldn't see my hand in front of my face. Had to drop to all fours, or I'd have fallen over. Even so, I still headbutted a tree – the back part of it's in woodland." He rubbed his head.

Farron took the wristband from Lucasz. "Lara, you're next," said Locksley, and the young woman walked forward, a little nervously. A few of the crowd were interested in us now; either they'd seen Lucasz crawl out of the Glory, or Jenks shoving the cult member. Lara seemed perturbed by the attention, especially as a few people actually moved aside to let her touch the Glory.

The rest of us were close behind her, wanting to see if she really could move it. She raised her left hand, palm flat, and touched the Glory, or at least as close as anyone but Lucasz had got to doing so. Everyone else's hands could get within about an inch of the rotating red lattice, no closer. Lara bent her arm a bit and began to push.

"EeeeeeeaaaaAAAAAAAHHHHH!" she screamed. Her whole body was shaking, seemingly paralysed. Frightened onlookers scattered. Lucasz ran forward, grabbed her waist, and pulled her backwards. The screaming stopped.

"My hand!" she wailed. "I can't feel my hand."

"It's probably temporary," said Locksley.

"How the fuck do you know?" Lara growled. "Get me away! Get me away from this thing! It felt me! It felt what I was trying to do and it didn't like it!"

"Bart, take her back to the bus."

"No no," said Lara. "Her. I trust her." She indicated me.

"Really?" said Locksley.

"It's either this, or I quit," Lara said.

"For fuck's sake, go then. And try not to get lost in the woods." Locksley nodded to Bart. "Go with them."

We started moving, Lara using me slightly for support. "I can carry you if you like, girlie," said the driver.

I thought Lara would scoff at this, but she said "Actually that would be good. My legs feel funny too." He scooped her up like she was a rag doll, and walked on as if he were carrying nothing. I paused for one last look at the Glory. Jenks was rising up the side of it, to the amazement of the crowd. I hoped the Glory wouldn't vanish while he was up there, and it occurred to me that Locksley had probably thought of that too, but decided she was happy to risk it.

Chapter 14: Time for a change

We reached the bus quicker than I expected. Bart had clearly taken quite a shine to Lara, who seemed rather wobbly now. It took both of us to get her up the steep gully to the road, and then she collapsed into Bart's arms.

"I don't know what's happening to me," she said weakly. "I feel so delicate, so vulnerable, I hope you don't mind if I ..." and she clamped her lips over his, snogging his face off, her hands running all over his body. He, clearly shocked, did not resist, placing his own hands rather more chastely around her back. Now her hands were probing around his bottom, fingers of one penetrating the top of his trousers, while the other dived deep into his pocket and drew out the minibus keys, which she then held out behind her. It took me a moment before I realised I was meant to take them. Then we heard a man's scream from the gully. Lara and Bart quickly disengaged, and he skidded down the slope to investigate. At the same time, Lucasz emerged onto the road just a little further on, pointing urgently at the bus. Lara and I ran towards it and got into the two passenger seats at the front, and I handed Lucasz the keys as he jumped into the driver's seat. He started the engine and reversed, gently bumping the car behind us, then was away along the road. I looked round to see Bart scrambling back onto the road and running after us.

"Shit," said Lucasz. A car was coming the other way.

"We're bigger, he'll have to give way," said Lara, beside him.

But the car was stopped in front of us, gesturing angrily at us to reverse.

Lara wound down the window. "The police are coming! They're going to arrest everyone!" she yelled. "So no, we're not going to reverse, you need to back up and get away too!" She thought fast, I had to give her that.

The other driver looked terrified, and reversed so fast he scraped another car, though still not fast enough for our liking. Behind us, Bart was gaining ground, and we knew how strong he was.

"I say, what's happening?" called Hector from the back.

"Not now," we chorused.

The car was still reversing, but now a second one had come up behind it, and our way was blocked. Bart had almost caught up. "Only one thing we can do," said Lucasz.

Bart was now alongside us, and about to pull open the side door, when Lucasz hit reverse. We saw Bart's surprised face whizz past us as the bus went backwards along the road, weaving from side to side slightly as Lucasz tried to avoid hitting the badly parked cars. "If someone comes up the other way, we're screwed," he said. But we passed a dozen parked cars, Bart now getting further away again, but still running.

"I thought that carrying me might get him out of breath," said Lara.

"Dammit!!" exclaimed Lucasz. A car was approaching from the way we were trying to go. Its driver hooted angrily as we stopped right in front of it. Lara jumped out and ran to talk to him.

"The road's blocked! You can't get closer. You need to park and go up through the wood. We can't find a space big enough for us, but look, you can go there."

Slowly the man began parking. Too slowly. Bart was running towards us, again. "Lara, get back in," cried Lucasz. She did. He gunned the engine forward, and Bart had to throw himself sideways out of the way; Lucasz hit the brakes the moment he did so, then we reversed back to where we were. The obstructing car was half-parked now, gingerly shuffling to and fro as it tried to waggle further into a narrow space. Bart was back on his feet and approaching again, his normally genial face now like thunder.

Lucasz hit reverse again, literally squeezing through the gap between the parking car on one side, and fence on the other. The awful screech of metal scraping against metal rent the air as the vehicles touched, the other driver screaming obscenities at us as we went.

"Well, next time park faster," shouted Lucasz, and then we were past him. The man jumped out and started remonstrating with Bart, who ignored him and ran past. "Thank God," said Lucasz, as we cleared the last of the clumsily parked cars, and reversed along forty metres of mercifully empty road, before a field entrance came up on the left. Lucasz reverse-turned into it, bumping the locked gate, then swung us back in a perfect three-point turn, and now we were away down the road.

Chapter 15: The kidnappers

Antony

The surface of the moon was incredibly detailed once we got close. I held back from touching it, standing just a few feet away from it. It was slowly rotating, the craters and features progressing past me from left to right at slower than walking pace. If you blotted out everything else, you could feel like you were in a lunar module, travelling over the surface, looking for a place to land.

"Hold my hand," said Sally. I did, loving the warm but slightly rough feel of her fingers in mine. Then she reached forward with her left hand to touch the Glory.

"No!" I said, and let go of her right hand. Her left pressed against the Glory's surface but couldn't go in.

"Hey," she said turning to me. "You let go."

"I think it was touching me that let you pull out a piece of that Glory."

"I know, so let me do it again."

"But don't you see? I think that's what makes people fall into them. Like a key. And if you do it, it'll be just the same. All those people there will fall into it!"

"S'pose," she said, her voice suddenly like a frustrated child's. More people were arriving all the time, their desire to get up close butting up against social distancing protocols, leading to an evenly spaced mass of people going many metres back behind us. A huge rottweiler dog was barking like crazy, then jerked its lead so hard, the owner lost his grip. The dog hurtled forwards towards the Glory, then skidded to a halt, growling and barking like fury.

"That dog can see it," I said.

"Well, yeah," said Sally.

"The other dogs I've seen, didn't see the Glory at all, just went straight through it."

The rottweiler was running from side to side, still looking at the Glory, and then sped off around the edge of the Glory, almost knocking people over as it went. As I returned my attention to the slowly moving lunar surface, I picked up snippets of what others were saying nearby.

"Some sort of trick."

"I think it's a real picture of the moon."

"Why won't it show up on my phone?"

"Look, a bird just flew out of it."

"People should control their dogs."

"It's God. God is here. He is coming today."

"Don't touch it. There's a story going round …"

"It isn't there, look! All I can see is the field behind it."

"Big crash on the way here."

"I can see my granny. Her face."

"Throw things into it!"

"Let's try and find the flag Armstrong planted."

"They're called Glories. The big Earth in the sky is one too."

"Get off my field!"

'He's not there either, look."

Chapter 15: The kidnappers

"I think this is it. The world's going to end. The four horsemen are coming."
"People running away from it."
"How can this be here?"
"How come they've not been in the news?"
"The virus is a hoax. To stop people finding out about these things."
"Grubber! Grubber, come back!"
"Get off my bloody field!"
"It's impossible."
"You're squashing all my crops!"
"Can't take a photo. Why can't I?"
"Not there at all, look."
"It's all smooth, even the cratered bits."
"Look, the stick just goes into it like it's not there!"
"I'm gonna take down all your bloody number plates!"
"Look at this!"
"Him, yes."
"That's him, look."
"Excuse me sir, you need to come with us."

Firm hands gripped both of my arms. A pair of tough looking men dressed in dark clothes had grabbed me. One had curly black hair and dark glasses, the other was squat with hair cut very short; both were wearing surgical face-masks. 'What's going on?" I said loudly. Looking round behind me, I could see that quite a lot of the watching crowd were looking at us. Many had their phones pointed my way, and were looking confused. *They've recognised me*, I thought. But the men didn't look like policemen.

"Are you police?" asked Sally. "Let's see some ID!"

"Stay out of this, chick," said the curly hair.

"You show me ID, or I shout 'paedophile' at the crowd and we see how far you get," she said firmly.

The man moved fast. Releasing my wrist, he swung round and hit Sally hard in the face. She fell back against the Glory's surface. Before I could move, he'd grabbed my hand again. "This kid's a super-spreader, we need to get him into quarantine," the squat man shouted. The watching crowd drew backwards.

"Now just a minute," said a tough looking man, striding forward.

One of the men pulled out a gun. "We are government operatives and authorised to use lethal force! This man is carrying a potentially lethal mutant virus strain!"

The tough man retreated, uncertain. Then the rottweiler came charging along out of the Glory, skidding to a halt, looking fretful and confused. Sally threw a large stone and struck it on the head. For a moment, the dog looked comically shocked, then turned and charged in Sally's direction, but by then she'd scampered round to put me and my captors between her and the dog, so it charged right at us, barking furiously.

The man with the gun swore in fear, and fired three times at the dog, but by then I was struggling furiously, so his aim was off, and he missed. Then the dog leapt up and sank its teeth into his arm, the gun falling from his hand as he bellowed in pain. Now I grappled with the second man, before Sally came up and drove her heel into the back of his knee, making him crumple backwards. I came down on top of him, smashing my knee into his groin. Sally kicked his head, for good measure.

Chapter 15: The kidnappers

"Peeeeeete! Get it off meeee!!" screamed the man with the dog on his arm. "Shoot it! Shoot the bloody thing!"

"That's my dog, don't you dare," said another man, running forward.

The tough man, who had challenged the men earlier, walked forward and picked up the gun by the butt. Then he looked from one to the other, and threw the gun into the Glory. It vanished through a crater. "You two OK?" he asked Sally and me, ignoring the battle with the dog.

"I think so," she answered. "Thanks."

"Bloody government," he said, and wandered off. Sally pulled some keys from the pocket of 'Pete', the man we'd tackled together.

"Come on, we've gotta go," I said.

"Just ... just a minute," she said, looking at the Glory. "Just let me ... look a little more."

"He's getting up," I said desperately. The man called Pete was moving, unsteadily, into an all-fours position.

I grabbed Sally's hand, and that seemed to shake her out of it. We ran back towards the roundabout, then saw the gridlock again, even worse than before, stretching well out of sight along all four roads into the roundabout.

"We'll never get away through this, even if we find their car," I said.

"Yeah, but ... wouldn't they have thought of that?" said Sally. "Parked further back, or something?" The side of her face was swelling up where the man had hit her, and she was limping now. Looking up, I could see yet another Glory hanging in the air, some way beyond the roundabout. It looked like a comet. There were plenty of people milling around among the trapped cars, some walking our way, some towards the comet. Perhaps we could lose ourselves among them?

I realised that Pete might be coming after us, and had a brainwave. I pulled Sally over to crouch down with me under a couple of hawthorn bushes. Sure enough, the thug appeared at the top of the slope, searching for us among the crowd, looking frustrated when he couldn't see us. Eventually he set off quickly down the slope.

"What's the plan?" said Sally.

"That bozo there knows we've got his car keys. I'm hoping that he'll forget we don't have a clue where his car is, and go to the car, hoping to catch us before we get in. We just follow him, and find out where it is!"

"Do you know, that's actually quite clever," she said with a smile. "Except for the obvious flaw."

"Umm, which is?"

"We'll have to deal with the bastard all over again. And I'm pretty much spent on adrenaline now."

"One problem at a time?" I said, apologetically. She nodded and we got up. Luckily, 'Pete' was very tall, and this plus his black jacket made it easy enough to follow him through the cars and people. On the other side of the roundabout, he headed up a slope into a field, a way that no-one else was going because there wasn't a Glory in that direction. We waited till he climbed over the fence at the top and went out of sight, before following. But as we reached the fence, we could see that he'd stopped just beyond it. A black car was parked some way along the side of the field, but 'Pete' himself was on the phone, wandering in small circles. We hunkered down on our side of the fence, concealed (we hoped) from his sight by a line of scrub alongside the fence.

Chapter 15: The kidnappers

" ... yeah, he was there just like the boss thought he might be. But he had some bitch with him and a massive dog, and they put up a fight. Boyd made a total hash of things, he's still there with that bloody dog biting off his arm ... no I didn't, because the boss made it pretty clear how important this kid is, so I left Boydie to it, and went after Blake. But there's a massive crowd here and he could be anywhere ... yes of course I'll bloody keep looking!"

He ended the call. "Move!" hissed Sally, and we went along sideways, hiding ourselves round a bend in the fence, just in time as the thug came back over his bit of fence, swearing profusely as the wire ripped his trouser leg. Then he tottered down the slope, limping slightly. Sally and I looked at each other gleefully, and climbed over our bit of fence, through the scrub, into the field, and along to the car.

"Would you like a ride, sir?" she said happily, holding open the passenger side door for me and bowing like a chauffeur.

"Why thank you, madam!" I replied, and got in.

On the dashboard was a printout satellite map of the area where we were, with a red cross roughly where the moon was. A dotted line showed how they'd got the car to where we were. Sally managed to turn it around in the field corner, and soon we were trundling along the edge of the next field. "Lucky I'm a farm girl, eh?" she said happily.

"Yeah," I said. "Thank you for rescuing me back there. That was a great trick with the dog."

"Used to throw stones at sheep when I was little, till my dad found out and stopped me. Oh, it was only little stones, they didn't even notice, usually. The game was to get them to stay in their fleece. But I'm a dead-eye aim!"

"You an only child?"

"Yup."

"Me too."

"I had plenty of company. But it was all four-legged, or had wings."

"How's the leg?" I asked.

"Not so bad now. Gonna have a fuck of a bruise tomorrow, but nothing more. One last thing that car did for me, I guess."

"Will your parents be mad?" I asked.

"They're stuck in New Zealand for now," she said. "Holiday of a lifetime, turned into a little bit more than they'd bargained for. But they're in a cottage with plenty of walks, so it could be worse. I dunno ... I don't know what's happening, Antony. The pandemic, and now the Glories. By the time they get back, I don't think they'll be worrying too much about one car."

"So you're on your own at the farm?" I asked. The prospect was not unappealing.

"I wasn't," she said. "Grandad was there, but he got Corona."

"Oh no," I said, feeling wretched because of my earlier hopes.

"It's OK, he's past the worst of it. But Aunt Flora's been looking after him since he came out of hospital. No way I could do that, and run the farm too."

"Maybe I could help out for a bit."

"Yeah, maybe you could." And she smiled at me like I've never been smiled at before.

Chapter 16: Get me to the church

Julia

"We did it! We're free!" said Lara ecstatically.

"Where do we go?" I asked.

"We can't keep the minibus for long," said Lucasz. "They'll be able to track it, I reckon. ANPR hits and stuff."

I had no idea what an ANPR hit was, so I took his word for it.

"You could stay at our place!" said Hector, jovially.

"Thanks, but they're bound to look there, since they know you're in the bus," said Lucasz.

"Hector, can you drive?" I asked.

"Yes, of course I can! How would I take Bluebell to the countryside if I didn't drive!?"

"How about this then?" I said. "We head towards Hector's house, but get out somewhere along the way, then call a cab or something? Go to a friend's house, someone Locksley wouldn't know about? Then Hector drives on. If they're tracking the bus, it'll send them the wrong way."

"Good idea," said Lucasz. "Except, I'd expect Farron to be all over our social media and our lists of contacts. They'll know everyone we might go to, and they'll be onto the cab companies too."

"We were just going to dump the bus in a service station, and try to catch a lift in a truck," said Lara. "Maybe split up. But I'm thinking ... look, this is the address that loony cult bloke gave me. It can't be that far, if they were at the Glory. We could join the cult for a little bit. Locksley would never think of looking there."

"You're kidding," said Lucasz.

"No, she's right," I said. I grabbed the road atlas that was sitting, largely unused, in the glove compartment. "First off, where are we?"

Lara checked her phone and told me.

"Now, do that satnav thing and key in a route to Hector's house."

"Fourteen spindle crescent, Salbury," Hector said.

"They can probably hack our phones," said Lucasz.

"Well we want them to, silly," said Lara. "For now at least. Look, here's the address the loony gave me. You need to find it in the paper atlas, not the phone, so we don't leave a trail."

"It's a church," I said. "I'd have expected some weird mansion, or a collection of battered tents."

The address read '*St Claudia's Church, by Yewford*'. We found Yewford in the atlas, a tiny dot on one of the pages. With some effort Lara and I managed to match up the satnav route on her phone with the ink roads in the atlas. "We pass within ten miles of it at the closest point," I said at last.

"Can we divert and get closer?" asked Lara.

"Not without giving a clue to where we're going," said Lucasz. "No, this is what we do. A short diversion here, into these services, and there we park right

Chapter 16: Get me to the church

by the edge where there's trees or a hedge, and switch drivers. Make it look like we got dropped off there. Then Hector drives us to the real drop-off point, which is on the satnav recommended route to his house. We pitch out there, and walk."

"Ten miles?" said Lara unhappily.

"Ten miles," said Lucasz.

"Maybe Lucasz can carry you this time," I said, which earned me a cold stare.

"It's tough and I'm sorry," said Lucasz gently, "but anything else and we'll be looking over our shoulders waiting for them to catch us. This way, we've got a real chance of getting away properly."

"S'pose," said Lara glumly.

"At least you don't have to walk it in your nightie," I pointed out. She almost smiled.

The plan worked like clockwork at first. We drove into another near-empty service station ("They're bound to have cameras here," said Lucasz) and then to a shady corner, where the three of us got out from the front and climbed over the wire fence between thorn trees, and then back again at a point hidden from any camera by the bus, and into the side door, keeping our heads down.

"Phones off," said Lucasz.

Lara herself had said that phones could be tracked, but she still wore an expression like a child who was putting her beloved pet to sleep, as she switched hers off and pulled out the battery. Hector strode round to the driver's seat, declaring "This is it, Bluebell! The outlaw Hector Margoyles, taking the wheel in the name of freedom!" He hadn't even asked why we were running away. He drove us swiftly and safely to the agreed drop-off point, a bend in the road where a little bridge crossed a stream with a narrow line of trees on one side, and we got out. But a thought had been brewing in my head, and I hurried round to speak to Hector, before he could drive off.

"They were drilling into our heads, in the night. Lara, and me. Tell Locksley that. Tell her that if she didn't know, then I'm truly sorry we didn't trust her, but we couldn't be sure. But if she did know, then shame on her. Shame on all of them!"

Hector's mouth formed a comical 'O', and Lucasz urged me to stop holding things up. I nodded, and Hector drove off.

"We shouldn't have given away that we knew," said Lara, as we hauled ourselves up a bank and over a fence into the wood.

"Why not?" I replied. "If Locksley knew about it, then she'll easily have guessed that's why we did a bunk. But if she didn't know, then my guess is she'll be too busy raising a stink with her bosses to come chasing after us."

"S'pose," said Lara.

Soon we were walking between the line of trees and a field of young crops, soon leaving the road behind us. We were free.

* * * * *

Chapter 16: Get me to the church

Freedom is all very well, but in practice it means trudging along field edge after field edge, climbing over gates and fences, and in my case feeling very silly in a nightgown and torn leggings. "I really hope this cult has a few spare bits of ladies' clothing to spare," I said.

"I think it'll be hoodies for everyone," said Lucasz.

We were navigating by the sun. With our phones deactivated, all we had was a hastily drawn sketch map taken from the road Atlas. Lucasz had worked out that if we kept the sun at four-o-clock, direction wise, moving to five over time, then we'd be heading towards Yewford. In between was the slightly larger village of Shelton, which would serve as the only useful marker along the way. We had a simple cover story, which we put into action when we saw a couple with a young dog walking towards us.

We stopped, three metres away from them. "I'm terribly sorry," I said, "but my daughter forgot to charge her phone, and now we're a bit lost. Are we going the right way to get back to Shelton?"

They looked at me incredulously.

"Don't mind mum," said Lara wearily. "She thinks lockdown's an excuse to dress like a scarecrow. I was really hoping we wouldn't meet anyone today."

The woman shrugged and indicated that it was in the direction they'd come from. Then the three of us squeezed into the hedge, so that the couple and dog could pass by at a decent distance from us. And on we went.

"Did it really hurt you? That Glory?" I asked Lara.

"Not exactly. But it did push back. As soon as I tried to move it. I could feel this strange anger, directed at me. Like a current running through me. I'd been planning to move it a little, then pretend to faint, so we could go back to the minibus. We were hoping they'd send the driver with us."

"You were very convincing," I told her. "Especially the snog."

"Did am-dram at school for a while," she replied with a smile. "Can't believe it came in useful. Gave it up pretty quick though, because there were too many drama queens."

We were now on a clear footpath. It passed through a small copse of trees, then we saw the town just below us. "Halfway there," said Lucasz.

In the little town, the streets were mostly deserted, most of the shops firmly closed, but a little corner shop was open. "Anyone got cash?" asked Lucasz.

Lucasz popped in and got us some sandwiches, with Lara's money. Apparently they could track credit card spending as well, though Lucasz assured me they couldn't locate our cards otherwise. As the town petered out, we continued along a narrow country lane, confident now that Locksley's people were unlikely to drive past.

The walk was pleasant, and even Lara didn't complain. Other than one boy racer who we had to dodge, the road was empty, and the few junctions we passed had signposts to Yewford. "Reckon Locksley must be spitting feathers," said Lucasz cheerfully.

I said nothing. It was stupid, but I felt guilty about running away.

"The government will be terrified of these Glories and what they represent," said Lucasz. "A loss of control, at the exact moment when they have us under better control than they could ever have hoped for. Look at how they were

Chapter 16: Get me to the church

suppressing the whole thing. Of course they're going to do anything and everything they can to find out more, what they are, and if possible how to control them. That's what they wanted from us. No wonder they went for you two first. Lara, you gave them a possibility of control. And Julia, you might have offered a cure for Corona. For everything else, too."

"They could be cloning us right now," said Lara.

"Oh come on," I said.

"Why not?" she said. "They took cells from us. They cloned that sheep, Dorothy."

"Dolly."

"Whatever. My point is they could do it, and I reckon they will."

"Be too slow to make much difference, I think," said Lucasz.

The discussion of possible clones veered into companionable silliness as we walked on. An hour later, our legs were aching for rest, but Lucasz urged us on. Eventually, we sighted a church, standing on top of a very small hill, a little bit away from a village. "Think that's it?" I asked.

"Could be," said Lucasz. "Let's take a look."

The lane we were on went straight to the village, but a clearly marked footpath came off it at right angles, cutting between two fields and up the slope to the church. We swung open a gate and entered a large graveyard from the side. Moving towards the main entrance, we saw a sign giving the name as *St Claudia's*. "We're here," I said.

"Look at this," said Lucasz.

A circle had been laid out, very neatly, in the middle of the churchyard. Its rim comprised plant pots of various sizes, gravestones, and logs standing on their ends. Flowering plants and fresh lengths of ivy were draped between these objects, forming a sort of fence. Within the circle were five chairs, arranged in a crescent such that all more or less faced the church. The circle opened at the front and back, where a path to the church door cut through it. By silent agreement, we entered the circle and sat down.

"They've used actual standing gravestones as part of this circle," I said. "There's no way any vicar would ever allow that."

"Really?" said Lara, pointing at a man who was now approaching. He was wearing some sort of loose white over-jacket, which looked like it had been stitched together with sheets. Corners of sheet hung loose beyond the wrists, and forming scraggly coat tail. I recalled a joke by Terry Wogan about some hapless Eurovision act: *'they made their own costumes, but they didn't have time to finish them'*. He also had a strip of sheet worn round his head as a bandana. He had a thin scraggly beard, and hair that looked like he'd given up combing for lent.

"Welcome, welcome, fellow searchers of truth."

"Hello," we replied, a little awkwardly.

"You are here seeking truth, are you not?"

"Well," began Lucasz, but I cut him off.

"We would like to know more about what's happening here, yes."

"Then let me tell you. You are sitting in the precise spot where the world changed for me, and for all of us. I do not believe that I am alone, or in any way

special. Others will have received the same message, or if not, they soon will." He paused, gazing at us with joyful eyes, clearly expecting us to contribute.

"And the message was?" I asked him.

"The world as we know it is changing – ending, in all probability. The time is coming when we must step beyond it."

"You're talking about Judgement Day," said Lara, sounding unimpressed.

"In a way, child," he replied. "Let me explain properly. The lockdown had just begun. I'd done one service in the yard right here, standing on a pulpit right in front of the church door, and then another online. My daughter set it up. And I was walking back to the church thinking about how we would hold our flock together in these frightening times, and it just appeared. A huge white bubble, hanging over the church, taking a bite out of the roof and steeple.

"It was pure white, yet somehow not bright or dazzling to look at. Perfectly circular. Because it was so utterly white, the surface looked flat, but as I walked around to the side, I realised it was a perfect sphere. After a while I went to get Millie."

"By which he means, banged on the door like a maniac, who forgot he had keys." We'd been joined by a woman in her late forties, round-faced with ample curly hair, and wearing a white neckerchief made of blanket linen.

"Ah, this is Millie, my wife," said the man.

"And my husband is Walt, I'm guessing that it hasn't occurred to him to introduce himself," Millie said.

Walt gave a brief, rather tolerant smile, and then resumed his story. "And she spread the word around the village. I stood there watching, while more and more of the flock came out to see it. Some of them asked me what it was, and of course I didn't know. We brought out chairs for the older ones, and the people kept coming. Half the village or more, and they were looking to me for answers, all of them. It was over my church. And though I had no answers to give, a moment arrived when I felt compelled to speak, and so speak I did."

He closed his eyes, as he recalled the moment, and began recanting as if to a far larger audience. "My people, I cannot explain to you what we are witnessing today, I have not been given the knowledge or understanding to convey the full message. But I do know this. We have been chosen. We have been spoken to. I stand before you at the house of our Lord, and I know in my heart that this is His doing, His will. He has told us that the Plague shall not be an end for our people, but perhaps it shall be part of a New Beginning. He has put before us a challenge, and Lord I say unto you, your challenge is accepted. I shall not rest until I have understood your message, and conveyed it to my people."

He stopped, arms outstretched, and opened his eyes. An awkward silence fell. Then Lara said, "So did you uncover it? The message?"

"I travelled deep into the electronic wilderness, seeking answers. I learned of Glories, other manifestations across the country. Foolish tales of alien worlds, other Earths, and Gods playing dice with the world. The playthings of credulous minds, no more. I was far from alone in invoking our Lord, yet I could see how others had succumbed to Hope but not Faith. I knew beyond doubt that when the truth was revealed to me, then I would know it for what it was. And so I searched on.

Chapter 16: Get me to the church

"I went one night without sleep, and then another. I wrote, I prayed, and eventually I painted. The church and the white bubble across a massive canvas. Yet when I came to the bubble I left it blank – nothing there, it was empty. A hole in all of creation. And then at last I understood."

Once again he paused, as if expecting us to fill in the gaps, like slow-witted kids before a teacher. If so, he was disappointed, so on he went. "A perfect, geometric gap in the weft of Creation. A perfect imperfection. How could I have taken so long to see it? If someone were to write you a letter, and cut out from the paper a perfectly hexagonal gap, what reason could they have for doing it?"

This time, at least, Lucasz felt able to answer. "A message. Some sort of code, perhaps."

"Exactly!! A message! And it could be from no-one but the being who created the fabric into which that message had been woven! The Lord himself!!"

"But lots of people have been saying that," said Lara, a little dismissively. "A message from God that we can't understand. It's the most popular explanation on Insta, even more than the Aliens."

Walt clasped his hands in glee. "But I *DID* understand it, don't you see? The nature of the message WAS the message. He was telling us that He was preparing to Unmake all of Creation. Or remake it. He was telling us all to be ready. He does not plan simply to end this world. He is looking to *upgrade* it. The Glories can only be witnessed by God's Children, and only those who have opened their hearts can understand the message. We have to make ourselves ready! When the time is right, he will pluck us from here and into a new world, perhaps a form of Heaven, or maybe to join Him in his own great Universe."

I was getting confused. "So you're saying it's Judgement Day?"

"Of a kind, yes and no. Maybe He'll let the world run on for everyone else, but surely you can see it is heading into darkness? He's offering the Chosen a way out!"

His wife spoke up. "We've come to believe that the Lord God may have built this world in the role of a computer programmer designing a virtual reality simulation, only infinitely more advanced and more powerful. The idea of a God, the idea of a computer programmer – the only difference is scale. Please understand, it doesn't make us love Him any less. The being in charge would be both these things, God and Programmer, yet best understood as something in between. And now He chooses to speak to us by carefully controlled glitches in the world we inhabit. We have to respond by catching His attention. He may at this very moment be building physical bodies for us, to exit His simulated world and to stand alongside Him! Or perhaps, He will allow us to speak with Him first. What we know is, we must be ready, and prepared."

"So the question for you is, are you ready to join us?"

* * * * *

"We're on the run," Lucasz told Walt and Millie. "We each have a special connection with the Glories, and there are people who are trying to exploit us. We need a place to hide, and your people were ..."

Chapter 16: Get me to the church

"Please," said Lara, cutting him off. "We're calling on you as a Christian, to give us shelter."

"It's more than that," I said. "We need to try to understand the connections between us and the Glories. Frankly, what you said to us just now makes a lot more sense than anything else I have heard. I'd like the chance to talk to you more, if I can."

Walt seemed genuinely pleased by this. "What sort of connection?" asked Millie.

"I can walk right through them," said Lucasz. "When other people can't. I've no idea what it means."

"I can push them," said Lara. "Well, one of them. The last one I tried, it pushed back."

"And you?" Millie asked me.

"Well I ..."

"Yes?" she eyed me curiously.

I'd been about to tell them of my cancer cure, but an image had flashed into my head of them decking me in flowers and parading me about as evidence of a genuine miracle. The idea appalled me. "I was feeling ill," I said, affecting a tone of slight embarrassment, as if I felt like an imposter standing next to the other two. "And then after I'd touched a Glory, I wasn't."

Millie looked unimpressed by this, as I'd hoped.

"All this means perhaps that we can help each other," said Walt, and that seemed to decide the matter. A younger woman was approaching now, with a round face, and a very neat brown haircut. "Ah, here's our daughter, right on cue. Helen, you'll recall how we were keeping the cottage free since you moved in with us, in case there might be someone we needed to care for?" He indicated the cottage at the edge of the churchyard, joined at one end to the vicarage.

"Yes, of course," said Helen. "But we were thinking of hospital patients, stopping people who might have the virus from being dumped into a care home."

"We were indeed," said Walt. "But it turns out that there are others who are in need."

"There's only two rooms," Helen said. "And I'm betting *they're* not married." She indicated Lucasz and Lara.

I saw a flash of venom in Lara's eyes, and I spoke quickly before she could say anything. "They're not a couple," I said simply.

"And I'll sleep on the sofa, it's fine," said Lucasz.

"Well then, that's all settled," said Walt happily.

Helen pulled a face, but decided not to argue.

So we moved into the Cottage. Helen gave us a quick account of the eccentricities of the place, and even a sort of tour from the outside. She and Lara pointedly ignored each other, like a pair of antagonistic cats. Once we were inside, Lara pulled exaggerated faces at the various Christian posters on the walls (*Do not fear the unknown, for I will always be with you*, that sort of thing).

"Honestly, look at posters like that for long enough and I swear they'd suck out your personality," Lara declared. "Always assuming you had one to start with."

Chapter 16: Get me to the church  97

Yet we'd barely settled in when we heard someone frantically knocking on the door. Lucasz ran to answer it, Lara and I following, and we saw Walt there, looking oddly ecstatic.

"Is it a Glory?" asked Lucasz.

"Balloon's gone up," he said. "The cat's out of the bag!!"

"What?"

"Trending. Apparently Glories are trending, whatever that means. Helen says that's never happened before. Turn on the telly!"

"We have," I said. "*Pointless* is on."

"Try ITV!" said Walt.

Lara switched the channels. The TV screen now showed a two-person zoom call, involving a rare afternoon appearance for Susannah Reid, and a scientist called Dr Griffiths.

Within moments we knew that Walt was right – the Glories were going public.

Chapter 17: The hay

Antony

Forty minutes after stealing the black car, we pulled into a motorway service station, and I got out to stretch my legs. The car park had scattered cars in it, and there were several families pottering around by their cars, looking dazed. One woman was talking on her phone.

"It's gone? Just like that? You're sure? How do you know it won't come back? No, we're going to keep going and stay with my sister, and to hell with lockdown, till someone explains just what on earth is going on."

Sally got out, hobbling a little. I was making a comically inept attempt to get the glovebox open, before she calmly opened the door on my side and clicked the box open in one go. "You're kind of two parts Indiana Jones, one part Mr Bean, aren't you?" she observed.

I smiled back at her, wanting to say something in return but I couldn't think of any beautiful young women who worked on farms I could compare her to. I got out and said, "What now?"

She was looking at some photocopied pages she'd taken from the glove compartment. "Thought these might tell us something about who those bastards were," she said. "Look, I need to grab some food, reckon the petrol station shop'll be open."

She supported herself on my arm as we tottered across to the petrol station. At the little window, she asked for some warm pasties, candles and matches, and an OS map of the area. She insisted on paying in cash, leading to a protracted argument with the man who was equally insistent that we paid by card, telling us our cash would be covered in germs. "Look, I'll leave you a twenty," she said. "Once you've laundered it, you can keep the change."

Perhaps it was her stern glare and battered face, or more likely the profit, but he acceded. She handed me the bag of stuff but I promptly dropped it, so she carried it herself with one hand while she stuffed the hot pasty into her mouth with the other as we headed back to the car. "You not hungry?" she mumbled through a mouth full of food.

"Strangely, no," I said as crumbs fell from her mouth.

"Suit yourself," she said, and she rammed the end of a second hot pasty into her mouth, and tore it off. I watched her chewing, crumbs falling from her lips, one of them reddened by blood. I watched other parts of her too. My mind was on things other than food.

"Where to now?" I said, as she opened the car door.

"A farm. It's about five miles that way." She pointed towards the grim looking hedge at the edge of the car park. Relieved that it wasn't too far, I moved towards the passenger door.

"We're not using the car, we're leaving it here." She ripped three pages out of the small road atlas she'd taken from the now open glove compartment, folded them and shoved them in her back pocket. She left the diminished atlas on the front seat.

"So how are we getting there?"

"Walk," she said, locking the car.

"But your leg," I said.

Chapter 17: The hay

"Is gonna hurt like fuck by the time we get there, probably. But if the bastards can track the car, they'll come to the farm. We can't leave a trail. So we leave it here, and they'll think we've hitched a lift up North." When I looked unconvinced, she showed me the road atlas pages she'd ripped out. All three of them followed the motorway northwards.

"Clever," I said.

"Hey, I'm not just a pretty face, you know!"

"Not *just*, no," I agreed, in a clumsy attempt at a compliment.

"Come on, we wanna be there before dark." She moved forcefully towards the hedge, her sore leg staying straight as she experimented with the most efficient way to lumber. We climbed through the hedge and over a wire fence beyond it. Following field edges at first, then lanes and footpaths, we slowly progressed westwards. Sally winced from time to time, but told me not to fuss if I showed any concern, though she did let me support her at times. After about two miles, she disappeared into the trees, and came back a couple of minutes later complaining that dungarees were great practical clothing, for all outdoor purposes except one. Then we sat down to rest, under some beeches, their young leaves bright green. The sun was setting in the distance, and the globe Glory was long gone. A few early bumblebees tootled past.

"We need to talk about why those men were after you," she said.

"Okay." I gave her the full story, leaving nothing out. The face in the Glory, the piece of it in my hand (which she knew about anyway), Daniel's disappearance, his father's rage and my own father's anger and refusal to believe me."

"That must have been awful," she said.

"He's always been a bit like that, you know, hard and distant, since Mum died. I always have to tell the truth, and I do, and then that's that, I get punished or I don't. But for all that, for all those years when I never ever lied to him, he still didn't believe me when it really mattered. He didn't believe me!"

I was almost crying, doing all I could to stop myself, but now she put her own hand on mine, warm and gentle, and I immediately felt stronger. I went on with my story, describing the various responses of Martha's little group to the Glories, and then the disappearance of Linda and Thelma.

"I understand now," she said. "I understand why you were so worried, when I was touching the first one."

"I didn't want to lose you as well."

"You won't," she said, squeezing my hand.

"But I don't know why they're after me," I concluded.

"Don't you? If you can make people literally vanish, then I can see how a few criminal outfits would find that really appealing. But they did go to a lot of effort to get you, and to pluck you out from a crowd like that, it seems like a huge risk. I suppose if all they knew about you was that you were likely to turn up where there was a Glory…"

"Yeah, that part makes sense," I agreed. "But not why they want me so badly."

Neither of us could come up with any better explanation, as we resumed walking. I was surprised when she said we had only a mile to go, because I thought I'd be recognising some landmarks by now. "Oh we're not going to *my* farm, she explained. Not yet, anyway. That's twenty miles away. We're going … somewhere that's empty. Me and Gramps were at a fiftieth wedding

Chapter 17: The hay

anniversary bash back in March. One of the guests must have had the virus. I think I must have caught it there, too, but it was barely a cold for me, same with Aunt Flora. Gramps, well, he got it bad, but he's a tough old boot. But Derek and Lily, the ones the party was all for, they ... they didn't make it. Some anniversary present, huh?"

"Both of them?" I asked, appalled.

"Both of them. Fucking bastard virus. Fifty years together, then suffocating to death in a room on their own. So their farmhouse is empty now. Farmer next door checks in on the animals, there's a few fields of wheat, they were winding it all down anyway. Family's going to sell it on, but it's all in limbo for now, what with ... you know."

"And we're going to just break in and use their house?"

"They were my godparents," she said, tears now rolling down her face. "And I bloody well wish they were still here. But they're not, and they'd want to help me any way they could."

"Well they are," I said.

"Yes. Good," she said, stiffly.

I realised that we were now holding hands. I couldn't recall how that had happened, but I made sure not to let go, as we continued towards the farm.

* * * * *

We walked up a dirt track through a thinly wooded valley and emerged at a long farmhouse with fields and a barn beyond it. Sally looked for keys under the doormat, over the front door and under various plant pots, but came up empty.

"I guess we could break a window?" I said

"I don't think I could do that to his house," she said. "I'm happy to use it, but I can't violate it. Fuck it, we'll sleep in the barn. I'm so bloody tired I could sleep anywhere."

The barn had seen better days. One of its huge doors lay flat on the ground, the other was half open and disinclined to move. Inside lay a scattering of discarded tools, and thankfully no large animals. There were hay bales stacked up at the back. We made for them and sat down, side by side. Outside the door, the sky had turned deep pink. "Sorry," she said, "it's hardly the Hilton."

I felt a reckless boldness. "Sometimes it's not where you are, it's who you're with."

She gripped my hand in hers. "After we saw that first Glory, I had this incredible feeling inside," she said. "Like I was complete, you know? I've been ... something happened to me a year or two back, hurt like nothing on Earth, like a part of me had gone, and I'd never be whole again. Oh, you keep on going, find ways to be happy, things to distract you and I thought, well, this isn't so bad, I could live like this. But that hole was still there, until today. Today I'm feeling whole again. Whole and happy, like I never thought I could be."

"Glories can do that," I said, squeezing her hand.

"Yeah, maybe," she said, turning towards me. "But the feeling was still there, after the Glory had gone. It's been with me all day since then. That's why I couldn't let those bastards take you. Because it wasn't the Glory at all, you see? It was you."

"Me?"

Chapter 17: The hay

"You."

She leaned in toward me, eyes wide, lips slightly open. Inviting. I moved my head towards her, paused, saw a look of encouragement in her eyes, and moved forward again. We kissed. She winced. I pulled away.

"Just the bruise," she murmured. "Better kiss the other side. Be gentle now."

I moved in again, kissing the side of her face. Her hand came up to the back of my head, and gently steered me as our lips caressed each other. After a while she seemed to forget about the bruise and was kissing me full on. I wrapped my arms around her. A little later she said, "Let's ditch this stupid coat, shall we?"

She tried to pull down the zip of my jacket but it seemed to stick in her hands. I gently prized her fingers away and pulled it down myself, tossing the jacket away from us. It was pretty dark now. "Reckon these dungarees are a bit in the way too," she whispered, and taking the hint, I moved my hands to her shoulders and tried to pull the straps to the sides. 'Tried' being the operative word.

"You haven't done this before, have you," she asked gently, as she swept her hands up her chest, and in one smooth motion removed the straps from her shoulders. She got gracefully to her feet and let the dungarees fall to the ground around her ankles. She stepped out of them, bending to pick them up, and I got a perfect view of the smooth white knickers around her bottom. She laid the dungarees out flat on the straw bales we'd been sitting on. "Not much of a bed, but it'll have to do."

"Your turn," she said with an inviting smile. "I think you're shy, I'll close my eyes if that'll help." It did – I had my kit off in no time at all. "Mmmhh, nice," she said, when she opened her eyes.

"I, uhhhh, don't have any protection on me," I admitted.

"I think I'm quite safe," she whispered. "It being your first time, and all that." In fact I hadn't even kissed a girl before, but I wasn't about to tell her that. "Hey, where's your jacket? I could use it as a pillow?"

I looked around, but couldn't see where I'd left it. "It must have fallen down between the haystacks," I said.

"Never mind," she said. Now her arms were around me again, her warm fresh skin pressed against mine, my hands free to explore all over her. From time to time she did something with her hand that calmed me down where I needed it, and we went on like this for some time. I tried and failed to undo the clasp on her bra ("Why are boys always so hopeless at that?") and she responded by shedding both items of underwear in quick succession, and then lying down on the dungarees, beckoning me towards her. I did as she asked, and entered the world of men.

Afterwards, Sally went off to a corner of the barn, and returned with a piece of slightly smelly tarpaulin, which would have to do as a blanket, she said, especially as I still couldn't find my jacket, or any of my clothes, in fact. I didn't mind. We went to sleep spooning, with my arms wrapped around her. I didn't want to sleep, I just wanted to stay forever in that moment. I, too, felt complete in a way I'd never known before. She accepted me for who I was, more than accepted me. wanted me. I gazed happily at the patch of starry sky beyond the barn doorway, and imagined shooting stars streaking across it.

Chapter 18: The day they told the truth

Julia

The TV screen was showing the presenter Susannah Reid, and a scientist in his fifties wearing a bowtie, each beamed in from their homes by Zoom. The scientist was speaking.

"*They are, by most accounts, astoundingly beautiful, but also dangerous, as today's events tragically revealed.*"

"*At least five people have died today,*" said Susannah. "*We expect that number to rise.*"

"*And that is on top of a steady but significant uptick in road accidents over the preceding days and weeks,*" agreed Dr Griffiths. "*Meanwhile, as we have seen, a Glory can appear anywhere, without warning, and that includes the middle of a major road. It could only ever have been a matter of time before one of them brought about a fatal accident, as occurred two days ago. However, today's events we did not foresee.*"

Lucasz and I looked at each other in shock.

"*In a moment,*" said Reid, "*we will be re-running this item from the start. But first, here is an artist's impression of a Glory, generated electronically.*" The screen showed a photo of a bracken-covered hill, with a pink cube hanging above it, rotating slowly. This stayed on the screen for a minute or two while banners scrolled across the screen telling us a special bulletin was coming, about unexplained optical phenomena appearing across the country. Then the screen went blank for a moment, before Susannah Reid's face filled the screen.

"*By now you will all be used to, or dare I say a bit sick of, every single news bulletin being about the Coronavirus crisis. Well, this news bulletin is going to be very different. Because there is another crisis going on in this country, a crisis even more strange and bewildering than the pandemic. A crisis that most of you will not even have heard about, because every media organisation in Britain has been obeying orders to maintain a strict news blackout. I have the letter we received – or one of them – right here.*"

She held it up to the camera.

"*Up until now, we have been happy to follow this instruction. We, like others, have agreed with the government's assessment that revealing this situation to the country could cause a rapid breakdown in the lockdown arrangement that is our best and currently only defence against the Coronavirus. But events today have changed that. The government has not yet formally rescinded the media ban, but we expect that to happen later today.*

"*Before we go any further, I want to urge you all: continue to follow government advice. Do not spend extra time outdoors looking for these things. Nor should you use your car to flee your home, if you see one close by. That was, in fact, a major contributor to the fatalities today. Do not drive unless absolutely necessary. As you will shortly see, road journeys appear to present the greatest threat.*"

Chapter 18: The day they told the truth

Reid paused, her face sternly calm. I found myself holding my breath as I waited for her to resume.

"For at least the past twenty-three days, Britain has played host to a series of phenomena that defy scientific or even rational explanation, which have been named the Spectral Glories, or simply Glories for short. They are, by most accounts, astoundingly beautiful, but also dangerous, as today's events have tragically revealed. A Glory is a colourful optical phenomenon, which can be as small as a football, or bigger than a tower block. They seem to always occur away from population centres, although no-one has any idea why. They may be a simple sphere or cube, or have a more complex geometric form. Some are one single colour, others have multiple colours, often in complex patterns. The colours may move across their surface, but Glories themselves always remain stationary. I repeat, they do not move. Most Glories look and feel solid to human beings; these are known as Type One Glories. A minority, however, have no surface of their own yet change the colour, or even texture, of everything within them; these are called Type Twos. We would love to show you pictures, but Glories cannot be photographed. If you point a camera at one, you simply get a shot of what you would see if the Glory wasn't there. Again, no-one has any idea why this should be.

"Rumours about Glories have been spreading on social media, although we believe that there are ongoing efforts to remove any posts that describe a Glory. Nonetheless, such posts provide almost the only evidence of their existence, through first-hand witness accounts. With one exception. The image we are about to show you was taken from a website dedicated to reporting these phenomena, which has so far dodged attempts to shut it down. We've had this photo checked by multiple experts and as far as we can tell, it is completely genuine, it has not been doctored in any way."

The camera cut to a photo, showing a sloping ploughed field with five people lying or sitting on nothing, about four metres above the ground. Others were standing and watching with awestruck expressions, although many were not looking directly at any of the floating people.

"Remember, the Glories cannot themselves be photographed. The five people hanging in the air had managed to get on top of a Glory. Eyewitness reports, of which there were plenty, all corroborate this account: a huge yellow circular slab had appeared, about one metre thick and thirty in diameter, its top absolutely flat, and touching the ground at one end because the ground was sloping; that was how those people climbed on."

The photo on screen changed, to show the Glory sketched in, with the words 'artist's impression' prominent below. It looked as if a giant frisbee had stuck itself into the sloping ground.

"Bystanders urged them to come down, because another aspect of Glories is that they both appear and disappear instantaneously, in each case without any prior warning. Three of those people had climbed off before it vanished; the other two fell when it winked out of existence. One escaped with minor injuries, the other remains in hospital with multiple broken bones and, we now understand, also Coronavirus.

Chapter 18: The day they told the truth

"These phenomena, as I say, defy any rational explanation that anyone has been able to come up with. Type One Glories physically repel human beings if we attempt to touch them, the effect having been likened by witnesses to the force when two very strong magnets of the same polarity are pushed together. The people who climbed onto that Glory report that they floated on top of it, but the hardest part was not sliding sideways. If you attempt to touch a Glory at ground level, it simply pushes you away. So I'd like to emphasise, as long as you remain at home, they present no threat to you of any kind, as far as any expert can determine.

"Why, then, are these phenomena dangerous at all? Well, until recently the only risk seemed to be that they would draw people out of their homes, and cause them to congregate in ways that might spread the virus. But at 11 am two days ago, an ambulance was called to a farm in the Scottish Borders. A young man had been seriously injured by a piece of farm equipment. The ambulance arrived promptly, with two paramedics and a driver, and the patient was swiftly stretchered into the vehicle. The ambulance then headed back towards the hospital at high speed, for the patient's chances of survival were time-critical. Upon rounding a corner on the A66, they ran straight into a Glory.

"No-one witnessed the crash. The ambulance was found, upside down, in a field beside the road. The body of the driver was crushed, yet the bodywork at the front of the vehicle was virtually intact. Regrettably, all four people involved were killed by injuries sustained.

"The fact that no-one witnessed the crash suggests that the Glory had appeared only minutes, or even seconds, before the ambulance hit it. Had it been there longer, then perhaps someone might have had the foresight to set up some kind of warning on the road. As it was, other drivers arrived only later, and our accounts of the Glory come from them. It was a flattened cone perhaps twenty-five metres across, and three metres high. Its colour was a perfect sky blue, with objects like cartoon clouds moving randomly across it. The key point here is, nothing other than humans can interact with Glories in any way. Animals pass right through them, and don't see them. Inanimate objects pass through them. So when the ambulance hit it, the vehicle would have gone straight through it, but the people inside could not. The Glory would have crushed them against their seats, and then their bodies would in turn have pushed the vehicle upwards and sideways, lifting it off the road and over the hedge beside the road.

"Now, if the driver had known about the Glories, perhaps she'd have had a better chance of avoiding this tragedy. Or maybe someone else would have seen the Glory in time to realise the danger, and blocked the road with their own car. On that day, we at ITV strongly considered going public about the Glories, but judged at that time that it would still do more harm than good. But then today, a huge Glory appeared in the sky above England. Millions of people saw it. It was shaped and patterned like an illustration of our planet, Earth. Estimates of its size vary wildly, but most sources put it between one or two miles in diameter. Unsurprisingly, the presence of what appeared to be a new planet in the sky, floating just a few miles above the ground, caused considerable panic, and a significant number of people responded by jumping into their cars and attempting to flee their homes. Tragically, there were also cars coming in the opposite

Chapter 18: The day they told the truth

direction, wanting to see the Glory up close. Inevitably, speed limits were ignored – not by all, but by enough to cause multiple accidents. We know of five confirmed fatalities, but fully expect that number to reach double figures by the end of today. Let me emphasise, those who remained at home were completely unharmed. The planet-like Glory simply hung in the air for a few hours, and then vanished.

"With this in mind, we at this channel have judged that there is now more danger in concealing these phenomena than in revealing them, and we are willing to accept what consequences will come from this. Let me emphasise, once again, that the best defence against both Glories AND the virus is to stay at home, and follow government guidelines. Nonetheless, we contend that there is also more safety in being informed, and we are not alone. We are now going to show you an interview that was recorded a few days ago, and sent we think to every TV news station, and also to the newspapers. Until this afternoon, we had all agreed to sit on it, but the tragedy today has changed our position. The gentleman you are about to see is Henry Carter, who was Home secretary under Theresa May for six months in 2018. He is being interviewed in his house by Miranda Grant, who'll be familiar to many of you as a retired former BBC presenter and journalist."

I could just about recall Henry Carter, or rather some comedian's take on him. *'Hello, I'm Henry Carter, Minister for being even more boring than all the other ministers. All my clothes have labels on them, to remind me who I am.'* Carter was perhaps the last of a dying breed of old school greyer-than-grey Tories.

The screen cut to Henry Carter, his morose face reminding me of an ageing bloodhound. *"My name is Henry Carter,"* he declared, *"and everything I am about to tell you is completely true. I am not, and have never been, given to flights of fancy. Yesterday morning I witnessed the appearance and disappearance of a Spectral Glory. If you have no idea what I am talking about, that is because the current government is imposing a news blackout on the topic, for reasons of their own. However, they are real and I have seen one, even touched it, after a fashion."*

The screen wheeled jerkily around, revealing the room to be a large one with floor-to-ceiling bookshelves, and then reaching the reassuringly familiar face of newsreader Miranda Grant.

"I'm guessing Carter couldn't work Zoom," suggested Lara.

"I doubt that he knows what a computer is," I replied.

"Please describe to us exactly what you saw, Mr Carter," she said calmly.

So Carter did, in his pedantic, exacting fashion. He began with a breathtakingly uninteresting account of what rich former ministers did with their mornings once they'd been put out to grass. Eventually he got to the point where he took his dogs out on a walk, following the same path at the same time every day, his attitude seeming to indicate that this behaviour was somehow exemplary.

"We were going along the rim of the quarry. My maternal grandfather used to be a foreman there, and I always remember him as we pass. So I was looking

Chapter 18: The day they told the truth

into the empty quarry, and then it ceased to be empty. In a single instant, the entire quarry appeared to fill with pink water."

"How deep is the quarry?" asked Grant.

"I would say forty metres at the highest edge, maybe fifteen at the lowest, where the track goes in. The pink water came up almost to the lower rim, where the track passes out of the quarry. Let me emphasise again – it appeared in an instant. The pink didn't flow in from anywhere, it did not fill from the bottom or fall from the sky. It simply came into being, instantaneously, before my eyes."

"What was the surface like?"

"Pure pink, but with speckles dancing across it, speckles of white or brightness, like on a swimming pool in bright sunlight. I couldn't tell if the surface was flat, or rippling, but the speckles seemed to move across it in waves."

"So what did you do?"

"Well, I called you, Miranda, as you know, and also my wife, then I took Gladstone and Disraeli around to the track, where it disappeared into the pink object. I tried to put my hand out and touch it, but I could only get within about two inches of it. I could see the surface more clearly now, and it was undulating gently, more like a flag in the wind than waves on water, and those white specks moved around as if they were some sort of small fish just under the surface. Then Disraeli ran right past me and disappeared into it. Right down the track as if the object wasn't there, and then Gladstone went in after him. I could hear them barking but not see them, and then they were back. I threw stones into it, twigs, even an ant, and they all fell through. But I couldn't."

"Jennifer, that's my wife, she got there twenty minutes later. She couldn't touch the object, either, but she could see it, clear as I could. We called a few neighbours, and then just sat and watched it. It didn't change, just stayed there. A few others arrived, people we'd called and people they'd told, and everyone said and felt the same thing. Then three hours and seventeen minutes after it appeared, the object winked out again. Vanished in a single instant, leaving behind the quarry, exactly as it had been. I was now able to walk into the quarry and out again, as if nothing had happened. But it did happen. I saw it, and so did eleven other people, including yourself."

The camera wobbled round to Miranda Grant, again.

"Everything Mr Carter says is true," she said simply. "I saw the Glory myself, having arrived forty minutes before it disappeared. I can add nothing else to Henry's account, except that what we saw was something truly exceptional, utterly outside of anything any of us had ever experienced before. The purity of its colour, it felt like magic. It felt as if someone was doing magic right in front of us – not the kind you see on stage, but real magic, producing an object of the utmost beauty. And believe me, I am being objective here. I am stating the facts as I see them, not exaggerating, not embellishing. This Glory was real, and it was utterly extraordinary.

"Certain of my contacts from television and radio have confirmed, on condition of anonymity, that the government has both ordered their silence and indeed pleaded for it, reasoning that knowledge of these phenomena would endanger the lockdown and destabilise this country at its most fragile hour. Yet I do not see how this silence can be maintained, as what evidence I have been

Chapter 18: The day they told the truth  107

able to gather suggests that these phenomena are increasing in frequency every day, possibly at an exponential rate. We believe, Sir Henry and I, that a time will come, probably very soon, when candour becomes a better strategy than concealment, for the government and for the people of Britain. That is why we are sitting here now, and why we have shared this account. So if you are seeing this, know that the Glories are real, and that the best defence, from this point on, is understanding, common sense and following government guidelines."

The video ended. *"We asked the government if anyone was willing to come on the show and talk to us about this, but were told no-one was available,"* said Susannah.

"Quelle sur-fucking-prise," said Lara.

Now the bulletin gave an account of the different types of Glory, and a graphic animation showing how many there'd been, on each day for the past fortnight.

"We're only including sightings that are corroborated by at least two apparently independent sources," said Susannah, *"which means this is probably an underestimate, even if one or two of the ones we did include could possibly be coordinated hoaxes. We have spoken to seven other people, all of whom we judge to be reliable witnesses, and all of whom describe Glories in convincing ways. These things are real. And as you can see, they are steadily increasing in frequency.*

"During recent weeks, Glories have been reported almost entirely within the UK, the only exceptions being two confirmed reports each from the Republic of Ireland, and France. We have no idea what makes Britain special in this regard, if special is the right word, and nor does anyone else we've spoken to."

"The Pertwee Paradox," I muttered.

"What??" asked Lara.

"I'll explain later," I said.

There followed a procession of scientists and former ministers, most of them backed by impressively laden bookshelves, giving their opinions on the Glories. The scientists were frank and open in their assessments, as the presenter summarised. *"You haven't got a clue, basically, have you?"*

"No, I don't," said one expert happily. *"And nor does anyone else."* His expression suggested that he found this rather liberating.

"There'll be lots more cars now," said Lara. "And lots more people trying to see them. It'll be chaos."

"But once the government accepts that they're real, what will they do?" asked Lucasz. "If they've already been willing to drill people's heads in secret?"

"Do you think the lockdown will hold?" asked Lara. "Now people know they've been keeping things from them?"

"I don't know," I said. "I've a feeling a lot of things are going to change."

Chapter 19: The lovers

Antony

Dawn light blazed in through the barn door. Sally was still in my arms, I hadn't dreamt it. "Hey, good morning," I said.

"Thanks for keeping me warm."

"I could make you warmer." Soon we were making love again, to the sound of birdsong coming in from outside. After that she got stiffly to her feet, then proceeded to retrieve her underwear from the hay bales.

"You OK?" I said.

"Better than OK. It's like there's some magic in the world – you and me, and the Glories. It's all linked together somehow. We're going to find your cousin and sort all this out. It's going to be brilliant." She pulled her t-shirt on, and I got up off the dungarees. "Much as I'm liking the view, you'd better get dressed too," she said.

"Uhh, yeah," I said, but I still couldn't find any of what I'd been wearing. "Hey, you haven't moved my clothes, have you?"

"Of course not, dummy! I've been wrapped in your arms all night, haven't I?"

"Well, someone's had away with them! You don't think, a fox or something?"

"Cute boy, animals only wear clothes in cartoons. They've probably just fallen down between the bales or something."

We searched for five minutes, but couldn't find a single thing that I'd been wearing. Then we heard a vehicle pulling up outside. We looked at each other fearfully. "Stay hidden, nude boy," she said. "I'll take a look."

She reappeared in the barn entrance a moment later. "Just the postman. I'll have another look for the key, while you try and find your underpants."

Ten minutes later she was back. "I found it," she said. "Their spare emergency key, I remember now, they had a secret spot for it." Her voice sounded different, and her eyes looked reddened.

"Are you OK?" I said.

"I will be. First time back in the house since ... you know. Being in the house without them, not the best feeling. Hey, you found your clothes."

"Oh," I said. "Yes." I was sitting fully dressed on the hay bales, though I couldn't remember pulling my clothes on.

"I found my old camera, little digital job," she said happily. "It was in the room I used to have when I stayed with them. Never thought I'd use it again, but since we're both phoneless ... can I snap you? Remember the moment?"

I was pretty sure I'd need no help at all remembering it, but I said, "Alright then."

"How about you try *not* to pull a ridiculous face?" she said, giggling with the camera just below her eyes. "Just look normal?"

I tried to look thoughtfully at a spot just to the side of her. "Right, here goes – oh. What the – what the fuck?"

"Not working?" I asked.

"It's w-w-working fine," she said, though she was sounding scared. She pulled it up to her eyes again, then down, then up, looking more and more

Chapter 19: The lovers

alarmed. I saw her mutter something under her breath, but couldn't make out the words. Now she was looking scared, as well. I jumped down from the bales and ran towards her. "Stop!" she shouted, and I did, standing there, confused.

"Y-your clothes," she said, voice wavering. "Where did you find them, exactly?"

"I don't remember," I said.

"How can you not remember? It can't have been more than ten minutes ago."

"I just don't! I don't know why."

"OK ... well ... how about ... what do you want to do now?" She still had that look of fear and alarm in her eyes that I couldn't understand.

"I suppose ... we should start making a plan, for how I'm going to find Daniel, if you're still willing to help me."

"Maybe," she said. "I was thinking of more basic stuff."

"A lie down in a warm bed?" I asked. I got the impression she was fishing for a particular answer, but had no idea what it was. "Or is there some housework that needs doing?"

"What I mean is, aren't you hungry?"

"Not especially," I said.

"How?" she asked, her expression incredulous. "How can you not be hungry? You've not had a single bite since I met you! I ate yesterday at the service station, and now I'm totally starving! When did you last eat?"

"Breakfast," I said. "The morning before Daniel vanished. But that was three days ago. I just haven't been hungry." Now that I thought about it, it did seem rather odd.

"And have you drunk anything since then? Or had a pee?"

"I don't think so."

"Then eat," she said, tossing me a cereal bar in a packet. I tried to catch it but it went right through my fingers.

"Mister Bean again," I said nervously. I turned away from her and bent to pick it up, but couldn't seem to grasp it. A stone plinked onto the floor in front of me, then another, then a third.

"Turn around," she said quietly, and I did. Tears were streaming down her face. She had two stones in her hand. Without warning she swung her hand and threw one hard, right at my chest. I tried to catch it but it flew right through my hand. And then through my chest. Then she threw the other, a little more gently. I had time to watch it sail towards me, into my waiting hands, and through them. Then through my belly, to hit the ground behind me.

"When I handed you the bag, you dropped it," she said softly. "You couldn't open the glove compartment. Couldn't even move the straps from my shoulders."

"I don't understand," I said. "What's happening?"

Trying to keep her voice steady, she asked me, "Can you remember picking anything up, or carrying anything, anything at all, since you saw that first Glory with Daniel?"

I ran my mind through all that had happened since, and one memory came to the fore. Me in that phone box, trying to call Gran. My hand not being able to lift the receiver. I'd told myself I was too scared, when the truth was, I had not been able to physically pick it up. "But I struggled with that man!" I said. "And you could feel me perfectly well, couldn't you!"

"Well, that's just it," she said, stony faced. Slowly, she brought up the camera, with the photo she'd taken, of me on the haybales. Except in the image on the screen, it was just haybales alone, with no me. "People can see them and feel them, but objects pass through them, and cameras can't see them."

"What? Who's 'they'?" I cried. "What are you talking about?"

"Oh Antony, I'm sorry. I don't know how it happened or what it means, but it has to have happened when Daniel disappeared, when you were at that Glory in the woods. When you somehow lost a day. There's only one explanation for any of this."

"What? WHAT?"

"Antony, you're one of them. You're a Glory."

END OF PART ONE

PART TWO

*"You've got the looks, I've got the brains,
Let's make lots of money"*

The Pet Shop Boys, "Opportunities"

Chapter 20: Julia Barnes, cult member

Julia

Lucasz whipped up some pasta, together with sauce from a tin, and I gobbled down two portions. It was not even eight yet, but I was already slumped on the sofa, thinking of sloping off to bed sooner rather than later. Then a knock on the door revealed Walt, who told us happily that there was a group meeting happening in the church yard. I felt too tired to go out, and Lara looked as if she'd sooner stick forks in her eyes, but Lucasz happily said he'd go along and report back. Still, I was able to open a window in my room, which looked out into the churchyard, allowing me to lie on my bed and listen in.

There were perhaps twenty people in the meeting, socially distanced around the churchyard, and they talked a lot about Glories. It was clear that racing off to try and see them close up was a big part of what this group was about, at least in practical terms. Anyone who had managed to see a Glory, or better still touch one, was asked to talk through the experience in as much detail as they could. Those who focused on the physical beauty of the Glories were soon interrupted with questions like "how did it *feel*?" One person described feeling incredibly small, like an ant looking up at a skyscraper.

"We are that small," Walt concurred. "All of us. This is a message we each must take to heart, for perhaps once we accept this, we will be able to rise."

One young man needed little encouragement to share his feelings. "I felt loved," he said in a wobbly voice. "I never really knew what it felt like, it was as if I'd been cold all my life, and then I was warm. My heart ... my heart was glowing."

"You were feeling God's love?" asked Walt.

"Every kind of love," the man replied. "Our Lord, a mother, a lover. I felt complete. And then ... then it was gone, and I was alone again, like I've always been."

"You're not alone, Ben," said Millie. "Every one of us is with you."

"But none of you truly love me," replied Ben. "I have never been loved, except then. Please ... when you get the next prediction, can you call me first? I have to see another one, I just have to. I need to feel that way again."

"You felt the love of our Lord," said Walt. "You must understand, you were blessed."

"Was I?" Ben almost shouted. "Then why do I feel so empty, huh? Tell me that!!"

"You'll feel it again, I'm sure," said Millie.

"Why would He do this to me?" shouted Ben. "Make me suffer like this? And don't you say He's testing me! Don't you bloody dare!!!"

"We don't understand it, Ben," said Millie gently. "We just have to have faith that in time, He will make you whole, and as you were meant to be."

For several seconds, there was silence, then Lucasz asked, "What did you mean by prediction'?"

Chapter 20: Julia Barnes, cult member

"We have a contact who can predict where they're going to be" said Walt simply. "Makes seeing them a whole lot easier. Ben, I'd like to talk to you one-on-one after the meeting, if that's OK."

"You know where I live," said Ben curtly, his voice full of bitterness and despair.

Other people took their turns at describing their experiences, including one involving a pair of naked and tattooed bald men dancing in mid-air in the middle of a wood, which was met with derision by Helen and several others. Alone on my bed, I sniggered at the memory. "Now, now," said Walt, "Jeremy is a most reliable witness, he would not lie about such things. But how did this make you *feel*, Jeremy?"

For a while I found myself drifting off to sleep. A raised voice from someone standing close to my window brought me back to alertness again.

"You have to see it, how fast the numbers of them are growing! Look, they could be doubling every day! Can you imagine what the country will be like by the end of the month! And we're just sitting here, waiting for another divine message?"

"I am, as I have always been, fully open to your suggestions, Keith," said Walt.

"I've told you! We have to recreate the original Glory, in the closest possible detail! Build a sphere, with gaps for the church, plaster it white with paper, haul it onto place! We have to play back the message, exactly as it has been played to us!"

"We don't have the physical resources to do that," said Millie.

"Then we should get them!!"

"Keith, I have told you before and I tell you again," said Walt. "You are most welcome to co-opt the assistance, both financial and otherwise, of anyone within this group and beyond it, to aid you in this enterprise. I shall make a contribution as a sign of goodwill."

"But you don't believe me, do you," said Keith. "No, just mad old Keith and his stupid idea, just humour him and he'll maybe go away. Either we all do this, or none of us do."

"Each person here is free to make his or her own choice," said Walt calmly.

"So who's with me, huh?" said Keith, far too aggressively. "You all know I'm right, just can't bring yourselves to take that final step, can you? Well, can you??"

I imagined myself standing out there with them, as they probably looked down at their feet. Shouting at people was never a way to win allies, but the poor guy couldn't see it. After a very awkward silence, I heard Keith stomping off alone into the distance.

The conversation quickly settled on how many Glories had been seen in the past two days, with no further mention of Keith or his plan. The consensus was that nearly thirty had been reliably recorded in the past 48 hours, all within the British Isles. Keith was right about one thing – if numbers kept growing at this rate, the impact of the Glories might very well begin to outstrip the virus.

A few people arrived late at the meeting, having been at a Glory some distance away. They described something that looked like a black hole, a gaping

disc of black with paler material swirling around its edges, and like many Glories, it looked the same from every direction. "Fascinating," said Walt. "But how did it *feel*, to be next to it?"

* * * * *

The next morning, Lucasz told us that he'd asked Walt for more details about the Glory predictions that he'd mentioned, but that Walt hadn't been very forthcoming. By the time we'd had breakfast, Lara was getting twitchy and irritable, sitting down and then getting up a bit and pacing around. I suggested she might go for a walk, but she acted as if I'd told her to eat pickled slugs. Lucasz, from behind her, cheerfully mimed texting on a mobile phone, and I realised what she was missing. I thought a bit of digital detox would probably be good for her.

A couple of hours later, Millie called to tell us that a Glory had been predicted some 65 miles away, and failed to hide her disappointment when we told her we wanted to lie low for a day or two. Again we asked how the predicting worked, and got no useful answer.

"I'm not sure I buy this 'predicting the future' stuff," said Lara, after Millie had gone.

"Maybe they're not," said Lucasz, thoughtfully.

"How come?" I said.

"It could be like weather forecasting. What if the Glory is actually there in some form, even when we can't see it, for perhaps a few hours before it becomes visible? Then it wouldn't be a prediction, would it? It'd just be like seeing black clouds rolling towards you from the distance, and knowing it's going to rain. We've no idea what these things are made of. All we know is, they've got someone who's more plugged into them than any of us.

"Locksley would probably kill to get her hands on this predictor guy," said Lara. And I think she meant it literally.

The mention of Locksley's name brought another twinge of guilt in me. "If they're not careful, she'll certainly be after him," said Lucasz. "If there's even a whiff of it on social media, Farron will pick up on it."

"We'll need to be very careful not to get caught by her lot again," said Lara.

"So we just hide out here, I guess," said Lucasz. "But what do we do?"

"Well, there's Scrabble," I said.

* * * * *

You can't spend the whole day playing Scrabble, especially if your two younger opponents don't enjoy being repeatedly trounced by hundred-point margins. By mid-afternoon, I had regressed to daytime TV, and then Lara suddenly announced to the world, "Fuck, I'm bored. Lucasz, do you want to go upstairs?"

She was speaking figuratively; we were in a bungalow. Lucasz' mouth fell open in delighted shock. "Umm, yes please."

"Which room do you think was Helen's room?" Lara asked casually.

"Yours, I think," I said.

"Good," said Lara. "Well, they do say Jesus sees everything." Then she turned to Lucasz. "Just to be clear, I don't do emotional attachments." Then she turned and strode into the room without a backward glance. Lucasz stood there for a moment with an idiotic expression on his face, possibly trying to work out if he was dreaming.

"Try not to drool," I told him. "I suggest you go on in there, before she changes her mind."

I decided that this would be a good time to go for a little walk and explore the village, but I was back in time for *Pointless*. Lara emerged during the first round, smiled at me (a first, I think), and plonked herself on the sofa. But within five minutes her fingers were twitching again.

After dinner, all three of us joined the outdoor meeting in the graveyard right by our cottage. I'd watched the news as I cooked, and they claimed that the number of Glories today had been a little down on the past two days. It was still very odd seeing them talking openly about Glories on the telly. I wondered if they were massaging the numbers to try and calm the public. However, when I joined Walt's group for their meeting that evening, they too said that there seemed to have been fewer Glories today. This time, most of the group had gone to see the Glory that Millie had offered us the chance to come and see. It sounded spectacular, a massive sphere made up of shards of every possible colour, each moving in and out at different rates. One by one they described their experiences as they'd seen or touched it.

"And we must mention Ben," said Millie. "He looked like he was in Heaven, poor thing. None of us dared move him, even when the police turned up. I'm afraid he got violent when they moved between him and the Glory."

"We managed to stop them from arresting him, just," said Walt sadly. "I managed to convince them he was my responsibility. But they took his name and address, and I was told that if he was caught leaving his local area to see a Glory again, then he would be arrested. You can imagine how he took it."

"But they can't do that," said Helen. "They can't do any more than fine him!"

"Not yet," said Keith. I knew his voice, of course, but now I could put a face to it. He was absurdly tall, wearing a long coat with fluffy edges at the sleeves and collar. His head was oddly rectangular in shape and his greying hair stuck out in many directions.

"What do you mean?" asked Helen.

"You haven't been paying attention, have you? Any of you, since the Glories went public last night."

"Now hang on," said someone, rather irately, but Walt cut him off with a wave of his hand.

"What have we missed, Keith?" Walt asked.

"In the newspapers this morning. Five different articles, five different authors – supposedly – but all saying basically the same thing."

Chapter 20: Julia Barnes, cult member

"ALL the newspapers were full of Glories," said Millie. "Now could they not be? They probably had a whole stack of articles ready to go the moment the government lifted the media ban."

"Yes, of course," said Keith. "And most of them were simply reporting on what we know about Glories."

"And what we don't," someone said.

"Well, quite," agreed Keith. "But there were also opinions. Not too prominent, only one of them was an editorial. But what I'm saying is, they all were saying exactly the same thing."

"Which is?" asked Walt.

"Which is that most or probably all of the road accidents we've been seeing are caused by a dangerous minority, who take leave of their senses when they see a Glory, or are trying to get closer to one."

"A lot of them were caused by people trying to get away from one of them," someone pointed out. "That big planet in the sky."

"Yes, but they dismissed that as a one-off, and anyone killed or injured trying to get away from it was a 'tragic victim'. The focus of these articles was on people speeding *towards* a Glory. One of them was arguing that people like that were going to be killing more people than Corona by the end of the month."

"But it's true, isn't it?" said someone. "Lots of people have been emotionally affected by the Glories, in lots of different ways. Look at our poor Ben. I've worked with drug addicts and some of the symptoms are the same."

"Don't you see?" said Keith insistently. "That's what they're banking on. They're setting them up as scapegoats. The 'Glory addicts.' Four of the articles used that exact term. Where did it come from? I hadn't seen it on social media before, had you? And now four articles, in three different newspapers."

"Scapegoats for what?" asked Walt.

"What does a government do when it's losing control? When there's a problem a lot of people are worried about, and they've not got a clue how to fix it? They find a group of people, a minority without much of a voice, and whom a lot of people don't like, and they pin the blame on them. Asylum seekers, trans people, Jews, immigrants. They got caught napping by the Corona, of course they did, but this time they were ready. Even before they went public, they would have been cooking up a strategy. This strategy. People were already starting to die on the roads. That ambulance crash on the news wasn't the first, you can be sure of that. So they can't stop the Glories, probably can't even stop people dashing out to see them, but they need to be SEEN to be dealing with the problem. So what do they do? They say '*Hey guys, it's all caused by a few naughty Glory addicts who can't control themselves, and drive too fast. We're going to be locking them up for their own good, to keep the streets safe for decent people.*' There's already one MP starting to push hard for this – he was on breakfast telly. And again – absolutely clear he'd been prepping for this for days, maybe weeks."

"Keith, you're being paranoid," said Millie.

"Think what you like," said Keith, who this time was keeping his cool a lot better. "But I know how these people operate. Why did the cops pick on Ben, today? He was just one person among dozens. They've already been told to look out for people who look like Glory addicts. Told they're a danger to the public,

Chapter 20: Julia Barnes, cult member

from speeding, or spreading the virus, or both. Soon they'll start arresting them. Pick up a few people like Ben, parade them on telly as they plead to be allowed to go see a Glory. *'Look, viewers, look how deranged these people are!'* Then as the Glory numbers keep going up, so will the arrests, just to show they're doing something. Eventually they'll come for groups like ours, just to bump the numbers up."

"You're being cynical," said Millie.

"Doesn't mean I'm wrong."

"Perhaps you might show me the articles you mentioned," said Walt, ever the diplomat.

"Gladly. I'll bring them round after this. The MP's name is Barry Collins. Keep an eye out for him."

"I think I was a bit short with you yesterday, Keith," said Walt. "Next time we have a quiet day, I'll pop round and give you a hand with that project of yours. It'd be nice if a few others would join me. You can show me the articles then."

"Oh. Thank you."

"Did you meet the connector woman?" someone asked.

"Sadly no, the Glory was the opposite side of us from where she lives," said Millie. "It was too far and she decided not to come. But a second Glory was predicted in the afternoon, only half an hour from her house, and she did go to that one. Phyllis, you met her, I think?"

"My husband, son and I went along," said a prim lady in her sixties, as if she were speaking about some tea party. "The Glory was simply green. A vertical sheet of green, with countless shades merging into one another and shifting slowly. I saw a woman fitting the description you gave me – mixed race, long hair in braids – arrive ten minutes after us. We asked if she was Siobhan and she said 'oh, you want me to *perform*, do you?' Really rather rude, if you ask me, but it takes all sorts, doesn't it? Brian and Ellie were there too, I'd rung them, you see, and this Siobhan woman had a little boy with her, so we all held hands, all seven of us, and she reached out and touched it. Brian, perhaps you could describe how it felt? You could do it better than I."

A young man with chubby reddish cheeks took up the story. "We could feel each other. Thoughts, feelings, what they were seeing. I closed my eyes and the Glory was still there in front of me, only from six different angles. I saw faces, people the other people know, I guess. I felt old, and I felt young. I could even feel Dad's arthritis, like it was mine. It was the strangest thing ever."

"That wasn't the strangest thing," said a deep-voiced old man standing next to Phyllis. "I'm colour-blind. Only when I was linked up with this Siobhan, I wasn't. I saw the world in full colour, the way everyone else sees it, until she broke contact. It was truly extraordinary."

"Then it's true," said Walt. "She can actually connect people's minds. That has to be part of it, don't you think? Part of how we get our message across. Perhaps if enough of us can connect at once, we can send a joint message that will be heard."

"There are stories," said someone. "Stories of people who can do special things when they touch a Glory. People said there's a man who glows, so bright

you can't look at him. If we could all do that, maybe that would be the message that we need.

Walt beamed. "We also know of a man who can walk through Glories, as if they aren't there." He waited, looking right at Lucasz, who sheepishly raised his hand, and stepped forward.

"He's talking about me."

"But that's amazing," said someone. "With him and Siobhan, we could all join hands, every one of us, and walk right into a Glory! Perhaps that's how we do it? Perhaps that's how we ascend?"

I noticed that Lara was looking at me, with her mouth hanging open. "*What*," I mouthed at her. But now Millie was staring at me too.

"Julia," she asked, "just how ill were you when that Glory cured you?"

"Ummm, quite ill," I said, cautiously.

"What sort of 'ill'?" she persisted.

"Cancer," I admitted. "Stage four."

A series of gasps went around the assembled people. Predictably, there was even an odd "Halleluyah!"

"I think she can cure herself of other things too," said Lara, rather unhelpfully.

"But don't you see," said Millie, eyes blazing now with passion and purpose. "This means that together, you, Siobhan and the Glories could very possibly cure anyone, of anything at all!"

Chapter 21: The meaning of a life

Julia

Sometimes, in life, there are moments when you feel you have a real purpose, that you might even have been put on the Earth for that one purpose. At school, there was one time when I decided I wanted to be a doctor, because I'd once helped an old lady who fell over, and it had felt like a moment that should have meaning. But I wasn't good enough at science, and I didn't get the grades. Still, I like to think that I have done good things by teaching, setting some kids who might have gone astray onto a better path.

Now, I was standing in a graveyard while too many voices were talking about me, each of them seeming to believe that they knew better than I did, what I'd been put on this Earth to do.

Walt let them prattle for a minute or so before raising his hand for silence. "I think we had better hear what Julia has to say, don't you?"

So I told the story of my encounter with the first Glory, emphasising just how unwell I'd been before, and how healthy I'd felt ever since. Other than a few more very unwelcome Halleluyahs, the audience let me speak.

"Only one man has ever healed the sick by His touch, and that was our Lord Jesus Christ," said Helen, when I'd finished.

"Well I'm certainly not Him," I replied curtly.

"Jesus healed other people, not Himself," added Lara.

"But it proves that the Glories are divine, and that Julia, like my father, is a Channel for God's power," said Helen.

"I don't think it does," said Lara. "It could just be technology we don't understand."

"Oh, and you're an expert, are you?" said Helen with a stare.

"As much of one as you are, yes," replied Lara, sweetly.

"Children, children," said Walt. "There will be time for philosophical debates later on. But let us focus on the here and now. We have been given the chance to heal the sick. Perhaps that might also be the way to send a message back to the Creator, that we have understood His intentions?"

"We don't know for certain that it will work," said Millie.

"All the more reason why we should seek to find out," replied Walt.

I slipped away from the meeting soon after that, signalling silently to Lucasz and Lara that I needed to be alone. I pottered through the village once more. It was pretty in places. I wondered what it was like to be a resident here who didn't buy into Walt's strange new religion. Probably you would just stay at home and pretend it wasn't happening. Mainly though, I weighed up this awesome new responsibility in my head. Myself, plus this Siobhan woman who could connect people somehow, and a Glory. Together we could very possibly cure cancer. Could we cure anything? How would that even work? I barely understood the conventional treatments I'd undergone in the battle against the dynasty of Bernards. I supposed that I hadn't needed to know how it worked then, and that

Chapter 21: The meaning of a life

I didn't need to know now, either. If we were living in some sort of divine computer simulation, as Walt believed, then perhaps it was as simple as turning a person off and on again. But going down that route messed with my head. Instead, I brought my focus back to the real world and real people.

Returning to the graveyard after the meeting was over, I saw Walt standing among the stones, hands clasped in front of him, looking contemplative.

"It is never easy to be called upon to serve, in any capacity," he said.

"No, it isn't," I agreed. "It's a good thing, of course it is. Just a shock. It's going to be hard though, really hard, getting the patients to where they need to be. But I know someone … I know someone who we could cure. Her husband has a car and they're not too far away. I owe him, you see. She's in a wheelchair. Catatonic, I think. He's so desperate to make her better."

"A wheelchair," he said, and I felt the fervour coming off him, almost like a glow. "If she could rise from a wheelchair…" he paused, pacing in a little circle, or rather rectangle, because he was terribly careful to step only between the graves. "Are you willing to try and do this tomorrow?"

"Yes. I should discuss it with the others though. If those people are still after us, then it affects them, too."

"Ah, well, you may need to wait a bit. Young Lara said something about wanting to desecrate my daughter's room again."

"Oh," I said, both embarrassed and amused. 'I'm sorry about that "

"I'm not," he said with a smile. "I have always believed that life is to be enjoyed. Funny to say it, but I think I'd have preferred it if my daughter had chosen to rebel in the opposite direction. Motorbikes, drink and boys, you know, instead of deciding I was too lax in my Christianity. I just want her to find happiness, really."

I nodded. "That's what all good parents want, religious or not."

"Do you Believe?" he asked me simply.

"I didn't before the Glory. But now? I feel like anything could be true, and that nothing makes sense. I suppose you'd call me an agnostic, for now."

"Perhaps you will feel closer to God, if we manage to heal your friend."

"Perhaps I will, yes."

"How about I pop round early tomorrow and we make a plan?"

I watched the late evening news for a bit, alone. It was odd, watching Glories spoken about in the same sombre tones as they discussed the virus. Considerable attention was given to a fatal car crash, in which two hikers on their daily exercise had supposedly been struck by a speeding car trying to get to a Glory. Then it cut to a Tory backbencher called Barry Collins. Wasn't that the name Keith had mentioned? He was advocating for stricter measures to make the roads safer, because *"we know that there are people who lose all sense of reason when they are trying to get close to a Glory. I'm only talking about a minority here, and I don't think it's even their fault. We have a second pandemic building up here, a pandemic of Glory addiction, and if we don't act soon our roads will become death traps."*

There was that term again, the one Keith had mentioned. *Glory-addict.* Collins also mentioned that a wealthy businessman was at that very moment

Chapter 21: The meaning of a life  121

setting up a treatment centre for them, with a view to understanding the condition, and hence developing a treatment for it.

"Which businessman?" asked the presenter.

"He prefers to keep his name out of it. I know it can be hard to believe in these cynical times, but not everyone does everything out of a desire for publicity."

"Hmm," I said to the screen. "But some people clearly do."

* * * * *

The next morning, we found ourselves sitting around in an odd little car park in the middle of nowhere, which someone had identified as a 'geographically optimal starting point.' The car belonged to Leo, a lad from the village who'd seen the white Glory above the church, and had been there at last night's churchyard meeting, though I didn't recall him having spoken. I found him refreshingly down to earth, though I suspected he would drive like a maniac, given the chance. All four of us were wearing face masks, though Leo seemed utterly unconcerned about the virus.

A call came through on his phone, confirming that Hector had agreed to the plan, and would drive Bluebell to the Glory as soon as we had a location for it; we'd already been told that Siobhan was up for it. Then the waiting began. Luckily, I'd brought a book from the house. Leo took pity on an increasingly twitchy Lara and lent her his phone to play with. Lucaz was looking rather forlorn, probably because Lara had barely spoken to him all morning. I suspected that he knew that he was being used, but couldn't help himself.

At 11.43, the call came through. A large Glory had been predicted on the west side of the Malvern hills, sixty-two minutes from now. We ran to the car and were off. Lara did the navigating – no-one was getting the phone out of her hands. She reckoned we could be there before the Glory appeared as long as the roads stayed clear. I reminded Leo to be very alert, both to possible Glories appearing in our path, and to people speeding.

We screeched to a halt in a small car park, fifty-four minutes later. There were a couple of cars there already – exercisers, we assumed. The predictor had sent us a few more details on where the Glory was to be expected, a wide area to the west of a particular peak, and we could do no more than walk in that general direction, and then wait and see.

"I wonder what would happen if someone's standing in a spot where a Glory is about to appear," pondered Lucasz.

"If it's you, nothing," I replied.

"But if it wasn't me. Would the Glory just wait? Would it appear somewhere else? Or maybe not appear at all?"

"Maybe that's why they don't tend to pop up in towns," I mused.

Ahead of us, Leo and Lara had stopped. She said something to him, and then they walked on a few steps, a little uncertainly. We caught up. Lucasz' manner changed, and he started looking up and around him. Only then did I start to feel it, a sort of expectation in the air, like when a thunderstorm is about to break, only not. It was no good trying to describe it, because it wasn't like

Chapter 21: The meaning of a life

anything else I'd felt before. I took a few steps back, and the feeling went. Forward, and it came back again.

"You can feel it too?" said Lara. "I think it's coming. We should probably all step back."

"Quickly!" said Leo, and he almost ran past me, Lara jogging behind. Lucasz seemed unminded to move, apparently enjoying the sensation, but Lara caught his eye with an urgent look, and he immediately complied.

No sooner had he stepped over the invisible threshold, than the path behind him vanished. In its place was a wall of what looked like sand, flowing upwards as if caught in a river current. Looking more closely, I could see that it was a mass of squares, hexagons and other little shapes, varying in colour from yellow to brown to purple, some brighter than others, moving at different speeds. I stepped slowly backwards. It was big. The wall of sand went some way up the slope, and down to its bottom and beyond. And towards the sky, as far up as we could see, from this close to it. Leo had grabbed the phone from Lara, and was making a quick call, telling the group that the Glory had appeared as predicted.

Lucasz decided to investigate how deep it was, and walked right into it. "Watch your footing," I said.

"It's only a couple of metres deep" came his voice, from behind it. "I've come right out the other side."

Sound travels through them as if they're not there, I thought. Looking behind me, I saw two groups of people approaching. One was a couple with a dog, from a higher path, and these had clearly been out walking when the Glory appeared. They took a few steps, then stopped and gawped, while the dog tried to work out why its humans weren't moving fast enough. The other group was four people, coming up from the car park. Walt was leading, but a cold chill of nerves ran down my back as I saw that a mixed-race woman with long braided hair was among them.

* * * * *

I stood there, heart pounding, as the four of them came closer. There was a breeze blowing, coming at my back right through the Glory, which was somehow unsettling me further. But there was no turning back now.

Soon, Siobhan was facing me, with a virus mask pulled down onto her chin, and looking as uneasy as I felt. "You're Julia?"

"I am. Pleased to meet you."

"I suggest we don't hang about," said Walt. "There's going to be a crowd here soon enough. Hector's on the way, maybe fifteen or twenty minutes."

"Are we all just going to link up?" I asked.

"I'm game," said Lucasz. Walt's party was completed by two teenage boys, both wearing masks, one who looked like he was Siobhan's son, and the other of Asian extraction, and sporting an arm in a sling. Both nodded in mute greeting.

Siobhan saw me looking. "Broke God knows how many rules to get him here, but if you want a test, he's it."

"Him and my friend who's on the way," I said.

Chapter 21: The meaning of a life

"Indeed," said Walt, "although in this case I feel a more visible demonstration may also be in order. Leo, if you would start filming?"

Leo nodded, and pointed the back of his phone at us.

"Hang on," I said. "I don't want my face going online, not with Locksley's people after us." In fact, I just didn't want it going online at all.

"And you do NOT include my face," said Siobhan, with fearsome vehemence.

"This is just for our people," Walt assured me, and I almost believed him, but I popped a face mask on as a partial disguise, just in case. "Oh yes, and one last thing before we start," said Walt. He drew out a very sharp pencil from his pocket, and clutched it in his left hand, the point digging into his palm. "Leo, make sure you get this!" he declared, voice wavering a little. Then he closed his eyes, and slammed the back end down onto the hard path with vigorous force, causing the sharp end to burst through the back of his palm. Blood spurted from the wound, and Walt gasped in pain.

"What have you done, you idiot?" cried Lucasz.

"A show of ... faith ..." gasped Walt, as he yanked out the pencil. "Now everyone but Leo ... join hands, Siobhan at the end, touching the Glory ... me at the other ... only one working hand just now ... quickly ... Leo, focus on the hand ..."

We linked up in a row: Siobhan, her son, the injured boy, Lucasz, me, and Walt. The injured boy was holding both Lucasz' hand, and his friend's, with his one good hand. Lucasz looked round at Lara. "Come on, join up," he tried.

"I told you, I don't do intimacy," she replied coldly, stepping away from us. So we did it without her.

"Everyone ready?" asked Siobhan? "Three, two, one ..."

Everything changed. For a moment I was floating in a peaceful black void, and then searing pain exploded in my left hand. I felt Lucasz' hand clenching around my other hand an instant later. I flinched but instinct told me to hold on, so I did. I was dimly aware of other thoughts, feelings and voices, children crying out in pain, and the fearsomely protective love of a mother. I could almost see the pain from the hand, a blazing ball of spinning fire, and I was the pain and it was me. But now it was shrinking slowly, a tickling sensation forming around it as the pain slowly lessened.

Now the other voices and sensations came to the fore. Thoughts and fears. Images of teenage girls the boys would very much like to kiss, and more. A glowing image of the pure white Glory above Yewford church, with the sun's rays coming from behind it, and an intoxicating tide of love and divine wellness seeming to flow from the glowing white orb. Brief flashes of Lara, in bed. It made me think of Malcolm, and I wonder if the others then saw flashes of him in the same way. They probably did.

But again, those are only the parts I can describe. Little points of reference among something far bigger, as if my mind had up until then been a little goldfish bowl of thoughts and experiences, but had suddenly become a small piece of water in a huge river, or a sea. I had let go of my individuality and floated free, drinking in the sensation of other people entwined together. Lara was right, this was true intimacy, freed from physical need.

Chapter 21: The meaning of a life

Then something shifted, a new stream joining the river, and I saw the faces of Hector and Bluebell, both much younger than I'd known them, each seen through the other's eyes. Thus far, all the images in my head had been fleeting and insubstantial, but what came next felt horribly vivid. The screech of brakes and twisting metal, a terrible car crash, the face of a little boy, eyes wide and unseeing among all the blood. And screaming, so much screaming, a scream that it seemed could never, ever, end. The mangled car with the child in it tumbled slowly through the grey abyss, with the young Hector and Bluebell clinging to it, still screaming, until Bluebell let go and then she was falling, drifting, away into the abyss, away from the terror, where nothing could hurt her. She wasn't screaming now. Hector cried out to her, even as he clung to the wreckage.

"Let go," a voice said. "Let go and you can save her."

"Don't want to," said Hector, in the voice of a cowering child.

"You said you wanted to save her," said a voice, and I realised suddenly that the voice was mine. "This is your one and only chance. Be brave, for Bluebell."

The young Hector gingerly detached from the car and moved a little toward the floating Bluebell. The car began to tumble in the opposite direction. Hector turned, distraught.

"Let it go," said the voice that might have been mine. "The past can't be changed, but the future can."

The tide of anguish that followed was almost too great to bear, but Hector hung there, allowing the car to gradually tumble sideways, and out of sight. Then he turned, slowly at first, and swam purposefully towards Bluebell. Their figures tangled together, and now they were coming back, arms around each other, united in sadness and hope.

The river of thought was ripped apart, and the world span around me. "Cops," said someone. "The cops are coming!"

I shook myself, trying to get my bearings. Where was I? I was on a path, on a steeply sloping hillside, with a lot of people around me, some of whom I knew. A woman in a blue dress was sobbing, cradled in a man's arms, close by. Hector, and Bluebell. But there were six approaching police officers coming up the path towards us.

Lucasz, as so often, seemed to come alive in moments of stress. "Siobhan, take my hand. Your boys, too. Get ready to walk and keep walking." The three of them obeyed, then a procession led by Lucasz walked into the Glory and vanished. Lucasz' head popped out of the Glory. "Lara, you next, take my hand." For a moment Lara looked like a cornered animal, head swinging fearfully from him to the police. Then Siobhan popped out too, and told her to pull herself together. Lara grabbed her hand instead, and dived into the Glory.

Some of the people around us – there were nearly twenty I think, scattered up and down the slope – looked on in astonishment. A couple tried to copy Lucasz, as if all you needed was confidence, but they bounced hard off the Glory, like Wile E Coyote hitting a fake railway tunnel "Julia, come on," said Lucasz, his face appearing again. But I was looking down at Hector and Bluebell.

"My fault," she was sobbing. "All my fault."

"No, my love," he countered. "I was driving."

Chapter 21: The meaning of a life

"But I told you to go faster. I was the one who'd made us late. Your beautiful boy."

"It doesn't matter now."

"Everyone please stay right where you are," said a policeman, loudly. I took one more look at Hector and Bluebell, then grabbed Lucasz's hand. My legs gave way under me as a smaller river of thoughts resumed, but somehow I found myself on the other side. I think perhaps I was dragged.

"You really need to work on staying awake when you do that," said Lara. There was a scattering of Glory-watchers on this side as well, who were looking at us with shock and disbelief, and keeping far more than a 2-metre distance. I guessed that to them, we might as well have stepped out of a flying saucer. I gave them a little smile and a wave, which caused several to step back ever further. At least there were no policemen on this side, yet.

Lucasz and Siobhan dipped into the Glory one more time, and came out with Walt and Leo. I could hear one policeman barking orders on the other side, while another voice asked, "how the fuck did they do that?"

"More to the point, how the fuck do we get back to the cars," said Siobhan.

"We split up," said Lucasz. "Me and Leo get the cars, the rest of you slip away quietly. Head for that church you can see, there, about a mile or two away. Walk in twos or threes, six people together attracts too much attention."

Walt looked a bit affronted that someone else was taking charge, and for a moment I thought he'd argue, but he simply said "Good plan."

"My arm's better," declared the Asian boy. He flexed his fingers as the other boy helped him take off his sling. "Need to get this dressing off!"

"Let's get down the hill first," said Walt, and we started walking. There was no blood flowing from his hand, it was completely healed.

Chapter 22: The Glory

Antony

Solemnly, I turned away from Sally and walked back to the haybales. I climbed up, and found the spot where we'd spent the night and sat down there, as if by returning to the spot, I could get back into the pure happiness I'd felt there, just hours before.

"They're not even sinking under your weight," said Sally softly, looking up at me with teary eyes.

"Yes, I've got the point, I'm a Glory, you don't need to keep throwing evidence at me!" I shouted.

"I'm sorry, OK? This is hard for me, too! I liked you! Still like you!"

"I don't even know what I am! Am I even human anymore?"

"You seemed pretty human to me, last night," she said softly.

"I don't understand how this can be happening to me," I said.

Slowly, she climbed up and sat on the bales a little way along from me. I could see now how they compressed a bit under her weight, but not under mine. I reached out a tentative hand towards her, and after a while, she took it. We sat like that for a long time, neither one speaking, nor looking at the other. Her hand felt warm. If I was a Glory, how could I still feel? Did that mean the Glories could feel, too?

"Does my hand feel cold?" I asked her.

"No. It feels warm. All of you does. Every part of you feels like a living, breathing person. Trust me, I did a thorough exploration." She offered me a weak smile.

"I don't know what to do," I said.

"Yes you do. You need to find your cousin. You've got a mission, and that hasn't changed. I think this might even make it easier."

"Easier? How can this make anything easier?!?"

"Think about it," she said, smiling gently at me. "Think about what you've managed to do without even knowing it. You've come all this way, visited three more Glories, fought off the bad guys, even got the girl. Probably made it easier, that you didn't need to eat."

"I guess it did. But I just had this hope, this silly hope, that once I found Daniel, I could go back to a normal life."

"Your life didn't seem that fun, from what you said."

"Even so." I didn't add that I'd been rather hoping I might live with someone other than Father and Gran, since last night. "Am I going to be like this all my life?"

"If it can happen one way, it can be changed back," she said, squeezing my hand.

We sat quietly for a little longer, hands still held. A few sparrows landed by the barn entrance, prospecting for seeds, and then flew off.

"I can feel my heart beating," I said.

"So could I, last night."

"It's like I'm human, yet not human."

"You're all human, trust me. It's just that you're somehow all Glory, as well."

Chapter 22: The Glory

"Look, I want to try something," she said. "Come with me." She climbed down, then held my hand as I followed her.

"How come I don't fall through the bales?" I asked.

"Huh. Good question." She stopped, let go of my hand, paced around in a little circle. "Same reason you don't fall through the ground, I guess."

"Which is?" I asked.

"No idea. But it'll be the same reason you didn't fall through the car, either. It's like objects affect you, but you can't affect them."

We walked slowly through the yard towards the house, holding hands again. "The door's unlocked," she said. "I want you to close your eyes, and see if you can grab the handle, turn it, and open the door and go through."

"But I won't be able to," I said.

"I want to see if you can do it better if you're not looking," she said.

I doubted that, but tried it anyway. Eyes closed, I stumbled forwards, reaching around until I found the handle. It took a few goes, but it moved in my hand, and I was through the door, inside the hallway. I opened my eyes and turned round, expecting to see her looking impressed, but instead meeting a closed door. I tried to open it, but this time the handle remained stubbornly unresponsive, my hand passing through it every time. Then I heard the sound of keys in the lock, and Sally opened the door, beaming at me.

"Why did you lock the door after me?" I asked.

"I didn't. It was locked already. You just walked through a locked door."

"What? But then how did I open it?"

"You didn't. Like I said, you walked *through* it."

My mouth fell open.

"Pretty sure you did that with the car door, the first time I met you. I was only half looking, but you somehow got in without me seeing the door open. It's like … you can go through doors as long as you think you can, without even opening them!"

Sally took the huge pile of mail that had been lying by the door, and put it all carefully in a corner out of the way. Apologetically, she set about feeding herself breakfast, which consisted of out-of-date cornflakes with a tin of condensed milk. Though I didn't feel hungry, I thought sadly about how I might never get to eat again, and left her to eat alone. In the corridor were photos of her godparents Derek and Lily, some young, some old. One was their wedding day, a black and white image of two young faces, full of joy and life. I wondered, if someone had told them on that day that they'd have exactly fifty years together, would they have taken that? Another photo raised a smile, it was a very young Sally with pigtails, laughing her head off while a pig looked on thoughtfully from behind her.

When Sally had eaten, she pulled up a chair for me and we sat down together and made a list of things that we knew about me, and how I now interacted with the world. She did all the writing, of course. Making the list took up much of the morning, with visits to the farm animals and upstairs bathroom all part of the process. A few hours later, the list looked like this:

- Looks and feels human.
- Acts human. Has full memories except ~24 hour period of first contact with Glory.
- Cannot move solid objects, and thrown ones pass through him (bulletproof?)

Chapter 22: The Glory

- Affected by gravity.
- Has heartbeat and pulse.
- Breathes when not thinking about it, but can hold breath indefinitely. I cannot feel his breath and he can't blow even a feather around.
- Can walk through closed doors, but only if he doesn't think he's doing it. Needs practice, we think.
- Feels the wind and the sun.
- Clothes he wears are part of him. Can switch to naked and back again. Cannot wear real clothes. Not sure yet if he can make other outfits part of himself.
- Does not appear in photographs.
- Does not need to eat or drink, and cannot do either.
- Brilliant kisser.
- Sheep, cows, overfed tomcats and chickens (all animals?) act as if he doesn't exist. He can feel them but they don't feel, see or hear him.
- Can feel pain when hit, pinched, etc. And pleasure, too. But does not appear to sustain any cuts or bruises, and pain quickly fades.
- Possibility that he could pass up and down through floors, but does not want to try it because then how would he stop?
- Surprisingly ticklish.
- Can move into Glories but feels resistance and gets pushed out again.
- Can pick up pieces of Glories, which might cause other people to fall into Glories, but maybe only if they are leaning on them.
- Can transfer above ability to at least one other person while touching them.
- Has no scent, even close up.
- Skin tastes salty, like normal slightly sweaty skin.
- Lips and tongue feel wet to touch, but leave no moisture.
- Possibly could train himself to move small objects, like Patrick Swayze in *Ghost*.
- Hasn't ever seen *Ghost*. Or *Dirty Dancing*. Urgently needs rectifying.
- Feels wet when in water, but does not displace water and cannot move it.
- Knows an unhealthy amount of *Doctor Who* trivia, but has never watched *Game of Thrones*.
- Can lift me, easily. Possibly stronger than he was.
- Cannot be heard by person on other end if speaking into phone (very confused insurance seller in Indian call centre).
- Mysterious organisation wants to capture him, for reasons unknown.
- Dynamite in bed.
- Weighs nothing according to weighing scales.
- Has shadow, but only when in full view. If positioned where he should have a shadow, but his body is blocked from my view, then the shadow disappears.

Despite Sally's injections of humour, I found making the list to be a draining task. Every line she wrote was a reminder of how different from her, from everyone, I had become. She must have seen this in my eyes, because she took my hand and said, "Come on you. Follow me."

She led me to what she said was her room. It had a huge picture of a long defunct boyband on the wall, and a few items dotted around that looked suited to a girl around Daniel's age. "I don't seem to want to get rid of all those," she

Chapter 22: The Glory

said. "I liked to come here and pretend I was still a little girl, you know? Derek and Lily, they never had kids of their own, they used to totally spoil me. I can't believe they're gone. But right now, we need to look after you. How about you do your disappearing clothes trick, again?"

An hour later, I was lying naked on top of her, blissfully half-awake, feeling properly human again. Perhaps there could be a life for me if I stayed like this, after all.

Sally had lunch (pasta with bottled sauce) while I went for a little walk. I found I could walk through wire fences if I didn't look at them, unless I'd fixed the position of the fence in my mind, in which case my body somehow decided it was solid and reacted accordingly. I wandered into a field with a small flock of odd-looking sheep, picked out a sheep that was walking purposefully, and stood in front of it. It walked right through me, its head appearing out of my crotch followed by its woolly body.

If sheep couldn't see me, was I even real? Was I some sort of illusion, existing only in the minds of human beings, including myself?

Chapter 23: After the miracle

Julia

The Glory was still there as we came to the bottom of the hill on our diagonal path, and we passed a lot of people coming the other way ("So much for the government's 'stay at home, they're dangerous' line," said Lucasz). One side of the lane was taken up with parked cars, their sides pushing into the hedge, while on the other, hooting cars squeezed past with barely enough room. It was lucky cars didn't need to socially distance, I thought.

The good news was, the police were very unlikely to pluck us out of this gridlocked chaos, but it also meant we couldn't just walk along the lane to the church, as we'd hoped to. We had to force our way through the thorny hedge on the other side, into a cowpat-infested field edge. Lara stepped right in one and looked horrified, and the cows themselves came up to see what we were doing. The two boys looked almost more amazed by the cows than they had been by the Glory, and I wondered if they'd ever actually seen a farm animal before.

We plodded along the rough and uneven ground of the field edge, climbed a gate and did the same again, before encountering a footpath that we followed even though it didn't get us much closer to the church. This eventually crossed another, less busy lane, and we carefully followed that, eventually reaching our goal. We sat on benches between graves, and watched as the occasional car whizzed past in one direction, or came disgruntledly back in the other. A couple of drivers gave up and parked by the church, which wasn't so bad an idea, for the Glory was perfectly visible from here. We could now see one of the ends, which was narrow, flat and vertical, and sticking out into a field beside the hill. It was blocking a lane there, apparently, which was adding to the parking chaos.

Siobhan's son Sammy and his friend Amit were enthusiastically unwrapping the dressing on Amit's arm, which did indeed seem to no longer be broken, while Siobhan fussed at them to be careful. Walt showed us the video Leo had shot, which mercifully included none of our faces, only our backs with arms linked, as Siobhan reached out and touched something that apparently wasn't there, and we all went stiff. Then it zoomed in on the palm of Walt's stricken hand, with its gaping wound (only now did I spot the deliberate symbolism), and then kept it on screen for long minutes as the flow of blood quickly stopped and it began, slowly but also impossibly fast, to heal. Leo sped up the video to 8x, and after 15 minutes had sped past, it had fully healed, and the video ended.

The wait for the cars went on, and I felt a little nervous. What if they'd been arrested? Then Lucasz phoned. "We're in the cars but we can't get out. Both ways in, it's gridlock."

"I guess we'll just have to wait," Walt said. "And perhaps park a little further away next time, try to anticipate this."

Siobhan was looking agitated. "Too many people here, too much attention," she muttered.

Walt looked troubled for a moment, then went to talk to Amit. "You and your parents will need to make a decision," he told the boy. "You may wish to

Chapter 23: After the miracle

keep this healing a secret, and I wouldn't blame you if you did. Or you could celebrate it as God's work, and join our little group."

"Mum and Dad think I'm out walking," said Amit.

"Oh."

"Don't worry, I've been out all day before."

"I believe that all Gods worshipped around the world are the same God, seen through a different lens," Walt continued. "That is why the Glories do not match the symbolism of any one religion."

"Have you got any crisps?" replied Amit.

* * * * *

The Glory winked out of existence about an hour after we'd reached the churchyard. I'd seen it happen before, but I'd always been distracted at the time. This time, I was looking right at it, drinking it in (they never got boring, no matter how long you gazed at them), and then suddenly, it wasn't there, like a crude film cut in an old TV show. I imagined, rather than saw, a handful of people who'd been leaning on it suddenly falling over forwards. The police had apparently given up trying to get people away from the Glory, and seemed to have headed back to the bottom of the hill. I could just about make out the scattering of people up and down the hill, mainly on the side we'd come down from, slowly starting to disperse. Lara, more animated than usual, was chatting to the two teenagers, probably enjoying the attraction towards her that neither seemed able to disguise. Walt was standing apart from us, gazing at the church, probably communing with the Lord, at least in his mind.

Thirty minutes later, the cars finally reached us. "Would have been worse," said Lucasz, "but the police changed their focus to turning all the cars around. There were just too many of them. Once the Glory went, we had to wait for people to come down the hill, then at last one of the ways cleared, and the police marshalled us all to go out that way. It was the wrong direction, but we eventually managed to loop back."

"I don't think I'll be doing this again," said Siobhan.

"What?" said Walt. "But we are doing the Lord's work here. Look!" he held up his hand, where only a scar remained of his self-inflicted wound.

"Your God, maybe. I don't have one. All I know is, we could have ended up in prison, and the whole thing was chaos. Look how many people there were! The cops aren't going to stand for this. They'll be more ready, next time. And we both know it won't be *you* they arrest first."

Walt gazed at her, dumbstruck.

"She's talking about white privilege," said Lucasz helpfully.

"Yes, I got that, thank you," said Walt angrily. "But we have a chance to save lives here! We've only just started! We could turn back the tide of the pandemic!"

"If you can come up with a better plan, then I'm listening. But right now, I'm taking my boys home."

"Um, it's my car, I'll have to drive you," said Walt.

Chapter 23: After the miracle

"Well then we'd better get going, hadn't we?" she replied. The two boys followed them to Walt's car.

"Well, that puts a spanner in the works, doesn't it?" said Lara.

* * * * *

The journey home was quiet and somewhat morose. Leo seemed preoccupied, Lara showed no interest in talking to anyone, and I felt empty. I hadn't realised at the time, sitting on the bench in the churchyard in the sun, how incredibly happy I'd felt. I'd cured three people – even if one of them would have recovered anyway, and another had only injured himself to make a point. Bluebell was better, and that was what mattered, even if she and Hector clearly had some massive grief issues to process. But now, with Siobhan's pronouncement, the idea that I might be able to do this again had been snatched away. I felt useless. When, forty minutes later, Lara answered Leo's phone and told us that another Glory had been sighted within driving distance, and asked if we wanted to go to it, I simply answered, "What would be the point?"

* * * * *

When we finally got back, Lara announced that she was depressed, looking meaningfully at Lucasz, and went into her room. He followed, like a dog after a thrown stick, fool that he was. So I went and found a seat in a churchyard, for the second time in a day. I missed Malcolm, the man who wanted me for me, not for my strange and mostly useless abilities, nor even as a fellow fugitive. Just wanted me. Would Locksley's people really turn up at his house, break down the door, and drag me off, if I went back there? I felt sure that someone from Walt's group would give me a lift if I asked for one. Perhaps I should just wait a couple more days. Events around me were moving so fast that if we didn't surface soon, then Locksley's lot would surely start turning their attention elsewhere.

An old laptop was sitting on the table in the living room, with the words "*In case you'd like to reconnect with the world – password is J0shua*" on a handwritten note beside it. Perhaps it would help with Lara's twitching fingers. It was switched on but asleep, and when I woke the computer, I found that Twitter was already open. It was chock full of Glories. I let out an expletive. Our Glory was the biggest story, not least because of its size. People had seen it from twenty or thirty miles away. That wasn't what bothered me. It was the stories of people walking into the sand wall, or emerging of it, and of people joining hands and apparently healing each other. A shaky bit of phone filming showed Hector and Bluebell staggering down the path, supporting each other, and then panned round to her discarded wheelchair, still lying on the slope *"She was in that wheelchair, an hour ago,"* said an excited voice. *"I swear to you, we all saw it. He was pushing her up the hill, really struggling and we couldn't help him because of the Two Metre Rule, but then he got up here and he joined her up with the people joining hands and when they let go, she just got up and started crying. That's what happened, right? That's what you all saw, too?"* The camera panned

Chapter 23: After the miracle

around to some milling people, a few of whom nodded, though others quickly hid their faces.

I went down the replies. Some accused the poster of lying, but not as many as when Malcolm had shown me tweets about Glories, what was it, just a week ago? Others expressed amazement, or said they'd seen the Glory but only from a distance. Someone said they would have been there but that the 'Fascist police' had turned them around. One commenter said that she too had been there, and confirmed the original account. Hector and Bluebell might well be celebrities by the end of the day. I wondered how they would handle it? And I started to feel a little sympathy for Siobhan's reluctance to keep doing this.

Helen came to talk to me an hour later. "I heard what happened," she said. "You performed a miracle. You should be proud."

"You dad stabbed his hand with a pencil," I told her. "There was blood everywhere."

"And you healed him. It was a miracle, Julia, a real miracle. And the woman in the wheelchair, too. Don't you realise how special it is? How special *you* are?"

"Not without Siobhan. She wants out, and I can't blame her. The attention is scary. The press are going to find us here, or the government, or the police."

"We could move you. Swap you into someone else's house. There's someone in the group who manages holiday homes. I'm sure we can talk Siobhan around. If we could get you and her into the same house, it would be so much easier."

"But I told you, she doesn't want to do it again."

"She'll come round. She's an Instrument of the Lord. However much we might fight against it, none of us can deny our destiny when it's outlined so clearly in front of us."

I was fairly sure that Siobhan would not take kindly to being told her destiny by anyone, but I kept this thought to myself.

"We're going to change the world," she told me. "When the word spreads of what you can do, everyone will Believe."

"The word seems to be spreading already," I said. "Thanks for leaving that computer, by the way."

"You're welcome. I wanted you to see for yourself."

"It's not me you have to convince," I reminded her.

"God will convince her," she replied simply.

* * * * *

Lucasz emerged, and said he was going to see if he could help Keith. Lara looked like a child on Christmas morning when she saw the computer, so I left her to it and went for a walk. I wanted to go home, to be with Malcolm, and to forget about Glories, God's plans for me and everything else. I wondered if I could hold Locksley at bay by threatening to reveal to the world what had been done to me while I was under her care. By the time I'd got home, I'd pretty much decided that I would talk to Walt tomorrow about going back to Malcolm. I

Chapter 23: After the miracle

skipped the churchyard meeting, didn't even bother having my window open to listen – I knew what they'd be talking about. I spent the evening with a book instead.

* * * * *

The following morning, no-one had called with any Glory predictions by ten thirty, and Lucasz announced that he was going out for a walk. He looked across at Lara in the apparent hope that she might join him, but she clearly preferred net surfing on Helen's computer, so he went out alone

Five minutes later the phone rang, and Lara answered. "It's for you," she said, and I wondered who on earth could be calling this number, specifically for me.

"It's Siobhan," said the voice on the other end.

"Oh," I said. "Hello. Are you OK?" Something in her voice suggested that she wasn't.

"I need to talk to you," she said. I wasn't sure if that answered my question, or not.

"All right, go on."

"I'm sorry if I ... well Helen said I'd rather left you in the lurch, that you were relying on me, and I'd totally let you down."

"Well she had no right to say that," I told her firmly. "You have no obligations to me or anyone else."

"I knew you'd understand. The pressure. I ... I mean we ... can do things. We can change peoples' lives. I knew a little girl who had cancer. But they said the government had kidnapped you and drilled holes in your head!"

"Well that's not exactly ..." I began, but she talked over me.

"And if they do that to me then who's going to look after Sammy, huh? They'll probably stick him in some kiddy care home where he'll catch Corona and die. I won't let them! I won't let them take me away from him, you understand?"

"I've got a son," I said. "He's grown up and moved away now, but I remember well enough. So yes, I understand."

"Then you won't judge me?"

"No, of course I would never do that."

"I've got to get away, you see. They'll find me, soon. But the trouble is, I've got to ... Oh I'm so stupid. I shouldn't have come."

I paused for a moment, digesting what she'd said. "Come? Come to where? Where are you?"

"I'm ..." her voice sounded lost, and guilty. "I'm parked in the little lane down the hill from your church."

"You wanted to see me in person? Why?"

"I think they might be listening," she replied.

I thought for a moment. "If they know to tap your phone – or mine – then they already know where one of us is, maybe both

"That's why I've got to get away! Please, you've got to help me!"

"I don't see how I can," I said.

Chapter 23: After the miracle

But she'd rung off.

"What's happening?" asked Lara.

"Siobhan. She's parked nearby. Wants me to talk to her in person. Sounded really worried, scared even."

"I could come with you," she said, though a trace of reluctance showed on her face.

"No, but let Lucasz know when he gets back, OK?" Whatever Siobhan wanted, she was more likely to open up to me on my own. I pulled a jacket on and walked down the path to where I could see her car lurking close to the footpath sign. As I got closer, I had brief visions of Locksley and a few minions jumping out of the hedge and putting a black bag over my head, but none of that happened. There was just Siobhan, in her little car.

"I'm sorry," she said. "I'm sorry to drag you out."

"Hey, I wasn't doing anything much. So what's brought you out all this way?"

"I'm scared. I think they're going to try and take Sammy."

"Your son? Why? Surely it'd be you they were interested in."

"Amit called me. Said he went out to the shops first thing, these two men in black suits went up to him and asked where his friend was. Right out!"

"They meant Sammy?"

"They always go round together. Except they don't, now, or at least not so much, because of the Rules. So he was at home with me. I made him promise to stay at home while I came to see you. But he doesn't always do what I tell him!! If they hurt that boy, I'm gonna …"

"Okay, okay. Calm down. Now tell me what I can do to help. Walt's people, they may be able to put you in a holiday home where no-one else would find you."

"But they'd expect me to do things for them, wouldn't they? We'd still get caught, soon enough."

I wondered what had happened to her in her life to make her so mistrustful of the world. Her tone changed to one that was steely and determined. "There's a way I can get away, hide me and my boy from trouble. A deal I can make, but only if you help me. There's a businessman, he knows about you and he knows about me. Don't ask me how, I don't bloody care, but he does. He's offering ten thousand pounds if we come when he calls us."

"To do what?"

"Cure some rich white guys, of course! What else can it be?"

"Or maybe just one," I pondered. "I had stage four cancer. A man would pay out his entire fortune to be rid of that." The thought repulsed me. I detested the very idea of the US health system, where treatment depended on your ability to pay, a system that certain people were all too keen to bring in over here. And now I was being asked to become a part of it.

"I felt you, you know," said Siobhan. "When we were connected. I know you're a good person."

And I'd felt her, as well. Felt the love she had for her son, which seemed to dominate her view of the world. And she was an honest woman, I was sure of it.

Chapter 23: After the miracle

I also knew how lost I'd felt when she'd drawn back from healing with me, and that was without any personal cost to me. For her, if I refused, it would have material consequences, even if some of her worries weren't justified. I didn't like either option. So it was the case of doing the most good, and the least harm. I knew then that, much against my better judgement, I was going to agree to it.

"I want ten thousand pounds as well," I said. "I'll give it to an NHS charity."

"They didn't say anything about paying you," she said.

"Well you can tell them next time you speak. If they need me, they can cough up. They've clearly got the money." She sighed, nodded, and typed a text on her phone. The reply came immediately.

"They say yes," she said. Another text came through. "They want us to drive to a service station, and wait."

"What? Why?"

"They explained it earlier. It's a good starting point to get anywhere quickly."

I sighed. "Let me nip back and get a few things."

"Please don't be long," she said. I nodded, and hurried back to the house. I found myself hoping that Lucasz wouldn't be there. He'd either try to persuade me to change my mind, or insist on coming with me. I didn't want the complications. Lara, I imagined, would simply look up from the computer screen and say 'OK, then.'

I opened the front door and went through to my room, grabbing a few spare bits of clothing, just in case. Then I rushed together a few sandwiches in the kitchen, and grabbed some fruit and a bottle of water. "Lara, I'm heading off with Siobhan, there's a plan to try and do some more healing," I said.

She looked up briefly from the computer, "OK, then."

Chapter 24: The gap

Antony

In the afternoon, Sally sat me down to make another list, which turned into a series of lists. She kept up her odd practice of writing about me in the third person, dispassionately, even though she tempered this with lovely sweet smiles from time to time. I started to wonder if her room at her home was full of lists. But these ones were important:

Where Daniel might be.

1. Back home, since Antony left (unlikely).
2. Walking around, with memory loss (but surely he would have been found?)
3. Memory loss, taken in by someone, living with them.
4. Inside a Glory, or maybe all of the Glories.
5. Transported somewhere else, by the Glory (but why no contact?).
6. Captured by people who hunt Antony, for same reason they want him.
7. In hiding because they *tried* to capture him?
8. Changed by Glory, like Antony but maybe in different way, e.g. invisible? (NB not mutually exclusive with 2, 6 or 7).

"Have you always looked out for your cousin?" she asked me, as she set down the list on the table. "I never really had anyone to look out for me."

I smiled. "Not really. Daniel never needed any looking out for. If anything, he looked out for me!"

"Really?"

"Yeah. There was this one time, about a year ago. This kid called Cronk, he was the school bully, well one of them. Tough, too. Liked finding an excuse to beat kids up. He found an excuse for me one day. I'd laughed when a teacher took the piss out of him. I mean, he's thick as pig shit and the teachers know what a bastard he is to the other kids, so some of them pick on him in class, ask him questions and try to humiliate him. I only laughed for a second or two before I stopped myself. He told me after class that he was going to beat me so hard I'd have to be carried home. He'd always wait a few days before he made good on his threats. For three days he'd just look at me, smile and nod.

"Every break, in those few days, I'd find a way to disappear. I knew every hidden corner, the bits behind buildings, the bushes. I couldn't think of anything else to do but try and avoid him day after day until maybe he found someone else who was easier to catch. But the fourth day, I walked out round the back of the science block and ran straight into him. I was cornered, and anyway he was a really fast runner. I was readying myself for a fight I knew I'd lose. Then this voice says, 'can I watch?'

"So Daniel saunters up behind him. He told me later he'd been following Cronk, because he knew he was after me. Cronk didn't know we were related. Daniel's got a different surname, and he doesn't look very like me. He's pretty, you know?"

"You're pretty," said Sally with a coy smile.

Chapter 24: The gap

"No I'm not. Maybe I can do rock band cool a bit, but I'll never be pretty. Daniel is. He could pass for a girl, like Roger Taylor in that Queen video with the drag. Anyway, Cronk looked at him as if he didn't understand what Daniel just said, but Daniel just leant against the wall and said, 'you know he's got protection, don't you?'

"Cronk looked around, trying to see who Daniel meant. But Daniel just holds up his phone, on speaker, and we hear the voice of Hackett, the toughest kid in the school, two years above me and Cronk. And Hackett goes, *'you lay one finger on him, you little shit, just one tiny fucking finger, and I'll break every bone in your body, you hear me?'*

"Daniel says, 'I dunno exactly what Blake does for Hackett, but it's gotta be good, don't you think?' And Cronk just stands there, tiny brain trying to make sense of it, then he looks me in the eye and goes, 'don't ever laugh at me again!' And that's it, he walked away."

"So what, did you really have Hackett on your side?" asked Sally.

"God, no. It was a voice recording Daniel had made, he never told me how he got it. My guess is, he threatened Hackett's pet hamster, or something. Cronk never bothered me again."

"Must have been great, having a guardian angel like that?" asked Sally.

"Yeah, a few times like that, it really was. But he also spent a lot of his time finding new and imaginative ways to embarrass me. Like spreading a rumour that I had a crush on Miss Hinton."

"Well, did you?" asked Sally with a knowing smile.

"Uhhh, a lot of us boys did," I said, blushing. "Daniel probably just picked the prettiest teacher and invented a rumour that he thought would stick. Funny thing is, any time he did me a favour, you could absolutely bet that he'd be playing some prank like that on me within the week. Almost like he felt the need for balance. He was like that."

"*Is* like that," she said firmly.

"Yeah."

She started another list, which turned into a trilogy.

Why Thugs might be after Antony.

1 They know he's a Glory (but how?)
2 They know he can cause people to vanish into Glories.
3 They think he has some power to do with Glories that they can use.
4 They have some grand scheme that they're worried he will foil (involving Daniel? Is his search a threat somehow?).
5 All-round cuteness.

How Thugs might know stuff about Antony.

1. Social media reports from onlookers (picking up pieces of Glory, not appearing on photos).
2. They know about 24-hour disappearance (police contact?).
3. They have someone/something that can remote-sense Glories, and detected a moving one (but they knew his face).
4. They have captured Daniel, who could have the same abilities.

Chapter 24: The gap

How to find Daniel.

1. Visit more Glories, see if Antony can detect them.
2. Search social media for sightings/images. Could he be visiting Glories too?
3. Find out what the Thugs know (how???).

The 'how to find' list looked depressingly short. I thought number 3 was a joke when she said it, but she shook her head. "Not saying we should do it, but it's not impossible. Look!" She produced the printed pages she'd taken from the car. "I think these ones are Glory locations, but one of them is a map of some sort of business estate area on the edge of a town, and look, one building is marked."

"Why would they have these?" I asked. "Seems dumb to carry around evidence like that. I mean, they were dumb, but whoever controls them clearly isn't."

"It depends," she said thoughtfully, "exactly what you're trying to hide from. If you're more worried about electronic surveillance, then old-fashioned paper maps are better than a phone, they can't be tracked. Sure, someone might hack the files on a computer, but the building is marked in pen, see, so all they'd find on the computer is a map of an area."

"I see."

"And if you could learn to walk through walls, then you could sneak in there and see if they have any information on Daniel, or even if they've got him, somehow."

"Uhhh, right."

"Don't worry, I'm not suggesting we do it tomorrow! More like a last resort sort of thing. But I do think you should try to memorise that map layout just in case, and also learn the whole walking through walls thing, if you can do it. Because if they do catch you, well it'll be kinda useful, won't it? Right, I need to nip to the bathroom – don't disappear!"

A bolt of terror shot through me, even as she sauntered merrily from the room. Why hadn't I thought of that before? I walked out of the house and around the fields, hoping it would somehow help, but it didn't. A few minutes later, Sally appeared at the door, looking worried and angry.

"Antony! Don't scare me like that! I said, don't ..."

"Disappear," I completed the sentence for her. "Because that's what Glories do, isn't it. Suddenly, without any kind of warning, they wink out of existence. And I'm one of them, which means I could be gone any second. Even talking to you now, I don't even know if I'll get through the whole sentence."

She ran forward and wrapped her arms around me, as if she could keep it from happening, just by holding me tight enough. "I'm sorry!" she said. "I didn't even think of that, I just meant don't wander off, it wasn't even serious!"

"I'm not blaming you," I said. "I would have thought of it sooner or later."

"But you've been walking around for what, three whole days now, since that blue lake Glory that we think must have changed you? Most Glories only last a few hours. You may be made of the same stuff, but you're very, very different. You could last months, years, decades ..."

"Centuries," I said. "Do you think I'll age?"

Chapter 24: The gap

"Forever young?" she said, meeting my eyes with a smile. "Well, I could live with that, though it'd be a shame not to see your silver fox stage in thirty years or so."

"Or I could be gone tomorrow."

"In this world, so could any of us. I could have died, yesterday, more than once."

"I'm scared," I said. We stood there, holding each other, for some time.

"If you do vanish," she said, "I don't think you'll die. I mean, these things must come from somewhere, mustn't they? They come, and then they go back. Wherever it is, it may be where your cousin has gone. Could be that you'll find him, just like that, without trying."

"Then I wouldn't be with you," I said.

"Well, you'd have to find your way back, wouldn't you? I could be your motivation."

We went back in, and she added a line to the final list.

4. Antony disappears, goes to where Daniel (maybe) is, and then comes back.

We agreed that neither 3 or 4 were appealing, whereas 1 hadn't worked so far, so we set about doing 2 – looking for sightings of him on social media. "I guess there'll be stuff about you, as well," she said. "Be prepared to come across that, but we'll focus on him. Crowd shots at Glories are our best bet. I mean, it feels a bit needle-in-a-haystack, but you visited three of them, and from what you've said, he's pretty smart."

"Smarter than me," I agreed.

"Question is, which days do we look at? Do we include the day you last saw him, or start with the next day, the day you came back and realised he was gone?"

"Let's start with that, from then to today," I said.

"Okay, so that's the 7th, 8th and 9th of May. Reckon Instagram and Twitter are best, so we can –"

"April," I said smiling at her.

"What?"

"It's April, silly, not May. Fairly sure it's not possible to read tweets from the future."

"No, it's May."

We looked at each other, each thinking the other was being very dumb. Then her expression changed. "Come on, I'll show you," she said.

"It's April," I said, as I followed her inside.

In a room upstairs, there was a computer that looked older than I was – a huge beige coloured rectangular thing under the table that had probably once been white, a chunky keyboard, and a screen that looked like an old telly. Sally reached down and pressed some button around the back, and a few whirring clunking noises signalled that the machine was slowly waking up. Very slowly. Sally muttered impatiently as it did so, not looking at me.

"It's April," I repeated. "I think I'd have remembered if a whole month had gone by without …" my voice trailed away.

"But would you?" she asked me softly. "The lockdown has been going on for six or seven weeks now. Virus cases are starting to drop, but only slowly. The Prime Minister's been out of hospital for four weeks."

Chapter 24: The gap

"Boris Johnson was in hospital?"

"You thought you'd lost a day. But I think you just assumed it was one day, because you went out on a Wednesday, and then you came back on a Thursday. But it wasn't one day, Antony! You were gone for a month!

Chapter 25: The American health service

Julia

On the way to the service station, Siobhan and I swapped stories and got to know each other. She and Sammy had been doing their daily exercise a week ago, on one of their regular routes, only to encounter a huge boulder blocking their way.

"It was as big as two houses, like it had rolled down from some mountain somewhere, except there weren't no mountain anywhere close. There were some guys walking around looking at it, and they said maybe it was a meteor fell out of the sky, but there weren't no crater. I told them if it had fell, there'd be a crater. I went closer and had a good look. There was something unnatural about it. Like it was CGI in a movie, you know? I got a bit worried, but my Sammy don't scare easy, and he went up to touch it. 'Mum, it's like a force field,' he said. Now I was proper scared, and I took his arm to try and pull him back. That's when it happened, the first time. I was in his mind, and he was in mine. Can you imagine? Seeing inside a teenage boy's mind?"

"Well I did," I said. "Two of them, in fact!"

She smiled. "Yeah, but this were just him and me. No distractions. I saw his thoughts. Lots of girls, mainly, and not many clothes on any of them."

"Well, I guess you know he's not gay."

"Knew that anyway. And that he loved me, but thought I fussed over him too much."

"Fussing over them is a mother's job," I said.

"Yeah. Then someone else must have tried to pull us away, because I felt a third mind, and then a fourth. Eventually someone knocked Sammy's hand away from the giant rock with a stick.

"There were a young man and a woman, said they were worried about us and tried to pull us away but got linked to us instead. We all looked at each other. I didn't know what the fuck had happened. Wanted to get away, to be honest, but Sammy just walked right up and touched it again. Thing is, it didn't do nothing when he touched it on its own. Then he asked the young man to touch his hand, and nothing happened to either of them. So it was me. Me that was having this crazy effect. Then the rock just vanished. Like it had never been there. We went right home, didn't go out for two days, wanted to forget it all. Well Sammy went out, I didn't. He found out about the Glories, one of his friends knew someone who'd seen one, and then of course it came on the telly. I thought that was it, as long as I didn't go near one again, nothing else would happen. But someone must have seen something, because I started getting phone calls. They knew what I could do, and wanted to know more about it."

"That happened to me," I said. "They actually came to my house. Well, my boyfriend's house. I've been living in sin."

"Me, it was just on the phone. Said they thought I'd been touched by God."

"Walt?" I asked. "Or Millie?"

"No, it was someone else."

Chapter 25: The American health service

By now we were parked in the service station, neatly into a marked space even though the parking area was huge and almost empty. The phone pinged, and Siobhan grabbed it immediately. She showed me the message, telling us that a Glory was predicted in fifty-seven minutes time, together with a precise location. She started the engine, and off we went.

"So this predictor person, the one who helps out Walt, is working for our 'businessman' as well?" I asked.

"How would I know? Maybe it's the same person, maybe not. If it even is a person."

"What else could it be?" I asked.

"A machine. Maybe the government made it, but someone sold off the design."

"They must have worked fast," I said.

"Hah! Not as fast as you think. They've known about the Glories for months, apparently."

"Months???"

"Yeah, well, they kept them secret didn't they? But Sammy turned up a handful of reports from all over the world, since about Christmas. He's bloody good at googling when he puts his mind to it. The one that got the most publicity was a lake in Austria that turned into something like custard. Kids were sliding across it, having a whale of a time, but then it changed back and they all fell in. Luckily it wasn't too cold that day, and they were all OK. There were stories of a spinning cloud in Texas that kept changing colour, a waterfall coming out of nowhere in the Himalayas. Then suddenly, they're all in Britain."

"How can a machine see them before they appear, when cameras can't even see them?" I asked.

"Don't ask me, girl."

"I can't see how a machine would … unless it had a bit of human in it …"

"Don't be sayin' crazy stuff. How'd they get a bit of brain in there?"

I didn't answer, but images flashed through my mind of that masked figure, drilling into my head.

* * * * *

The location we'd been sent to turned out to be a small car park between a golf course and its clubhouse. Ours was the only vehicle there. We got out, and nervously circled around the large building, which showed no signs of life.

"Ms Smith, and Ms Barnes, delighted to meet you."

A second car was now in the car park, and a small man was standing beside it. He removed his hat to greet us, as he spoke, and even bowed a little. He had black curly hair and a big smile; I didn't like the look of him at all. He had to be the 'businessman' Siobhan had spoken of. "We have, I would estimate, another eight minutes before the Glory appears," he said. "Our patients should be with us very shortly, but I'm given to understand that you can sense it when a Glory is about to appear?"

"I think anyone can," I said.

Chapter 25: The American health service

"Well, let us perambulate a little. The location indicated was, I believe, in the vicinity of the third hole."

I wondered, not for the first time, how this predictor, be it man or machine, could possibly be so precise. But there was nothing else to do but walk with him across the deserted fairways. "Golf course near me has been turned into a public park," the man said. "Families, dog walkers, everything but golf. Doesn't make sense, of course, but better than standing idle. But this place is exclusive and out of town, so we shouldn't be disturbed here. In fact, I'm making sure of it, we're putting '*police – road closed*' signs on all the access roads. I know how the two of you aren't keen on publicity.

"No need to thank me," he added, after a pause.

A little further on, I felt that same tingling I'd felt on the side of the Malvern Hills. "Do you feel it?" I asked Siobhan.

"Yes."

"We need to step back a bit," I said. "It's going to be here. Don't want to risk making it turn up somewhere else instead, do we?"

The man looked at me with interest. There was something about his eyes that looked oddly familiar to me, but I couldn't work out what. "Would that happen?" he asked.

"I've no idea, but I'm guessing you wouldn't be too keen to find out."

A horn tooted behind us. "Aha!" Said the man. "Let us go and meet our patients."

There were now five cars in the car park. A thick-set Asian man with greying hair was pushing forward a frail old woman in a wheelchair, while a tall silver fox of a man was pushing another wheelchair, this one containing a young woman whose head lolled awkwardly to the left. All four wore surgical masks. Two suited men in sunglasses walked towards us and handed the businessman two large wads of money. "Count out ten thousand for each of our ladies here, if you would, gentlemen,"

The young woman in the wheelchair tried to speak, but it was all unintelligible moans. "It's all right, Debbie, these are the people who are going to cure you," said the silver fox.

Debbie made a few more noises, but she did not sound reassured.

The businessman addressed them. "Quentin, perhaps you might position your niece with a view across the first nine holes, and ask her to alert us when the Glory appears?"

"Yes, Mr Collett," said the man, who then spoke gently to Debbie as he moved her.

"Late stages of motor neurone," explained Collett, the businessman. "She won't last the year without a miracle. Nor will Mrs Kumar here," he said, gesturing to the old woman. I didn't need him to tell me that she had cancer – one look told the story. Another car was entering the car park now, a battered little Vauxhall, looking rather intimidated as it parked beside the two huge status symbols that the Kumars and Quentin had come in. Three people got out, a man and woman in their thirties, and a pale little boy with no hair. The two parents looked like neither had slept in a week, and they had walked halfway towards us before the father ran back to the car and collected a package from the boot.

Chapter 25: The American health service

"We couldn't get it all," he said to Collett in a pleading voice. "We tried everything but it's really hard to get cash in hand with the lockdown. We can give you the car as well."

"What would I want with *that* little car?" said Collett. "It's fine, I'll take an IOU. With interest, of course."

"I'm not giving you a penny unless it works!" said the father, with fragile determination.

"And *I* shall not be taking a penny unless it does!" replied Collett in an avuncular voice, slapping him on the back. "But rest assured, that particular point will soon be well and truly moot."

Debbie made a noise, and we turned to look. A rippling curtain of light and fire had appeared, right over the third hole. It was small for a Glory, perhaps ten metres across and slightly taller, with dazzlingly bright whites, yellows and reds playing across it.

"Mummy, is that ... is that the door into heaven?" said the bald boy.

"You're not going to heaven for a very long time," his mother replied, with a confidence in her voice that was not reflected in her eyes.

Collett turned to his two suited colleagues. "Don't let anyone else park here, but have the van wait here when it comes." Then he led us down the slope towards the Glory. "Come on folks, it's showtime." The patterning of the Glory changed as we got closer. Or rather, it *didn't* change. You'd expect the flames to appear larger the closer you got to it, the way anything would, but they didn't. They seemed to move further inside the Glory, as we approached it, so that they appeared to always be the same distance away. "Everyone join hands," said Collett. "Well, it's only the patients and our two walking miracles who actually need to be touching, but the rest of you can be part of it if you want to."

I took Siobhan's hand in one hand, the little boy's in the other. In his other hand, he grasped the inert hand of poor Debbie. Neither Quentin nor Mr Kumar seemed inclined to touch anyone, so eventually the boy's mother walked up and served as a link between Debbie's other hand, and Mrs Kumar. "Everyone ready?" asked Siobhan. She took a quick look around, and then leant forward and touched the Glory.

I felt a sickness worse than when Bernard was at his peak, and was assailed by images of hospitals, so many hospitals. There were sounds of parents weeping when they thought I couldn't hear them, music and dancers in colourful costumes all seen through a foggy veil, a morose-faced consultant delivering terrible news, arguing families, and a strong (all too familiar) sense that I'd be leaving this world behind before too long.

Then, unexpectedly, I was back on the golf course. Collett had used a walking stick to break Siobhan's contact with the Glory. "That was half an hour," he said. "I've really no idea how much time this process needs, though apparently a self-inflicted stigmata-type wound requires under fifteen minutes. Perhaps, if the patients might let me know how they are feeling?"

"I feel fi – OH!" said Debbie. She leapt from the chair with a whoop, jumped up and hugged her uncle in mid-air, and then attempted a cartwheel on the grass, before collapsing into a heap.

Chapter 25: The American health service

"You might find it better to take things a little more slowly at first," said Collett happily. Meanwhile, the old woman in the other wheelchair had ripped off her mask and was arguing at high speed in some Indian language with the man who'd brought her. I turned my attention to the boy, who was still holding my hand. His hair hadn't grown back, but his skin looked a normal shade of pink.

"I'm not feeling sick anymore," he said. "Mummy, daddy, I think I might be better!"

His parents both rushed to hug him.

"Money?" said Collett, and a hand detached itself from the hug, presenting the envelope. Meanwhile the high-speed Indian argument went on. "Mr Kumar, am I to take it that your mother, also, is recovered?" asked Collett.

"Oh yes, sir, thank you, sir. Totally her old self again," said Kumar, beaming broadly, before turning back to his mother and resuming the argument.

"I think we can call that a resounding success," declared Collett, producing the two wads from his pocket. "Ten thousand each, like we agreed." He handed one to me, and one to Siobhan.

I swear the money felt slimy to the touch, as I took it. I told myself it wasn't for me, but even so I felt violated by its presence in my hand. How was I going to get it to the nurses? How long would I have to carry this vile package around? Then I looked again at the bald boy's hugging family.

"Excuse me, can I ask you how much money you were short by?" I said to the father.

If he was surprised by the question, he didn't show it. "About three thousand."

"How are you going to find that money, now?" I asked gently.

He snorted a laugh, as if I'd asked a mouse how it was going to build a nuclear reactor.

"Right," I said, and counted off 60 fifty-pound notes from the wad I'd been given, and stuck them under Collett's nose. "It's from them," I declared. "The balance of their payment." He looked puzzled for a moment, then raised his eyebrows a fraction, and pocketed the money. Again, I got the faint notion that I'd seen those eyes before. I turned back to the family, and handed them the rest of my wad. "Here, you can use this to start buying your life back."

The woman answered, "But we can't accept this! You've just given us back our son's life! We can't possibly take this from you!"

"And I can't possibly live with myself if I've been party to bankrupting you. Take it, for me. If you don't want it, give it to the NHS, but your son should come first. And get yourselves home now, this isn't a good place to be."

The father took the money from me, mouthed the word 'thanks' with teary sincerity, and then led his wife and son back up the slope. Debbie was getting better at cartwheels, and Mrs Kumar had stood up, taken a little walk around, and then decided that since they had the wheelchair, she was damned well going to ride back up to their car in comfort. Collett had taken a few steps away from us, and taken out his phone.

"Are the next lot ready? ... Good. When I wave my arms, send them down."

"I can't believe how you just gave all that away," Siobhan said to me. There was a hardness in her eyes I hadn't expected.

Chapter 25: The American health service  147

"Well, they needed it, and I didn't."

"You've never been poor, have you?" she said sternly. "Never lived week to week, not knowing how you'd get through. What it must be like to just be able to give away money like that."

I thought she was being grossly unfair, but I held my tongue. It wasn't my fault she was poor, was it?

"Now, ladies," said Collett, "I get the clear impression that you're none too impressed with my – let's be honest – rather capitalist way of doing things. Which is why our second batch of patients are not going to be paying customers at all. You may of course say no, you have discharged your duties for the day most admirably, but I have brought along a group of care home residents who regrettably have all become infected with Coronavirus when it got into that home. The residents have been dropping like flies, and the staff expect few if any of this group to make it through the week. Which is why they let me borrow them for our 'experimental treatment'. Are you OK to proceed?"

Siobhan and I looked at each other, bemused, and nodded. The businessman gestured with his hand. I'd expected a group of tottering figures in white gowns, but instead a van just came trundling across the fairway. "I may need to send a little money to the groundskeeper by way of compensation," said Collett happily. "But I'm afraid these patients are in no condition to walk, or even be pushed."

"They're in the van?" I asked, a little appalled.

"As comfortable as they can be, on mattresses in the back. We gave them something to help them sleep through the journey. I hope it doesn't affect the two of you two much, but I imagine you'll clear that out of their systems, too. Now when they get here, we'll just quickly tape the hands of our patients together into a sort of human chain, and then my two colleagues in the van will link with the pair of you, as they have been exposed to rather a lot of the virus in the past few hours."

The two men from the front of the van hopped out, opened the back, and climbed over the sleeping patients, taping hands to those of their neighbours. Then one man took the hand of the patient at the back, the other took his hand and mine, I took Siobhan's, and she reached out and touched the Glory.

* * * * *

I woke as if from a dream. I felt sore all over, but this quickly passed. I had dim recollections of cloying headaches and spinning rooms, of gasping for breath, and again that sense that I was on my way out, coupled with flashbacks to lives that weren't my own. The Glory was gone. Croaky old voices from the van were asking where they were. Bemused, but healthy voices.

"Well, there you go," said Collett. "A cure for Corona. How about that?"

I felt rather tired, and lowered myself into a sitting position. What if all this healing of others was taking energy out of me? Energy that the Glories couldn't restore? Well, I'd been near to death myself a couple of weeks ago, so I really couldn't complain.

"Of course, that's only six people, in a country where hundreds are dying each day," said Collett thoughtfully. It was only the three of us on the grass now,

Chapter 25: The American health service

the van had trundled back up towards the car park. "Just think how many more we could cure, if we could get a proper system going!"

"I only agreed to this one time," said Siobhan.

"But you know, now that we have proof of concept, we can charge a whole lot more for the paying customers," he replied. "Much more! I'm sure our patients from today will be only too willing to supply us with glowing testimonials. I think – indeed I am quite sure – that I shall be able to pay you ladies twenty-five thousand if we do this again. Each!"

"Please don't think I don't appreciate the offer," said Siobhan, "but I am gonna have to think on it awhile. Speak to my boy. Now I know you got it all right today, kept all prying eyes away, but you'll not be able to do that every time. We're taking a risk doing this. *I'm* taking a risk."

"Ah," he said. "I fear that creates a little bit of a problem. You see, the clients we had today were willing to gamble on a little uncertainty, and the level of payment we could ask for reflected that. However, the clients I have lined up for the imminent future are not those kinds of people. They pay for certainty. An hour of their time is worth more money than many of us earn in a year. I hope that you can see how they would react less than favourably to me telling them that we *might* be able to cure them tomorrow, or we might not, depending on one person's whims."

His voice was chatty, matter-of-fact, and almost friendly as he drew the gate shut on his trap.

"I'm sorry about that," said Siobhan, "but you had no right to promise my involvement in anything to anyone beyond today. The answer is no."

He shrugged. "Ah well, perhaps it's for the best. I know that Ms Barnes is less than enamoured with my rather American approach to healthcare. So, perhaps the nationalised model is the better one after all, especially during such times of crisis. You may be aware that there is increasing momentum behind a movement to treat what some are calling the increasing menace of Glory addiction. When I say 'treat', I fear that's a bit of a euphemism, for I gather what they do is closer to experimentation."

"Experimentation?" I cut in, sharply. "What do you know about that?"

He ignored me, still addressing Siobhan. "They're looking for test subjects, of course. That boy of yours, Sammy, he's managed to find his way onto a list of suspected addicts. Thus far, I've managed to persuade them to leave him alone, on the grounds that you are being useful to me. I have connections, you see. But were you to cease being useful to me …"

"You bastard," said Siobhan. "You total, utter piece of filth."

"Now is that any way to talk to a man who has been doing his best to protect your son from human vivisection? And as for you, Ms Barnes, I believe that you are now on several such lists, but as long as you're helping me, I shall tell none of them where you are. All I'm asking is a few more days of working with me, and I will have your son's name removed from the list, Ms Smith. Indeed, I shall aid you both in the art of disappearing, should you so wish it. Now what do you say?"

Chapter 25: The American health service  149

I looked around, briefly considering whether we could simply run away, across the golf course. But I could see the two suited men lurking a little up the hill from us.

"So now we are your prisoners?" said Siobhan, icily.

"I would prefer to view you as my slightly reluctant business partners," he said happily. "Your payments will remain undiminished despite this lack of enthusiasm on your part. Shall we go?"

We trudged after him up the slope, towards the clubhouse, noting the ruts left on the golf course by the van. I decided that if I got the chance, I would be sure to tell the golf club exactly who was responsible for it. Small victories.

Siobhan was made to surrender her car keys, and the two of us were invited into the back of Collett's large Mercedes.

* * * * *

We arrived at what looked to be a run-down motel on the edge of nowhere. It was surrounded by battered fields, waste ground and the edge of a grim-looking industrial estate. Waiting there was a tall, thin and humourless man whose name was apparently Pridgeon, but his grey clothes, hair and pallor reminded me of a starved pigeon, so that quickly became what we called him, Siobhan and I. Without a word from Collett, the Pigeon motioned for us to get out of the car, and led us into the building. There was an unoccupied reception desk, but a man clad in leather was lounging on a seat opposite.

"You planned all this, didn't you?" I asked the Pigeon, who was still walking silently in front of us. He didn't answer, of course. It seemed crazy, but I found myself wondering if it had been one of them who'd come and assaulted Lara and me in the night, knowing it would cause us to run away. Had they then somehow followed us to that Glory, and gone round handing out addresses for the Acceptors of Light? Because no-one else in that group walked around in hoodies with white discs sewn onto their fronts. Did Collett's people have a spy in that group, too? It would explain so much. Had they been manipulating me, all this time, all the way into their clutches?

Of course, these sorts of brilliant insights are of very limited use after the event. The Pigeon pointed to a room, with a large padlock and attachment newly screwed onto the outside of the door, so that the occupant could be locked in. I went in as instructed, and heard the padlock click into place. One more uselessly brilliant insight struck me then, as I stared miserably at the locked door. There didn't need to be a spy in Walt's group, if the Glory-predictor worked for Collett. The connection had been in plain sight, all this time.

I sat down miserably on a small double bed in a grotty little room. At least it had a small bathroom, and a telly. I turned it on and watched *Pointless*.

Glories and the Virus competed for space on the news. A minister told the programme that there was no truth in the rumours that Glories occasionally caused people to vanish without trace, nor that many people were becoming sick or mentally unbalanced after looking at them.

I imagined Malcolm's response (how I missed him!)

Chapter 25: The American health service

"The best way to start a rumour, Julia, is to deny that it is true. Especially if you're a politician."

They were trying to get people to stay at home, of course they were. Later that evening (for what was there to do but watch TV?), a more junior member of government was pontificating on the Glories, via zoom of course. She appeared to be sitting on the toilet in her bathroom.

"Well, of course it's early days, and much of our attention is on the pandemic, which of course represents a far greater threat. But you know, about these Glory things, I have to say that there is no evidence as yet for the idea that it is some sort of weapon or device being tested by a hostile power, or a side-effect of the 5G network. And I think it's really silly to say, as some people have been, that it's just mass hallucinations caused by the Coronavirus or collective population trauma, I mean that's completely absurd, isn't it. And they haven't been making people sick who look at them for too long. The danger to human health remains the virus, and only the virus."

Again, I found myself imagining Malcolm, perched on the bed beside me, being knowledgeable.

"I'm actually impressed by that," I imagined him telling me. *"They picked possibly the most guileless minister of the lot, and between you and me, that's a pretty crowded field, and sent her out to unconvincingly deny a bunch of lunatic conspiracy theories that people are now going to start to believe. Anyone who thought the Glories were made up, well they're going to buy that hallucination baloney, aren't they? Or just take it as confirmation that they were never real in the first place. And for everyone else, that same denial that they're dangerous, plus a couple more conspiracy theories to build up the fear a little more."*

"But they're trying to keep people safe," I said to him, in my head. I had no love at all for the current government, but felt that they'd been doing OK since the lockdown started.

"Yes, I think they are, but they're playing a dangerous game. Once a conspiracy theory gets out of the bottle, you can never get it back in. What if, somewhere down the line, they really need people to believe in the Glories, to keep them safe? What happens then?"

Chapter 26: The politician

Antony

Sally held me for quite some time, while I slowly absorbed this latest shock, and the old computer continued the process of waking up. Eventually she got a screen (the machine was so old, there was no password), and quickly found a news story on the BBC website. Staring out from the screen, at the top of the article, were me and Daniel. I looked shifty and uncomfortable – it was a school photo. Daniel of course was beaming at the camera, he had probably been telling the photographer to make sure they got his best side. I read the story.

"Missing teenagers: Antony Blake seen alive, claims to have seen Daniel Blue the day before"

One month after they disappeared, multiple eyewitnesses report seeing Antony Blake (16), the older of the two missing teenaged cousins, in their home town of Swinton, on the afternoon the 7th May. Blake came to Blue's house, asking if Blue was there, though he also claimed that he had been with Blue just a day earlier, appearing to confirm suspicions that the two of them had gone off together. When challenged by Blue's parents, and then his own father, Blake had simply run away again.

With the government ban on reporting Glories now rescinded, the police have revealed the contents of a one-word text that Blake had sent to a school friend, about an hour after he and Blue had left their respective houses. The word was 'Glory'. The parents confirm that Blake tried to use Glories to explain Blue's disappearance, and although no-one else had reported a Glory in Swinton on the day the boys disappeared, that does not rule it out.

One expert suggested that Blake, and perhaps also Blue, could have been mentally altered by an encounter with a Glory. "We're seeing increasing numbers of people being profoundly affected by contact with a Glory, or even just seeing one. Personality changes, religious conversions, depression, elation, and pertinent to this case, I think, memory loss. One or both boys might have forgotten who they were, or where they lived."

One possibility, which the police declined to comment on, was that one or both boys had somehow been absorbed into one of the many Glory-related cults that are springing up. "It's hard to see where else they could have gone, for a whole month, with the country in full lockdown," said the expert. The police are believed to have chosen to ignore lockdown breaking by such cults as part of a wider strategy to avoid publicising the existence of Glories, although there is some indication that this policy may now be changing.

The public are asked to report any sighting of either teenager to the police, immediately.

Our eyes were drawn to another news story, the 'top story,' which referred to the globe Glory of the previous day. The main image was a mock-up of the Globe, basically a view of the countryside taken from the air, with a computer-drawn globe hanging above it. The image was quite accurate – not too detailed, no ice caps. Well, I supposed that a very large number of people had seen this

Chapter 26: The politician

one. More interesting was a map, showing all of the Glories in that area that had been reported. There were eleven! There was the moon, the comet, the blue diamond, and many others, most of them somehow associated with space and the solar system. I was sorry to have missed the replica Saturn.

There were two paragraphs about the panic the Globe had caused, and the multiple traffic accidents that had resulted, as cars fleeing the Glory had met others coming equally fast in the other direction. Seven people had died, with many others in hospital. A senior minister was quoted, reminding people that the safe course of action was to stay at home, and that Glories only presented a threat to life if people drove around trying to get to them, or indeed away from them. There was more detail on the accidents and traffic chaos, but the final paragraph was rather different:

```
Several witnesses reported seeing the missing teenager Antony Blake
among the crowd around the second-largest Glory of the cluster,
which was a half-submerged moon. We have not been able to confirm
this, because he does not appear in any of the photos we have seen.
However, several onlookers report two men attempting to abduct him,
an attempt that was thwarted, according to conflicting accounts,
by either a young woman or a dog. "He looked exactly like the boy
in the photos, and they knew precisely who they were after. And I
tell you, they weren't police," said one eye-witness. In response,
a police spokesman merely asked that people obey the rules and stay
away from Glories, but that anyone who thinks they have seen the
missing teenagers to contact them immediately.
```

Sally had dragged the photo of Daniel onto the desktop. Now she told me that we needed to divide our resources, because there was only one computer in the house. She would search social media for images or mentions of him, while I watched a rolling news channel on the telly downstairs, to see what else I could learn. She had to turn it on for me, of course.

The first programmes were more general news. I caught up with the events of the past month, the horrendous virus death tolls (calmly delivered, as if it were now routine), the support for people unable to work, the strains on the NHS, now compounded by all the traffic accidents. And the Glories, for which the story was being filled in retrospectively after weeks of denial. One scientist caught my full attention.

"*There were a few scattered reports of them from around the world between January and March, but from early April there was a shift, both in range and in frequency. From that point on, they were reported almost exclusively from the British Isles.*"

"*The so-called Pertwee Paradox,*" said the presenter.

"*I'm sorry?*"

"*It's a reference to 1970s* Doctor Who, *I believe. The point being, all the paranormal activity on Earth is mysteriously centred around southern England, for which no convincing explanation has been put forward.*"

"*I think you'll find that 'no convincing explanation' also applies to the Glories themselves,*" said the expert. "*But yes, the 'Pertwee Paradox,' as you call it, has indeed birthed its own subset of strange theories, many of them suggesting the Glories must be man-made in some way. I'm afraid the answer is, as usual, that we simply do not know, but there is no technology in existence,*

Chapter 26: The politician

or anywhere close to existence, that could produce these things. If I were to speculate..."

"Please do," said the presenter.

"I would suggest that whatever is causing these phenomena would have to have some sort of anchor point, probably somewhere in England, which would resolve your paradox. Science will explain all this, I promise you, it just may take a little more time. Remember, a couple of centuries ago we had no idea that diseases were caused by microorganisms."

Half an hour went past without anything much of note. Sally came down looking a little unsettled.

"Everything alright?" I asked.

"Just missing you." And she gave me a big hug, which seemed to fix her mood, then off she went upstairs again.

A little later, a longer interview was on offer, with someone else billed as "a bit of a Glory expert," who I was surprised to learn was a Tory MP. The female presenter opened with, "Well, all the talk in the past 24 hours has been about one thing and one thing only – the Glories. And I'm happy to say that we've got a guest here who knows more about them than most – Conservative MP Barry Collins."

"Hello, Jessica."

"Barry?" I said, to the screen and the empty room. "Whoever heard of a Tory MP called Barry?"

The man didn't look posh, though. He had a thick-set, northern look to him.

"Barry, perhaps you could tell our viewers why the government decided to keep the Glories secret from them, for as long as you did?"

"Glady, Jessica, but let me start by saying it was not just our party. We consulted with the leaders of all the main parties about this. Put simply, we felt that public knowledge of these phenomena presented a significant threat to lockdown. The public have been doing such a great job, truly excellent, Jessica! A great job of staying home, riding out the virus crisis and slowing transmission, and also leaving the roads clear for essential vehicles, greatly speeding up food deliveries for those who are shielding. But once people know about the Glories, well then there's this perfectly understandable temptation to be out all day looking for them. Of course, most of us knew that the cat would get out of the bag sooner or later, with numbers of Glories increasing. That's why I pushed so hard to have a plan for when it did."

"Barry, forgive me for saying so, but you are quite a junior MP. How did you come to be on the – until recently – very secret committee dealing with the response to the Glories?"

"I forgive you, Jessica! It's very simple, I was one of the first people to see a Glory, and almost certainly the first MP."

"What was it like? Many of our viewers still haven't seen one, or certainly not up close."

"Jessica, imagine showing a widescreen colour TV to a prehistoric caveman. That's how gobsmacking it was – for me and the few others who saw it when I did. But afterwards, of course, I was utterly bemused. What had I seen? I didn't dare tell any of my colleagues, they'd think I was barking! I tried to research strange phenomena that could explain it – Brocken spectres, ball lightning, nacreous clouds, the works – and none came close. Then a few days

Chapter 26: The politician

later I started coming across accounts on social media. So I reported it to the PM's office. He was in hospital by then, of course. I'm afraid it took quite a few days for them to believe me. Once they did, well, I was so far ahead on researching these things that it just made sense to have me on the committee with some far more senior people."

"You said they're increasing in frequency," said Jessica. "The Glories. Can we be sure of that?"

"Very sure," said Collins. "Yesterday we had what may be the first ever cluster – at least eleven within one area, at one time, and one of them easily the largest that there has been so far. I'd estimate that a fifth of the country would have seen it. Like I said, the cat was always going to get out of the bag. So yes, they are increasing, and while that's good news for anyone who wants to see one, it does create all sorts of concerns if the trend continues."

"But they're not dangerous, are they? I mean, unless they appear on a road, as we sadly have learnt recently, then the danger is all from people driving too fast, isn't it?"

"Jessica, try telling that to the parents of Tina Gregg."

"Tell me about her," said Jessica.

"A child with all of her life in front of her," said Collins. "Out for her permitted daily exercise with her parents. Then a car came screaming along at well above the speed limit, on its way to see a Glory. It left the road and hit them. Tina was killed instantly. Her parents ended up in hospital where they both contracted Coronavirus, though I believe they are now on the mend."

"Can you be sure that the driver was trying to get to a Glory? I understand that the police have not released many details."

"A Glory had been reported half an hour earlier, in the direction he was going. What other explanation could there be?" said Collins. "Listen – the main, indeed only danger from Glories is people driving too fast, trying to see one. So I have to say to all your viewers, stay within the law. Do not exceed the speed limits. Otherwise, we would have to increase police presence on the roads and ramp up penalties for speeding offences. Fortunately, the vast majority of the Great British Public are sensible, rational, law-abiding people."

"And those who are not?" asked the presenter.

"Strange as it is to say it, some of those who have caused these accidents may not be fully responsible for their actions," said Collins.

"What do you mean?"

"I mean that we are rapidly coming to realise that close contact with a Glory can have strong mental or emotional effects on a minority of people. This is another reason why people should think twice before driving out to see one. I've heard stories of memory loss, permanent anxiety, depression. Yet there is also a condition that may make the person a risk to others as well – through no fault of their own, I must add."

"And that is?" said Jessica.

"Glory addiction. A compelling, often completely irresistible urge to be close to a Glory. We are seeing more and more cases of this. Our government has been far too slow on this I think – perfectly understandable, with all the other challenges of course, but nonetheless it requires more attention. These people, unfortunately, pose the greatest risk, because they will stop at nothing to see another Glory, speeding and – in one case I've been told about – even stealing someone's car at knifepoint. It's not their fault, because unlike drug addicts

Chapter 26: The politician

they did not become this way by making poor decisions. But nonetheless they are ill and should be treated, because they are, I think, creating a very real danger on the roads."

Sally was standing in the doorway, looking unsettled. "They're going to stop us all," she said. "Lock us all indoors, like they did in Spain. So no-one can get to any of the Glories."

"That wasn't what he was saying," I replied. "They're just talking about addicts, people who go cold turkey when they're not looking at a Glory."

"For now, yes. But I promise you, he's got an agenda. Whether it's his, or the whole government's, who knows. They want to stop people going to see Glories. The addicts are just an excuse."

"Why?" I asked. "Why would they do that?"

"Control. They can't control the Glories so they'll control us, instead."

I decided she was being paranoid. The presenter was now asking Collins why no-one nearer the top of the government was talking about Glory addicts, if it was such a big problem. Collins said that they were all still '*very understandably*' preoccupied with the virus, which was '*at present*' still the greater threat. The words 'at present' lodged in my head, making me wonder what would happen if Glory numbers kept on increasing indefinitely.

We agreed that we'd had quite enough of news and current affairs for one day, and went off for a siesta that didn't involve any sleeping. Later, Sally managed to find the movie 'Ghost' on a pay-per-view website, and we watched it on the screen of the old computer, upstairs. She spent much of it blubbing her eyes out, which apparently counts as enjoying a film if you're a girl, while I tried and failed to pass her some tissues. As we watched the movie, I kept trying to acquire the Patrick Swayze character's talent for picking up and moving objects with his ghostly hands, but I got absolutely nowhere. So I consoled myself at the end by picking up Sally and moving her to the bedroom.

* * * * *

The next morning, we headed out for a walk. It was a beautiful day, and we both felt that a long trek might clear our heads. Plus, there was always the outside chance that we might happen upon a Glory, and somehow learn something useful for my quest to find Daniel. For miles and miles we walked, seldom letting go of each other's hands, making a game of trying to keep them held even as we negotiated styles and kissing gates. I felt utterly, blissfully happy. I daydreamed that we'd come home to the news that Daniel had somehow turned up and returned to his home, meaning that Sally and I could just stay in the cottage and not worry about anything other than loving each other. I knew it was a silly dream, and I couldn't shake off the thought that my quest to find Daniel was going to rip us apart, sooner or later. Every time a thought like this flicked through my head, I held onto Sally's hand just that little bit tighter.

We were in no great hurry. We kept to the high ground wherever we could, giving us the best chances to see any distant Glories, but we saw none. We didn't care. I was already thinking that we might just do this every day, and sooner or later one would pop up. I was fine with later.

As lunchtime approached, we were heading along another path running along the top of a long hill. Beech trees loomed majestically above us, but the

Chapter 26: The politician

slopes going down on either side were a mass of shrubs. We'd stopped to watch a treecreeper bird working its way up a trunk, when we both heard a distant crashing sound among the shrubs on the right-hand slope below us.

"Is that an animal?" asked Sally.

"Bloody big one if it is," I said. The sounds were getting closer, we even saw a young tree wobble at one point. Whatever it was, was coming right towards us.

"Let's get out of its way," she said. We jogged along the path for a bit, as the hill curved round to the right. Figuring we'd gone far enough, we stopped, panting, out of breath. Well, she was out of breath, I guess I just panted in sympathy.

Then we heard the crashing again. Moving through the bushes in a new direction, again heading straight toward us.

"Whatever it is, it's tracking us!" said Sally. "It's coming for us!"

Chapter 27: Julia Barnes, slave

Julia

The following morning, some time after breakfast had been brought to my room, the door was unlocked again. "Showtime!" said a goon, gesturing at me to come out. I went for a pee first, just to annoy him.

Siobhan and I were driven in separate cars. My driver, a leather-jacketed young man named Feodor blared out horrific modern music at full volume from the car radio, and I wondered if the idea of this was to stop me calling for help. On balance, I decided, I'd much rather be gagged.

We parked in a lane that ran past walls and high fences, behind which I supposed rich folk must be sitting out the lockdown in their huge houses, not knowing or caring about my own predicament. The two men with me escorted me down a dirt track leading to an empty campsite, where the other cars were waiting together with Collett, the Pigeon, Siobhan and a few of Collett's goons. Collett was telling off one young goon for something or other.

Siobhan and I were encouraged to walk across the field, past a fallen wire fence, and into a looming mass of rhododendrons.

"You two, hack a way through, would you?" demanded Collett, pointing at a pair of his men. But the goons were no match for the plants, whose branches were far stronger than they looked, and the hapless duo could do little more than break off smaller twigs to clear a sort of tunnel. So we progressed slowly, sometimes upright, sometimes on all fours, for about ten minutes until we reached an unexpected clearing, flanked by rhododendrons on all sides. Tussocky patches of rush alternated with rank grass, and a couple of large pieces of weird looking farm equipment were rusting in one corner. *They could kill us here*, I thought, *and no-one would ever know*.

"Aha!" said Collett. "Right on cue."

The wall of rhododendrons on one side had changed. The best way to describe it is to visualise the plants as a sort of three-dimensional water-colour painting, and then to imagine that all the ink had started to run, and twist into a spiral getting tighter and tighter towards its centre. Bits of sky and grass were mixed in there as well, and the proportions of these changed if you moved your head. It made me dizzy to look at it. At five metres across, it was even smaller than the previous day's Glory. Were they deliberately picking smaller ones, to avoid attention? Or maybe most of the Glories were small and hidden, with only the big ones getting found, except by this mysterious predictor that they had. I wondered how he – or she, or it – was doing it. If only Locksley could get her hands on whoever or whatever it was, then everyone might start getting some real answers as to what was going on.

The sound of someone crashing about in the rhododendrons brought me back to the present. It was coming from a different direction to where we'd come from. A man with a large machete burst clumsily from the foliage, followed by a second, older man.

Chapter 27: Julia Barnes, slave

The second man looked utterly incongruous in this setting. He wore a suit, for one thing, indeed he looked the sort of man who never wore anything else. A virus mask and sunglasses (slightly askew) concealed much of his face, but even so, he oozed wealth and power. He took an angry step forward and pitched over, with flailing arms, into a ditch that he hadn't seen. Feodor and another man rushed forward to help him, but the suited man brushed them off impatiently.

"Now see here, Mr Collett, I am a sick man, and I expected better treatment than this," he snarled, before dissolving into a coughing fit.

"My apologies, sir. I shall knock one percent off your fee for the inconvenience. I am afraid that I have no control over where the Glories choose to appear, and very limited warning of where or when they will do so. Given more warning, I would have bulldozed a path through these troublesome shrubs for you. Nonetheless, as you can see, everything is ready, and in just thirty minutes you will once again be a healthy man."

"Dear God," said the rich man. "Is that ... that's a Glory ...". He raised his sunglasses onto his forehead to get a better look. So I could see his eyes now, but I didn't recognise him.

"You'll need to get a little closer," said Collett. The man nodded and moved forward, unsteady on his feet. He didn't look anywhere near as sick as I had been, nor the old Mrs Kumar from yesterday, but I knew that it was perfectly possible for terminal cancer patients to appear healthy, at least for a little while. Or, perhaps he wasn't even at that stage, merely 'battling' cancer, as the media always called it. If you were rich enough, you'd splash a fortune just to banish your Bernard early, save yourself months or years of fear and misery. I wondered if he knew that Siobhan and I were being forced to co-operate. I wondered if he'd care.

Siobhan took my hand, and I was going to take the rich man's, but Collett shook his head, and beckoned forth the young man he'd been telling off, before. "Ryan, come here a minute, would you?"

"Yes boss?" said Ryan. Collett punched him hard in the face, sending him sprawling to the ground with blood spurting from his nose.

"Bot duh buck dud yer do dat fur," said Ryan.

"Science, my boy. I'm sure our client would like to see physical confirmation that the treatment we provide will be genuine. In fact, Sir, if you might like to make a little cut in Ryan's hand, yourself, to serve as further proof?"

"I'd just like to get on with it," said the rich man.

"Fair enough," said Collett. "Take Ryan's hand, and Ryan, you join with Ms Barnes. Good. Now Ms Smith, if you would touch the Glory?"

Again, that swirling maelstrom of thoughts and feelings that weren't mine. My nose hurt, and linked to it was Ryan's indignant embarrassment. There was a sense of acute anger, from Siobhan, mixed in with love and fear for Sammy, at home on his own. Oddly, the man we were curing was the one I could feel the least. Distant flashes of boardrooms, golf courses, exotic holidays, a stoic wife he had no fondness for, and several much younger women that he clearly did, made up a superficial vignette of his life. Lurking below all this was fear, coupled

Chapter 27: Julia Barnes, slave

with a sense of outrage that his ongoing rise in the world was being cut short by something as sordid as illness.

We detached. Ryan's nose, though slightly askew, was no longer bleeding. "How do you feel?" asked Collett pleasantly.

"My nose doesn't hurt any more, but ..."

"Not you," said Collett angrily to Ryan. "Our client," had added, more softly.

The rich man ran his hand around parts of his torso, under his jacket. "Well, it feels like it's gone, but I shall have to see my consultant to be sure," he said.

"You do that," said Collett happily. "And when he declares you all clear, you can send the second half of the payment."

"We're being forced to do this against our will," declared Siobhan, suddenly.

"What concern is that of mine?" replied the rich man. He walked across the clearing, no longer stumbling or unsteady, and followed the machete man through the bushes in the way that they had come.

"Now that was foolish and unhelpful," said Collett to Siobhan. "Our client knows that we are bending the law a bit, and appreciates the need for complete discretion. He cannot blow the whistle without implicating himself. Now, I believe I owe you both 25 thousand pounds, but given your behaviour today I shall keep that money on the tab for the time being, and give it to you once our business relationship is dissolved."

"And when will that be?" I asked him, coldly.

"Given the rate at which things seem to be changing, I suspect that the window for making money in this fashion will prove to be fairly limited. We must take advantage while we can. Now, we had only the one client today but I intend to have several lined up for tomorrow, so let us return to our base and have a good rest."

We tunnelled our way back through the rhododendrons. I wondered about fleeing, but even if I briefly got ahead of the pursuers, the noise of crashing through these bushes would quickly have them upon me.

Soon we were heading home, a grim procession of two cars (Collett and the Pigeon had gone off in another direction, no doubt to solicit more business). Once again I was in Feodor's car, and the one in front had Ryan driving and another goon in there with Siobhan, no doubt to keep her in line. Then their car suddenly swerved, and careered into a ditch.

Feodor swore in what sounded like Russian, and stopped the car. "You, out," he said, opening the door of the back and yanking me onto the verge before I'd had a chance to obey. He propelled me into the ditch, locked the doors, and ran forward towards the stricken car. I saw a back door open, and Siobhan staggered out. She took one look at Feodor, and pointed a shaking gun at him. Feodor also drew a gun, pointing his at her.

"Now now," he said. "I really don't think this is a good idea. Only one of us knows how to use a gun, and it isn't you."

"Yeah?" she replied icily. "Well, your boss only needs one of us alive, and it isn't you!"

Chapter 27: Julia Barnes, slave

"That is a fair point," he said. "Maybe I'll just shoot you in the leg. Then you can lie there in agony until Mr Collett is kind enough to find you a nice Glory to get you better."

Siobhan squeezed the trigger, but nothing happened. Then I whacked Feodor on the back of the head with a stick. His gun went off, blasting the ground right next to Siobhan's foot. He staggered forward two paces, and turned around towards me. Panicking, I barged into him, pushing him over and landed on top of him as he fell onto his back. The impact stunned him enough for Siobhan to run forward and grab the gun from his hand. By now, both Ryan and the other goon were struggling their way out of the car in the ditch.

"Get back in the car!" Siobhan shouted. "Both of you!" And she fired a warning shot. They obeyed, struggling back into the car stuck in the ditch. "Get his keys," Siobhan said, and I took the keys from Feodor's other hand. He was clearly still conscious, but made no attempt to resist. "Get up, and go lie in the ditch," commanded Siobhan, and he slunk across the verge and into the ditch, crawling on all fours. Then she jumped into the driver's seat of the other car, and I got in beside her. Feodor's phone was still in the holder above the dashboard, and it pinged as we sat down. We ignored it. "We drive to the nearest town, dump the car, disappear," she said.

"What about your son?"

"I'll call a friend, have them move him from the house, until I get there."

She started the engine and we seared off down the road. "I told the guy next to me that if he shot me his boss would cut his balls off," she said as she drove. The phone in the holder pinged again. "Then when I could see that the message had sunk in, I whipped out a rope I'd made from my bedsheets and worn round my waist all day, and got the driver round the neck. Boom! We went right off the road. Hurt like fuck but at least I was braced for it."

"That was incredibly risky," I said, though I couldn't help admiring her gumption.

The phone pinged again.

"Wasn't it?" she declared, face alive with triumph. "No bastard fucks with me!"

The phone pinged twice more, and a recorded voice told us to *proceed to the route*. I realised that the satnav on the phone could tell us exactly where Collett's base was, which would be useful for the police to know. But the screen was partially obscured by a series of text messages:

```
Mummy, it's Sammy.
Mummy, are you there?
I'm scared mummy.  Sammy.
Mummy, Mr Collett wants to talk to you.
```

They were bluffing, I thought. Please let them be bluffing.

Ping!

```
Mummy, there are two men in the house and they say they're going to hurt me if you don't stop the car.
```

"What's it saying?" asked Siobhan. "Julia! What is it saying?"

"They're saying they've got Sammy."

Chapter 27: Julia Barnes, slave

"WHAT?" the car screeched to a halt, and she grabbed the phone. Frantically she tried clicking it, but she couldn't get it to unlock.

Ping!

```
They say you have to turn around the car and go back.
They already pulled Mr Plumpkins' arm off.
```

"No, no, NO!" yelled Siobhan, banging the wheel in frustration.

"They could be bluffing?" I tried.

"Mr Plumpkins was Sammy's favourite toy when he was little. No-one knows that name 'cept him and me! They've got him!! They've got my boy!" The rage bled out of her voice, and she began to sob.

"I guess we'd better turn around then, hadn't we?" I said gently. "Do you want me to drive?"

* * * * *

"You're very resourceful, I'll give you that," said Collett, as we sheepishly got out of the car. He, the Pigeon, and two others had joined the three hapless goons that we'd got the better of. "So I fear we will have to make a few changes how we do things. Ms Smith, I have two employees in your house, keeping your son company. Don't worry, he's not been harmed, nor will he be, as long as we have no more instances of ... resourcefulness. He believes they work for the government, and is quite unaware that they will shoot him if you misbehave again. I think it suits both of our purposes that things remain that way.

"Now Ms Barnes, I understand that you were not the instigator of this little escape plot, but nonetheless I'd like to ensure your own co-operation as well. This is a friend of yours, I believe?"

He showed me a picture on his phone. It was Lara, eyes bulging in fear, with duct tape over her mouth. "I'd been hoping she might be useful in moving Glories into more convenient locations, but it turns out her abilities are rather hit and miss. But I'm sure I'll find a use for her. Exactly what sort of use, rather depends on you."

"I get the message," I said icily. Siobhan and I had our hands tied behind our backs, and were put into the back seats of separate cars while the goons tried and failed to pull the car out of the ditch. One suggested towing it, but Collett decided to leave it there.

"We'll buy another one out of the ladies' share," he said simply. Then a goon got in either side of me, and I was driven back to base with loud music blaring in my ears.

As I was walked to my room (hands mercifully freed), I asked to be allowed to see Lara. "She's not in this house," said a goon. He let me talk to her briefly on the phone – she sounded scared, but alright. As far as she knew, she said, they didn't have Lucasz.

"OK, that's enough," said the goon, and snatched the phone away.

Confined to my room once more, I saw that a few weedy sandwiches had been dumped on the tiny little table: insubstantial bread, a slice of cheap ham and

some rubbery sliced cheese. They would have cost about forty pence each to make, I reckoned. How miserly was Collett, really?

That got me wondering just how much money he'd made, today, and indeed yesterday. He'd been (allegedly) willing to pay us fifty thousand pounds between us, even though he had us under his control. Not to mention being willing to leave a perfectly decent looking car lying in a ditch, as if it were not worth retrieving. The conclusion, clearly, was that his money was chickenfeed compared to what they were getting from their clients. A round million, perhaps, from the man today?

Again, I turned on the telly to pass the time. It was both reassuring and absurd that daytime TV quiz shows were still being shown, normal as anything, while I was a prisoner, fearing for my life. I recalled something else Collett had said, that he didn't expect this operation to last more than a week or so. Would he really let us go, after that? And was he right that things were changing so fast, now? Were there more and more Glories, each day? The BBC news was cautious about Glory numbers, and while Channel Four gave an "at least" figure, it felt like an under-estimate.

Channel-hopping, I found a specially commissioned current affairs show, in which 'experts' from various backgrounds discussed the Glories. The word 'experts' was of course a bit of a joke, since no-one on the panel had a clue. A scientist tried to claim they were electromagnetic disturbances, and that perhaps our planet (and solar system) was passing through an anomalous region of space.

"Then why are they only happening in Britain?" someone asked him.

"They're not," the scientist said snootily. *"Other countries are simply doing a better job of keeping it quiet than we are."*

"Why can't you accept," said a man in a dog collar, *"that these phenomena simply cannot be explained by science? Tell me, what is the difference between a human eye, and a camera?"*

A female biologist answered. *"There is no great difference. Both capture and focus light. Of course, the receptors are different, but I would argue no more different than a digital camera is from a film camera."*

"Exactly!" said the priest gleefully. *"Which means science can offer no explanation for why only human beings can see these things! Why only our flesh can interact with them, when animals are blind to them and go right through! It is the soul! That which has a soul, sees and touches the Glory. That which does not, cannot!"* He folded his arms as if to declare the argument thoroughly won. I had to admit, he had a point, and I thought fondly of Walt and his little group.

"As ever, religion seeks to capitalise on anything that science does not, YET, have an explanation for," replied the male scientist, drily.

"While you have tried for centuries to dismiss us because you claimed you COULD explain everything," the priest shot back. *"Well, this time you can't, and more and more people are seeing the truth. The Lord had stepped back from our lives for a long time, leaving us to mind our affairs, the affectionate father leaving his children to make their own mistakes, but now He is back. The message could not be more obvious."*

The female biologist stifled a snigger.

"What?" said the priest, affronted.

Chapter 27: Julia Barnes, slave

"Well actually, assuming you're right, which I seriously doubt, I can think of one or two ways that He could have made it a little *more obvious."* She adopted a deep, avuncular voice. *"Well Holy Ghost, it is time to return to the world of Men and remind them of My message."* She switched to a spooky voice and wobbled her hands. *'Shall I carve new commandments into a big mountain, or perhaps write them across the sky, my Lord? Or perform a miracle and purge the pandemic overnight? Maybe a big star in the sky like before?'* She switched back to the avuncular voice. *'No, no, what I want you to do is scatter a load of strangely coloured objects around the countryside where not many people will see them, and make it impossible for them to share images of them too. Oh, and don't do it everywhere, only in southern England.'"*

The male scientist sniggered, and so did I.

"It is not for us to question the ways of the Lord," said the priest, who looked furious that his killer point had not settled the matter.

"Oh, right, shall we all go home, then?" mocked the biologist.

* * * * *

After a miserable lonely night, I spent most of the morning waiting for something to happen. It was almost lunchtime when they finally unlocked the door and told me to move. "We're not gonna tie your hands this time, but if you try anything funny you'll be bound and gagged in the boot," said one of the two goons, gruffly.

"Noted," I replied. They had the look of squaddies, with crew cut hair, muscles and no brains. How many goons did Collett have working for him? The number had certainly increased since that trial run on the golf course. I'd counted at least eight, and there were probably one or two minding Lara. And Sammy, too. All had to be paid, and not trivial amounts, either. Again I wondered just how much the very rich were willing to pay for a complete cure.

As I got into a car I saw Siobhan, hands tied, walk out with two more goons beside her, and a very battered looking Ryan, with two black eyes and his arm in a sling, injuries from the crash, looking daggers at Siobhan. The ones who'd walked me from the room squeezed in either side of me, and we were away. Feodor was driving, with the Pigeon beside him in the front, and we were clearly in a hurry. Was the Glory more than an hour's drive away, or had they been given less warning than usual?

Half an hour later, Feodor swore in Russian. A tornado was rising up some distance ahead of us, and then ballooning outwards into a mushroom shape at the top. "That will be seen for many miles!" he exclaimed.

"But I think it will provoke fear, rather than a desire to visit," the Pigeon replied. "In that respect, we are fortunate. I shall text the clients and confirm it as our destination."

Ten minutes later we were practically underneath it, parking on a minor road under a bridge where a dual carriageway passed above us. The car with Siobhan in it joined us. "Well, would you look at that," said Collett, happily. A graffiti artist had spray-painted the words 'STAY HOME' across the concrete bridge

Chapter 27: Julia Barnes, slave

support in huge letters, accompanied by a stylised version of the Grim Reaper. "That's what I call community spirit."

We started walking up a footpath with a lot of brambles either side, and Siobhan's hands were untied. The sun was completely blotted out by the giant swirling tornado, but we could feel its warmth, and see the shadows it cast. Far more disorientating was the virtual absence of wind – the breeze was barely sufficient to move a blade of grass, yet the broiling maelstrom surface of the tornado raced past at terrifying speeds. It had to be twenty metres across at ground level.

"Remarkable," observed the Pigeon, almost reluctantly. We had entered an area that looked like it had once, long ago, been buildings, before being mostly ceded back to nature. Thorny shrubs competed for space with burnt-out cars, slabs of concrete, dirt tracks rutted by motorbikes, and other sundry chunks of human detritus. Further on it gave way to a wood, only part of which we could see, because the Glory had swallowed the rest. Sprigs of shrub and tree sticking out of the tornado in a few places simply hung there, unmoved.

"He wants you two to be touching it, before the clients arrive," said the Pigeon.

I expected Siobhan to protest, or at least offer some sort of comeback, but she simply nodded, gestured at me to follow, and we walked towards the Glory. I felt wobbly on my legs, still unable to process the absence of wind.

"It's hard to look at," I said.

"We won't have to in a minute," she replied. "I'll go first." She walked right up to it, the first time I'd seen her touching a Glory without me doing it with her, and put her hand onto its surface. The effect was extraordinary. At first, the swirling grey lines near the point where she'd touched it changed direction, forming into spinning circles around her hand. Then the Glory started to expand around her, swallowing her hand, her arm, and her body.

I turned to the others in alarm. "Th-that's not meant to happen, is it?"

"It always happens that way, you fool," said Feodor. "You just don't see it. Now touch her!"

I obeyed. For a few fleeting moments I saw the Glory respond, and watched it slowly engulf my hand and arm.

Chapter 28: The addict

Antony

The crashing thing in the bushes was almost upon us now. I thought about running away again, but Sally still hadn't caught her breath. So I moved between her and whatever was coming, and faced it.

A man stumbled out from the bushes. His hair was scraggly and a thin beard was starting to grow, matching his unkempt clothes. His face had multiple scratches, and his eyes looked haunted. His left trouser leg was badly ripped in one place, and I could see a long scratch in the flesh below the rip. He looked perhaps forty years old.

"Is it here?" he asked, staring at us with wide eyes. "Is it here?"

"Is what here?" asked Sally.

He looked around, jerking his head this way and that. He seemed in a state of panic. "The Glory, of course! It's here, it has to be here. It didn't just disappear, did it? It has to be here!"

"We haven't seen one today," I said. "But we can help you look."

"It's close," he replied. "Very close. I can feel it, I can always feel them!"

"Maybe this one's harder to see than usual?" I walked over to a wide holly tree, and circled around behind it. I saw nothing out of the ordinary.

The man followed, saying "Yes, yes, it's this way, it's here somewhere. I think it moved!"

"You can feel them?" I asked. "You can feel where they are?"

"That's what I'm telling you! There's one right here!"

Sally shot me a meaningful look, and the penny dropped in my head. There was a Glory here, of course there was. It was me.

"Listen," said Sally. "Perhaps we've found an invisible Glory. I dunno, maybe it's ultraviolet in colour or just invisible. Or maybe it hasn't appeared yet, or something. There's a few stories out there of people who know where the Glories are going to be, before they appear."

"But it's here, now," said the man. "I can feel it. Can't you?"

"I'm not sure," Sally said. "You seem to be very well tuned to them?"

"Hah!" said the man. "Well-tuned, I like that. Yes, I can feel them. I can always fucking feel them. Day and night. It's like there's this massive hole in me. You ever been in love? I mean properly, break-your-heart-forever-if-she-leaves-you in love? It's like that but a hundred times worse. It gnaws away at me, day and night. I wish I'd never seen that fucking thing. Got this phone call, three weeks ago. An old mate telling me, 'hey Rick, there's a Glory four miles from your house! You gotta go see it!' I don't do social media, waste of fucking time, and frankly when he tried to explain it, it sounded like he was having me on, except he doesn't have that kind of imagination. I'm stuck at home on my own with fuck all to do, so I think, why not. There's nothing to lose, is there? How wrong can you fucking be. So I jumped on my bike, don't have a car since the ex left me, then suddenly there's all these cars parked up along the lanes, and other ones hooting and hawing because they can't get past. I went right through on my bike, and there it was. A burning ball of deep blue, with ice blue flames flickering all around the edge. Bigger than a house. But if you looked into the middle, there were circles and spirals of different hues, drawing you

Chapter 28: The addict

down into it. I got as close as I could, felt I had to, getting far too near to other people, but it was like nothing else mattered. I think I stared at it for hours. We all did. I felt total peace, contentment. I could have stayed like that forever. Then it vanished. And there were just dozens of people looking confused and a bit embarrassed, and the sound of a police siren coming from somewhere. I jumped on my bike and made myself scarce."

He seemed determined to keep talking, so Sally and I nodded for him to keep going.

"The first hour or two after, I felt OK. Better than OK, in fact, like the warm glow you get after … well, you know, I think," he looked at us then, as if noticing us properly for the very first time. "But by the evening, I was starting to feel a bit weird. Empty. I went out on the bike, not even knowing why, rode around for two hours, but when I got home I felt worse. I was shaking. I kept seeing the Glory in my head. I couldn't eat, didn't sleep all night. Ended up walking around in the dark. It got even worse the next day. I managed to eat, but everything tasted like cardboard. Gradually I realised that only one thing would make me feel better, and that was seeing another Glory.

"Oh, I'm not stupid, I know what addiction is. I stayed at home, I fought it. Read up on grade A drugs, cocaine and heroin, cold turkey and how long it lasts. But it didn't stop. After a week I felt just as bad as that first morning after seeing it. I dreamt of the bloody things, whenever I could sleep, which was hardly at all. Managed to see a doctor – virtually of course – and he said it was all in my head. Fucking moron. Eventually I did the only thing I could do, and gave in to it. Went out looking for more Glories. I had this crazy idea that seeing a second one would fix me. I didn't really believe it, but also didn't think it could make me any worse. By then I knew that I could feel them. A few days later I'd felt this pull, coming from the northeast, and I knew there was one close by. Later I learned that there had been, fifteen miles away. So I saddled up my bike and went riding, got the feel of one on my second day out, followed the feeling all the way to this hidden dell in some forest estate. There was no-one else there. Just this giant ruby the size of a chair hanging a metre off the ground. No-one would have known about this one if I hadn't been drawn to it. I wonder how many there are out there, that nobody sees?

"I was with it for three hours. I felt absolute, total bliss. Then it was gone, and the same thing happened – a few hours of feeling OK, and me daring to hope that I was cured, but then it all came back, the addiction and longing, just as bad as before. That night, I almost hanged myself.

"Next morning I packed up a sleeping bag and some supplies, and went out on my bike. There was nothing for me to do but look for more Glories. I've found three more since then, one of them was that moon in the field."

"We were there too," said Sally with a smile.

"A few hours here and there, of feeling totally alive. That's all there is for me now." He sagged, his story completed.

"How do you feel now?" asked Sally, cautiously.

"Do you know, I feel OK," he said, as if he were a little surprised by the fact. "Really good actually. I think you must be right, there's an invisible Glory here. I'd been so busy looking for it, I hadn't even realised. I feel great!"

"You look hungry," said Sally. "When did you last eat?"

Chapter 28: The addict

The man – Rick, his name was – looked for a moment as though he didn't understand what Sally was talking about. "We can spare you a sandwich or two," she said.

Rick accepted the offer, biting the sandwich cautiously at first, and then tearing into it like a lion at a kill. "This is great!" he declared. "Got any more?"

She gave him two more of her sandwiches. After all, he did look half-starved.

With food inside him, Rick seemed keen to engage in small-talk. Sally gave him a very simplified account of our last few days together, telling him merrily how the two of us had joined forces to try and see the big earth Glory, and ended up falling in love. He didn't seem to recognise me as a missing person from the news.

"Not hungry?" Rick said to me at one point, as Sally tucked into a sandwich.

"Do you know, I've hardly ever seen him eat," said Sally jokingly, and that seemed to satisfy him.

An hour passed. It was a lovely day, and it felt good to rest, but I was starting to feel that I wanted Sally all to myself once more. But Rick, of course, showed no inclination to move. By now he was convinced there had to be an invisible Glory very close by.

"There could be hundreds of invisible Glories around," said Sally. "Most people would walk right through without even knowing it."

"Huh," said Rick. "Look at that, I've got a special power. A completely useless one."

"Might not be," said Sally, with a meaningful glance at me. "I mean, scientists are probably desperately trying to understand these things even as we speak. A man who could find them would be very useful to them."

Rick's face exploded with anger. "Are you fucking kidding? Haven't you seen what they're saying in the papers? That bloody Collins bloke? *Glory addicts are the enemies of society*! One of them ran down a little girl, well that's what the bloody tabloids are saying. '*Lock 'em up!*' Blaming us for every fucking road accident. They're building a gulag, right here in England, you know that? Of course, they're not *calling* it that. So no, I'll not be turning myself over to the government, thank you very much. I'm not spending the rest of my fucking life in an insane asylum. Luckily it's just me and my bike. It's the drivers they'll be going after."

"I'm sorry," said Sally gently. "I've read a bit about this addiction to Glories, but I steer clear of tabloids."

"Did you say Collins?" I asked. "The Tory MP?" Rick nodded. "He was on a chat show yesterday, and you're right, he's a smarmy git. I'm not even sure it's only the Glory addicts that they're going to be targeting."

A little later, Rick stood up and announced that he needed to 'visit some bushes'. As soon as he was out of earshot, I quickly asked Sally:

"What are we going to tell him?"

"About you?" she asked.

"Yes, of course about me. If he finds out I'm a Glory he'll probably follow me around for the rest of my life! But I don't see how we can get away from him! He's not going to leave, not as long as he feels there's a Glory here. And

Chapter 28: The addict

if we try to leave, he'll feel the Glory moving and he'll start following us! And then he'll work it out."

"Even tying him to a tree wouldn't work," pondered Sally, half-seriously. "Because as soon as he got away, he'd still be able to sense you. But you know, he could be exactly what you need, if you want to find Daniel. I've been thinking that ... oh, he's coming back. Look, follow my lead, OK?"

Rick waddled back, asking Sally to pour a little water so he could wash his hands. "I have a suggestion," she said. "We live on a farm about eight miles from here, and there's an annexe with a bedroom in it. Do you want to stay there for a couple of days?"

"I don't know," he replied. "Once this invisible Glory goes, I'm not going to be good company."

"I was wondering," said Sally. "Could it be that it's just human company that you're needing? I'm not denying the Glory addiction, not at all, but I'm wondering if just being around other people is making you feel better.'

Rick shrugged, looking unconvinced.

"We've both been in contact with Glories," said Sally. "Do you think you might be feeling that? They clearly affected you. Maybe they somehow attached to us as well? Let's try walking a bit together."

Rick was reluctant to leave the spot where we were. "OK, well, it's your choice," said Sally. "We've got an eight-mile walk to get home, so we'd really better get started."

"I'm staying here," he said. "It was good to meet you. And thank you, for the food, and the company."

So Sally and I walked away, wondering what Rick would do now, and wishing we could help him. Forty minutes later he turned up again, out of breath and bedraggled, running along the path behind us.

"It's you," Rick said, gasping. "One of you, or both. You were right. You've got Glory attached to you, somehow. When I'm close to you, the withdrawal effect goes away."

"Okay," said Sally. "Well, I guess the offer of a room in the annexe is still open."

"I want to know which one it is," said Rick, looking from Sally to me. "Would you mind? Would you mind walking apart for a moment?"

Sally and I looked at each other, but I couldn't think of a good reason to say no, and it seemed neither could she. We nodded, and I went one way down the path, and she the other, as if it were some Victorian duel. I'd gone maybe twenty metres when Rick called "Stop!" We stopped. Rick was gazing at me. "It's you," he said, face beaming with a strange form of awe. "They're all on you."

"OK," said Sally. "I guess you can come back to the farm with us, and we can talk about it some more."

"Oh fuck," said Rick.

"What?"

"My bike," he said sheepishly. "I left it about three miles that way. Don't suppose you'd be willing to walk with me and get it, would you?"

* * * * *

Chapter 28: The addict

We finally got back to the farm at about 5 pm. I could tell Sally's legs were getting stiff from the way she was walking, but she didn't say anything, probably because both of us were getting pretty sick of the constant apologies from Rick, for causing so much trouble, for being a gooseberry, for taking us so far out of our way, for imposing on us ... the list went on. But I felt sure that if I pointed this out to him, he'd have apologised for all his apologies. Still, I did feel genuinely sorry for him – he'd clearly been through hell, and somehow being around me was the only treatment that worked.

We settled him into the room in the annexe, a newer part of the building that I'd barely been in, and then Sally set about cooking, while I watched telly. Another fatal accident was on the news, with three people dead. There was Barry Collins again, who seemed to spend most of his life doing zoom interviews on telly, saying once again that something had to be done. It had happened three miles from the location of a widely reported Glory, somewhere in the north. Sally carried a portion through to Rick in his room. We couldn't eat together, of course, because I couldn't eat and we were a long way from being willing to tell him what I really was. But we did all sit together, a little later, to talk about plans. By that point, Rick had renewed his acquaintance with things like hairbrushes, shaving and personal hygiene, and he looked like a different man. But this only emphasised how unhealthily thin he was. He munched through a jar of stale biscuits as we talked.

"We're very keen to visit some Glories ourselves," Sally told him. "Antony has some sort of connection to them – we know that, thanks to you. We can't see any other way of understanding it, except to go to one, maybe even touch it. Have you actually touched a Glory?"

Rick had to think about it for a moment. "No, I don't think I have. It's funny but my memories of when I've actually been close to one, they're pretty hazy, like a night on the booze. But I think I was just happy to look, all three times."

"Do you think that touching one might fix you?" suggested Sally. "That maybe something's attached itself to you, that could be detached again?"

"Do you really think so?" he said, a little pleadingly.

"I honestly don't know," said Sally. "No-one understands any of this. All we can do is try, experiment a bit, see if something works."

"But how do we get to a Glory?" said Rick. "We can't all fit on my bike. Have either of you got a car?"

"Would you count a broken heap of metal lying in a ditch somewhere, maybe 20 miles away?" asked Sally.

"Not really, no," said Rick with a weak smile.

"Then we haven't."

"Ah."

There were two practical problems, we realised. One was locating a Glory, preferably in time to get there before the crowds, and the other was getting to it. Rick found a simple solution to the second problem, by calling a friend (once he'd charged his mobile, whose battery had been dead two days).

"Rob? Rick ... much better thanks. ... Yeah, I think it was a stomach bug, not the Corona. Hit me pretty bad but I'm a lot better now. Look, do you think, would it be possible to borrow your car for a few days, if you're still not using it?"

There followed a bit of small talk about how Rob hadn't much use for the car, having little love for the countryside and living just round the corner from a

Chapter 28: The addict

small supermarket, and how Rick would now owe him a pretty big favour, but the upshot was, Rick would come to Rob's garden the following day, and Rob would throw him down the key from an upstairs window.

"Well done," said Sally. "Now the big question is, do you think you'll still be able to feel the things, when being around Antony takes away the withdrawal effect?"

"I don't know," said Rick. "The effect around him is different from a proper Glory. I'm not compelled to gaze at him like he's something impossibly beautiful."

"For which I'm very grateful," I said.

"I do that sometimes, when he's not looking," said Sally, fondly.

"I don't know how close I have to be to feel them. The two I actually felt my way to were four and sixteen miles away, from the moment I first sensed them. Could be that I sense them just the same, even around Antony. But it could be I don't. I guess all we can do is wait and see."

"What if we went away from you, or you went away from us, for a bit? I know it would be hard, but it might help you detect them."

I watched him clench his fists, digging his knuckles into his palm. "It would be horrible," he said, "The withdrawal came back must faster when you two walked away from me today. But if there's no other way, I guess I'd be willing to try it."

"Well, let's give it a few days," said Sally. "See if you can sense them without having to do that. And I guess we can watch social media to look out for reports of one close by. Once we've got the car, we'll have a decent shot at getting to one."

The conversation wound down, but Rick didn't seem in any hurry to go to his room. Eventually Sally and I dropped increasingly unsubtle hints like brushing our teeth, and retired to our room.

"Are you OK?" she asked me quietly, once the door was closed.

"I feel sorry for him, and I'm glad we're helping him," I replied.

"Yes, but what about you? Is it weirding you out at all?"

"I guess it is, a little. Like having a very polite and apologetic stalker."

"How about I try and take your mind off it for a while," she said, looking at me with that meaningful smile that I've come to love above all others.

* * * * *

We woke to find Rick sleeping on the sofa in the living room. He somewhat wretchedly explained that he'd needed to move closer to our room – and me, because he'd started to feel withdrawal symptoms after an hour in the annexe. It seemed the further he was from me, the worse he felt, and the faster the symptoms came on.

The town where Rob and Rick lived was eighteen miles away. Walking seemed the only option, as he wouldn't go without me, and we only had the one bike. Sally told us she'd have to stay home, because her feet were sore from the previous day's walk and her legs were stiff; 18 miles would be too much for her. She said she'd use the time for some research on Glory addiction, to see if there was any other way that we could help Rick.

The prospect of spending the bulk of the day with Rick hardly filled me with joy, but in fact once we were under way, I found his presence a lot less

Chapter 28: The addict

annoying, given that he wasn't getting between me and Sally. To pass the time as we embarked on our long trek, he told me a bit of his life story.

"Mister ordinary, that's me. Or at least it was, until that fucking Glory turned me into a headcase. Met my wife when we were eighteen, and married by twenty-one. We just couldn't get enough of each other, back then. But then came kids, and careers. Looking back on it, I guess I can see how we fell apart in slow motion. We just had less and less time for each other. It was always the kids, her work or my work, the odd evening with friends. Sometimes we talked about stuff we'd do when the kids left home, or we retired. Yeah, we'll love each other later, when we've got a bit more time. Then last year, this woman started coming on to me at work. Younger than me, and hot, I'm telling you. Fucking hell, I felt like a proper stud just 'cos she was looking at me. I didn't do anything, then one night I was a bit drunk and I told the wife, I dunno why, I think maybe I was thinking that she'd think, blimey, my husband's still got it, and she'd rip my clothes off or something."

"But that wasn't what happened?" I said.

"Course it wasn't. What happened was that she burst into tears. Told me she'd been seeing this bloke. No kissing, no touching or anything, just walks and cups of tea. But I could see it in her eyes, right from the start, where it was fucking going, but it took a whole load of waffle before she got to it. That she was in love with this man. The very next day, I went to a hotel with the hot woman from work and bonked her brains out. It lasted about three weeks after that, because as soon as she got wind that my marriage was breaking up, she lost interest. The wife and I had a no-faults divorce. And then it was me, alone, ever since. Rob's divorced too, and the drinking sessions with him kept me going. I was just starting up a thing with a woman I met online, when the lockdown hit."

"And the Glories," I said.

"Yeah, funny how they both came together, isn't it? It's like the world's turning sideways. Kind of like my life, I guess. Forty-two years, following the normal path, boring and predictable. School, college, girlfriend, wife, bad job, good job, kids, promotion. Thought we'd grow old together, then she throws me a fucking curveball like that, and everything changes. The pandemic's done that to everyone, hasn't it? All the rules we lived by, boom! Gone or changed. Then the Glories come along, and it turns out we can't even trust the laws of fucking physics to stay how they were. Maybe we'll wake up tomorrow and dogs will wear clothes and speak English, or plants will start walking, or West Brom won't be shit anymore ... sorry, I'm rambling. Hardly slept the last few weeks. Except last night. When you can't sleep, then your mind goes to all sorts of weird places. So what's your story, kid? How'd you land yourself a cracker like that Sally?"

I wasn't at all keen to share my story in detail. So I let myself divert into long accounts of all the things I loved about Sally, like a lovesick idiot with verbal diarrhoea. It did the trick, and Rick soon ended the conversation. We pottered on in companionable silence for a while, remarking on the odd bird, plant or view, and pausing to check directions.

He did reveal snippets of his two weeks as a roving Glory-addict. Criss-crossing the countryside on his bike, seldom eating, sleeping poorly and at odd times of day. "Thing was, whenever I was moving it didn't feel so bad. Then when I stopped ... well I didn't stop for long."

Chapter 28: The addict

We made good time, and reached his village mid-afternoon. We stopped briefly at his house for supplies, which turned into half an hour of throwing out perishable food items from the fridge and kitchen that had turned into festering masses of mould. He collected his laptop, too.

Finally, we moved on to Rob's house. I suggested that I hang back out of sight to avoid awkward questions, and he was fine with that. "There you are, mate," called Rob from the window. "I left you a beer in the garden, look!"

"I'm driving, you moron," replied Rick happily.

"Oh, gee, I didn't think of that!" said Rob sarcastically. "But one won't take you over the limit, dickhead!"

"Well, maybe a few sips, you reprobate!"

I waited patiently while the banter went on, and at one point had to move into the road to let an old lady with a face like thunder shuffle past me. Finally, Rob tossed the keys down, Rick thanked him profusely, and walked to the car with the half-drunk bottle of beer in his hand. He got into the driver's seat while I slipped into the back behind him, hoping he wouldn't notice that I'd done it without opening the door.

"We – are – MOBILE!" declared Rick joyfully, as we pulled out onto the road.

"Yeah, but let's keep the speed down," I replied. "Last thing we need is police attention."

Rick clicked on the car CD player and sang along to a series of rock songs all the way home. Before long we were parking at the farm, and I was very much looking forward to getting thoroughly re-acquainted with Sally. I realised that we'd never really been apart since I'd met her. She'd clearly heard our car arrive, because she opened the door and came running out to meet us. But her eyes were puffy, her nose was red, and tears were streaming down her cheeks. "I'm sorry, Antony", she stammered. "I'm so very, very sorry."

"What?" I said, with fear and dread racing through me. "Sally, what is it?"

Chapter 29: Children, money and choices

Julia

I was sitting on the ground, with Siobhan beside me. Three men were staggering around close by, two of them in hospital gowns. Collett and his men were looking satisfied. The Glory was gone.

"Well, gentleman, how do you feel?" asked Collett, walking forward with a smile on his face.

The oldest man began flexing his arms and legs experimentally, turning a little and kicking an imaginary ball. "Do you know, I think the arthritis is gone completely? As for the other ... well I don't seem to have any gaps in my memory."

A young man in hiking gear came out of a path through the wood where the Glory had been. He came towards us and said "hey, were you a part of that? I touched that Glory and I could feel a connection with a lot of other people. And the headache I had is just ... gone! He turned towards me, still sitting on the ground. "You!" he said. "You, I saw your face. I touched the thing and I was sort of dreaming, and I saw your face!"

Collett walked forward, and spoke to the hiker. "Do you know the time?" Collett asked. "We've rather lost track." The hiker pulled out his phone to look, and Collett grabbed it from him in one swift motion.

"Hey, what the fuck are you doing?" said the hiker angrily. A goon held him still while Collett casually grabbed the man's right hand, and pressed his index finger against the phone, unlocking it.

"Mum ... Dad ..." said Collett, scrolling down the man's messages. "It's good to stay in constant touch with your family, now that we can't visit them. Ah! Now, who's Lizzie? Lots of messages from Lizzie. Goodness me! You lucky bastard!!" he slapped the hiker on the back. "I have to pay through the nose to get anyone to do that with me! Although, ah I see, you don't live with Lizzie, hence all the saucy texts. I'm guessing the two of you make some very interesting use of Zoom, as well. Well, we all have to get through it however we can, don't we?"

Collett handed the phone to the Pigeon, who was lurking nearby. "Copy down the man's name and number, and the numbers for Mum, Dad and Lizzie, would you? Just the landlines will do, I think."

The poor hiker looked angry, bewildered, and a little scared.

"Now," said Collett. "You and I need to have a little chat. You just had a free sample of a very special service that these gentlemen over here paid a very, very large sum of money for. Don't worry, it's *gratis*, but I do require your absolute assurance that you will say nothing of what you have seen here, and especially who. You can talk about the Glory all you like, but you don't talk about *us*. You saw the Glory, a great big tornado mushroom cloud thing, and it was very, very impressive. You didn't meet, see, or feel, any people, have you got that?"

"Uh, right," said the hiker, uncertainly.

Chapter 29: Children, money and choices

Collett put his arm round the man's shoulder, while one of the goons casually brandished a gun. "Now, if I get even a sniff that you've told anyone about what happened here today, the tiniest sniff, you understand … well, your mum will be getting the first visit, then we'll do your dad next. Sad that they don't live together any more, isn't it? Nothing ever seems to last these days. And as for young Lizzie, well let's just say you'd have to learn to share. Now, do we understand each other?"

"Uhhh, wh-who's 'we'?" said the hiker, with a terrified grin. "Th-there's no-one here but me."

"Hah!" said Collett happily, and he clapped the hiker on the back so hard, the man stumbled forward two paces. "Smart man! You get yourself off home now, and give your Lizzie a virtual one from me!" The Pigeon handed the man his phone. The hiker took it, backed away a few paces, turned, and then ran like the wind.

"Wise man," said Feodor, as they watched him go. "Much less trouble than beating him up or shooting him."

"Won't always work, though. We were lucky he was on his own. Have a couple of men check the other side of the wood, just in case."

The Pigeon was talking to another of the men in gowns, who had an expression like a kid on Christmas morning.

"I feel great!" he said. "I didn't honestly believe you could do it!"

"I'm happy for you," said the Pigeon. "Now you need to arrange payment, and you can be on your way."

"O-of course," said the man, a little less happily.

"Or you could come back with us, until the money comes through," said the Pigeon.

The third gowned man, who was much younger, had less to say but was flexing his arms and legs, and looking very confused. "Where am I?" He kept asking. "How did I get here? Where's Fi?"

Collett brought a phone over to him. "Perhaps you might like to speak to your mother, here? She's rather keen to hear that you are back with us," he said.

"Mum?" said the man. "Where the hell am I? What's going on? Where are you?"

I could just about hear a series of ecstatic shrieks from the other end.

"Mum? Are you alright? Yes I'm fine, I'm walking around, there's nothing wrong with me – why would there be? Is Fi there? What? My eighth birthday? I got stung by a wasp on my lips during a picnic in the zoo, you know that! Why are you asking me that?"

"I think she wants to make sure it's you," said Collett, taking the phone from his hand, and speaking now to the woman on other end. "I hope that dispels all doubts? Good. As soon as the money is transferred, we will deliver your son home to you."

"Listen, mate," said the man. "I don't know who you are or what we're doing here, but why are you demanding money from my parents? My father is a very powerful man, and …"

Chapter 29: Children, money and choices

"Your father and mother contacted me," said Collett. "Or rather, they responded to a discrete enquiry from my people. You were driving with your fiancée to Cornwall, I believe?"

"Yeah I was. I remember leaving, stopping off for lunch." He scratched his head, thoughtfully. "Where is she?"

"Ah. Now, perhaps I should start with the evidence. Paper, please?"

Feodor produced a newspaper from his small backpack, and handed it to the man.

"What's all this lockdown stuff?" he said, confused.

"Look at the date," said Collett.

I watched the exchange with interest. Siobhan and I were still sitting on the ground, a little way apart, while a couple of goons kept an eye on us, one casually touching the gun in his pocket from time to time. The oldest of the three patients had left, while the middle one was still worriedly holding animated discussions with the Pigeon. The youngest patient looked angry and confused.

"What the fuck is this?" he shouted. "The year's 2015! It's October, 2015!"

"Then why are all the trees just coming into leaf, instead of dropping them?"

The young man looked at the trees, and pulled a few faces as he tried to process all this information. "If this is some hidden camera shit ..."

Collett sighed. "Sir, you tried to overtake a car on a bend, at sixty miles per hour. You saw an oncoming car too late, and had a rather nasty crash. Your car, I'm afraid, was a write-off."

"Don't be ridiculous," he said. "I'm not hurt, not even a scratch. Now will you finally tell me, where's Fi?"

"Your fiancée suffered multiple injuries but recovered from them all. She waited for about two years before succumbing to the attentions of another man. Sir, you have been in a coma for four and a half years. Minimal brain activity."

"Some things haven't changed," smirked Feodor.

"Your parents, however, did not give up on you. They tried everything, up to and including the very exclusive therapy that my people have just performed, which restored you to full health, I'm pleased to say. Even seems to have fixed the muscle wastage – you were skin, bones and flab when we wheeled you here, let me tell you."

"Money's come through, boss," said Feodor, looking at his phone.

"Excellent! Ryan, drive this gentleman home, would you? No, actually, drop him at a service station halfway. I'll have his parents come and pick him up there. They'll like that."

Ryan, who was now free from all injuries, led the confused young man away. "Come on, people, we have lingered here long enough," said Collett. Siobhan and I got to our feet and started walking before anyone could push us.

"That one doesn't have the full amount," said a goon to Collett, indicating the worried man who was walking alongside the Pigeon.

"Oh?" said Collett, pleasantly. "How much does he have?"

"About sixty percent of what he promised."

"Ah. Now that is quite a shortfall." Collett hung back and positioned himself on the other side of the worried man.

Chapter 29: Children, money and choices

"Now Sir, you realise that we cannot simply give you back the cancer. So you must find some other way of …"

The rest was out of earshot as we got too far ahead of them.

"People watching from the flyover," observed a goon.

"Glory-watchers," said Feodor. He waved at the figures up there, and they waved back.

Then we were driven back to base, where another lonely night beckoned.

* * * * *

The following day began in a similar way. I found myself sat between two goons in the back of Collett's own car, which at least was a bit roomier. Collett had seemed a little agitated as we'd got started, but once he was driving, he seemed to calm down.

"Ms Barnes," he said. "I thought it was time for you and I to have a chat."

"If you wish," I replied.

"I am wondering," he said, "if you and I might be able to come to some sort of more amicable arrangement. One where, once our current operation comes to its end, we might part, if not as friends, then at least with minimal enmity."

"Perhaps you might make a start by not tying us up, or threatening my friends," I suggested.

"I might," he replied. "In truth, the tape was only on young Lara's mouth for under a minute, and do please recall that Ms Smith managed to overpower three of my men and dump a car in the ditch. You can, I hope, understand my caution on that front."

"Threatening her son is cruel," I said simply.

"The boy is quite happy," he replied. "Unlimited computer game time."

"I meant to the mother."

"But for the greater good," he said.

"I notice there haven't been any more Corona patients to cure, since the first time."

"Alas, they have been surprisingly difficult to source. Ironically so, given that during a pandemic we ought to be swimming in them. Hospitals are a no-go, and it turns out that the first care home was something of a fluke. No, unless we can make some sort of breakthrough, we shall have to focus our efforts elsewhere."

"Have you murdered anyone?" I asked. "I mean, in the course of your current, what did you call it … arrangement?"

"Operation, and no. I have not murdered anyone, nor ordered anyone else to."

"What happened to the man yesterday, the one who didn't have all the money?"

"Oh, him? Mister 60%? Ms Barnes, despite all of our differences, I do believe that you and I have one strong feature in common."

"Really?" I enquired. "And what might that be?"

"Honesty. We both value it. As a businessman, I consider it to be essential. I am honest in all dealings with clients, and expect the same in return." I noticed

Chapter 29: Children, money and choices

the '*with clients*' caveat – which meant he was not extending that same guarantee towards me or Siobhan. "To row back on a promise, that creates a problem. To make a promise that one never intends to keep, that is a bigger problem. Deliberate dishonesty. I take a very dim view of it."

"He was clearly desperate. Did he have terminal cancer? A man will do anything to survive, surely you must know that."

"Had he been honest and upfront, I'd probably have offered him a discount. As it is, I shall be giving him the opportunity to make good his debt to me. But we are getting off the topic, I think. I would like to make you a more willing participant in our arrangement, enough that you would choose not to contact the police about me when we go our separate ways. I'm thinking about helping children. Sick kids. Much easier to source, funnily enough, and we've already learned that you have a very soft spot for such families. So tell me, how many terminally ill children would I have to cure, to win your willing cooperation?"

I thought for a moment. "All of them," I concluded.

"Har har," he said humourlessly. "And I would like to be richer than Gates and Zuckerberg combined," he replied, "but this is reality, so we must find a way to compromise. How about one for one? One child cured, for each paying client?"

I thought about it. The image of that little bald boy, telling his weeping parents that he felt better. I had to admit, I might have acquiesced for the life of just one more such child. But I said, "Including all the clients we cured so far."

"One of those *was* a sick kid," he pointed out.

"Whose parents you nearly bankrupted with your fee," I countered.

"Then one sick kid for each paying client, past and present, excluding him. Do we have a deal?"

"Alright," I said. "But I can't speak for Siobhan."

"But perhaps you can speak *to* her," he suggested.

"If you can find something to offer her," I replied.

"I'm open to suggestions," he said.

"Remove all threats to her son, and replace them with the promise of a very large college fund?"

"What I like about you, Ms Barnes, is your sense of humour."

It felt unreal, to have had such an open and dynamic discussion with a man who was keeping me prisoner, and whom I strongly suspected to be an outright monster. It wasn't his treatment of me, Siobhan or even Lara that made me think so, nor even the threats about Sammy. It was the casual way in which he'd issued those threats to the hiker. I felt sure that none of us watching had been in any doubt about his willingness or ability to carry them out. Collett hadn't made any attempt to conceal what he'd said to the hiker. He'd acted like Siobhan and I weren't there, but he'd known we could hear it all, indeed had probably made sure of it. *This is what I'm capable of, and you'd do well to remember it.* I'd done a deal with the devil, even though logically it seemed an incredibly good deal. I had given him nothing he couldn't already take by force, and he was going to let us save the lives of children. Still, I felt sure there had to be a catch, even if I couldn't fathom what it could possibly be.

Chapter 29: Children, money and choices

* * * * *

"Up ahead," said the Pigeon. "That's got to be it."

Collett swore with gusto. "The bloody thing's huge!" he growled. "Again!"

I leaned forward to try and see if through the front windscreen. A series of enormous spheres were progressing upwards towards the sky. From this distance, each one looked about as big as the moon did in the sky, though it was impossible to tell how far away it actually was. Each sphere almost touched the one above and below, and each was a different colour: red, blue, orange, green, pink, yellow, purple, cyan.

"He said it would be a medium-sized one! He said that!" roared Collett, losing his cool in a way I'd never seen before. "How the fuck is that thing medium-sized? It's got to be visible for fifty miles around! It'll draw the crowds like bloody flies on shit!"

"I recall him saying something about the predictor being less accurate in the third dimension," observed the Pigeon.

"And that makes it alright, does it?" screamed Collett. "You know how much Client Seven is paying for today! You know what kind of man he is! You told me yourself how little he trusts us! And now I have to choose between performing our service in front of God knows how large an audience, or crying off for the day knowing that we'll probably never persuade him again!"

"Cancer is cancer, though. It's a powerful motivator," said the Pigeon.

"But it's not terminal yet. Means the bastard still has other options."

"So what do we do?" asked the Pigeon.

"Haven't you been listening?" Collett's voice was now getting comically high pitched, which would be funny if he didn't look like he was about to crash the car, or strangle someone. "I have not the slightest fucking idea what we are going to do, because for the second time running we've been sold a bogey!" He went silent, and the car trundled on, his driving mercifully unaffected by his mood.

"I see it now," he said in a calmer voice, the anger now more controlled. "I'm being played. How could I not have seen it before? Like a bloody teenaged greenie, buying his first drugs! The first hits are free, and you get the really good stuff. Then once you're hooked, it's like '*Oh I'm sorry, the good stuff's not there anymore, we've only got the crap stuff, I'm afraid. Unless of course you can pay me a bit more – well quite a lot more actually.*' Call the bastard. Call him now. Ask him how much he wants!"

The Pigeon apparently lacked the imagination to understand who or what Collett was talking about, and I enjoyed watching his very tentative expression as he said "Um, just for clarity, who are we talking about here?"

"Dexter, of course!" roared Collett, the self-control vanishing again.

The Pigeon winced just a little. He dialled the number tentatively, as if he were defusing a bomb. The phone rang and rang, while Collett muttered, "Answer, you bastard!"

Finally, the bastard did. "Put him on speaker," growled Collett. "Now listen here," he said loudly. "The last two Glories you found for me – yesterday and

Chapter 29: Children, money and choices

especially today – have not been suitable. Too big, too visible, too public! We have already had one near miss with an accidental onlooker. I need small Glories, and concealed locations, not bloody great light shows streaking up into the sky. If you want a bigger cut, then that can be discussed, I fully appreciate that you are an essential part of my arrangement. But I need a new prediction for today!"

"I will pass the message on," said the man on the other end.

"I want to speak to the organ-grinder, not the monkey!" said Collett, trying not to shout.

"Mister Dexter will consider your request," said the man, then he ended the call.

Collett swore again. "How far are we from the Glory?"

"Assuming the coordinates are correct, about fifteen minutes," said the Pigeon. "We'll get there ahead of most of the Glory-spotters, but probably not all of them."

Collett said, "Turn back the other clients. Tell them the truth, that this one's too public, and we'll alert them the second a better one is predicted."

The Pigeon began texting, rapidly. "And Polnukov?" he asked.

"I want to try. I know it's a risk, but if we can, I want to find a way. He doesn't look too ill, he can pass for healthy, we can try to do it all under the radar."

"And the kids?"

"We can't do it, too public. They think they're on a special trip to see a Glory," said Collett. "That's just going to have to become the truth, after all."

"Hang on," I said. "You had already lined up some kids for curing?"

"Call it a gesture of faith," said Collett. "Have they texted back yet?"

"Dexter's lot? No."

"Dammit! Tell them I'll pay them a hundred thousand for a discrete Glory prediction, today!"

The Pigeon texted. A response pinged through rapidly. "Same response, I'm afraid."

"What do they *want*?" snarled Collett. No-one in the car was dumb enough to say anything.

I found myself thinking of that bus full of kids, coming so close to salvation without even knowing it, and being denied. Then I thought of the Glory wrapping itself around Siobhan and then me, making us look like we were a part of it. And then finally, those two men who'd pretended to be cult members, being ignored by all the Glory-watchers as they marched around handing out addresses.

"I think …" I said carefully, "I think I might have an idea."

"Well, share it," said Collett, grumpily.

"If I do, and it works, then you cure the kids as well."

"If we possibly can, we will. Now share."

"If Siobhan and I were to press ourselves against the Glory," I said, "we might become almost invisible. You saw the way it wrapped around us. If we could get to it without anyone noticing? And then your client and the kids, too."

"Other people will touch the Glory, though," said the Pigeon. "They always do! They'll get caught up in the effect!"

"Yes, but if they don't know it's us causing it, it'll just be another Glory story that most people won't even believe," said Collett. "Our client can just act

Chapter 29: Children, money and choices

the role of a bystander. Seeing the Glory wrap around people will probably scare a lot of them off from doing it, anyway. The only problem is how we get the women to the Glory at the start, without them being seen."

"Oh, I thought of that," I said happily. "We pretend to be some crazy cult. I thought 'The New Age Luminarians' has a nice ring to it. Put pillow cases on our heads and go '*om om om*' as we walk towards it, have a few of your people aggressively tell the onlookers that they have to join us if they want to be Saved."

I knew it was risky to help them, and I could see so many ways it could go wrong. But those children deserved a chance. Perhaps that's why Collett brought them. Suddenly, exactly as he'd suggested, I had become a willing collaborator.

"And where exactly are we going to source all these pillow cases at very short notice?" asked the Pigeon, acidly.

"I think I can see a way of doing it," said Collett.

Collett had a mass of brown packing paper in the back of his car. I thought it best to not think about what it was intended for. He instructed everyone to wrap a piece around their faces, having first cut out two eye holes, and then secure it in place with duct tape. The effect was then completed with a second, conical piece put on top, and a randomly chosen symbol taped to each person's front. We all looked idiotic, and the goons looked deeply uncomfortable, which made me rather happy. The Pigeon had tried to argue his way out of it ("Someone needs to stay with the cars"), but Collett was having none of it, and the Pigeon's now thoroughly morose face was wrapped like everyone else's. Collett seemed to be having the time of his life organising all this. Siobhan seemed more co-operative than I'd expected, putting on the ridiculous garb with no fuss at all, and barely a word. I found myself wondering rather unhappily what they had been saying to her to take the fight out of her like that.

So, ten minutes later, we parked on an anonymous roadside spot, separated from the Glory by lines of trees, which kept us clear of crowds. The Glory, according to the prediction, was in the grounds of some huge estate that was open to the public, so most of the Glory-spotters would head for the estate's main car parks, the Pigeon reckoned. Our paying client had been told to do the same, act like a normal Glory-spotter, and keep touching the Glory until something happened.

We hurried along a slightly overgrown footpath in our stupid outfits. Through one line of trees, across a rough meadow, and through more trees, the colours of the Glory glinting through ahead of us. And then we were out, looking up a gentle grassy slope towards this truly remarkable sight. Every new Glory one sees is extraordinary, but this one, close up, was a little bit mind-blowing. Each new coloured sphere was a hundred feet across, emerging at a steady pace from the ground, so that the top was there first, before growing outwards as it rose, becoming a dome then finally a full globe, all one pure colour yet still clearly three-dimensional. As soon as one globe left the ground another started, each one taking perhaps fifteen seconds to emerge, and then proceeding upwards, indefinitely upwards, until they were too far away to see.

"Everyone copy my hand movements," said Collett, again clearly loving this pantomime that he and I had cooked up. We walked towards the Glory. I could

Chapter 29: Children, money and choices

see eight people already there, and more than a dozen approaching, some ahead of us, more from further away. Closer up, I saw that some kind of ruined folly was sticking out of the side of the Glory, with a faded information board dutifully holding court beside it, and right now garnering no attention at all. Those parts of the folly that were within the circular area of the Glory did not reappear when each sphere started to leave the ground. The space between the rising spheres was empty, except for a thin mist.

"We are the Servants of the Immortal Spectrum!" shouted Collett at the top of his voice. "Join us and be elevated to the higher plane of Chromatica! This world and all who remain on it will soon be ended by the energies of Tinctura! Join us and be saved! Join us! Join us!"

I joined in happily. His goons reluctantly took up the chant.

"Bit more enthusiasm," I told the one next to me. "We're supposed to be happy fanatics!"

Collect's performance had the desired effect, causing all the Glory-watchers to give us a wide berth. The Glory was big enough that it could easily be watched from various angles. Soon we were right next to it. Close up, the mist between the spheres revealed more texture, as if it were a collection of fluids that subtly differed in colour, and which flowed around each other rather than mixing fully. The overall effect was like a colossal, invisible tube of liquid, within which giant balls floated upwards while the fluid around them flowed down. Collett turned to me and Siobhan. "Flatten yourselves against it, like you said, Ms Barnes. Do it now."

We obeyed, and the Glory soundlessly swallowed us up once more.

Chapter 30: The breaking

Antony

Sally stood there, dishevelled and streaked with tears, by the farmhouse door.

"Rick," she said, "c-can you leave us alone for a bit?"

To his credit, Rick nodded and immediately made himself scarce within the farmhouse.

I reached out with my arms to hug her, but she shook her head and went inside, motioning me to follow. We sat down, facing each other, in the kitchen.

"Sally, what is it? Please tell me!"

"Wuh-wuh-when you went out this morning, I was OK at first. Went on the c-c-computer, looked up stuff about G-Glory addicts like I said I would. Th-there's some vile, vile people out there."

"Glory addicts?" I asked.

"No, you fool! People saying they should be locked up, chained up, caged, even lobotomised, one of them. That MP Collins, writers in the tabloids, all whipping them up. This *hatred*!"

"Sally, the country has always had its share of bastards," I told her.

"That's not the point! I started feeling sick, about an hour later. Nuh-nuh-nauseous. Thought I was gonna throw up, nearly did. Luh-like my heart was being pulled out of my chest. It got worse and worse. I was … at one point I was lying on the carpet, ripping into it with my nails …"

She showed me her fingers, scratched with blood, and with blue carpet fibres sticking out from under her fingernails. "I couldn't think straight. Thought maybe I'd got the Virus. Thought muh-maybe I'd die before you even got back. I didn't want to give it to you. Th-thought maybe I should go outside, c-get into the cow shed and just lie there until it was over."

"Oh, Sally," I said. I was crying too now, and I didn't even understand what was wrong.

"B-but it wasn't the virus. I think p-part of me already knew, but I couldn't admit it. A-a-and then, ten minutes ago, as your car pulled up, s-suddenly it got better and th-then I knew. I couldn't deny it any more, Antony." She looked at me, wide puffy eyes beseeching me to understand.

"Deny what?" I asked.

"Oh, you're so sweet," she said, as tears streamed down her face. "But so epically dim sometimes ... Antony ... I'm a Glory addict. I'm the same as Rick."

* * * * *

Sally and I stared at each other across the kitchen, as I tried to think of something to say. "When I met you," I said. "When I first met you, you were fine then, weren't you?"

"I wasn't fine, but I wasn't as bad as Rick. I'd seen one by then, but I hadn't been that close to it." Her voice was almost a whisper now, but she'd stopped shaking. "I'd felt empty and depressed ever since, and hadn't know why. I thought it was because I was alone, and maybe I was remembering the baby."

"Baby??"

Chapter 30: The breaking

"I was a very silly girl when I was sixteen. So I ended up having an abortion. Thought I'd got over it pretty well at the time. But it doesn't matter. Then I met you and I didn't feel depressed anymore."

I felt the world start to spin and shift, as if everything that was good in my life was falling away. "Hang on, hang on ... are you saying that ... the way you feel about me ..."

Her tears began anew. "Thing is, I don't know, Antony. I actually don't fucking know! All those feelings ... I thuh-thought they were love. When you feel good around someone and bad when you're away from them ... buh-but ... I don't know anymore. I don't know if it's you, or if it's the Glory in you."

"So you don't know if you love me," I said quietly.

"I don't know what my feelings mean," she said, which I took to be agreement.

"So what do we do now?" I asked her.

"I don't fucking know!!!!" she almost screamed at me, eyes burning with something like hatred. "I didn't ask for this! I didn't ask for any of this!!!!" Her tone softened. "I know you didn't either, and I know it's not your fault. It's just ... it's just ... I don't know what it is."

I reached out to take her hand, but she jerked it away. "No, don't touch me!"

And at that moment, I knew. I knew that whatever romance there'd been between me and Sally, was dead. Anger was rising within me, yet I knew it wasn't her fault, and that made it worse. There was no-one to take it out on. "I'm going outside," I announced.

"Don't go far," she replied immediately, her eyes wretched and pleading. Then her hands went up to her face and she began to sob, with tears and bogies flowing between her fingertips. But if she wouldn't let me comfort her, what could I do? I left her to it.

Outside, I found Rick, sitting with his back against the wall to the kitchen where I'd been, sipping the last dregs of his bottle of beer.

"Did you hear all that?" I asked him. "Did you listen in?"

"Heard her shout at you," he replied, sympathetically. "I'm really sorry, did I cause this?"

"No, of course not," I snapped, because the last thing I needed was yet another apology from Rick. "Ask her yourself." And then I strode off.

Part of me wanted to leave the farm, choose a direction, and keep walking. There was nothing left here for me but misery and dependence, and the ghost of murdered love. It wasn't Rick's fault. It wasn't Sally' fault. But if he hadn't forcibly attached himself to us, then Sally would never have learned she was a Glory-addict and we'd have had more days of bliss together. Now everything was broken, and I wanted to be anywhere but here. But even trembling with rage and loss as I was, I couldn't bring myself to inflict pain on either of them. So I ended up circling the farm in some stupid kind of orbit, not too close and not too far away, repeatedly climbing over the same fences and gates, passing the same animals and dried-up pools of mud.

More than an hour passed before I was finally ready to go inside. By then all I cared about was to negotiate some way out of this trap of people that I'd somehow fallen into. I walked in to find Sally in Rick's arms. I felt a brief surge of furious jealousy but it quickly passed, because it obviously wasn't like that.

Chapter 30: The breaking

She was sobbing against his chest and he was holding her like a father would, looking nobly towards the wall as she soggified his clothes.

"I've been comforting her," he said.

"I know," I replied stiffly.

"I've got daughters, you see."

"And you understand what she's going through."

"Pieces of it, yes," he replied.

"Well, I'm glad she's got you," I said coldly, and went outside again.

* * * * *

I walked the same circuit, again and again, trying to think about anything but Sally. It was difficult because I kept seeing her face in my mind, loving me, kissing me. Making me believe that I could be loved. I'd been OK until I met her – not happy, but OK. At least I had been before Daniel disappeared. My life had been alright. But now I felt utterly empty. I began to feel a sucking feeling inside my gut, as if someone's hand had gone in and started to squeeze. I was getting short of breath, which was ridiculous as I didn't need to breathe. Yet there I stood, gasping like a stranded fish. I shook my head, told myself to stop being an idiot, and started walking again. The breathlessness passed, but the pain in my belly got stronger, my organs seeming to all clamp together inside me. Now every step I took was hurting. Eventually I thought of Rick, and realised that maybe I knew what was happening.

I found him in the kitchen, sitting alone.

"Where's Sally?" I croaked.

"In bed. Suggest we let her rest, for now."

"I think I'm one too," I said.

"One what?" he asked.

"An addict. Like you and Sally."

He cocked his head sideways a little. "How come?"

I glared at him like he was stupid. "How you feel – the pain when you're away from Glories. I'm getting it too. So maybe it works the other way round with me, with me needing humans in the same way. Or one human. Her."

"That's got nothing to do with Glories, Antony."

"Of course it does, you fool! I *am* a Glory."

"No, you just picked up the essence of them, Sallys' reacting to it, same as me."

"That was a lie, you idiot," I shouted. "Oh, for goodness sake, look!" I snapped, and I walked into the middle of the kitchen table, my legs vanishing from view beneath it. His mouth hung comically open. "That's why you need to be around me, see? I'm not just touched by Glories, I am one! And no, I don't wanna talk about it, not right now. But if people can be addicted to Glories, then it's gotta work the other way round, hasn't it? I've got the same thing. I feel sick, like I can't breathe half the time, and this pain inside me like I've swallowed a fucking black hole and it's crushing me bit by bit from the inside!"

We stared at each other in silence for about a minute, all the time with my top half sticking right out of the middle of the kitchen table.

"Mate, you're just lovesick," said Rick gently.

"What?"

"What you're feeling is perfectly normal."

Chapter 30: The breaking

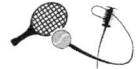

"This? How can *this* be normal?!?!"

"Love is like an addiction. At least in the pain you get when it's ripped away. Trust me, I know. It hurts like hell, you feel like you're gonna die, but it passes."

"I just want her back," I said, my voice wobbling. "You can talk to her. I don't care if she's addicted to Glories or anything else." Tears were streaming down my face. "I just want to be with her."

The answer was in his eyes, so I knew what he'd say before he said it. "I already talked to her. She said no. Said she can't trust her feelings, she's terrified of the addiction getting worse, she's scared that she'd fall deeper into it, every time she's with you. I'm sorry, I know it's not what you want to hear."

I strode from the room, blinded by tears.

* * * * *

I don't really want to say much about the two days that followed. Of course, eventually Sally stopped crying and the pain in my gut slowly deadened, but one look in her eyes was enough to tell me things could never go back to how they were. Meanwhile, Rick did his best not to look pleased about his elevation from unwanted gooseberry to peacemaker and comforter-in-chief. So in the end we sat down at the table like three colleagues who'd been thrown together by a disinterested manager to solve some difficult problem between us. The problem, of course, was how to get us to a Glory, and bring all three of us into contact with it. Unlike Rick, Sally had of course touched a Glory before, and this didn't seem to have had any effect on her addiction, but by unspoken consent none of us mentioned this. We each had our own reasons for wanting to do something practical, because otherwise we'd be stuck in this rut together for ever.

My quest to find Daniel gave us a noble purpose, beyond anyone's individual needs. Now that Sally and I were over as a relationship, Daniel dominated my thoughts again. His disappearance was linked with my becoming a Glory and losing a month – it had to be. In a way it made the puzzle a lot simpler, he was hardly going to hang around for five weeks waiting for me to move again, was he? But he hadn't gone home, unless his dad had been lying. Could he have been lying? I'd never liked Daniel's dad. I don't think Father really did, either. All that anger, when I'd gone to their house asking for him. His mother, she'd been all tears, as you'd expect of a parent who'd lost a child. But why had the dad been so angry?

It had to have been the Glory. I'd caused Linda and Thelma to fall into one, so the obvious answer was that the same thing had happened to Daniel. Except, I had to assume I'd only become a Glory during that lost month, and it followed that the ability to pick up pieces, and make people fall into Glories, had come along as part of that. So unless Daniel had been frozen there beside me, until I changed and made him fall in, then it didn't fit. More likely, what happened to him had been more like what happened to me. Could he still be there, frozen in time? Would the Glory appear once more, and him with it, unaware that five weeks or more had gone past? If so, all I'd have to do was wait. But that was a guess, and guesses could be wrong. I couldn't just wait.

I hadn't touched a Glory since I'd learned that I was now made of the same stuff. Perhaps that would make all the difference? Would we now be able to

Chapter 30: The breaking

communicate? If I learned how, would I be able to pull Daniel, Linda and Thelma back into the real world?

The first day after we got the car, we agreed, would be spent with Rick simply focussing himself on trying to sense a Glory that wasn't me, while Sally scanned social media for reports of a Glory that was close enough for us to get to. Both came up empty. With nothing to contribute, I alternated between watching telly and my now routine walking orbit around the farm.

We tried the same thing the following day, again without success. On the third morning, there came a very loud knock on the front door.

Chapter 31: The cost of a life

Julia

The sun was out, and I was pitching forward to land on my knees, with Siobhan beside me. There were children's voices coming from various directions, sounding frightened. I could see a group of six young children, two of them without hair, looking at us fearfully. A man I recognised as Ryan was trying to herd them back towards the distant car park. Had Collett come through on his promise after all?

A tall, fierce looking man in his fifties strode towards us. Somehow, he picked out Collett despite the brown paper masks we all wore.

"I am feeling that your treatment was success," the man said. He had a Russian accent, so I assumed it must be Polnukov. I'd heard of super-rich Russian oligarchs, men who were supposedly buying up half of London. I presumed I must be looking at one.

"OK, well, transfer the money as soon as you can," said Collett.

"About that," said Polnukov. "Who is Sammy Smith?"

"What?" said Collett. "I'm not sure I know that name."

Polnukov reached forward, and in one fast movement ripped the brown paper-bag mask from Collett's face. "You are not so good a liar as you think you are," said Polnukov.

"I'm not sure I see the relevance of this." said Collett. "We performed a service for you. Now we expect payment. That's how business works in this country." I could tell that he was trying to keep the agitation from his voice. Collett's goons, still looking ridiculous in their fake cult disguises, watched the exchange, not certain what to do.

"I will tell you the relevance. You have, I think, kidnapped a child. His name is Sammy Smith, and I now know the address where you are keeping him."

"I don't know where you've been getting this information," began Collett, but Polnukov cut him off.

"How or why, is not important. But I can see from your eyes that this is true. The police in this country are very opposed to the kidnapping of children."

"We are simply minding the child, while his mother assists us," said Collett.

"The deal has changed. I cannot be leaving a trail that can connect me to this vulgar type of crime. The price for my treatment will not be paid in cash. It is being paid in the form of my silence. Good day to you."

Polnukov turned sharply, and started walking away. One of Collett's goons reached for a concealed gun, but Collett stopped him. "No, you fool, it's far too public!" Then Collett ran to catch up with Polnukov. "It's not just me you're betraying," he said. "It's Claude Dexter, too. You've heard of him, haven't you?"

Polnukov stopped, but didn't turn around. "Mr Dexter and I have our own arrangements." He resumed his walk, and Collett swore loudly.

Chapter 31: The cost of a life

"You!" I turned to see a very large and muscular man stomping towards us, and based on his buzz-cut hair and general bearing I'd swear he was ex-army. He was followed by a boy with short cropped hair, and a slight, rather pretty woman. The big man had clearly watched the earlier discussion, for he went straight to Collett.

"Is it true that you've been kidnapping kids?" said the big man.

"All membership of our group is voluntary," said Collett, "We are a peaceful organisation."

"Yeah? Well why did my boy see it, clear as day, when he was touching that ... thing? Black kid sitting terrified in his own house, while you and your men threatened him?"

"Glories cause all sorts of dreams and hallucinations," said Collett.

"Funny that, cos it sounded like the guy you were just talking to there saw exactly the same thing," growled the big man. "Holly, call the police!"

"Now hang on a minute!" said Collett.

"Let's just go," said the Pigeon.

"You're not going anywhere," said the big man to Collett, and his arm shot out to punch Collett's face. Then there was a sudden crack, and blood exploded from the big man's forearm. Several people started screaming. The goon who'd wanted to shoot Polnukov was pointing the gun at where the big man's arm had been. The big man reacted instantly, spinning around and slamming his other fist into the gunman's covered face. The goon staggered backwards, firing his gun wildly, then the big man kicked him in the balls so hard that he doubled up and dropped the gun. All this had happened in two or three seconds. The big man was about to strike a third time when the pain from his shattered arm hit him. His face contorted in silent agony, and he dropped to his knees.

The big man's wife ran to him, screaming his name, while their son wailed where he'd been standing. Two more goons had drawn their guns, and all the other bystanders were fleeing in any direction but ours. Siobhan was tugging at my arm. The Pigeon was shouting. And Collett was sinking to the ground, with blood oozing out of his chest.

Collett gasped out three words. "Secure ... the ... women."

"What are you doing?" I asked desperately, as I was hoisted upright and my hands were tied. "He needs to get to a hospital!" The only response was having my brown bag hood pulled up, to allow a piece of tape to be slapped clumsily over my mouth.

"Not ... hospital ... need ... Glory ..." rasped Collett. "Find ... ask ... Dexter ..."

"Police!" said Feodor, pointing. In the car park far below, two police cars had arrived, and plenty of people were running in their direction.

The Pigeon ripped off the paper mask from his face. "You two!" he said to a pair of goons, "get the women to the car! And you two, carry the Boss! And you ..." he turned furiously to the stricken goon who'd accidentally shot Collett. "Stay here and hold them off."

"What?" said the hapless goon.

Chapter 31: The cost of a life

"Shoot at them. Distract them. Draw them off in another direction. Redeem yourself. Then disappear. Say a word about us, and we WILL find you. Goodbye."

By now I was stumbling down the slope with a goon gripping my arm to both propel me and stop me falling over. Behind us, another goon dragged Siobhan, and two more struggled with the weight of Collett. The police had split up, two were heading towards us, the others towards the goon with the gun. There was no way Collett's men would get us to the car before the cops caught up. Could this finally be over?

We tottered into the woods, the goons carrying Collett now grunting with the effort. "Stop!" came a shout from behind us. The two police, one male and one female, were hurrying towards us, then halted abruptly when Feodor pulled a gun.

The goons kept forcing me along, and I glanced back to see Feodor and the Pigeon using the hapless cops' own handcuffs to lock the pair of them into an embrace around a large oak trunk. All in all, it hadn't been the world's most effective rescue attempt.

Before long, Feodor and the Pigeon caught up with us again, and they decided to carry Collett between them and two goons, holding one limb each, which sped things up. We reached the cars, and following Collett's rasped instructions, poor Siobhan was shoved into the boot, while I was put in the back of the same car, with Collett slumped against me. Looking at the red sticky mass on his chest, it was hard to believe that the poor man had any blood left.

Feodor and the Pigeon got in the front, and they started the engine. "Don't go too fast, there'll be more police soon," said the Pigeon. "Those cops were probably just coming to disperse the crowd. That's why they got there so soon, but they'll have called for more. But they have no way of knowing which car we're in."

"Plus, they've lost contact with their mates," said Feodor with a crooked smile. Not long after, a police car sped past us in the opposite direction, sirens blaring.

As Feodor drove, the Pigeon was texting. "No response from Dexter's people. I'll have to call them," he said. He put the phone on speaker. I could feel the extra tension in Collett's body as it rang, rang, and rang. I would have stroked his forehead gently had my hands not been tied. Finally, someone answered.

"*There are still no more predictions for today,*" the voice said, rather curtly.

"Listen to me," said the Pigeon furiously. "Mr Collett has been shot! Everything went wrong because the Glory was too big and too many people were there! If we don't get to another Glory – and fast – he's going to die! Do you understand me? Name your price!"

"*OK, hold the line.*"

Long moments ticked by, punctuated only by the rumbling of the car and croaking gasps from Collett. Then the voice on the phone returned.

Chapter 31: The cost of a life

"You will owe Mr Dexter a favour, the nature of which will be his to determine, at a time of his choosing. Agree, and we will give you a current prediction."

"I ... agree." rasped Collett.

"*I will text through the estimated location. It will be small. It will appear in twenty-nine minutes.*" The phone went quiet, then pinged.

"What ... he ... wanted ... all ... along." rasped Collett quietly.

"Forty-three miles away. That'll be nearly an hour," said the Pigeon.

"You hear that, Boss! Sixty minutes, and you'll be right as rain!" Yet Feodor's voice betrayed his fear, and he was now driving like a maniac.

The frantic, terrified look that had been in Collett's eyes faded into one of simple agony. I guessed an hour was a very long time when you were in that state. He looked up at me.

"I am ... sorry ... for what ... I have ... done to ... you," he said, wincing with every word. Somehow, and it looked like the movement cost him a lot of pain, he reached up and managed to pull the tape from my mouth.

"It might be a good idea to give him some painkillers?" I suggested.

"Well sorry, we forgot to pack any, because we *weren't expecting this to happen*!" said Feodor angrily.

"Doesn't matter," rasped Collett. "Deserve ... pain. I'm a bad ... man. Sorry. But kids. Did you see ... kids?"

"I saw six children. I think your man Ryan was with them."

"That's ... right. They were ... dying ... but not ... now." Every word seemed an agonising effort.

"You kept your promise," I said. "Thank you."

"Not ... all bad ... then."

"We all have good and bad inside us," I told him. "Ultimately, what matters is what we do. I wish we could have found a way to do this without all the threats and nastiness."

"I was ... going to be rich," he whispered. 'So very ... very rich." His eyes were starting to glaze over.

"Stay with me!" I said. "Stay with me! Tell me what you were going to do with all that money you were going to make!"

Collett murmured, head lolling on my lap.

"We're losing him!" I shouted.

"What do you expect me to do?" screamed Feodor. "We're still more than thirty miles away!!"

"Ask them if there's anything closer," I said. "Big, small, anything! He's not going to last that long!"

"No need," said the Pigeon. "Look! On the left!"

It was like a tidal wave, frozen in time. A great edifice of blue, just a little darker than the sky, rearing across the fields in the distance on the left.

"They didn't tell us about that one!" shouted Feodor.

"I'll try and work out the fastest route," said the Pigeon, desperately tapping on his phone. "Look for a turning on the left!

Chapter 31: The cost of a life

"Mister Collett's losing consciousness," I observed.

"I cannot. Go. Any. Fucking. Faster," bellowed Feodor. But the road widened into a dual carriageway and, as it turned out, he could go fucking faster, as the car seared along at over a hundred miles an hour.

"This turning! This turning!" yelled the Pigeon, and Feodor slammed on the brakes, yanking the car onto the side road as the tyres screeched their protest.

"Stay with me!" I told Collett. "Stay with me!"

"Are we close?" yelled Feodor.

"I don't have a precise location!" said the Pigeon. "I'm guessing five minutes!"

"Call it two!" We bombed along a winding lane at nearly sixty, honking the horn constantly, then almost went into the back of a little hatchback tootling along in front of us doing thirty-five. Feodor hooted a symphony at them. They ignored it. He pulled out his gun, wound down the window and fired three times into the road by the hatchback. The hatchback immediately swerved left and buried itself in the hedge, blocking half the road. Feodor mounted the narrow grass verge on the other side, hawthorn branches scraping the car as it tried to squeeze past. "Come on, come ON!" he raged, as briefly the car seemed to stick, then somehow we were speeding on again, back on the road, leaving the stricken hatchback behind us.

Ahead our road joined another, and Feodor swore blue murder as a car passed the junction just ahead of us, going our way. But it was going nearly as fast as we had been, so we settled in behind it. "Almost there," said the Pigeon.

"You hear that?" I told Collett, but he was unconscious.

"SHIT!" cried Feodor, slamming on the brakes. I had no seatbelt, and I was thrown forward into the back of the passenger seat. Collett rolled off the seat. I heard a crunch as we rear-ended the car in front. Looking up, I saw a traffic jam of cars on the lane, all here to see the Glory.

"Must have been here a while," said the Pigeon.

"Damn, damn, DAMN," said Feodor. He honked his horn uselessly.

"We'll have to get out," said the Pigeon.

"We can't carry him," I said. "He's barely breathing. The manhandling will kill him!"

Feodor gunned the engine and the car shot backwards, smashing into a Toyota that had just come up behind us. He swore, moved the car forward a few metres, then reversed to the side, squeezing past the car he'd just hit as the driver shook his fist at us. He reversed for two hundred metres, managing not to hit anything else, stopping when he saw a gate on the left. He backed up about ten metres, gunned the engine and swung the car straight into the gate.

"Unlock it first!" shouted the Pigeon, but it was too late, we hit the gate with a sickening crash. It gave way beneath us and the car trundled over, but with an unhealthy clunking sound. It lumbered into the field at barely walking speed.

"Niet, niet, NIET!!!" cried Feodor, thumping the dashboard.

"Stay calm and think," said the Pigeon.

Chapter 31: The cost of a life

Someone was knocking on the windows.

"Are you alright? Did you crash?" said a man there.

The Pigeon, to his credit, was thinking fast. "The steering went. And I think John in the back got hurt. No seatbelt, the idiot!"

"Don't listen to him!" shouted another voice. "Guy's a fucking maniac! Almost ran me off the road!" It was the Toyota driver we'd reversed past.

Feodor jumped out of the car, and the Pigeon followed. I looked round. A Land Rover had stopped by the gate, and the first man at the window had clearly been its driver. The Toyota driver was now furiously telling him what had happened. I could do nothing, hands tied with a half-dead man by my feet. And my nose was bleeding from the impact. A banging sound was coming from the boot – Siobhan.

"Julia! Can you hear me?"

"I'm here! Are you OK?"

"I'm fine. Got my hands free but I can't get the boot open. Can you do it?"

"My hands are still tied. And we can't let Collett die."

"Why not, for fuck's sake!?"

"He's a human being."

"He threatened my son!"

The door beside me was thrown open, and I was pulled out. Feodor was both pointing a gun at the other two drivers, who stood there, shocked, with their hands up. the Pigeon clicked open the boot, and Siobhan scrambled out.

"Now you two, lift our colleague into the Land Rover," said Pigeon to the drivers. "Quickly and carefully, my friend here is getting quite nervous and that makes him trigger-happy."

The two drivers hauled the inert Collett out of the damaged car and into the Land Rover, supervised by the Pigeon. Siobhan managed to free my hands as Feodor marched us over to the Land Rover, while the Pigeon ordered the two drivers into the boot of our stricken car (there was barely room, they complained) and shut them in. Then we were in the back of the Land Rover, with the near-dead Collett between us. Feodor gunned the engine. "I will not let him die," he yelled, as we thundered across the field. The vehicle smashed through another gate, then thrashed its way through a mass of oilseed rape, the looming hulk of the Glory getting closer and closer. Feodor picked out a thin looking spot in the hedge ahead of us, turned towards it and smashed the vehicle through it. The field we came into had forty or more people in it, plus some very confused cows, and beyond them was the wall of blue, gently streaked with darker lines, so very like an enormous wave about to break.

"You see, Boss?" yelled Feodor manically. "We did it, we'll not let you die!!" He honked the horn repeatedly as we sped towards the Glory across the field at high speed, and both people and cows rushed to get out of our way. One woman didn't move, standing stock still, and Feodor had to swerve hard around her, screaming obscenities through the window. He hurtled the car towards the Glory.

Chapter 31: The cost of a life

"Slow down!" yelled the Pigeon. "You can't drive right into it!"

Feodor didn't seem to hear, he was still swearing as another two motionless watchers didn't get out of the way. He pulled the car left, then right. The Glory was just metres ahead.

"SLOW DOWN!!!" screamed the Pigeon, then he opened his door and jumped out. At that moment, Feodor finally realised the danger and hit the brakes, but he did it too late, and the car went into a skid. The wall of impossible blue hurtled towards us at high speed, and swallowed the bonnet as we all braced for impact.

Chapter 32: No good deed

Julia

The blue wall of Glory rushed up towards the bonnet and right through it, through the windscreen, and into Feodor. His cry of shock was cut short as the Glory squashed him like putty against the back of his seat, which bent backwards under the force. The car spun clockwise, sending the left side where Siobhan sat towards the Glory wall. The blue passed through the passenger seat and the side of the car, then into her. But instead of squashing her, it flexed around her like rubbery jelly, as the car came to a halt. I touched Collett with one hand, and Siobhan with the other, then everything dissolved.

* * * * *

The engine was roaring. The Land Rover shot forward. I tried to shout in surprise but I couldn't, because my mouth was taped shut, under what felt like a surgical mask. Behind us a siren came on, and a police car emerged from the hole in the hedge that our car had created, and headed straight towards us. Confused cows and people were milling around, getting out of its way. Everything stank of raw meat for some reason.

"Brace yourself" said the Pigeon from the driving seat. "We're going through a fence!" There was a thud, and a fearful twang as wires whiplashed against the windows. We were gaining ground on the police car, which wasn't built for off-roading.

"Where's Feodor?" asked Collett. He was sitting up beside me, right as rain, though his clothes were soaked in blood. On the other side of him sat Siobhan, wearing a virus mask for some reason.

"I'm sorry, sir. He died saving you," said the Pigeon.

I remembered the impact into the Glory, and now the pink and red goo all over the driver's seat came into horrible focus. The Pigeon was sitting in it. My hands were tied again. For a moment, Collett scrunched up his face in evident grief. Then it passed. "I take it you have a plan?" said Collett.

"Tara's parked on the other side," said the Pigeon. "And some more of our people. We get us into her car and they'll never spot us among all the Glory-watchers. Turns out this one was a biggie – and there's a few others around, it's a spate. Gonna be chaos on the roads. I think the police were waiting for armed back-up, I fired a couple of warning shots and then they sat and waited, thinking we were cornered. Well we were, until the Glory disappeared. How are you feeling, sir?"

"Alive, and angry."

The car passed through an open gate and through another huge field. On the far side of it, a thinning crowd of people were climbing over a wire fence, beyond which was a mass of parked cars. A few of the crowd turned in puzzlement at the Land Rover hurtling towards them.

Chapter 32: No good deed

"Right," said the Pigeon calmly. He wound down his window. "Get the Hell off my land!" he yelled at the top of his voice. "If you're not gone in thirty seconds I'll bloody well shoot you and the law says I can!" He kept on bellowing words to this effect, and the crowd scattered in panic. Quite a few of the cars had already left, but it was a slow process because there were so many.

"There," said Collett. "Over on the right, look, there she is!" The car veered right, heading towards a point where a woman in a baseball cap was cutting a gap in the wire fence that bounded the field. Amid the panic, no-one else noticed it, but the Land Rover went straight through the newly cut gap and bumped onto the road, into a chaos of people and cars. The woman ran behind us, catching up as we got caught in the traffic.

"Cops'll have trouble getting through all this," said the Pigeon.

"So'll we," said Collett. "Give us away, either of you, and young Sammy will regret it. Understand?" Siobhan and I nodded. It was distressing, seeing all those people just beyond the car window, not even aware of our plight. The police car didn't seem to have followed us, maybe it had got stuck somewhere.

The traffic started moving, and suddenly we were next to another car, doors were opening, and Siobhan and I were pulled from the Land Rover into the other car. I looked across the gap as this happened, hoping to catch a bystander's eye, but I couldn't. The Pigeon threw the Land Rover keys into the hedge, leaving the vehicle blocking the road, and jumped into the new car with us. Then we were moving, slowly, with the other cars.

"Our fingerprints will be all over that car," said the Pigeon. "And your blood, and Feodor's."

"Then it's lucky we've got an exit strategy, isn't it?" said Collett.

"Feodor?" asked the young woman driving, sounding worried and upset. "Dad, is he alright?" I recognised her voice.

"I'm sorry, love," said Collett. "He died saving me. I know, I know, he was like a son to me."

"You said it would be fine! You said there'd be no risk! And now you've fucking killed him!" She turned round, eyes blazing with tears and fury. They were eyes I knew, on a face I knew. It was Lara.

* * * * *

"How about I let you two get re-acquainted?" said Collett, pulling the tape from my mouth.

"Lara," I said. I couldn't think of anything else to add.

Lara, or whatever her name really was, paid me no attention. "What happened, dad? How did Feodor die?"

"You know that I got shot?" said Collett.

"Yes, of course I fucking know that! Why do you think I dropped my cover and came bombing on out here! I thought you were gonna fucking die!"

"I would have died," he said gently, "but for Feodor. He drove like a maniac to get me here on time. But we hit the Glory, in the car, at speed. It was quick, he wouldn't have felt a thing."

Chapter 32: No good deed

The cars in front were gradually speeding up, and so did we. In the front, the Pigeon suddenly ducked down, as we passed a police car coming the other way. They weren't expecting a female driver, and we sailed on past it.

"But how?" Tara persisted. "How did you end up getting shot? This was supposed to be *properly planned*!"

"Do you know, Tara, that is a very good question," said Collett. "One that I'm hoping your friend, Ms Barnes, might be able to answer." He turned to me, meaningfully.

"Well, there was this huge bloke, ex-army maybe, and he got into a bit of an argument with you, and then your goon got a bit trigger-happy," I said.

"Don't play games," said Collett. "You know exactly what I am talking about. You, Ms Smith, Mr Polnukov, and various bystanders were connected through the Glory. Then, when the connection was broken, everybody was suddenly accusing me of kidnapping Ms Smith's son. Mr Polnukov first, then that aggressive ex-squaddie, and quite a few other people pointing and looking as well. Tell me, Ms Barnes, did you also see vivid images of Sammy, his house, the address written down, and myself being there?"

"It's all a bit of a blur," I said. But now that he mentioned it, I did find that I had an extremely clear picture of Siobhan's house in my mind, despite never having been there.

Collett persisted. "I did see flashes of your thoughts, and Ms Smith's, while you were healing me. The name 'Malcolm' popped up. But it was, like you say, a bit of a blur. Which again asks the question, how did everyone get such a very clear image? The *same* image?"

By now I knew the answer, but he spelled it out. "Well, it could only have come from one person, couldn't it, Ms Smith?" He turned towards Siobhan, who was still gagged with tape under a virus mask. "Was it another of your daring and imaginative escape plans? I must admit, full marks for ingenuity. Unfortunately, you caused the death of a very good friend, and almost killed me. There will be consequences."

Siobhan turned her head towards him and met his gaze, eyes full of defiance.

* * * * *

"So your name's really Tara, not Lara?" I asked.

"That's me," she replied, eyes still on the road.

"And you've been lying to us about pretty much everything."

"Sorry. That was the gig. Invent a Glory-related power, get picked up by some group collecting such people, and find someone that dad could make money from. I was texting with him all the time. As soon as he learned about Siobhan Smith, well, he quickly worked out that the two of you together would be gold dust."

I thought for a moment, working things out. Far too late, once again. "It was you, wasn't it? Drugging me in my bed and making little holes in my head. Making sure I half woke up, so I'd see it all."

"You fell for it hook, line and sinker. Lucasz too, and I didn't even have to touch him."

Chapter 32: No good deed

"As I recall, you touched him rather a lot later on."

"Well, yeah, like I said, I was bored. Wasn't lying about that."

"How is he now? Really?"

"Perfectly fine when I last saw him this morning. Worrying about you, of course. I've been pretending to search for you online, looking for clues, feeding him red herrings. But any time he started asking the wrong questions I just told him I was feeling bored."

"And I thought they were threatening *you*."

"Just stuck a bit of tape on my mouth and did a selfie, in a side room of the church," she said casually.

* * * * *

Collett was on the phone again. "Listen, that place you got the virus patients from, I need you to get onto them. Tell them I need a bag full of tissues soaked in Corona snot. Yes, you heard me. About ten will do, full of liquid virus and bogey. Say it's for research, and we'll pay a hundred quid. Got it? Good. Make it happen. Fast."

"Daddy?" Asked Tara. "What are you doing?"

"Feodor's dead, and Polnukov was part of why it happened. I nearly died too, and the bastard didn't pay me. Yet. Because believe me, he is going to pay for it."

"You're going to infect him?"

"Damned right I am. He goes jogging first thing every morning. I'm going to have a man shove a fistful of Corona into his face."

"Dad, he'll kill you! You know how dangerous he is! You told me yourself!"

"Oh yeah, bastard has his own private army, I know that. But they can't cure Corona, can they? Only I can do that. He'll be at my mercy."

"But he'll probably just recover. We both did."

"Yeah, but I'm pretty sure getting a load of it right in your face means you're gonna get very ill, and very fast. I know the type – he's a control freak, not a gambler, so he won't be able to leave it to chance. He'll come crawling to me, all right. And I'll be asking for five million pounds!"

"*Five million*?!"

"I'll let him haggle me down to two or three, but he'll pay. And when he does, we can wrap this whole thing up and disappear."

"Dad, this is completely fucking crazy. You're not thinking straight. You almost died, we lost Feodor – come on, please, just stop. Stop and think. This isn't you. You're always careful. Clever, but careful. This is fucking reckless!!"

"Tara. My love. Clever and careful is what I've been doing all this time, and as you so rightly observed, it almost got me killed. It also got the police chasing after us, which means we have a narrowing window to get the money we need to put ourselves out of harm's way."

"Dad, he'll kill us! You don't go round making men like him angry."

Collett turned to her, his eyes with a darkness in them I'd never yet seen. "*He* made *me* angry. And now he's going to pay. And then if I deign to leave

him alive, he'll have no way to follow or find us. Bridges burnt, my love, bridges burnt."

Tara looked neither mollified nor reassured. For a moment I thought she even looked scared of him. But then I stopped thinking about her, because those last few words of Collett's were echoing through my head, like a prognosis of doom.

Bridges burnt, my love. Bridges burnt.

Chapter 33: The hunters

Antony

On the third morning after that terrible day when Sally learned she was a Glory addict, there was a knock on the door. It was just after breakfast. Sally immediately looked worried.

"Post?" said Rick.

"Doesn't knock that loudly," said Sally. "You two, hide yourselves, quickly!" We couldn't get from the kitchen to the rest of the house without being glimpsed through the front door window, so we ducked into the scullery, off from the kitchen, and then Sally opened the front door.

"We've had reports of lockdown-breaking at this address. May we come in?" The voice was firm, authoritative.

I could just about hear Sally agree, then they walked with her into the kitchen. She offered them tea or coffee, but they declined.

"Who lives in this house?" said the firm voice.

"Just me, officer," replied Sally.

"Yet you do not appear to be the registered occupant," said a second male voice, this one oddly croaky.

"The owners were my Godparents," said Sally. "The virus killed them both. I'm minding the farm for them."

"I see," said Firm Voice. "So is that your car outside?"

"I'm borrowing it."

"Who does it belong to, then?" asked Croaky Voice.

"Friend of mine called Rob," said Sally.

"Rob who?" asked Croaky voice.

"So if we were to call this … 'Rob', he would confirm that he has lent you his car, and that you are legally insured to drive it?" said Firm Voice.

"Fuck," whispered Rick, beside me. "They've got her."

"Yes, of course," said Sally, but her voice betrayed uncertainty.

"No doubt you'll have his number on your phone," said Firm Voice. "Anyone who trusted you enough to lend you his car, would certainly be on your phone contacts."

"And would tell you his last name," added Croaky voice, with a hint of amusement.

Beside me, Rick whispered urgently, "Be ready to run. If it comes to it, just run. Don't worry about me or Sally." Then he stepped out of the scullery.

"It's alright, Sally, you don't need to protect me," he said. "I'm afraid you're quite right, officers, we have indeed been breaking lockdown rules. I know there's a bit of an age gap here, but we're both consenting single adults who live alone. I'm willing to pay any fines, on behalf of both of us."

"How very noble," said Croaky Voice. "But I'm afraid we may be forced to take you both into custody."

"What?" said Rick. "Why?"

"Because you are still not being straight with us," said Firm Voice. "Because we know for a fact that you are harbouring a fugitive from justice named Antony Blake."

"Who?" said Sally and Rick together, quite convincingly.

Chapter 33: The hunters

"Him," said Firm Voice. "You recognise this photo? He was in the news quite a bit when he and his cousin disappeared, then he popped up a few days ago hanging around Glories causing trouble. He's wanted in connection with his cousin's disappearance."

"I remember the stories now you show me the photo," said Rick carefully, "but I don't recall any suggestion that he was a police suspect."

"I don't know where you got the idea that he's here," said Sally, "but he isn't."

"If you're lying, and I'm pretty sure you are, you will go to prison for a long time," said Croaky Voice, with a hint of sadistic glee.

"For aiding and abetting a murderer," said Firm Voice.

"Murderer?" asked Sally. "Who's he supposed to have murdered?"

"His cousin, of course, and maybe two others," said Firm Voice.

"Why are you so interested, if you've never met him," asked Croaky Voice.

"Stay here," said Firm Voice. "We're going to have to sniff him out." I heard him leave the room.

"What do you mean, 'sniff him out'?" asked Rick.

"Oh, you'll see," said Croaky voice.

My heart was pounding, even though I wasn't sure I technically had one.

Firm Voice returned, and someone else was with him. "He's close," said a scratchy female voice. "In there!"

"What?" shouted Sally, oddly loudly. "Are you telling me she can see THROUGH WALLS?"

"She's about to prove that you're both a pair of liars," said Croaky Voice. They were walking towards the scullery door.

"But how can she see Antony – *through walls*?" Sally repeated, emphasising the last three words.

The scullery door began to open as I finally worked out what she was trying to tell me, and I closed my eyes and ran straight through the wall, stumbling into the yard outside. I heard Firm Voice shouting, through the small scullery window. "You said he was here!"

"Well, now he's there," said the scratchy-voiced woman.

I waited just long enough to see one of them burst out through the front door, before I ran round to the back of the house. Footsteps thundered after me, but I slipped through the wall back into the kitchen.

"Antony, you have to run," said Rick.

"He's right, don't worry about us – we'll cope, somehow," said Sally.

"How did they find me?" I asked.

Behind me, through a half-open window, a voice shouted, "he's in the kitchen! I see him!"

"They've got a Glory-addict," said Rick quickly. "Like me! You have to run away!"

"But then they'll follow me," I said. "Wherever I go!"

"We'll hold them off!" agreed Sally, rummaging in a kitchen drawer.

"Run away for half a mile, then loop back," said Rick.

"Why?" I asked.

"Just do it! Quickly!! Go!!!"

"Enough of this!" roared Firm Voice, who'd come in through the front door. He was six foot three, in police uniform, but brandishing a gun. "You come with me, or I start shooting!"

Chapter 33: The hunters

"Okay, okay," I said. I raised my hands and walked past him to the front door, then at the last moment slipped through the corridor wall into the next room. Firm Voice swore like crazy and ran around to the door of the room I was in, but just as he got there, I went through the outside wall into the farm yard. I came face to face with a middle-aged woman in a track suit, face pinched and eyes sunken. She saw me and yelled "I've got him! He's here!"

Firm Voice came running from the front door again, but I was already sprinting away into the distance. He and the woman went after me. "If you don't stop running, we'll hurt your friends," Firm Voice shouted, but I had to hope Sally and Rick could look after themselves. I vaulted fence after fence – I could have run through them but vaulting was actually faster, because I didn't have to think. Firm Voice came after me, matching my speed, the woman losing pace behind him.

I was out of the farm now, crashing down a slope through thick grass. How long did it take to run half a mile? Would I get out of breath? Firm Voice was still behind me, but the woman was falling out of sight. I was aiming for a plantation I recalled seeing on an earlier walk, with a high deer fence around it. I closed my eyes and ran straight through that fence, and Firm Voice shouted several rude words. I wondered if he'd wait for the woman, and then follow at her pace. I ran between the trees, dead side branches passing right through me, until I met another deer fence, which I ran through as well. Now I was running through a big field newly planted with some sort of cereal crop. I was nearly at the far end before Firm Voice and the woman appeared in the corner behind me, pointing my way and shouting. They headed towards me, Firm Voice half dragging the woman. The field edge my pursuers were running along had a thick high hedge on their left, with a ditch beyond. Let them struggle through that, I thought, nipping through a gap in the hedge and jumping over the stream into a field full of cows. The cows munched contentedly as I ran between them, diagonally up through the field and back towards the farm. A few minutes later I was vaulting fences at the edge of Sally's farm, then rushing back towards the yard in front of the house, where a figure lay bound and bleeding on the ground.

* * * * *

I later found out from Rick what had happened after I'd run from the house with Firm Voice after me. Croaky Voice, without any warning, had smashed his fist hard into Rick's face, sending him crashing into the corner of the kitchen. Then, covering Sally with his gun, he'd grabbed Rick's arm and handcuffed it to a kitchen table leg. Then he'd advanced on Sally, marching her out of the house at gunpoint, before locking his right arm around her neck and shouting out,

"Blake! Either you surrender now, or your girlfriend gets it!!"

"P-please don't hurt me," whimpered Sally.

"Then you'd better hope your boyfriend comes back."

"I think he's over there," she said weakly, pointing to a shed.

"I don't see anyone," said Croaky Voice.

"We keep a shotgun in there," she said.

"What?" Without thinking he swung his gun towards the shed. Then Sally brought her heel down hard on his toes. "Arrghh!!" he said angrily, loosening his grip on her neck. Then with her right hand she whipped out the kitchen knife

Chapter 33: The hunters

she'd been concealing, and stabbed it into his left shoulder. "Aaaa-aaaarrrgghhh!!" he yelled. He'd somehow managed not to drop the gun, until Sally slashed the knife again, cutting his wrist. The gun clattered to the ground. For good measure she stepped back, spun around and kneed him hard in the groin.

"I'm nobody's fucking hostage," she snarled.

By this point, Rick had freed himself from the kitchen by the simple dint of lifting up the kitchen table and sliding the cuff off the leg. "Fucking hell, Sally, remind me to never piss you off!" he said.

Blood was spurting from Croaky Voice's wrist, which he was clutching at, moaning.

"Oh fuck, I hit an artery!" yelled Sally, her rage dissolving into distress. "Fuckitty fuck, he's going to bleed out! What do I do?"

"Run in and get bandages, straps, belts, anything!" said Rick. As she did so, he picked up Croaky Voice's gun. "Who are you working for?" he asked the wounded man.

"None of your business," snarled Croaky Voice.

"We could let you bleed out," said Rick. "You could die here."

"No you won't, you're not that kind of people," he replied.

Sally came running out with a handful of leather belts. "Your lucky day," Rick told Croaky Voice. "Give me your wrists, no, both of them! Sally, roll up his sleeves." This done, Rick pressed the man's wrists and hands together, palm against palm, the uninjured wrist pressed tight against the bleeding slash in the other. Then Rick tied them together as tightly as possible, using belt after belt after belt. When he was done, the flow of blood was reduced to a trickle. "Want us to bandage your shoulder, as well?" he asked.

"I'll ... pass," said Croaky Voice, who was looking a bit pale by this point. The shoulder was soaked in blood, but it wasn't coming out in spurts.

"Sally, shoot the tyres on their car," said Rick, handing her the gun.

Sally walked over to shoot the two nearest tyres, then began shooting speculatively into the car's bonnet, again and again until her ammo ran out. Meanwhile, Rick asked Croaky Voice once again, "Who do you work for?"

"Fuck off."

"How about I cut off your balls?" asked Rick, waving the kitchen knife menacingly at the man's crotch.

"Fucking amateurs," said Croaky Voice with a crooked smile. "Nothing you jokers could do would come close to what Dexter would do to me if I blabbed!"

"Dexter?" said Rick. "Thanks!"

"Oh, fuck!" said Croaky Voice.

"Antony's coming," shouted Sally.

Rick threw Croaky Voice to the ground, and ran with Sally to get Rob's car. As I ran into the yard, the car reversed up to me, and Rick shouted "Get in!!" from the driver's seat. I did, and we sped away. Rick filled me in on what had happened as we went.

"He actually said his boss's name?" I laughed, when he got to the end.

"He really did," said Rick happily.

"*'Don't tell him, Pike!'*" we chorused, in our best Captain Mainwaring voices.

"And he called *you* an amateur?" I said.

Chapter 33: The hunters

"Yeah – if he doesn't die of blood loss or get crucified by his boss, he may just expire from embarrassment," said Rick.

"What a moron," I cackled.

"To be fair, he had lost quite a bit of blood," said Rick. "Maybe he was getting a bit light-headed."

"Do you really think he might die from blood loss?" asked Sally, who'd been rather quiet and hadn't joined in with the jollity.

"Of course not," said Rick. "If you slash both wrists and do nothing, it takes maybe twenty or thirty minutes, I don't know. But we only slashed one, we stopped it pretty quick, and the shoulder wound wasn't bleeding that hard. His mate will call an ambulance, or maybe another car from this Dexter bloke, and get him the help he needs.

"But who is this Dexter?" I said, feeling the joy at our escape ebb away. "I don't know anyone with that name. Why's he after me?"

"I think," said Sally, and then she paused. "I think I may have seen that name, though it might not be the same person. He's a businessman. Something about building treatment clinics for Glory Addicts."

"If he's got one of them working for him, then that'd make sense," said Rick thoughtfully.

"At least one," I said. "Maybe that's why he's building these supposed treatment centres, so he can find people who can find me."

"Not just you, though," said Rick. "At least some of us can find Glories, as well. I've heard rumours about Glory tourism. Man could make a lot of money if he could lead paying punters to a Glory before anyone else knew about it."

"You weren't tempted to try that?" I asked.

"I was too ill to remember to eat," he reminded me.

"They must be putting that woman through hell," I pondered. "The one they were tracking me with."

"Very probably," said Rick.

"Even with just one working for them, they could track me anywhere," I said. "And maybe they've got more than one. They're going to keep coming after me, and there's nowhere I can hide."

"Yes there is," said Sally.

"Where?"

"Close to a Glory. They're drawn to you because you're a Glory. Get close to a real one, and it'll probably confuse them."

"But how do we do that?" I asked.

"Well, one's just been reported on social media, seventy miles north of here," said Sally.

"Then that's where we're going," said Rick

We'd covered about half of the distance to the Glory before we spotted the helicopter in the air, heading towards us.

* * * * *

Sally had noticed the helicopter first. The lockdown had grounded most commercial flights, though by no means all of them. One of the TV programs I'd watched during the miserable past two days had included a debate about whether it was ethical for people to fly every week between Belfast and London so they could do 'essential work'. An economist had tried to defend the flights,

Chapter 33: The hunters

while an epidemiologist argued that it made a total mockery of the sacrifices everyone else was making.

"*And what happens if a Glory appears on the runway, too?*" the epidemiologist had asked.

The economist had stated that even if Glories were real (he wasn't convinced), then the chances of one popping up on a runway at the exact wrong moment were something like a billion to one.

"*I'm not sure the airlines* agree," the presenter had said. "*Since the government admitted that Glories were real, the number of commercial flights taking off and landing in the UK has dropped by more than half, and it was very low already.*"

So the skies were now mostly empty, and perhaps that's why Sally had spotted the helicopter so quickly. "It seems to be coming our way," she said.

"Maybe it's nothing to do with us," I said.

"Maybe," said Rick. "But if I were Dexter, and I had the resources, then a helicopter is exactly the way I'd track you – with an addict on board, of course. No danger of being caught in traffic, and the freedom to go in whichever direction the addict points. Let's see."

He took a right turn, and continued that way for several miles. The helicopter changed course, and continued heading towards us. Then he turned left, resuming our northward progress towards the reported Glory. The helicopter corrected its course again.

"Can we outrun it?" asked Sally.

"Not a hope," said Rick. "Even on a motorway, it can do twice our speed. Our only advantage is it can't actually do much from up there, other than follow and report our position."

Sure enough, the helicopter gained on us rapidly, but once it got close it merely lurked in the sky, tailing us, a few miles behind. "They're probably calling more guys, and they'll be coming on the roads," said Rick. He was trying to hide it, but I could tell he was enjoying the hell out of this chase. I supposed that he deserved a bit of fun after what he'd been through, and I truly appreciated all his help.

"Another Glory!" said Sally, who'd been scrolling the feed on Rick's phone. "It's massive, like a disc-shaped iceberg, not too far. And a third one's been reported too, further north. I think it might be a spate!"

"Spate is good," said Rick. "No way those creeps can feel out our boy, when there's multiple Glories around!"

"We just have to lose this bloody helicopter."

"Look!" I cried. I'd seen it wink into existence, a column rising up from the ground to the clouds, narrowest halfway up, then widening near the base and top. It was made of broiling, burning orange light, and the narrow part in the middle was so bright I could hardly look at it, like the sun through a gap in the clouds.

"Can you tell how far it is?" asked Rick.

"Can't be sure," I said. "Past those hills, though."

"Nothing on social media yet," said Sally. "Won't be long, though."

Rick made a decision, taking a sudden right turn, towards the orange Glory. The helicopter followed. Driving fast, we reached the top of a hill and saw the stunning view beyond it. The base of the Glory was sunk into a

Chapter 33: The hunters

patchwork of fields and woods, a small river emerging from one end. "It's massive," Sally said.

"Utterly incredible," agreed Rick, his voice full of reverence.

There was a clunk as the front of the car glanced off a barrier at the side of the road. "Fuck!" shouted Rick. "Fuck, I'm sorry! Rob's gonna fucking kill me!"

"Come on Rick, stay focused, you're doing great," I said.

"But I don't know how long for," he said, a note of panic in his voice. "Dammit, I need fucking blinkers! If I get too close to that fucking thing, I may lose it completely! Sally, you need to drive!"

"But the same might happen to me," she protested.

"You weren't affected like that," I reminded her. "You were totally rational, even up close to that moon Glory."

"Alright then," said Sally. Rick swung the car into a half-space by a gate in the fence, and he and Sally swapped places. The helicopter came in closer, I could almost see the pilot's face. But then we were away again.

Sally had driven like a demented Lewis Hamilton when I'd first met her, but she was more cautious now. Still the Glory loomed closer, and closer. "Gotta be a mile across," said Rick, eyes wide, mouth hanging open. The pillar of flame was starting to look like a wall as we got closer.

"How close will you come, huh?" muttered Rick, looking up at the helicopter. "How close do you dare get to it, you bastard? He's not giving up yet. I was hoping if we got close enough, he'd back away."

"I've got another idea," said Sally. "There's a big wood right up ahead. If we can get into it, they won't be able to see us!"

The trees were just about all in full leaf. We veered off from the road, along a dirt track running under the trees. "What now?" I said.

"We wait. They'll either hang around in the air until their fuel gets low, or they'll land and try to come after us on the ground." She took the car down a turning off the dirt track on the right, then stopped in a spot where the canopy above was quite dense.

"We can't take too long," said Rick. "Not if they've got cars coming as well."

"Can you see the 'copter?" I asked. We couldn't. So we got out of the car, and moved about a little, until Sally caught sight of it.

"Still lingering," she said. "Waiting to see if we come out, I reckon."

"I've got an idea," said Rick. "If we're right, and I think we are, if they can't detect Antony this close to a Glory, then they'll be following us by sight, and sight alone. So I'll just drive off in the car, and they'll come after me!"

"Then we'll be stuck here," I said.

"You can get to the Glory, once they've gone off after me," said Rick.

"Might work," said Sally. "If they're as dim as the last lot."

"I'm not sure they are," I said. "Hang on, I think I've got a better idea."

Two minutes later, our car emerged from the wood, with Sally driving it. The helicopter took a moment to spot it, then swung over to hang above the road in front of her, closer than it had come before. Then, it rose up and flew back towards the wood, and Sally drove on. A few minutes later, she said "It worked! You can come up now!"

Chapter 33: The hunters

Rick emerged from where he'd been hiding under a blanket in front of the back seats, and I managed to pass through the back seats, out of the boot, to join him. "You were right," Sally said. "They did think of our plan A."

"But they totally fell for your plan B," said Rick, slapping me on the back. "I make that two-nil to us!"

"How long before they realise?" I asked.

"Could be a while," said Sally. "They've got a whole wood to search. As long as we're close to another Glory by the time that one vanishes, I don't see how they can find us!"

Julia

Collett's phone rang. "Oh, for fuck's sake, what now?" he said, answering it.

I could just about hear the voice on the other end. *"Mr Dexter wishes to call in the favour from earlier today."*

I saw Collett silently shake his fist for a moment, before replying. "What does he want?"

"A young man named Antony Blake. We will text you a photo. He is somewhere among the cluster of Glories you are heading away from. Mr Dexter would like you to turn around, and capture him."

"Is Mister Dexter aware that the area is likely to be crawling with police, who are looking for *me*?"

"That is not his concern. You owe him a favour and he expects you to honour it. You have resources, and more to the point, they are already in the area. Deploy them all. Mister Dexter himself is sending a couple of cars. Of course, if he catches Blake first then your favour to him will remain outstanding."

"But how are any of us supposed to find him? Those Glories are spread over a pretty wide area! If you want us to find him, we need more information!"

"There are two people with him, a middle-aged man and a young blonde woman," said the voice on the phone. *"We'll send you the locations of each Glory in the area as we get them, and the license plate of the car they were last seen in."*

"I knew it!" said Collett, covering the phone with his hand. "I knew they were holding back! They can predict any Glory they want to, whenever they want!" Then he spoke into the phone again. "Any other information that you suddenly feel willing to share?"

"Mister Dexter strongly expects him to turn up at one of the Glories, and attempt to place himself inside it."

"In*side*? Why would anyone do that?"

"Again not your concern. You are to capture Blake and hold him until Mr Dexter is ready to collect him. ... Ah, yes, Mr Dexter would also like to mention that having Blake under your control could be exceedingly helpful for both the profitability and the practicality of that little operation you've got going."

"Really?" said Collett. "Why?"

Chapter 33: The hunters

"*Because he's a Glory. A walking, talking Glory. Of course, these benefits will only be available to you if you can catch him before our people do. Mr Dexter says, may the best man win!*"

"How can a person be a Glory?" said Tara, driving.

"I don't know, but they're right, we could make a fucking fortune in no time at all," replied Collett, suddenly animated. Then into the phone, he said simply "tell him we agree!"

He ended the call. Tara screeched the car to a halt, and executed a three point turn.

"Why does Dexter never speak on the phone himself?" Tara pondered, as the car sped back in the direction we'd come from. "It sounded like he was in the room with the person calling. I reckon he's someone famous. A prominent businessman, or politician. A voice you'd recognise."

Collett didn't reply.

Chapter 34: The baddie

Antony

A patch of land had appeared in the sky. It was ordinary British countryside: fields, woods and hedgerows, only it was hanging there like a cloud, roughly circular in shape but with irregular edges, as if someone had ripped out a piece of a painting and stuck it to the sky. Of course, it was no use to us, we needed one at ground level.

"It's useful in a way," said Sally. "It'll draw attention, while we look for one that's smaller, more out of the way. The bright orange column had winked out ten minutes earlier, which probably meant that our pursuers now knew they'd been duped. But the helicopter had not yet been seen.

"Those woods," said Rick, pointing ahead and to the right.

"You sense something?" Sally asked.

"Not sure, just instinct. Could be imagining it."

We had no better leads, so we turned right and took a small road through the woods he had mentioned. A few minutes later we were out the other side, and driving along a lane with high hedges. Then Rick yelled, "Stop!". Sally braked. "We just passed an opening on the right. Can we back up?"

Sally did, and we turned into an almost empty car park, flanked by hedges and the odd tree, except at the far end, where it opened out into a patch of flat heathland, with a Glory sitting right in the middle. Happily, we got out and ran towards it.

It was the size of a small house. The colour was not easy to describe. Imagine how the brightest, most vibrant shade of purple would look next to a dull greyish blue. Well, that gives you an idea of what this colour would look like, next to that vibrant purple.

"It's like no colour I've ever seen," said Sally. "It's a colour that doesn't even exist."

"Like purple, only more," I said.

"Ultraviolet," said Sally. "Normally only bees can see it. I think it might be ultraviolet."

"But we can't see ultraviolet," I said.

"Glories don't follow the rules," she replied.

"It's beautiful," said Rick. "So very beautiful." He got out of the car and began walking towards it. Sally jumped out, and caught up with him. I followed.

"Rick?" she said. "Stay with us, Rick!"

"Sally?" his voice sounded dazed and confused, like he'd just woken up. "Beautiful," he added. "So beautiful."

"Sally," I said. "I need you to walk all around it and check no-one's leaning on it. I can't let anyone else fall into one because of me."

"What about Rick?" she asked.

"I'll look after him."

Rick wandered closer to the Glory, but stopped about five metres from it. He dropped to his knees, eyes wide as he gazed at it, with his arms outstretched. His face was a picture of rapturous ecstasy. I walked towards the Glory cautiously, looking back several times to check he was OK, but he stayed exactly where he was. I was right by the edge of the Glory now. The

Chapter 34: The baddie

surface wasn't smooth, it was a patchwork of irregular triangles a foot or two long, each tilted differently so that some vertices projected out slightly, and others inward. Each was a slightly different shade of this impossible purple colour.

Sally appeared coming around the side of it, taking a glance at where Rick was still kneeling. "Just two people at the other side so far, I told them not to lean on it," she said.

"OK, I'll do it now. Can you check on them again?" I asked.

"Alright."

As she walked around the edge of it once more, I stuck my hand into the Glory. It passed through the surface easily enough. Then I bent my fingers into a scoop, and pulled out a piece of it. There was no resistance. Now I had a shard of impossible purple in my hand. I looked at it, expecting something to happen, but nothing did. Maybe I needed to touch it against my head, I thought, so I tried that. Nothing.

Maybe I had to walk into it. I had epically failed at that the only other time I'd tried, but perhaps this one would be different? I held the hand with the detached piece away from the Glory, and tried to walk into it with the rest of my body. I got about halfway in, before the pressure against me sent me tumbling out again, landing in an undignified heap. Rick, eyes still fixed on the Glory, didn't notice anything at all.

Then I recalled how Sally had been able to pick up a piece, when she'd been touching me, and a different idea formed. If I could give the piece to Rick, make him hold it in his hand, would that make the Glory open up for me? Maybe he could somehow hold onto that piece, which would fix his own problems, as well? It had to be worth a try. I walked up to him, aiming to pass the Glory fragment into one of his hands. But the second it touched his skin, he immediately jerked awake, gripped my wrist, and swung his head round to face mine.

"They're calling!" he said, almost shouting. "They're calling for YOU!"

"For me?" I asked.

"They're calling for you!"

"Who are calling?" I asked, urgently. "I don't understand! Who's calling for me!?"

"The Ones! They're not all the same. It's vital you understand this! They're *not* all the same!"

"Who aren't? Who's calling? Who isn't the same, and as what? Please! This isn't making any sense to me!"

Rick's body had gone rigid, but was shaking and juddering. From his expression, it looked like he was in pain.

"The Ones ..." he said, unhelpfully.

"Is Daniel there? Is Daniel with them? Where's Daniel?"

"Claude Dexter," said Rick. That name, again.

"Dexter? The man who's after me? Are you saying Dexter's got him?"

Rick shook his head, violently.

"Dexter ... the Others ... terrible plan ... monstrous ... my daughters. Oh my God, my children!" he was shouting, now, his face screwed up in agony.

"Please," I said. "I know it hurts, but I don't understand. I don't understand what they need me to do! I just want to find my cousin. Do they need me to

Chapter 34: The baddie

come? To walk into the Glory? I'm happy to do it, I just don't know how! Can they show me how?"

"Wrong stuff," gasped Rick. "Made of the wrong stuff ... too difficult ... need a bridge ... aaaaaarrrhhh!!!" With what looked like an agonising effort, he brought his free arm around and pulled my hand with the Glory piece away from him, breaking the connection.

"Oh God, oh God, oh God," he said, shaking like crazy but otherwise talking more normally. "Oh God, I felt them!"

"Felt who? Felt who, Rick?"

"Most of them are good," he said, looking at me with pleading eyes. "But that's not going to be enough to stop it. They don't know how to talk to us! Those women you sent them, they learned a lot but they couldn't save them. Think next time they'll do better. They need a bridge. But it can't be you."

"Rick, I don't understand."

"I have to go into it. I have to make contact. I understand now. They've been calling to me, all this time, but they're different, so very different. Only now do I think it makes sense. This is the right thing for me, Antony. Don't be sad."

He stood up, awkwardly, and took a step forward. I grabbed his arm, careful not to touch him with the Glory piece. "Wait," I said. "We have to talk about this. Linda and Thelma, you said that they died."

"I think so, I'm sorry. They didn't understand us enough."

"But Daniel went in *before* them," I said

"Daniel isn't dead."

"You're sure?"

"I'm sure," he replied. "I saw him but ... it's hazy now. Antony, I have to go now. If I don't go soon, it could be too late."

"I could be sending you to your death," I protested.

"This is my choice," he replied. And he began walking forwards.

"That's far enough," said a voice from behind us.

I turned around to see two large cars, and a man with black curly hair standing in front of it, pointing a gun at us. Beside him was a pretty young woman with an icy expression. "You see, T, our luck did change, after all," the man told her. Then he directed his gaze towards me.

"Antony Blake, I presume?"

"Who are you?" I asked him.

The man with the gun said, "Step away from the Glory please, or I may be forced to shoot your friend."

I was still holding the fragment of Glory in my hand. I clenched my fist, hiding it, then raised both my hands, putting myself between him and Rick. If Rick could just take a few more steps forward, he could still get into the Glory.

"Stop!" shouted Collett. "Yes, you, the other one. One more step and I will fire."

"What do you want?" I asked him.

"You," he replied. "But I also don't intend to let your friend there get up to any tricks with the Glory. Ah, now there's the third member of your little party."

He looked to the side, and Sally walked around towards us, hands in the air, followed by two men, one of whom was pointing a gun at her. "Sorry,

Chapter 34: The baddie

Antony," she said. "They told me they were just ordinary Glory-hunters. Then they pulled a gun on me."

One of the men marched Sally towards the car, the other went and grabbed Rick by the arm, dragging him there as well.

"Tell me, Antony," said Collett. "Which of these people do you care more about?"

"What?" I replied.

"If I told you I was going to shoot one of them, which one would you save?"

I knew the answer of course, but I didn't say anything.

"Oh, come on, Dad," said the icy-faced woman. "It's obviously the girl. I can feel the sexual chemistry from here."

"Right, good," said Collett. "We take the girl, stick her in the car. The man looks like a Glory addict to me. Call Dexter, tell him we've got one for his collection, free of charge." Then he turned to me. "It's very simple, kid. You cooperate with me, she'll be fine."

A thug was dragging Sally towards the back door of the car. The piece of Glory in my hand was now tugging, hard, like it was attached to the Glory by invisible elastic. The further I got from the Glory, the harder it pulled. "You want me in the car too?" I asked sullenly.

"I think you can get in the other car," said Collett.

I nodded, and walked past him as if to get in the car, but now he was between me and the Glory. I let go of the fragment and it flew towards him, hitting his belly. He staggered back several steps, waving his arms around comically.

"Dad!" said the ice woman, alarmed.

"Millions," said Collett, his face full of confusion. "There are millions!"

I ran, straight through the car as if it wasn't there, and drove my head into the chest of the thug gripping Sally's arm. He lost his grip on her, and Sally swung round and broke his nose with her fist.

"Stop them!" shouted a gaunt, older man, as Sally and I began running. Bullets smashed into the ground all around us, then Sally pitched forward, screaming. Blood spewed from her ankle. I span round and lifted her up, but now four people were pointing guns at us. Back by the cars, one other thug was standing beside Rick, watching the action. That was a mistake, because Rick smashed his elbow into the thug's eye, kneed him in the groin, then balled his fists into one and brought them up so hard into the thug's face that he flipped over onto his back.

"Rick, RUN!" I shouted. "Don't worry about us!!"

Rick paused for a split second, then sprinted off towards the side of the Glory. He tried to run into it but bounced off, stumbled, regained his footing and hared off into the wood.

"Let him go," ordered Collett. "We've got what we need."

"Please," I said. "We need to bandage her ankle."

"No we don't," replied Collett. "Put her in the car." I carried Sally back to the closer of the cars, lifted her into the back seat, and got in with her."

"At least Rick got away," she said, through gritted teeth. She clutched my hand, tightly.

"Does it hurt?" I asked her.

Chapter 34: The baddie

"Of course it fucking hurts, stupid!" But for a brief, precious second, she managed to look amused at the dumbness of my question. Then she said, "He got away ... and he wasn't acting like an addict anymore."

"We drive," said Collett. "Find a quiet spot and stop.

So the two cars drove in convoy, but after ten minutes both pulled into a layby under some trees. "Everyone out," said Collett. "Except the one in the boot, open it but leave her there."

The thugs, the gaunt man and the ice woman all got out, along with a kind-looking woman my Father's age, who looked totally out of place in this company. She favoured me with a sympathetic smile. "I'm Julia, fellow hostage," she said.

"I'm Antony, and this is Sally."

"Hi," winced Sally. I was again carrying her in my arms, as blood dripped from her foot.

The last to exit was the thug who'd had his nose broken by Sally. Another thug sniggered at the bloody mess she'd made of the man's face.

"Nod fuddy," the stricken thug mumbled.

"Oh, come on, it is a bit," said Collett, and then he started laughing out loud. The third thug, whose eye was starting to blacken thanks to Rick, joined in, along with the gaunt man and the ice woman. Even I laughed a little, though I've no idea why.

"Shall we get on with it," said Julia, with the air of a teacher in a playground. "This young woman is losing quite a lot of blood."

"Yes, yes, fun's over," said Collett. "You two link with Smith in the boot," he said to the two bloodied thugs. For the first time, I noticed the woman bound and gagged in the boot. The black-eyed thug grabbed the bound woman's hand, and linked his other hand with the one we'd all laughed at. Julia took that man's other hand.

"Now I need to touch Sally," she said to me, "and you need to make sure you're touching her, flesh to flesh." I obeyed. Then everything dissolved into a dream.

I was still standing there, with Sally in my arms. "What the hell just happened?" she whispered. "My foot doesn't hurt anymore. Can you put me down?"

I did so, carefully, but she could stand on both feet just fine. Both thugs' faces were no longer bleeding, and they were running their hands over themselves, looking puzzled. Collett was rubbing his hands with glee. "We are going to make some *serious* money," he said.

Chapter 35: The visitor

Julia

Back at base, I lay in bed alone, processing everything that had happened. We'd saved lives – six children! But a man had died, not a nice man, but a man nonetheless. And then there was Antony. Tara's question now echoed in my own head – how could a man be a Glory? Collett had been animatedly making phone calls all the way back, talking about a clinic with a miracle cure for exorbitant prices, available only for one day. Eventually I slept.

* * * * *

"Cooo-eeee! Mrs Barrrrnes!"

I opened my eyes. I was in bed. "You might want to turn on your bedside light," said a man's voice. I fumbled around on the bedside desk, knocking the water bottle onto the floor, then found the switch. Squinting in the light, I saw the man. He was perched oddly on the room's only chair, feet on the seat, bottom on the armrest, head tilted as he looked at me.

"Sorry to wake you, but I thought we ought to have a chat," he said cheerfully.

I felt a stab of raw fear. This man was very different from Collett. He had a neat ginger beard, reminding me somehow of Prince Harry, and slightly frizzy ginger hair. He was in his thirties, perhaps, and dressed in a pale blue suit with a yellow tie. He was grinning at me and didn't seem to blink.

"Who are you?" I asked, blinking.

"Well, that's a good question. How about you have a guess?"

I thought for a while. Only one name came to mind. "Claude Dexter?"

"*Pinnngg*," he said happily. "You've got one hundred pounds!"

"What do you want?" I asked.

"Straight to the point, I like that. I'm auditioning. I've got my leading man already, but he's proving a little slippery, not to mention out of form, so I thought it might be useful to find myself an understudy."

"Leading man?" I asked, recalled Collett's earlier phone conversation. "You're talking about Antony, aren't you?"

"*Pinnngg!* You've got two hundred pounds!"

"What is it you want him for?" I asked.

"Ah, well, you see, we're still wading through what's known in the business as 'development hell'. Could be some while before the product is ready. We have to assemble all the extras, as well. Are you deliberately avoiding the obvious question?"

I sighed, because I was. "Just tell me whatever you want to tell me."

"Are you a teacher?" he asked. "Because you talk like a teacher. I need an understudy, in case Antony does a bunk, or we can't get him ready in time. Someone with a very firm link to the Glories, a foot in both worlds, as it were. You've had more contact than most, have you not?"

"I've touched quite a few," I said.

"More than touched. Been healed, and done healing on others. It makes me wonder, what exactly is your body is made of, now?"

He slid down from the chair, and started moving towards me.

"Stay back," I said.

"Or you'll do what, exactly?" he said with a smile, continuing towards me. I felt myself trying to shrink down under the bedclothes. "Don't worry, this won't hurt, at least I think it won't," he said. "Now hold still. He reached out and placed his hand on my forehead. I felt myself falling into a dream.

I opened my eyes, and he was perched on the seat, once more. "Back with us?" he said. "Good news is, you seem to be all human, although changed somehow. I think there is a link, but it's weak. But maybe you'd do at a pinch. I popped in on Siobhan, but she wasn't very talkative. She's got a connection too, but yours is a little stronger, and anyway I can't see her surviving long given Collett's current mood. I had a word with him last night, but he's very impetuous, isn't he? Too emotional to be a *really* successful businessman. He seems oddly fond of you, though. I'm getting off topic, aren't I? Point is, I think you're the best candidate available, so you've got the part! The understudy role, I mean, so I'll no doubt be seeing you again, nearer the time. Toodle-pip!"

Then in a blink of an eye, he was gone. I got up and walked over to the door. It was firmly locked, as it had been all night.

Antony

Sally and I were taken to rooms in some large, isolated building that Collett was using as a base. I pleaded to be allowed to share a room with her, but he refused, before magnanimously saying that she could have a room 'quite close' to mine.

"I'll be fine," she said, before she was led away from me.

Collett addressed me. "Now, I know that you can walk through things. But your girlfriend can't. Make any attempt to escape, and she *will* be hurt, do you understand?" I nodded. "Cooperate, and she'll be treated well."

I was marched along a corridor, noticing that several doors had padlocks on them. The room they ordered me into didn't, I guessed there wasn't much point. Two thugs went into the room with me, and Collett told them they'd be relieved in four hours' time. They found a very violent movie on the telly and settled down to watch it, one either side of me. There was little I could do but watch it with them. It mainly involved one man winning protracted fights with a long sequence of opponents, who had the decency to only ever attack him one by one. It didn't seem to occur to my captors that they were exactly the sort of people whom the hero was beating to a pulp. At the end, a lot of things exploded and the credits rolled. The thugs channel-surfed until they found something similar, and away we went again. Eventually I went to bed and tried to sleep, which is difficult when two people are in the room sitting up.

Chapter 35: The visitor  215

Early the next day Sally, Julia, Siobhan and I were taken in two cars to a new location. We got out into a small private space behind a grand-looking building, and were marched through the back door, along corridors that smelt of antiseptic, and eventually into a large room with huge windows and a high ceiling. It was divided into two halves by a thick blue curtain. "Okay, let's get set up," said Collett.

Two medical examination couches lay behind the curtain, and Julia was made to lie on one, and strapped down tightly, though her arms were left free. Siobhan was strapped to the other, with one of Julia's arms gaffer-taped to a bare spot on her shoulder. On the other side of Siobhan were two seats – I was told to take one, and a thug the other. Julia's other hand was taped to the top of a chair, just behind the curtain. "I'm afraid it's going to be an uncomfortable day for you," Collett told her as he applied tape to her mouth. "Can't be helped. But you'll be doing some amazing things for our patients."

Julia

When I was little, the school would very occasionally show TV documentaries. It was on something that kids today would not even recognise as a television – a box on legs made of Bakelite, with opening doors in front of the screen. Someone from the class had to volunteer to stand in a precise spot holding the aerial to minimise the fuzzing snow on the screen so we could actually see what was happening. The programme that I remember the most was about the future of farming. The narrator kept his tone formal as he talked us through the bold new innovations on show, but it was clear that whoever made the film thought this was progress in its most perfect form. There were lines of cows having tubes attached which sucked out their milk, and endless cages full of chickens ("They have everything they need, and are completely safe from foxes") forming an egg production line. Food came from nozzles at the top, and the eggs rolled along little tubes and gutters, which the class thought were brilliant. It was only later, when one of the other girls volubly expressed her opinion, that I found myself agreeing with her, and wondering how it felt to be a cow or a hen, deprived of all choice or agency in life, merely a machine for supplying the needs of others.

Well, I didn't need to wonder now.

I could move my legs a little, and my head and neck, but that was about it. Siobhan and I were battery hens, strapped down to be used, reused and eventually thrown away. Antony was seated next to Siobhan, his cooperation assured by the presence of Sally in a nearby room, and continued threats to her person. A goon kept an eye on him, and the Pigeon watched over us all. Collett was dressed as a doctor and sat self-importantly in front of an old oak desk, while Tara cosplayed a nurse. Then a thick blue curtain was drawn between them and me, and I could see no more.

There was nothing to do but try to forget the discomfort of my body, and focus entirely on what was happening outside. One by one the patients came. Like listening to a radio play, I formed pictures of them from the tone of their

Chapter 35: The visitor

voices and their choices of words. The first man, I decided, was tall, grey-haired and probably never took his suit off except to bathe, and possibly to make love.

"Cancer," he said simply. "Fifty-fifty survival rate, but that was before the new virus. You got something that works, I'll pay 500K. You don't, you'll hear from my lawyer for wasting my time."

"You brought the money?"

"Half of it."

"This treatment is experimental," said Collett, and I could tell he was affecting a much posher accent than his normal speaking voice. "Connected to the Glories."

"How?"

"I don't know the details. I was given a limited number of doses in exchange for information on whether they worked or not. An unofficial trial, as it were."

"I am not paying you a penny to be a guinea pig!"

"Apologies sir, you misunderstand. We already used ten doses on persons of lesser value than yourself, with a wide range of ailments. 100% cure rate and no appreciable side effects. We have 14 doses remaining. If you do not wish to purchase one, we have a long list of reserves."

"I see." In those two words, I could hear all the resentment – not at Collett, I guessed, but at being in the situation of having to ask for something, rather than wading in and taking it. Of having to enter into a business arrangement where he was the one taking the risks. "We will proceed," he said after a while.

"Good. The treatment involves a single pill. You must swallow it whole – I'm told if you break it, the effect is lost."

"They've put something inside it? A tiny piece of Glory?"

"I am not at liberty to say any more. Are you ready?"

The man must have nodded.

"You will experience a series of hallucinations. Memories that are not yours, possibly even voices talking to you. They are not real. The boffins, I gather, have had a field day trying to explain them. Ignore them. In fact, I would keep everything that has happened here very strictly under your hat, unless you feel like spending the next few years of your life as a research subject. OK? Right, here you go."

I could just make out what sounded like him swigging water and putting the glass down. "We just need to take your pulse, you should feel the effects within seconds," said Collett. Moments later Tara's hand reached through the gap in the curtains and touched mine. The Pigeon then signalled to Antony, and he obediently reached out and touched Siobhan. I guessed that Tara was secretly touching Collett with her other hand, completing the connection to myself, Siobhan and Antony, sending me into the now familiar healing trance. I experienced the waves of sickness of this posh man, the fragile hope of remission, the crushing despair at the news that it was back. And through it all, the indignant fury that his body had brought him so low, coupled with a childlike terror at feeling so helpless, a sensation he thought he'd banished from his life forever. Either Collett or Tara seemed to judge correctly the precise moment when the cure was complete, and broke contact.

Chapter 35: The visitor

"Sir?" said Collett. "You zoned out completely there. That happens sometimes. How do you feel?"

"Did you hypnotise me?"

"No. I gave you a pill, remember. Please stand up and walk around. Tell me how you feel."

"I feel ... well, it's very hard to tell." Yet I could detect a tone of fragile elation in his voice.

"You'll want to see a specialist as soon as you can, of course," said Collett. "When you do, he'll confirm that the cancer is gone. The sooner the better from my perspective, as I'd very much like to get the second half of my fee."

"So that's it concluded?"

"Completely. I fully accept your skepticism, but rest assured, you are cured."

"If that turns out to be true then you will have my gratitude. And the remainder of the fee, of course."

With that, he strode from the room, and very soon another man came in, and the scene was played again. It was impossible to keep track of time, but we got through six patients before anyone got a break. A procession of rich men and (less often) women seeking to prolong their lives. Only one touched my heart, the exception, a young woman in her early twenties reduced to a paraplegic by an accident that apparently wasn't her fault. The family had scraped together ten thousand pounds, which her tearful parents told Collett they had been planning to spend on some spinal regeneration treatment they'd heard of in the States, but the pandemic came and the flights were all cancelled. And that meant he, Collett, was the girl's last chance.

I thought Collett would haggle, for this was far less than the other patients had paid.

"I know this is less than you asked for," said the father. It sounded like he was crying, and I was glad I couldn't see his face. "But it's all we have. If you cure her, we'll work to pay the rest of your fee, however long it takes."

"Now, now," said Collett. "I believe there is a little scope here to vary the fees according to ability to pay. Furthermore, the treatment has not yet been tested on a serious spinal injury of this kind. Therefore, we will do the treatment, and if it works, we will accept your money and no more. If not, there will be no charge."

"Seriously?" said Tara. I imagined the petulant look on her face. It was the same old Collett, I thought, pivoting from his default setting of limitless greed and attendant violence, to playing the part of a virtuous man.

"Yes, nurse, seriously. Now, the pill needs to be swallowed whole, and I am sure you will be much better placed to assist her with that than I would be." The parents were, and moments later came the now familiar signal of "Now I need to take her pulse," and Tara's hand on mine.

I'll never forget my glimpses of the girl's despair when she'd woken in hospital, and gradually learned that she would never again feel or move anything below her neck. The long periods when she'd lain there, helpless and wanting to die, interspersed with phases of heroic determination as she tried so hard to find some purpose for her shattered life.

Chapter 35: The visitor

"My hand! I can move my hand! My legs!! My legs as well!!!" For several minutes there was shrieking and whoops of uncontrolled joy.

"Now, now," said Collett, smugly. "Remember social distancing. Save your hugs for each other, please."

For perhaps the first time since I'd done it, I felt truly glad that I'd saved Collett.

"You're going soft, Dad," said Tara, once the happy trio had left the room.

"And you, my dear, need to find your own gentler side."

"You taught me not to, remember?" she said coldly.

"But soon, we'll be starting a new life where we won't need to be hard all the time."

"Provided you don't give too many more impromptu discounts," she muttered.

"I think we'll take a break," said Collett.

Chapter 36: Julia Barnes, commodity for trading

Julia

Siobhan and I were fed and allowed a toilet break. I moved my arms around as much as I could to get the blood flowing, and then we were strapped and taped down, and it all started up again. More patients, more games of guess-what-they-look-like. One had a weak, reedy voice and I imagined him to be about a hundred; he wanted a heart condition fixed that he'd been told he might drop dead from any day now. He sounded so old that he would probably drop dead from something else soon enough, even if they cured his current complaint, but it was his money to do what he wanted with, I supposed. There was a man who'd decided his much younger wife would look a lot better without the burn mark on the side of her face. A middle-aged woman had terrible eczema, and at first I was amazed she'd pay 25 thousand pounds to be rid of it, but I changed my mind after I'd experienced with her what it felt like.

A young man with a booming voice came in, announcing like a tannoy system that his new baby had cystic fibrosis. Curing the child was a strange experience, sharing the barely formed mind of a newborn. It was a genetic condition, I knew, and I wondered whether the actual genes of the baby were being altered.

By now I was intimately familiar with the ceiling of the room, imagining that the hanging light was some sort of exotic flower, growing from a white desert where occasional cracks were the only other suggestion that there might perhaps have once been water there. I guessed that it was late afternoon. The latest patient had hobbled in, a man with a thick fruity voice whom I pictured as about sixty, very rotund with florid cheeks and a wide bristly moustache. "Arthritis!" he declared. "Absolute bugger, especially in the winter. Bloody doctors say I just have to live with it! Well I've got two hundred thousand here if you can prove them wrong. And I'll throw in this bloody walking stick to boot!"

"Just the money will be fine," said Collett. "Now this is highly experimental medicine, very hush-hush, Glory-related technology you see, your money buys you one pill, but one is all you're going to need."

The Pigeon's phone vibrated. Without a word, he walked through the blue curtain.

"Text from our *erstwhile patient*," he told Collett.

"Oh. Colonel Forster, I'm most terribly sorry, but I must ask you to wait outside while I attend to this." I heard a chair scraping, and then Forster's slow progress towards the door.

"Now," said Collett hopefully, the instant Forster closed the door. "Has our Russian fare-dodger agreed to cough up?"

"He is extremely angry," replied the Pigeon. "He is demanding that we call him immediately."

"Tell him we will speak within the hour. Colonel Forster, unlike someone else I could mention, actually intends to pay for his treatment, and we have kept him waiting long enough."

Chapter 36: Julia Barnes, commodity for trading

The Pigeon's expression was priceless as we came back through the curtain: exasperated, and a little fearful. He was even shaking his head woefully as he typed into the phone. I couldn't say anything, of course, but Antony did.

"Is this some crazy revenge plan your boss has got going?" he asked the Pigeon quietly.

"Mr Collett is going to ask for five million pounds," said the Pigeon, stiffly.

I made a deliberate giggle through my gag. "You think that's funny?" the Pigeon asked me.

"Why don't you take off the tape and ask her?" said Antony. Then he dropped his voice and continued just audibly. "She thinks it's a mad vendetta that will get you all killed. I can feel it in Collett's head, we all can. You and your men would be better off taking your cut of the money, and running away before it all kicks off."

The routine of healing resumed, albeit briefly. Curing Colonel Forster involved brief flashes of conflicts and decimated human bodies, mixed in with smoking clubs and fox-hunting. Two more patents followed, and having totted up all the sums of money I'd heard mentioned as the day went along, I calculated that Collett had made several million pounds today alone.

* * * * *

The Pigeon walked solemnly through the curtain to join Collett and Lara. "We'll call him now," said Collett, who sounded excited. But the Pigeon said, "I suggest we do it on the road, just in case he can trace where we are."

"But we're not going to use this place again," said Collett.

"Even so, why give him that information?" said the Pigeon. I could tell he sounded rattled.

"All right, if you insist," replied Collett. "You will take Blake and Ms Smith back to the base. Tara and I will take the other two. Just to be extra careful, we'll even take a round-about route, while I make the call. Does that satisfy your nerves?"

"I'll get going as you suggest," the Pigeon replied stiffly.

Soon, Sally and I were in the back of Collett's car, with our hands tied and a large goon for company. Tara was driving. "OK, showtime," said Collett, with again that edge of glee in his voice as he dialled Polnukov's number.

The phone was answered immediately. "Mr Pulnokov," said Collett, in the delighted tones of an owner greeting a beloved pet. "How delightful to hear from you again."

Polnukov's voice, by contrast, seethed with palpable fury as he ranted about the assault he'd received early in the morning, and ferociously demanded that Collett administer a cure. He was almost shouting, so I could easily hear every word.

"Now, don't be like that, Mr Pulnokov," said Collett. "I provided you with a quite considerable service, for which you neglected to pay, and you responded instead with unpleasant allegations. You're aware that I got shot, as a direct result of our argument? That I lost a man who was like a son to me, as he heroically battled to save my life? I think I am being perfectly reasonable. That could have

Chapter 36: Julia Barnes, commodity for trading

been a knife, not some tissues, we both know that. All I am doing is giving you the chance to make good your debt to me. Plus interest of course, and compensation for my losses. Hence a round five million. In cash. Upfront."

"You are playing with fire, Mr Collett, and you will regret this."

"Or," said Collett, "you could just sit back, relax, and play the Corona lottery. Mind you, the experts are starting to think that the bigger the dose you get infected with, the faster you get sick, and the more likely you are to die. Would you like to test that theory?"

I noticed how tightly Tara's hands were now gripping the steering wheel.

"You think that you have the upper hand in this negotiation, Mr Collett?" said Polnukov.

"Only one of us is facing the prospect of an extremely unpleasant death in the next week or so," said Collett.

"Maybe not in the next week," said Polnukov, "but you too will be marked for death, because I will find you. Wherever you go, whatever name you might try to hide under, my people will find you. You and your daughter. You will spend the rest of your short lives looking over your shoulders."

Tara pulled the car into a layby. "Dad, we've got more than enough money, even after we've paid the men," she told Collett. "Let's just go! Give him what he wants, and go!"

"What about Feodor?" said Collett. "He won't be coming with us, will he?"

"I'm sad about him too, but this bastard's powerful! I don't wanna spend every fucking day on the lookout for bloody Russian hitmen!"

Collett did not reply to Tara, instead speaking into the phone. "Mr Polnukov, we are businessmen, not a pair of drunks squaring off outside a pub. There is no need for these threats. I too have the resources to hire hitmen, if you force me to go down that route. The inevitable end point will be both our deaths. Is my offer really so unreasonable?"

"To deliberately infect a man with a fatal virus, that is unreasonable."

"To accept an extremely difficult and exclusive treatment for a fatal condition, and then refuse to pay for it, is equally unreasonable," said Collett.

"You will administer your cure free of charge, or face the consequences," said Polnukov.

"Dad, pleeeease," said Tara.

Collett sighed. "You drive a hard bargain, sir," he told the phone. "Let me revise my offer. In exchange for the money, I will give you the operation. The means not only to heal yourself, but to make large sums of money very quickly. You could make back your five million in a day or two, with the contacts that you have."

"You mean, the two women," said Polnukov.

"I mean, the two women."

They were horse-trading Siobhan and me, as if we were cattle at a farmer's market.

"Had you come to me with that offer at the start, a lot of this could have been avoided."

"Had you paid for your treatment the first time round, I probably would have done," replied Collett.

Chapter 36: Julia Barnes, commodity for trading

"You also have a third component," said Polnukov. "One that allows you to administer your cures without rushing to visit a Glory."

"How well informed you are," said Collett. "But that component does not belong to me. It is on loan from mister Dexter, so you would need to discuss that with him."

"Without that component, we would not have a deal."

"Mister Polnukov, you could be pointing a chainsaw at my balls, and I still would not even consider giving you something that belongs to mister Dexter. If I did so, I'm betting both of us would be dead within a few hours, 24 at most."

I expected Polnukov to ridicule Collett for this, perhaps even laugh out loud. But there was silence from his end of the phone. Perhaps he, too, had been visited in the night by Claude Dexter? No amount of money or power could protect you from a man who could walk through walls.

Collett said, "How about this. We will use the third component to administer your cure, but you only get to keep the two women. Unless of course Mr Dexter agrees otherwise."

There was a pause. "Then I accept," said Polnukov. "But one hint of betrayal, just one, and it will go very badly for you indeed."

"I'll be in touch with arrangements first thing tomorrow," said Collett. "Good doing business with you." He ended the call.

"Dad, he's going to kill us," said Tara.

"He's almost certainly going to try," said Collett. "But he can't afford to do anything that might jeopardise his cure. So it's really very simple. We send a few men to exchange the two women for the five million. Once we have the money, Blake goes along and gives them his magic touch one last time, and cures the bastard. We keep his girlfriend to ensure cooperation. And we have Dexter's people on hand to take custody of Blake, once it's done! See, he gets what he wants, but you and I don't have to be anywhere near."

"What's to stop him sending a hitman after us, later?" said Tara.

"Dexter. I'll pay him half a million or so, to kindly ask Polnukov not to," said Collett.

Tara seemed reassured by this. "Okay. I'm sorry I doubted you, Dad"

"Hey, that's OK, little girl. This time tomorrow, it'll all be over." And with that, she started the car again and drove us back to base.

By now, Sally was beginning to look distinctly unwell, though she was staying resolutely silent. "How are you doing in the back there?" asked Collett, turning around to us happily. "I'm sorry to have to sell you on, Ms Barnes, but you know how it is. I have to protect my daughter, you know."

I looked straight ahead, not offering him the satisfaction of a reply. He turned his attention to Sally. "I say, Sally, you're really looking rather peaky. Not getting travel-sick, are you?"

"I told you, Dad, she's a Glory-addict," said Lara. "That's why Blake keeps insisting she stays close to him."

"Well, well," said Collett. "I'm sure Mr Dexter would pay us a small sum to add another one to his collection."

Chapter 36: Julia Barnes: commodity for trading

Antony

I spent the day as a tool in Collett's production line of healing. It was impressive in a way, to be part of such an enterprise. I got vague senses of the people we were healing – emotions and a rough idea of how they saw the world – although much of this faded from my mind as soon as we broke contact. Still, it seemed that most of them were the sort of very rich, self-entitled types that Father would occasionally rant about to no-one in particular, when he wasn't railing against benefit scroungers or all the other kinds of people who annoyed him. But a few of the ones we cured were people I felt that I would like, if I got the chance to meet them. I didn't, of course.

Throughout the day, I cooperated meekly, doing everything that was asked of me, without complaint. That had been my deal with Collett, in exchange for Sally being kept in the neighbouring room. They'd let me see her at lunch time, but with two goons for company, so neither of us had felt like saying anything. The only brief ray of joy for me was the opportunity to verbally needle the Pigeon, who was looking comically nervous about having to send a text to someone called Polnukov.

Finally I was driven back to base, squashed in between two thugs, while poor Siobhan was again stuffed in the boot. She'd obviously done something to anger these people, and it was clear from the look in her eyes that she'd do far more at the first chance she got. Sally was driven in another car (my protests about this were ignored), and soon I was back in my prison room, with two thugs searching the TV channels for a suitably violent movie.

* * * * *

The attack began just after eleven. My minders and I were probably the last ones to become aware of it, on account of all the gunshots and random exploding that was happening on the telly, as the latest film approached its climax. But I realised that some of the sounds were coming from outside.

"Is that shooting?" I asked.

"Course it's fucking shooting," said one of the thugs. "See that thing he's holding? It's called a gun."

"I meant outside, dickhead."

"Wot?"

At that moment, the film went briefly quiet, as the hero ran along and jumped from one roof to another. That allowed all three of us to hear a series of pops that were clearly coming from outside."

"Oh, fuck," said one thug, and he clicked off the TV.

"Whadda we do?" said his mate.

"They told us to wait here."

"I know, but … do you think it's the cops?"

"It might be Mr Polnukov's men," I said. "I heard that your boss infected him with Corona this morning. He sounded pretty pissed off on the phone, for some reason."

"Polnukov?" said one.

"Fuck!" said the other.

"I'm not fucking going up against him. Let's stay here."

Chapter 36: Julia Barnes: commodity for trading

Damn, I thought.

So the three of us sat there and listened to the sporadic pops that we assumed were gunfire, accompanied by shouts and the occasional cry of pain.

Then someone knocked on the door, and a voice shouted, "There's too many of them! They're killing all of us! Get up and run!"

"What the?" said one thug, but the other had had enough. He whipped out his gun and ran to the door, throwing it open. Then a tall man standing behind it punched him hard in the face, while his other arm grabbed the thug's gun hand, pulling it upwards. The gun went off, hitting the ceiling. The second thug sitting beside me whipped out his own gun, aiming for the man, but I grabbed it and tugged it to the side. As I did so he fired twice, and both bullets hit the side of his mate, who the tall man had just thrown back into our room. The tall man then swung his boot upwards and broke the second thug's jaw. Between us we smashed his gun hand down against the floor until he let go of the gun.

The first thug was lying moaning and bleeding in the corner, and the tall man had already turned away from me. "Where have you been?" he asked, addressing a young man in a leather jacket who'd just appeared in the doorway.

"She was tied to the bed," he replied. "Took ages to cut her free! Is this your son?"

"That's him," and the tall man turned back towards me.

It was Father.

* * * * *

Father didn't do hugs, even in life-or-death situations. "It's good to see you, son", he said, and reached out to shake my hand.

"And you," I said. "How did you find me?"

"Lucasz did most of it," he said.

Siobhan had appeared in the doorway. "I need to call my house! Give me a phone!" she demanded.

The leather-jacketed man, Lucasz, said, "Sammy's not in the house, we think they moved him."

"Fuck!" shouted Siobhan.

"Lucasz, free the others," said Father. And then to Siobhan, "you help him."

"Excuse me?" said Siobhan, indignantly. "I've got other things to do!" She grabbed a dropped gun from the floor of my room, and then stormed off down the corridor, a projectile of avenging fury aimed at Collett.

"I understand her position," said Father. Lucasz was already trying to break the padlock on another door along the corridor. Thankfully, all the shooting seemed to be happening outside.

"She'll get herself killed," I said to Father. "I have to help her. You help Lucasz!"

Father raised one eyebrow – was he impressed that I was taking charge? But he said nothing. I ran down the corridor, and he followed behind me. There was no point arguing, not with Father. One of Collett's thugs lay moaning in the corridor, his belly a mass of blood. "They're inside," said Father. "The attackers."

"Hang on," I asked him. "They're not with you?"

Chapter 36: Julia Barnes: commodity for trading

"Of course not! We were waiting for the chance to break you out quietly, then they turned up and all hell broke loose. We realised we couldn't wait any longer."

"Polnukov," I said quietly. "He's a violent oligarch that Collett's been pissing off."

"To us, he's just a diversion," said Father.

"There's a chance we might be able to heal him," I said, looking at the bleeding thug.

"Good lad," replied Father. We went up some stairs, and along another corridor, with me making sure I was the one to look round corners. We approached a partly open door at the end of a corridor, but before we went through it, we heard voices from within.

"Get out of here, this doesn't concern you," said Siobhan, again sounding fearsome.

"I am afraid that it very much does concern me," replied Polnukov's voice.

"How about I pop out of the room for a bit, leave you two to discuss it?" came Collett's voice, with a rather forced cheerful tone.

Father moved to go into the room but I held him back. "Let me watch," I said. "Until we know what's happening, we can't make a plan." Again, he responded with raised eyebrows and a nod.

I sank to my knees and slowly moved my head into the door, until my eyes peeked through and I could see. Siobhan was pressing a gun into the side of Collett's skull, while her other arm was clamped tight around his neck. Facing them, with his back to me, was a man who had to be Polnukov.

"This man's got my son," said Siobhan, addressing Polnukov. "You got kids? So I'll tell you what's going to happen. This piece of shit is going to pick up his phone, and call whoever he's got minding my son. He's going to instruct them to give my son that phone, and allow him to leave the house or wherever they are holding him. When my son confirms that he is safe, then we will move on to whatever your business is. Mr Polnukov, isn't it? We connected before."

"We did," said Polnukov. "But since then, the Piece Of Shit has arranged for me to be infected with a large dose of Coronavirus. So I will be requiring your curing services for a second time."

"Fine by me," said Siobhan.

"In that case we can do business," said Polnukov. "Collett, do as she says, arrange for the release of her son."

With two guns now pointing at him, Collett obeyed. After a minute, Siobhan was talking to her son on Collett's phone, as tears streamed down her face. "Are you sure?" she was asking him. "Are you sure you're away from him? Start running, son! All the way down the street, get into a shop! Is he following? Make sure he's not following!"

Then a sound like a firecracker went off behind me, once and then again, and Father collapsed to the ground. I looked up and saw Tara, accompanied by the Pigeon. She had a smoking gun in her hand.

"Faaather!" I wailed. "You've killed him!"

Chapter 37: Those whom the gods love

Antony

"I aimed for the gut," Tara said, icily. "You do as you're told, and he'll make it."

The door to Collett's room swung open, and Polnukov's gun fired twice. The Pigeon's head exploded in blood, but Tara dived to the side. "Drop your gun, then come in and join us, little daughter," said Polnukov. "Or I start putting bullets into your father, kneecaps first."

A moment's silence, and then Tara laid her gun on the ground, and walked icily down the corridor. Ignoring me and my crumpled Father, she stalked into the room.

"And you too, Mr Blake," said Polnukov. "Please join us. I am meaning you no harm."

"Go," rasped Father.

Shaken, I walked in. Siobhan's gun was still pointing at Collett, and Polnukov's at Tara. "We need the other one. The older woman," said Polnukov.

"She's in a room downstairs with two of her friends," said Tara. "I locked them in."

"Then I suggest you go and unlock her. Tell her that if she does not come, this woman dies." He indicated Siobhan. "And of course, if you don't bring her to me, daughter, then your father dies."

Tara strode angrily from the room. "When he's done, he'll kill all four of us," said Collett to Siobhan. "He doesn't like loose ends, this one."

"Only you will die," Polnukov told him. "Unless you annoy me, in which case your daughter dies also."

I couldn't work out what to do. Siobhan was still pointing her gun at Collett, who was now in a kneeling position. Polnukov's gun was aimed at both of them. Whatever I did could get Siobhan shot. It was better to wait and hope that the three of us could heal Father. I took a step backwards towards the door.

"Stop!" shouted Polnukov. "I can see your reflection. Do not take another step."

"I just have to check on my father," I said, trying to keep my voice steady. "They shot him! And then I'll come back, I swear it." I stepped through the door before he could argue. But Father wasn't there.

* * * * *

"There's no blood," I muttered, looking at the spot where he had fallen. "Why's there no blood?"

"Antony?" Julia was coming down the corridor, with her hands in the air. Tara was behind her. I walked back into Collett's room.

"How did you find this place, by the way?" asked Collett, as if to pass the time. "I really wasn't expecting that you would, at least not so soon. Was it – Dexter?"

"That man you abandoned, after he shot you, at the Glory," said Polnukov. "I had people there, posing as sightseers, just in case you caused trouble. One of them picked him up. We convinced him it was in his best interests to talk."

Chapter 37: Those whom the gods love

"Julia's coming," I told Polnukov. "The girl's sticking a gun in her back."

"Drop the gun, daughter," said Polnukov loudly, "or your father dies."

"I don't think so," replied Tara. "Because if I shoot this woman, you'll be dying of Corona by the end of the week, remember?" Julia walked into the room with Tara behind her.

"Siobhan, dear, your hand is shaking," said Collett. "Your son is free, and I don't think you have it in you to kill a man. Why don't you put that gun down. Then the three of you can heal Mr Polnukov, and we can all walk out of here alive."

"Don't do that, Ms Smith," said Polnukov, also pointing his gun at Collett. "Daughter, if you shoot that woman, then I will perhaps die this week, or next. But if you do not drop your gun by the count of ten, then your father will certainly die today."

"Oh shit, police!" said Tara, suddenly looking towards the window.

Polnukov swore in Russian, turning his head to the window, and his gun too, just for a moment.

Tara fired three times from the gun she was now holding by Julia's side. Blood exploded from Polnukov's chest. Siobhan's gun went off too, hitting Collett in the neck. She dropped it immediately, hands flying to her face in shock and distress.

"Fucking CUNT!" screamed Tara, throwing Julia to the ground and pumping four bullets into Siobhan, one of which went straight through her eye, killing her instantly. Far too late, I leapt forwards and barrelled into Tara, throwing her to the ground. Collett was gasping and rasping as blood pumped from her neck. Polnukov was also somehow still alive, hand flapping across the ground, looking for something.

"You stupid girl!" Julia was yelling at Tara, her normally kind face full of fury. "We could have saved him! We could have saved your dad! All you needed to do was not shoot her! YOU killed him, you understand that? Well now you have to live with it!"

"Come on, we have to go," I said, pulling her away.

"Not ... going.... Anywhere ..." said Polnukov, whose bloodsoaked arm was now holding a gun in our direction. "Heal me."

"We can't," I told him. "Without Siobhan, we can't."

"You will try," he croaked.

"Antony, come on!" the door flew open and Sally ran in. Why did she run in? Polnukov shot her. I'm not even sure if he meant to, but he did. I screamed in fury, and kicked him hard in the hand, sending the gun flying. Sally was slumped against the wall, gasping and coughing blood. The bullet had hit her lung, it looked like. Lucasz ran in, looking horrified, and then he and I half dragged, half carried Sally from the room.

"I tried to stop her running in," he said helplessly.

I thought about the Glory addiction. Maybe it had dulled her reasoning. I should have focussed on her, not Siobhan. "We have to get her to a hospital," said Julia. "That's her only chance, now."

"I can help," said Father, coming up the stairs to meet us. He looked perfectly healthy.

"I saw you shot," I gasped.

"She missed. I played dead. Sorry I scared you, but it worked."

"All the money's in the car, boss," came a male voice from downstairs.

Chapter 37: Those whom the gods love

"Quickly, Antony," said Father. "You've done well here."

"What?" I replied, incredulously. "I really haven't!"

"Boss! Did you hear me? It's all in the car. Did you get the kid?"

"Boss?" I asked him. "Father, why's that man calling you 'boss'?"

"You didn't think I'd attempt this on my own, did you?" he said, with an odd smile. "I had to hire some help."

"They're off duty cops, or something," said Lucasz.

By now, Lucasz and I were carrying the stricken Sally down the stairs, with Julia behind us.

"And what's all this about money?" I asked Father.

"Let's get the girl outside, then I'll explain. There's a fire exit just along this way – yes, there it is."

A man I didn't recognise was holding it open. We all hurried through to the car park. A car was there with its engine running, and a man in the driver's seat. "Come on Antony, I'm taking you home," said Father, his voice now back to its usual no-arguing-with-me tone. He grabbed my wrist.

"Don't be stupid," I said, trying to wrench myself free. "We've got to take Sally to the hospital!"

"Your friends can do that. You are coming home with me. No more crazy adventures for you." He began pulling me hard towards the car.

"Get her to a hospital," I shouted to Julia. "Don't worry about me." There were other cars there, I had to hope they'd be able to get into one of them.

"Open the back door for me," commanded Father to the man who'd been at the fire exit, as we reached the ready car.

"Why don't you open it yourself?" I asked him.

"Do it," said Father, ignoring me, and the thug obeyed. Father dragged me into the back seat alongside him. An image flashed through my mind, of Sally throwing a stone and it going right through me. Then another, of Tara firing at Father. She'd hit him, I'd have sworn that she had, unless ... but how could *he* be a Glory, too?

The thug jumped into the front seat and the driver gunned the engine. I closed my eyes. The car only pushed my Glory-body because I somehow expected it to. If I could convince myself that this *wasn't* the case ...

The seat gave way, beneath and behind me, and I fell right through. "Wo-aaahhh!!!" yelled Father in surprise, but he released his grip and suddenly I was sitting on the road, as the car screeched to a halt some way in front of me. Father's head stuck out of the window. "Go back! We have to get him!"

Then bullets began smashing into the boot of the car. A furious, tear-stained Tara was standing there, firing at us. One of Collett's men stood beside her, his left side spattered with blood. I ran like crazy, straight through a hedge.

"Fuckitty fuck-face!" yelled Father. "Forget the kid, just go, go, GO!" and their car sped away.

"SHIT!" screamed Tara. "Maybe it's in one of the other cars." She wheeled round to see my friends, who had somehow got the door open on one of the two remaining cars. Tara brought her gun round to fire at them.

I ran at Tara, screaming. She turned and fired at me, but I'm guessing the bullets went through me, as I felt nothing. I crashed headfirst into her belly, sending her flying back into the corridor. The thug pulled me off, hoisted me up to my feet, and smashed his fist into my face at the exact moment my knee hit his groin. We fell apart from each other, him back into the building and me onto

Chapter 37: Those whom the gods love

the tarmac outside. My nose hurt like hell, but there was no blood. Then a car swung round to beside me.

"Get in!" shouted Lucasz from the driving seat.

I dived into the empty front passenger seat. Lucasz yelled "Hold on!!" and he floored it. Bullets smashed into the back windscreen as we accelerated away.

"Carefully, Lucasz!" said Julia.

Sally moaned.

"But fast!" I said, because Sally looked deathly pale. "Where's the nearest hospital?!"

"Never make ... in time ..." muttered Sally. "Hold ... my hand."

"Use my phone, Julia," said Lucasz. "Navigate for me!"

Then the rear window disintegrated as another bullet hit. We looked round to see headlights behind us.

"They're after us!" I said. "They think we've got the money!"

"She's angry," said Julia. "Too angry to think."

"They won't catch us," said Lucasz.

He drove like an utter maniac, making Sally's driving seem like Gran after a big Sunday lunch. The lights of the chasing car were still there, behind us. "Have you found a hospital?" I shouted.

"Nearest one doesn't look like it's got A&E," said Julia. "Even at this speed, our best bet's half an hour away – oh my!! Look ahead!!"

A rippling blanket of flames was hanging in the sky some way ahead of us.

"Sorry ... Antony," muttered Sally.

"What for?" I asked angrily.

"Being ... stupid."

"There's another one, look," I cried, pointing at what looked like a yellow firework hanging in the sky, some way to the left of the rippling fire. It was like a little sun, repeatedly exploding out rings of yellow which grew and faded like ripples on a pond.

"It's a spate," said Lucasz. "Been happening a lot since the Globe – at least one a day, somewhere. Means there'll be more, lots at ground level."

"And cars too," said Julia. "The roads will be a death trap."

"We can't let her die!" I shouted.

"We'll have to try and use a Glory," said Julia.

"But you said you couldn't without Siobhan!" I shouted.

"Can you think of anything better?" she replied. "Maybe somehow the three of us – you, me, and Lucasz – could do something?"

Could I do something? Then I realised that I could, although I really didn't want to.

Another bullet whizzed past, and Lucasz increased our speed even more. We hurtled down the empty road until we came up rapidly behind a small car trundling along at a mere fifty-five. It was just coming to a bend as we caught it, "Come on, come on," said Lucasz as we sat on its tail and dropped speed, the headlights behind us now getting closer. Then we were round the gentle bend and the road opened up, Lucasz hit the gas and we swerved around the other car, gaining speed as we swung back into our lane. Behind us, the pursuing car shot past the small car, too. There was a flash as we went passed a speed camera, then another behind us. I caught the face of the driver behind

Chapter 37: Those whom the gods love

us, in that flash. Tara, her face set in furious determination, with the blood-splattered thug beside her, looking scared.

"Turn left," said Julia, and Lucasz performed a screeching handbrake turn.

"What are we after?" asked Lucasz, as Tara's car turned into the road behind us

"That!" said Julia. Ahead of us, looming over the darkened horizon, sat a huge blue cloud that appeared to be illuminated from all sides. "I think it goes down to ground level!"

"Must be *massive*," said Lucasz.

"Watch out for people coming the other way, running away from it," I said.

"I'll try, but you can bet the bitch behind us won't be," he said.

A car shot by going the other way, then another. What would it be like, to look up and see that hanging above you? Would you think you'd gone mad?

"Shit!" Lucasz slammed on the brakes. An approaching car was being overtaken at speed by another, veering wildly into our lane. Lucasz wrenched the wheel sideways and we mounted the verge, then a sickening whack as the car made contact.

"Wing mirror's gone!" shouted Lucasz, yanking our car back onto the road.

"Well, we know what's behind us," I said, craning round. The chasing car had got a lot closer.

"Julia, try social media," shouted Lucasz. "We need a precise location on one at ground level."

"Dammit, I'm no good at this," said Julia as she fiddled with the phone.

"Keep trying," I said.

"No cars coming," said Julia, as we came to the top of a slope. "There were cars coming at us along this road, and now there aren't."

"Well, that's good," I said.

"No, it isn't! It means the road must be – STOP!!!"

The road had plunged into a steep descent, and ahead of us was a mass of glowing white ice, which had swallowed the road entirely and the verges either side, right in front of us. We were hurtling towards it, at eighty miles an hour.

Chapter 38: Into the Glory

Julia

The screeching of brakes rent our ears as we hurtled towards the Glory, but the slope worked against us – we were barely slowing down, and the Glory rushed towards us.

"Julia, jump out!!" yelled Lucasz.

I was halfway through saying "What?" when Antony joined in:

"Do it!" he yelled, and images flashed through my mind of what happened to Feodor. I grabbed the door handle, threw open the door and jumped out into blackness. My knee hit something hard, my body cartwheeled in the air, then my arm hit something even harder, and my face slapped into tarmac. The car screeched on into the Glory.

Antony

I saw Julia jump out. Sally was twitching, her face deathly pale. The screech of the brakes filled my ears as the ice-coloured Glory bore down on us. I stuck out my hand and grabbed desperately as we went into it. Blackness engulfed me, and invisible forces pushed hard against me, so hard I thought I would break. Then seconds later, it was over. I was still in the car. We skidded on some way further, then came to a stop. The road had levelled out. In the driver's seat, Lucasz gasped with relief. He was OK – the man who could walk through Glories.

In my hand was a piece of glowing white ice. I opened my fingers and it shot back towards the Glory. Then I turned to look at the back seat. Sally was gone.

Julia

The car vanished into the Glory ahead of me, then a second set of headlights came screaming towards me from behind.

I rolled to the side, away from the beam of the headlights. That car's brakes were screaming too, but like our car, the slope was against them. They smacked right into the Glory, but this car didn't go through it. Instead, the sound of twisting of metal almost drowned out the human screams.

Then the pain hit me. Shooting agonies, from my right leg and left arm. I thought both of them were probably broken. Something in my torso felt wrong, too. The world was tipping repeatedly on its side, and there was blood in my mouth. I coughed, and splattered salty blood on the road in front of me. Something invisible felt like it was dragging me down, away from the pain, into blissful slumber.

No.

Chapter 38: Into the Glory

No, I couldn't give up.

How far away was the Glory? Its luminous icy wall rose up in front of me. Of course, it could disappear any minute. The back end of the chasing car stood still on the road, maybe one car-length in front of me. It wasn't that far. But my right leg wouldn't take my weight, and my left arm erupted in agony every time I tried to move it.

But it was downhill, so I rolled. Like a kid on a slope, I straightened myself and turned, over and over, trying to protect my left arm with my right, gasping and yelping with pain as I went. I was level with the back of the car now. "Don't go! Don't go, Glory, don't go!" I implored in my head. I rolled on again, and again, then at last I was touching it, and the pain washed away.

Antony

"Where is she?" said Lucasz. "Where's Sally?"

"I sent her into the Glory," I told him.

"You did WHAT?" he looked furious.

"She was dying. There was nothing else we could have done." Tears rolled down my face. "There was this guy, Rick, he made contact. Told me they needed a bridge, that he might survive it. I didn't know what else to do!"

"What the fuck are you even talking about? She was your friend, and you vanished her!"

"I *TOLD* you, she was dying!" I shouted.

He flung open the car door and strode away from it. I got out too, saying nothing. After some moments he shook his head, still not looking at me. "We'd better find Julia," he said, curtly.

"Yeah, good idea," I said. And we walked in silence towards the Glory. I stopped just before we reached it, but he just walked on through, as if it was nothing.

Julia

Sally was standing in front of me. Why was she there? How was she unhurt? "Julia, listen, I've very little time. They're going to call to you, and you have to be ready!"

"Ready for what?" I asked.

"What's coming, what they're going to do … the Others … we have to stop it!"

"Sally, you're talking in riddles, for goodness' sake."

"Be ready." Then she fell away into the blackness. I opened my eyes and the Glory was gone.

"Oh, God," said Lucasz. He was standing quite close to me, looking at the wrecked car that had been following us. The middle was crumpled, but the bonnet intact, its headlights still blazing.

"Lara … she's dead," said Lucasz.

Chapter 38: Into the Glory

"Her real name was Tara," I told him. "She was working against us the whole time."

"I know, but ..." he didn't finish the sentence, turning to face me with tears in his eyes.

"Come here," I said, finding that I could stand up without any trouble at all. I stretched out my arms, and embraced him.

"Sally's gone, too," he said.

"Gone?" I asked.

"I dropped her into the Glory," said Antony. He was walking towards us through where the Glory had been.

"That was your plan all along, wasn't it?" I asked him gently.

"Not at first," he said. "But I couldn't see any other way to save her, and if I hadn't done it the impact would have killed her anyway."

"That's hardly 'saving her', said Lucasz.

"She spoke to me," I said. "I didn't understand what she said, but she's in there, somehow."

"Thank God," said Antony, sinking to his knees. "Thank God." Now he was crying, too.

I gently disengaged myself from Lucasz. "You've been through a lot, haven't you," I said to Antony, gently.

"Lost so many people," he muttered. "My cousin, I think he went into a Glory, too. Linda and Thelma, Siobhan, and now Sally. Not sure if I can do this anymore."

Lucasz decided to change the subject. "That man who helped us escape, was that your father? He said that he was."

"Him?" said Antony. "Well, he looked like Father and he talked like Father ... but he did things my Father would never do. Father never gave up, you see. Never backed down in an argument, never admitted a job was beyond him. At chess ... I mean, he didn't play very often, but you had to scrape him off the board when he did. You should have heard some of his ding-dongs with Gran. Most of the time he was just grumpy. Rules, rules, rules. *'If you don't do your work, son, you'll fail. You'll fail at life.'* If he was sure he was right, which was most of the time, it took a force out of Hell to shift him. You had to lay out the evidence piece by piece like a lawyer, and then maybe, just maybe, he might admit you were right. No wonder he didn't believe me, about that Glory, when I ran away from Daniel's house. I went there, you see, and Daniel wasn't there, and his dad blamed me and then Father came, and I said it was because of a Glory, and he didn't believe me. Well, of course he didn't.

"Would my Father have run through a hail of bullets to rescue me? Yes. Would he have tried to save all my friends as well? Yes. Back to the wall, Father would do what he judged to be right. And yes, he'd have dragged me off against my will, if he thought it was the way to protect me. But then he gave up. I had this moment of doubt and I got away, and Tara came out shooting and I ran, and he gave up. They had all the money in that car, didn't they? Over a million. But Father would have jumped out and ran after me, to see I was safe or to drag me to safety, even if it meant giving up all the cash. The man who raised me would

Chapter 38: Into the Glory

never back down, and he wouldn't give up. So you see, whatever he looked like, it can't have been him."

"So ... what?" asked Lucasz. "You think he'd been hypnotised? Someone was controlling his mind? Or some lookalike?"

"I don't know, and I don't understand," said Antony. "But that man was not Father. And Tara, she shot him before. I saw her do it. He went down like she'd hit him, but there was no blood and then suddenly he was fine. He said she missed, but she didn't. Lucasz, did you see him carry anything? Or open a door for himself?"

"I don't know," he said. "I don't think I did, come to think of it. He showed up at Walt's place, said he was looking for you and he'd heard a rumour that maybe you were there, and of course we got talking about Julia and Lara. So we joined forces. He worked out where you all were, I've no idea how. I was all for getting Keith and a few others to come along and help, they were up for it. But your father said no, he'd get his own people, a couple of ex-cops he liked to drink with."

"Father doesn't have drinking buddies, and he doesn't know any ex-cops," I said. "I think ... I think that man was a Glory, like me. It means I'm not the only one."

"No, you're not," I agreed. "Claude Dexter appeared in my room last night, without opening the door. I'm starting to think he might be behind a lot of what's happening. Maybe even behind the Glories themselves."

But Antony wasn't listening. He had turned away from me, to look at the far verge of the road, where a new Glory had winked into existence. It was a shimmering deep blue lake, with waves rippling across it. It lay on the sloping verge like a giant blanket that had been dropped there, or a piece of ocean. The water looked like it should flow down to the road, but it didn't.

"It's the one," said Antony. "The first one. The one that took Daniel." His back was to me, and his voice has a strange reverence about it. He stretched out his arms, and started walking towards it. I ran forward.

"Antony," I said, catching up with him. "Antony, what are you doing?"

"I've found him. I've found Daniel," he replied. He didn't take his eyes off the Glory.

"You can't know he's in there," I told him.

"But I do," he said, simply.

The blue Glory was just a few metres away from us now.

"The man I was telling you about, Claude Dexter," I said. "I think he knows where Daniel is. He was after you too, he told Collett where to find you! But if you find him first, then you can find your cousin! Please! There's no way of knowing if you can even survive this."

"Daniel did." His voice lacked emotion, as if he'd been hypnotised; he was still looking straight ahead at the Glory. "I can see his face now. *'Jeebus, Cuz, what took you so long?'*"

We were at the bottom of the road verge now, with the edge of the Glory just a metre ahead. "Lucasz," I shouted. "Help me."

Chapter 38: Into the Glory

I grabbed Antony by the waist, trying to pull him back, but his hands gripped my wrists and easily pulled them to the sides. Then he turned, said "I can't let you stop me," and pushed me hard in the belly. I landed in a heap on the road.

Antony stepped onto the Glory, digging his toes in and somehow not losing his footing among the rippling waves. I was back on my feet now, helped upright by Lucasz. "Antony, wait," I said helplessly.

He turned around. "Thank you for everything," he said, addressing us both with a tear in his eye. "But I have to do this."

He dropped into a squat, leant to the side to stick his left hand into the Glory and bring up a piece of it, then he fell into the blue water and was gone.

PART THREE

*"And the stars reach down and tell us,
there's always one escape"*

Spandau Ballet, "Through the Barricades"

Chapter 39: Julia Barnes, free woman

Julia

Lucasz and I were lying on the grass together, watching the waves break across the surface of the Glory hanging in the sky above us. It was a pale blue ocean, with white wave crests appearing and disappearing, only of course it was upside down. It got less disorientating if you looked at it for long enough, provided you didn't look at anything else. Occasionally I thought I'd caught glimpses of Antony and Sally among the waves, but I was probably imagining them. I could see the first rays of light from the new day, coming over from the east.

We had got back in the car and left the spot where Antony and Sally had vanished, and Tara died, simply because we didn't want to stay there. We'd driven on for a while, in silence, before it occurred to either of us to discuss where we were going, or what we were going to do. The car decided things for us, at least in the short term, when the petrol ran out.

Without a word, we'd both got out, noticed the great sea Glory above us, and simply found a spot on the grass to rest. Lucasz told me a bit more about the rescue attempt, and we discussed whether the man had been Antony's father or not. We didn't really get anywhere, and somehow deviated into small talk. I even let him waffle about Marvel movies for a good ten minutes. After all, he had just rescued me.

We didn't talk much about the people we'd lost. There'd be time to grieve for Siobhan, but as for Antony and Sally, we didn't even know if they were dead. We talked instead about what we hoped for from the immediate future. In my case it was Malcolm, rest, a few gentle walks, more rest, lots of good food, some rest, and an *Archers* omnibus.

"I don't want to go back to my parents' house. They just argue and argue," said Lucasz.

"I remember you telling me," I said gently.

"Maybe I could go and rejoin Walt's little group."

"Really?" I asked.

"I don't know, maybe. I was sort of happy there. But a lot of that was Lara, even though she kept me at arm's length most of the time. It was worth it for when she didn't. But of course, that person didn't really exist, did she?"

"I wonder," I said. 'She told me that her times with you, she really did do it because she was bored. So maybe you got the real her."

"It's such a waste," he said. "So many people dead, and for what? Most of them were just trying to get rich, and instead they got dead, and Antony's dad ran off with the money instead – or whoever he was."

"And Siobhan," I said. "She was so bloody angry. She had reason, of course, and she saved her son. It was almost the last thing she did. But if Collett hadn't treated her so badly, then she might still be alive. Both of them would be. Instead, they ended up on a collision course, and neither of them could stop it. God, that poor boy. Someone's going to have to tell him his mother's gone."

Chapter 39: Julia Barnes, free woman

"We need to go to the police, don't we," said Lucasz.
"We do," I agreed. "I've had enough of running and hiding."
"Okay, but not yet," he said. "Let the sun rise, first."

* * * * *

We looked for anything useful from our erstwhile car, but the only thing worth taking was a packet of biscuits, which we shared. It was daylight now, though still before seven, and for the first time in some while, we couldn't see a single Glory in the sky. Lucasz dialled 999 and explained that we'd witnessed a series of fatal shootings, and were now in the middle of nowhere, doing his best to describe our location based on the map on the phone. The person on the other end didn't seem to believe us. It was cold, so we started pottering along the road.

The sun continued to rise. I told Lucasz about my son and grand-daughter, to pass the time. He was content to listen, and admire the countryside. He seemed less of a boy now than when I'd first met him, and more comfortable in his own skin. I wondered if Tara had been his first woman. The few cars that passed did so at a normal speed. I noticed twin streaks of rubber tracks in one place, swerving from one side of the road to the other. I found that I was enjoying the walk. For the first time, I started to really believe that I was free from the cancer, and might actually live to a ripe old age. As I stroked the dew off the cow parsley flowers that massed along the roadside, I dared to dream of a future with Malcolm. We would travel. I'd always wanted to properly travel the world. But I wondered what sort of world there would be, now, as the certainties we'd all lived by seemed to be falling away.

After about half an hour a police car tootled up behind us. "Are you the ones that called about the shootings?"

The first hour in the police station felt like some kind of surreal tragi-comic farce. Every police officer we talked to looked exhausted or haunted, and the ones who took our statements did so with perfunctory reluctance. I told them about Sammy and his mother, able to recite their address. I even confessed everything about Locksley and her group, including how Tara had tricked us into our dramatic escape. Some of them looked at me as if they were waiting for me to start talking a language they could understand. "Nine people have died on the roads in the past 24 hours," said one. "Can you tell us anything about that?"

"Well, one of them was Tara Collett," I said, "the daughter of the man we were telling you about. Only I'm not sure that's her real name. Two days ago, a man died at a Glory. His name was Feodor. He drove a Land Rover right into it, which he and others had hijacked a few minutes before. They pointed guns at people. The Land Rover would have been full of blood – another man's too. That man was Collett. There'll be fingerprints, including mine. You must know about this – surely?"

They didn't seem to.

I asked to be allowed to call Malcolm, but they kept putting me off. Eventually I found myself alone in a police cell, eating chewy toast and tasteless

Chapter 39: Julia Barnes, free woman

marmalade. Then the door opened again, and a woman said "Boss wants to see you." I followed her up to an office, where two senior-looking officers faced me.

"We've found the place where you were held," said the man, who'd introduced himself as Inspector West. "It's a bloodbath. Not a single person left alive. I'm sorry if our officers were sceptical, earlier."

"I understand. A fellow hostage, Siobhan Smith, she was shot. They were holding her boy, Sammy, but I think he got away."

"The boy is fine," said the female officer, Inspector White. "Well, as fine as he can be, under the circumstances."

"Poor kid."

"We need you to think very carefully, Ms Barnes," said West. "Was there anybody else involved in this operation?"

"One or two of his goons might have got away, but otherwise everyone involved is dead. And Polnukov, the guy who led the attack, he was either killed or badly wounded."

"He's dead. Anyone else?"

"Well … there was Claude Dexter, of course. He was the one pulling the strings. He seemed to have some way of predicting where Glories were going to be, and I tell you, it actually worked. More than once we arrived at the predicted spot before the Glory appeared."

"We're familiar with the name, but there is no such person," said White.

"He's real," I said firmly.

"As far as we can tell," persisted White, "the name is a construct, or an alias. It's been cropping up across various enterprises during the past month, he's claimed as the author of the Glory Tower website and organisation. But the name is a smokescreen."

"I met him."

For a moment, they both look shocked. "You met someone who *claimed* to be him," West corrected me.

"Perhaps." I described the encounter as best I could, including the fact that he got into and out of a locked room, and they listened but didn't really ask questions. Instead, they moved on to the money. My estimate of their takings from the previous day came in useful.

"Do you know where it is, now?"

"We think that a man claiming to be Antony Blake's father drove off with it."

"This man?" West passed me a photo of Antony's father.

"Yes, him."

"Extraordinary," said West.

"Frank Blake insists he was at home all evening and night. His mother backs him up. Yet both you and Lucasz swear blind it was him."

"To be accurate, I can only swear blind that it looked exactly like him, and that Antony Blake was convinced it was his father, at least for a while."

"Ah, yes," said West meaningfully. "Antony Blake. We need to talk about him."

* * * * *

Chapter 39: Julia Barnes, free woman

"Frankly, what you are saying is utterly preposterous," said West.

"A human being who is also a Glory," said White. "You do understand how absurd that sounds."

"I do," I told them. "So ask yourselves this: why would I make up such an unbelievable story when I have absolutely nothing to gain from it?"

They looked at one another, thoughtfully.

"Tell me," I asked, "have there been sightings of him, since his cousin disappeared? Around Glories, for example?"

"There might have been," said White.

"But I'm guessing not a single photograph," I said.

"That proves nothing," said West.

"I'm just telling you what I know. And let me emphasise, just before he vanished, he told me he was certain that the man we met was *not* his father. So I imagine that Frank Blake really was sitting at home last night."

"And then Antony Blake deliberately fell into a Glory," said White.

"He did. I wouldn't bother looking for him, for a while."

I wondered what on earth they would make of it all. They told me I'd been very helpful, but I suspected they both wished I had talked about nothing but shooting, cash and kidnapping. We spent a while trying to wring from my brain the names of some of the people we'd cured. Then there was a firm knock at the door, and Locksley walked in.

* * * * *

"I'm sorry," I said, as Locksley sat down in a small room with myself and Lucasz.

Locksley gazed at me impassively.

"I'm sorry we ran away," I continued. "We were played. Lara – that wasn't her real name – broke into my room, drugged me, drilled a little hole in my head. Then convinced us you'd done it to her as well. Made us think we were guinea pigs. That's why we ran away."

"I see," she replied.

"She's dead now," I added.

"I heard."

"I honestly thought that you probably weren't in on it," I told her. "But I couldn't be sure."

"How noble," she said.

"You probably got all that from Hector," I said. "Have you spoken to Bluebell, by the way? You know that we cured her?"

"Yes, we know," she said curtly.

"What would you have done, in our position?" asked Lucasz.

"Been less of an idiot," she replied.

I sighed. "If you've come here to enjoy the moral high ground and marvel at our gullibility, then bully for you. But I did have you down as a practical person. I'm truly sorry for whatever harm we may have done to your operation, but what's done is done, and it was an honest mistake. Since then, I have been

Chapter 39: Julia Barnes, free woman

kidnapped, tied up, broken several limbs, repeatedly feared for my life, and seen a woman I cared about shot dead in front of me."

"Okay," she said. "I would like to debrief you on everything you experienced during your contacts with the Glories. You can start by telling me everything you can about these Glory predictions that I've been hearing about."

* * * * *

Locksley actually drove me to Malcolm's house herself, with Lucasz along for the ride. Locksley told us her operation had been terminated by her bosses soon after our escape, but she seemed oddly unconcerned by that. "Pretty sure the funding would have been cut anyway. As soon as the bloody things went public, everything changed. No-one was interested in Glory-powered oddballs anymore, it was all about how many Glories there were, and how they affected the general population.

"Glory addiction?" I asked.

"Not at first, but it went up the agenda pretty fast. To start with, it was how we would stop half the people from running to see them, and the other half from running away. But Glory addiction caught the attention of the media, and whatever they say about it in public, the government – or at least some of them – are taking it seriously. So Farron and Bart and I have been going round to interview people who've been identified as addicts, just to try and get some sense of what's going on. It's a real thing, I can tell you that much. And someone *is* setting up treatment centres for them."

"Claude Dexter," I said. "The police said he was some sort of alias, but I met him."

"That name does keep cropping up, and trust me when I say he's on our radar, but technically speaking they're right, he doesn't exist. There's a few people who actually have the same name, but we've accounted for all of them. The name is an alias, but whether it's for one person or a group, I don't know. There may be no single 'Claude Dexter.' But your report says this man can walk through walls."

"He got into and out of a locked room, when I was in it."

"So he's a Glory," she said simply.

"You believe me?" I said, surprised.

"Of course I do. I know an honest person when I see one."

"Apart from Lara," said Lucasz.

"She did a number on us all," admitted Locksley. "So tell me more about Blake. I gather he's a Glory too."

I told her everything I could about him, though in truth I hadn't known him for very long. I asked if the government would take seriously the possibility that there might be multiple human Glories walking around.

"I'm really not sure," she admitted. "But *I* will. I'd like to stay in touch, I may have more questions, and I think perhaps that we could help each other."

"I'd like that," I said. It felt good to finally stop feeling guilty about deserting her. I shared my home number, then remembered that I wasn't planning

Chapter 39: Julia Barnes, free woman

to live there anymore. "And my mobile's sitting in a cottage somewhere with the battery taken out."

"What about you, Lucasz?" asked Locksley. "Where will you be staying, and can I have your contact number?"

"About that," he said. "Did you say your house was going to be empty, Julia?"

* * * * *

First we dropped Lucasz off at my house, with keys and the customary instructions of how to navigate its oddities. Then Malcolm greeted me with delight as I walked up the path to the front door. He nodded respectfully to Locksley, and she returned the gesture with a rare smile, before going on her way. The smell of roast beef wafted from the kitchen. "They told me you were coming," Malcolm said. I ate three whole portions, then we cuddled on the sofa, and my eyes began to droop. Malcolm helped me up the stairs and left me to sleep.

* * * * *

Three days passed, full of joy yet also blissfully restful. I was surprised to see how modestly the season had advanced while I'd been away, and when Malcolm told me it had only been a week, I had to count the nights on my fingers before I believed him. Most days involved two or three zoom calls for me, some with police, some with government scientists who were itching to learn more about the healing process. They had tracked down a few of Collett's patients, one of whom I even got to say hello to on a group call. Of course, I could tell them very little of note, other than that it seemed to work on every injury, illness or complaint that it had been tried on. I found that I had to keep telling them that I could heal no-one but myself unless they found someone with the same gift as Siobhan, which so far they hadn't. I had very mixed feelings about this. I loved being able to help people, but I also loved my simple lockdown life with Malcolm, and had no desire to go dashing after Glories again.

The one thing I didn't enjoy so much was the telly. Even *Pointless*, which I used to love, suddenly had bad associations for me. But the main reason was current affairs, which was what Malcolm still watched a lot of the time. Yet I often put up with it, just because I loved hearing the wry comments Malcolm made at the television, and thought he'd be sad if there was no-one to hear them.

Barry Collins was still all over the schedules, even cropping up on GMTV, the show all the ministers refused to go on because they might get asked questions. Collins and Piers Morgan went at each other like strutting peacocks trying to out-smarm each other, while Susannah Reid tried to get a word in edgeways. She ran through all of the government's failings, reading out the statistics on road deaths. "*The roads are nearly empty,*" shouted Morgan, "*and yet the death rate there is three times what it was before lockdown!! What are you going to do about it?*"

"*Well I'm just a humble back-bencher,*" Collins began.

Chapter 39: Julia Barnes, free woman

"Humble in the same way as I'm young and Chinese," growled Malcolm. Soon Collins was launching into his pet topic of Glory addicts, and the threat that they posed, even though (as he never failed to mention) it wasn't their own fault.

"*So you approve of the building of unregulated, privately run treatment centres for these people?*" asked Morgan. "*Unregulated, and doing God-knows-what to them?*"

"*Firstly, the treatment centres are entirely voluntary,*" said Collins. "*Patients are free to come and go as they wish. Secondly, it may just save lives. And thirdly, the NHS is, as you have so frequently pointed out, just a little bit busy at present. If help is forthcoming, we'd be fools to turn it down.*"

"*Yet the people at the top of your government consistently seem to be playing down the Glory addict 'problem', as you call it,*" said Reid.

"*They don't think it's a problem, do they?*" demanded Morgan.

"*They are focussed on tackling the Coronavirus, at which they are doing a magnificent job, though perhaps they might have underestimated the role that Glory-spotters, and addicts in particular, have played in spreading the virus. No-one seems to remember social distancing when they dash off Glory-spotting. Some of them even share cars!*"

"*So you blame all the road deaths, and all the virus deaths, on a few Glory addicts?*" barked Morgan.

"*Not all of them,*" said Collins. "*Just some. But I do say that these people are undermining the effects of the amazing sacrifices that the rest of the Great British Public are continuing to make.*"

"Soon he'll be blaming them for the failing economy and global warming as well," muttered Malcolm.

"Yet for all his uncountable flaws, Boris doesn't seem to be buying it," I observed. I still could not quite believe that Boris Johnson was our Prime Minister.

"The question is why, though," pondered Malcolm. "Why, when they've got a well-publicised problem and a readily available solution, are they backing away from what looks like an easy win?"

Twenty-four hours later, an explosive news story appeared to provide us with the answer.

Chapter 40: The tears of a clown

Julia

The story was broken by the *Guardian* and *Daily Mirror*, but soon it was dominating the news. The Prime Minister's special advisor, Dominic Cummings, had violated the lockdown rules by inexplicably driving all the way from London to a place in the north called Barnard Castle. The story did not speculate on the reasons behind this strange trip, but that didn't stop everybody else. The question was whispered at first, beginning as suggestions on social media and the comments area underneath online news articles. By the evening, it had built up to a roar:

Is Cummings a Glory Addict?

On every evening news program, and on every political talk show that evening, the question was asked. It screamed out from tabloid headlines the following day. Malcolm of course was entranced by the drama, and I had to do my morning walk alone. By lunchtime that day they were bored with that question, and a new one took over:

Was Prime Minister Boris Johnson protecting him?

"*It's understandable,*" said Barry Collins, turning up for the third time that day. "*Cummings has done a huge amount for this country, and the Prime Minister's loyalty to him is commendable in its way. But the first duty of any government is to protect its people. If Cummings stays in post, then we're sending out a message that obeying the lockdown is somehow optional.*"

"He's breaking ranks," said Malcolm.

"*But hundreds of people have been leaving home to see Glories,*" said the presenter. "*Is it fair to single one man out?*"

"*Firstly, the sheer distance he drove is quite exceptional. Ordinary members of the public do drive to see Glories, even against our advice, it is true, but they seldom venture that far from home, only Glory Addicts do that.*"

"*You're saying Mr Cummings is a Glory Addict,*" said the presenter.

"*I'm hoping that he can give us a better explanation. But I'm also calling on the Prime Minister to restore trust in our leaders, and at the moment I'm struggling to see any path to doing that, which involves Cummings staying in post.*"

A Labour MP had been waiting patiently for her turn. "*Yes, of course Cummings should be sacked,*" she said, her expression implying that it was a stupid question. "*He broke the rules. The reason he did it doesn't matter. We can't have leaders who don't follow their own rules.*"

Throughout the day, not a word was heard from Boris Johnson.

* * * * *

The next day's *Sun* had a cover showing thirty faces of people they claimed had been killed on the roads by Glory Addicts. Dominating the cover was a large photo of the 8-year-old girl called Tina who was killed in the first weeks of

Chapter 40: The tears of a clown

lockdown, and whom Collins had made his *cause celebre*. "Actually, you'll find that the police aren't even sure the driver who killed that girl was going to a Glory, let alone a Glory addict," Malcolm told me. "But when did the facts ever get in the way of a surging bandwagon of self-righteousness?"

A few hours later, Malcolm was jumping around with excitement like a small boy desperate to show off a new toy. "Julia! Julia! Come and see this!" A little reluctantly, I descended the stairs from where I'd been happily reading, to see Dominic Cummings on the telly, sitting incongruously on a chair on a lawn, with roses behind him.

He was providing a rambling explanation for his journey, which somehow involved his wife being ill, and then some extraordinary stuff about an eye test. It seemed wholly unconvincing to me, and before long he was being asked, outright, if he was a Glory addict. He denied it vehemently, pointing out that he'd been in the Durham area for several days.

"*So you were just dodging the rules because you felt like it, then?*" shouted one reporter.

"*It's hard to spot Glories from central London, is that the real reason?*" shouted another.

Cummings appeared to hold his nerve, and the press conference eventually ended. "Do you know," said Malcolm, "the slippery bugger might actually survive this?" His prediction was reinforced when Boris Johnson himself turned up on screen in bullish form, declaring that mistakes should be forgiven, and then unexpectedly launching into a defence of Glory addicts, stating that he wasn't convinced by the evidence for the condition, and that it was un-British to persecute those with health conditions, real or imaginary. In his view, the problem was caused by recklessness and selfishness among a small minority of Glory-hunting drivers, and these people should be dealt with by the law. Therefore, he was drafting emergency legislation which would cut the speed limits on all roads to forty miles per hour, with exceptions of course for emergency vehicles and certain key workers. Anyone caught breaking those limits could expect to be banned from driving until the Glory crisis was over, at a minimum.

"I hate to say it, but the Fat Waffle Machine's got a point," admitted Malcolm. "We know that addicts are real, but if I were called upon to estimate a percentage, I would be going with perhaps 25% of Glory-related road accidents being caused by them. I think the agenda might just shift now. I predict a few 'lock 'em up' type headlines tomorrow morning."

It was a fair prediction, but also completely wrong. Instead, every single newspaper carried a large photograph of a garden party on the cover, which they told us had happened in Number Ten Downing Street, just a few days before. Visible in the picture were the PM, his wife, the health secretary and nearly 20 other people. The headlines connected it to the Cummings saga, with phrases like '*One rule for them*' or '*How many more rules did they break?*'

"I'm more interested in who leaked the photo," said Malcolm.

Chapter 40: The tears of a clown

"People are going to start ignoring the lockdown rules, aren't they?" I said worriedly. "I don't mean discretely, I can't really criticise anyone for that, can I? But I mean, flagrantly?"

"They are," agreed Malcolm. "I wonder if that's the idea? But who? And why?"

The following morning, a new image was leaked, of the health secretary snogging and groping a woman who was most certainly not his wife. Within hours he had resigned over his 'error of judgement.'

"That's a new one," I said happily. "Randy young girls will be asking boys if they want to sneak into the cupboard for a little '*error of judgement.*'" That made me think sadly of Tara and Lucasz. By now the quality papers were asking the same questions as Malcolm: who was doing the leaking, and what was their goal?

* * * * *

The Glories were becoming steadily more common, with often two or three spates recorded per day, plus dozens of isolated occurrences. Glories were now appearing in northern France and Belgium, as well as Ireland and Scotland, but nowhere near as many as England. Still no-one was any closer to explaining the reason for the Pertwee Paradox, let alone the Glories themselves.

A Glory popped up three miles from our house. There was an app you could get, that pinged when a Glory was reported within a set number of miles from your location. Malcolm said they were trying to ban it. We drove most of the way, sedately, then parked and walked the rest. It was a patch of black, starry sky, the size of several houses, hanging there in bright daylight. We met a man who was furiously trying to map the exact locations of every star within the patch, because he reckoned it might give us a clue about the origin of Glories. "What if it's aliens?" he asked excitedly. "Projecting to us from another world, even another galaxy. This star map could show us exactly where they are!"

We left him to it, and found a spot where we could sit down and simply admire it. "Our excitable friend might be right, you know," said Malcolm. "It doesn't look like any patch of sky that I'd recognise. I suppose it could be southern hemisphere." But he checked a book when he got home, and concluded that it wasn't. "It was the night sky seen from somewhere else."

The lockdown was beginning to collapse. "It was all about consent, from the start," said Malcolm knowledgeably. "Most people locked themselves down *before* the government imposed it, remember? There was this rare and precious sense that we really were all in it together – rich and poor, governors and governed. They've shattered that."

"The leakers, or the government?" I asked him.

"Both."

Suddenly there were commentators urging for the lockdown to be scrapped altogether, claiming that the threat from the virus was greatly exaggerated and that government transgressions clearly proved it. Some of these argued that the Glories constituted the much greater threat, because their numbers kept on

Chapter 40: The tears of a clown

increasing and we knew nothing about them – and would continue this way, until we stopped cowering indoors.

One even went as far as to suggest that the Glories had only appeared in our countryside *because* it had suddenly been emptied of people.

"There's this idiotic dichotomy starting to form," pondered Malcolm. "Between those who say fear the virus and ignore the Glories, and the ones who say fear the Glories but act like the virus is over, or was never that bad. Honestly, it's like none of them can hold two separate thoughts in their heads at the same time."

Over the next few days, there was a clear sense that Boris Johnson had lost control of events, and that the lockdown could not be restored unless he was replaced with someone who had himself followed the rules. Barry Collins was still popping up regularly on screen, advocating for continued lockdown yet defending Johnson, while also pushing his Glory-addict agenda. Voices from the left told Johnson to resign because lockdown was failing. Voices from the right told him to resign because he should never have imposed it in the first place. Yet still he clung on.

Then an anonymous website appeared, publishing Boris Johnson's entire Whatsapp message history for the month of January, 2020, with the promise that all messages from February, March, April and May would be released in turn over the next four days. An MP called Nadine Dorries appeared on the telly, ranting breathlessly about a plot to take down her beloved Boris, reeling off a list of suspects, many of whom I suspected did not exist. It was to no avail. Within 24 hours, Boris Johnson had resigned as Britain's Prime Minister.

Upon hearing the news, Malcolm rushed upstairs and returned with a book of UK history, and a calendar. He was trying to work out where Johnson sat on the all-time chart of the UK's shortest serving Prime Ministers.

"I think it's second, or maybe third," he said with that wonderful childlike delight that sometimes escapes from his normally serious exterior. It was announced that, in view of the country's desperate need for stable leadership, the contest to succeed him would be truncated, involving MPs only, and would begin immediately. Contenders were given 48 hours to throw in their hats. Then a series of daily votes would whittle them down to the top four, three, two, and finally one.

"How about I order in a large supply of popcorn for you?" I told Malcolm.

"Yes please," he said, not realising that I was joking.

Barry Collins was among the nine contenders who entered the fray, declaring that none of the other candidates took the Glory problem seriously enough, and that he felt compelled to put himself and his ideas forward for consideration. As Tory MPs prepared to vote, the papers reported what seemed to be a spike in hit-and-run accidents in the country, including one that hit an ambulance. Glory addicts were blamed by several right-wing tabloids.

"It's going to be Collins," said Malcolm.

"But he's the outsider," I said.

"Precisely."

Collins made it to the final four along with two frontbenchers and a well-known former minister. The chancellor, suddenly distrusted after the photo leaks, missed the cut. Editorials in several papers openly backed Collins. Another batch of leaked Whatsapp messages caused one of the candidates to drop out of the race. Footage emerged of a supposed "Gladdie" (the new slang word for Glory addicts) physically dragging an old lady off her bicycle and riding off in the direction of a nearby Glory. '*Who will stop this menace?*' thundered an editorial piece. Collins got through to the final two.

A hastily arranged TV debate pitted Collins against his remaining rival. Collins devoted much of his pitch to the problem of Glory addicts, and to a lesser extent reckless Glory-hunters. "*As Britain gets back on its feet, we cannot afford for our road network to become a death trap for decent people!*" he declared. His rival agreed that the addict problem needed tackling, but then waffled a lot about the economy. Collins presented his 'Twelve Point Plan' to deal with Glories, Glory addicts and the virus. His rival conceded that she would be looking carefully at whether to implement some of Collins' measures.

"That's a mistake," observed Malcolm. "Why choose the tribute act, when you can have the real band?"

"Collins seems a lot more well-prepared than she does," I noted.

"Yes, he does, doesn't he?" agreed Malcolm thoughtfully. "Almost as if he'd been practicing for weeks."

At the end, each candidate got to make their final pitch, uninterrupted. "*Ultimately, this is not about me,*" said Collins. "*It's about Tina Gregg, and all the other people who've been killed on our roads. It's a time to talk about the essential work carried out by delivery drivers, who deserve to be able to keep our shelves stocked without risking their lives to do it. It is time to talk about how the sacrifices made by the British public during these long, hard weeks of lockdown are in danger of being undone. It is time to talk about action. If you decide to trust me with this awesome responsibility, then I shall do my upmost to deal with this menace, and deal with it in full. On my first day in office, I would table emergency legislation, establishing special centres where Glory Addicts will be treated and cared for. Suitable locations have already been identified, and the one existing private and voluntary clinic will be made a public-private partnership. That will help us to have this policy up and running in two or three days. We will also be creating the power to detain Glory Addicts by force if they are judged to pose a danger to the public. Any person caught speeding in the attempt to reach a Glory will be detained and assumed to be a Glory Addict until they can prove otherwise.*"

I gasped. "Detention without trial."

"You're surprised?" said Malcolm. "That was always the way this was going. First Muslims in America, then refugees, and now Gladdies."

"I don't understand why this addict issue is getting so much attention," I said to Malcolm. "The virus is still killing at least twenty times more people every day."

"That's exactly why they're making it an issue," he replied. "Don't you see? The Tories hate the virus because it's an invisible enemy. They're shifting attention from a problem they've handled abominably, to another one where they

Chapter 40: The tears of a clown

can be seen to be doing well. And mark my words, you really won't want to be a Gladdie after tomorrow. Because Collins is going to win. But I'm not sure he will be the one in charge. Collins is the means, not the end, though I wish I knew what for. Someone's engineered all this, someone very powerful and extremely clever. Someone so Machiavellian, he or she makes Dominic Cummings look like Baldrick by comparison."

"Claude Dexter," I said.

"That would be my guess. I've been trying to find out about him, who he is and what he does. But Locksley was right – there's *nothing*."

The following day, Barry Collins was introduced to the world as Britain's new Prime Minister.

Chapter 41: A good time for a holiday

Julia

Within days of Collins' elevation to PM, well over 100 'Gladdies' were reported to have been moved to what the press were now calling Collins' 'Gladcamp'. The location was kept secret ("*These patients are entitled to their privacy, and we do not want any risk of reprisals,*" said Collins). Collins proudly declared that the roads were already getting much safer.

"Probably true," said Malcolm. "He's given the police emergency powers to arrest anyone going even slightly over the speed limit, and potentially send them to Gladcamp. So of course the roads are getting clearer, most people won't be driving at all!"

"It's authoritarian," I said. "Like a new kind of lockdown,"

"That's just it," said Malcolm. "That's why they can get away with it. They're relaxing other restrictions at the same time. Good news for the virus of course, and the economy. But it also makes people more willing to accept this new restriction."

A hotline was set up, for people to report suspected Glory addicts. A massive pale purple hexagonal column appeared over the Pennine hills, looming high above the few clouds in the sky. Perhaps over a million people saw it from their homes or gardens, but few took the risk of driving to get closer. The government expanded the official definition of Glory addict to include anyone who had had an unusual reaction to contact with a Glory. Malcolm and I looked at each other in silent alarm.

The press reported an attempted breakout from the Gladcamp. Someone had smuggled in a mobile phone and got an alert for a Glory just fifteen miles away. A group of nearly twenty patients had overpowered a delivery driver and tried to smash through the gates of the grounds, only to find that the gates were stronger than the van. Five of the inmates, who were crammed into the back of the van, were hospitalised. Collins willingly accepted that mistakes had been made ('*we've been doing all this very fast, you know!*') and vowed to tighten security there. But he looked anything but upset by the development.

Within a week, the number of reported Glories was starting to drop. "Our working hypothesis," said a government scientist, "is that these things somehow respond to human contact. If we deprive them of that, we believe it is likely that their numbers will continue to fall away, ultimately to nothing."

"Baloney," said Malcolm. "Numbers are dropping because people aren't going out to see them, and even if they do, they're not reporting it for fear of being labelled a Gladdie."

Chapter 41: A good time for a holiday

Locksley called, and I put her on speaker. "Don't worry, I'm not trying to recruit you. I'm just thinking, it might be a really good time of year to go on holiday, don't you think?" she said.

"My last holiday turned out to be a bit more stressful than I'd intended," I replied.

"Did it really?" she asked. "I wonder whose fault that was. Anyway, you may well get the chance to discuss it in detail, soon. They're working systematically backwards now, looking at anyone who had a past reaction to a Glory, or was a member of a cult. Or both."

"Me and Lucasz," I said.

"But you know, a holiday might be just what you need. Somewhere a bit off grid, perhaps. Where you won't get too many unwanted visitors. In fact, you might even think about going tomorrow. Before the weather turns." She rang off.

"They're going to come for you, and Lucasz," said Malcolm.

"But what did she mean about the weather turning?" I asked.

"The forecast is sunshine for most of the week," he replied. "So she meant the political 'weather'. You know how they've been ramping up the rules every few days. Turn the screw another notch, and see how the people and papers respond. Lock up the addicts? Great. What about people caught speeding, shall we sling them in there, too? Fine by us. How about we include historical speeding offences as well? Yes, what a good idea. And just to be on the safe side, anyone who's ever acted weird around a Glory? Yes, Mr Collins, we're with you all the way. Tell you what, let's just ban longer road journeys altogether. Just until the Glories are gone. We'll give essential workers a special road pass, but everyone else has to stay within two miles of their home. If not, it's a one-way trip to the Gladcamp."

"A travel restriction?" I said. "That was in the papers?"

"No. But I've been trying to second-guess what they might do next. And a policy like that, they couldn't give any warning about it, because that would cause a mad dash before the rule came in. So they'll be drafting the law in secret, before presenting it as a *fait accompli*. Locksley could have meant that they'd be coming to our house very soon, but I'm willing to guess she was telling us that we need to travel tomorrow, before something happens that stops us. In fact, I suggest we don't wait till tomorrow. I think we should pick up Lucasz, and go today."

We called Lucasz, and spent the next two hours organising ourselves with military precision, with Malcolm as our logistical commander. I joined the socially distanced queue to get into the local supermarket, snaking its way through an improvised maze of trolleys. Most people were silent, but I caught snatches of conversation between two old ladies. They clearly liked Collins and thought that both the virus and Glories would be gone by August. "And I always knew that Johnson was a wrong-un," said one, unconvincingly. I filled my trolley to the brim with supplies for our trip, but thanks to the lockdown habit of shopping in bulk once a week this didn't look out of place, and no-one commented as I lugged it all out to Malcolm's car.

Chapter 41: A good time for a holiday

"A friend of mine keeps a few holiday cottages in South Wales," Malcolm explained. "I spent a week in one on the Gower Peninsular last year. The key's kept in a little combination box in the outside loo. I still remember the combination. I can pay him for it later. There'll be nobody in it now."

By 2pm we were ready, and I said goodbye to the house once more.

* * * * *

Malcolm showed me the road map. "It'll take longer, but we'll stay within urban areas as much as we can. Anyone stops us, we're a family on the way back from a big shopping run." Only then did I understand his insistence on placing all the food items, unsorted in their shopping bags, on top of the suitcases of clothes that we'd packed into the car.

The roads were largely clear, and we made good time. Traffic lights patrolled junctions that were almost bereft of cars. "It's funny," I said, "I really thought the lockdown wouldn't hold. All the people rushing out to see the Glories."

"I know what you mean," said Malcolm. "And if Johnson and Cummings were still in their jobs, I'm not sure it would have. But Collins is letting people visit the house of one designated friend or relative, each week. That, and the fear of being labelled a Gladdie, has kind of brought it back again. But it's a fragile balance."

"All the leaks have stopped," said Lucasz, who it turned out also followed current affairs.

"Yes, I'd noticed that," said Malcolm. "As soon as Collins took office. Mission accomplished, one might say."

* * * * *

We planned to cross the river Severn at Gloucester, although it added nearly an hour to the journey, in case the police were checking all cars crossing the Severn bridges. As we passed through Stroud, Lucasz spoke up.

"We may have a problem."

"What is it?" said Malcolm.

"Reports of a Glory just west of Gloucester. By a place called Caldicott Green. It's right by the river."

"Is it close to where we'd cross the river?" asked Malcolm.

"Very."

"So what do we do?" I asked. "Ignore it and hope they don't pull us over? Wait till it goes away?"

"We can't risk being taken for Glory hunters," said Malcolm. "Some zealous cop might decide we'd been speeding even when we weren't, and there's no burden of proof for the Gladcamp. No, we'll have to go round it. Go up through Cheltenham, and cross the river at Tirley."

Malcolm drove with extreme care now, slowing down before every junction in case a speeding car came barrelling out. One time a car did whizz past, and we all held our breaths in case a police car dashed past in pursuit. We caught

Chapter 41: A good time for a holiday

glimpses of the Glory, which appeared as a population of brightly coloured stars appearing and disappearing seemingly at random, stretching up towards the sky. Carefully skirting it, we headed west out of Tirley until we crossed into Wales near Ross-on-Wye. Then at last we turned south. It was well into the evening when we pulled into the driveway of a cottage at the edge of a little village. The keys were exactly where Malcolm remembered them, and soon we were in.

That night, Barry Collins appeared on TV for a special broadcast, bemoaning the fact that some Glory addicts and Glory chasers were still escaping justice. *"Therefore, as of this moment, we have brought in a new rule. Any person or persons who are caught driving more than six miles from their registered place of residence, without good reason, will be apprehended and treated as possible Glory addicts."*

We looked at each other, open-mouthed.

Chapter 42: Talia's place

Antony

I was in a playground. Little girls swung, slid, rocked and ran around happily, while adoring mothers watched. Flowers bloomed along the edges. Birds sang in the trees among the cherry blossom. I couldn't quite recall how I'd got here, but I was sure it'd come to me. I'd been doing a lot of running and needed a rest, and this place seemed as good as any for that. One bench at the edge of the playground was empty, so I sat down there.

One of the little girls detached herself from whatever she was doing, and strode up to me. "What are you doing here?"

"Me?" I said. "I'm sitting down."

"You don't belong here. Go away." She was only about seven but the vehemence in her deep brown eyes was incredible. She had smooth dark necklength hair, and a thin face that would be pretty if it weren't so angry.

"Oh, I'm sorry," I told her. "I was just on my way home but I took a wrong turn, so I stopped for a rest. Do you know the way to Swinton? That's where I live. It's where I need to get to."

"How would I know? Go away!" She stood there, arms folded, glaring at me. She looked like she was prepared to do it all day. I wondered if any of the women there might be her mother, but they all ignored us, so I assumed they weren't. The staring went on. I got up and left.

The playground was part of a park. I passed more flowerbeds blooming with tulips, crocuses, big daisies of various colours, and all manner of other pretty flowers that I couldn't name. Beyond them some mothers and children were feeding the ducks at the edge of a pond, while a couple of others raced motorised model boats across the water. I tried to catch someone's eye, hoping to get some directions, but none of them paid me any attention as I walked past. This didn't bother me too much; I felt oddly relaxed, and other than a vague notion that I probably ought to be finding my way home, I didn't really have any other questions forming in my head.

I found a mass of rhododendrons, with children climbing merrily in the branches while others chased through the tunnels underneath. How many children had I seen here? It had to be twenty or thirty. Groups of rose bushes bloomed red, wafting over their glorious scent. In between were patches of grass where dogs of all shapes and sizes chased ecstatically after sticks thrown by old ladies. I passed under some trees, just leafing out, and letting through shafts of warming sunlight.

Further on, the park was a lot less interesting – lines of trees, the odd little building, and wide featureless lawns. No-one was walking or playing there. With no idea what to do or where to go, I walked on in a straight line, vaulting a fence onto the pavement beyond. It was a road, but no cars drove past, and the pavements were empty of people, too. I crossed the road. Ahead stood a line of houses. They all looked the same. I walked further along to a junction, to see more streets, and those houses looked the same as the other ones, for as far as I could see. Feeling unnerved by this, I vaulted the fence back into the park.

Chapter 42: Talia's place

I followed the fence, which soon became a high wall, around the inside edge of the park. Occasionally the wall was interrupted by gates, but beyond these were always the streets of identical houses. Eventually, I started to hear the sound of children playing again, and somehow I was back at the playground with the 'go away' girl. There was another path I hadn't tried, and this brought me at last to a street where the houses had different-coloured front doors. I walked down that street, then another where the houses differed from each other in colour and shape as well, and finally a cul-de-sac where each of the houses had its own distinctive brickwork, window shapes, and gardens. Among them, I identified one house that had more character than any of the others. The garden path had a series of cracks in it, a few weeds and lots of flowers, big and small. A child's bike lay under a window box from which dark leafy stems emerged, festooned with deep purple flowers that looked like propellers. There was a porch with peeling paint. I looked up at the front door. It was large and forboding, with creeping plants climbing up on either side of it. The number 16 hung on it in faded red letters.

The curtains were open but it looked impossibly dark inside, and I couldn't see anyone moving. My finger hovered over the doorbell, which was twisted slightly and had what looked like mould in one corner. My hand began to shake. I drew it away and went back to the road. I forced myself to admit it: this house terrified me. And I had no idea why.

I continued my wanderings, eventually picking up another trail of non-identical houses to follow. Eventually this brought me out into the countryside, onto a lane that passed under a very distinctive crooked tree, past a junction and then some flowering blackthorn bushes which dropped their white petals like confetti onto the lane. Beyond these a gravel driveway caught my attention, and it took me to a row of cottages. Each had its own character, but one seemed to radiate life, its garden a riot of flowers and birds, while I could almost feel warmth emanating from the windows. This time I walked straight up to the door and without really thinking, pulled the little chain beside it. I heard it working an actual bell on the other side of the door.

I saw a figure moving through the frosted glass of the door and took a step back. The door swung open. An old lady wearing about three cardigans stuck out her arms towards me. "My darling, how good to see you, well don't just stand there, come on in, come on in!!"

It seemed rude not to, so I nodded and went inside. "It's nice to feel welcome," I said, as I followed her along the corridor. The walls were crammed full of all manner of pictures and decorations – paintings, embroidery, children's drawings, mementoes. You could barely see the wallpaper. A very well-fed tabby cat purred loudly as it rubbed itself incessantly against my legs.

She led me into the kitchen. "Now, a little bird told me you might be calling, so I've got your favourite right here in the oven. And do you know, I think it's just about done? Sit down, sit down."

This wasn't like any kitchen I'd ever been in. The walls and most of the furniture were darkly coloured wood, but a big black metal stove dominated one corner, with flames dancing beyond a soot-encrusted window. Soothing warmth shone out of it, filling the room. Laundry hung on some complicated contraption above our heads. I sat on a rickety stool, next to a thick wooden pole in the middle of the room, and the fat tabby cat was settled on my lap within seconds. There was an oak table in the room, slightly warped with age, and

Chapter 42: Talia's place

utterly covered in plants, pots and utensils. There was a shelf sticking out from the pole in front of me, and onto it was placed a large steaming portion of chicken pie, accompanied by roast potatoes with brown crunchy edges. "Come on, eat! But leave room for pudding!"

I couldn't remember the last time I'd eaten, and I honestly didn't think I'd ever tasted anything as good as this pie. When the plate was clean, I asked for seconds, but she ignored that and served up a mound of ginger pudding with treacle instead. I wolfed that down as well, while she looked on approvingly. She seemed to know me, but I was as sure as I could be that I had never seen her, nor this house, before in my life.

The next thing I knew, we'd gone through to the sitting room, where we sat together watching *Babe*, a film about a talking pig, which the lady seemed sure was my favourite film. The cat purred on the sofa between us. As I sat back, watching the pig improbably learn how to herd sheep in a non-violent fashion, I found myself relaxing, feeling safer and more secure than I had in a very long time.

When the film ended, the atmosphere changed, just a little. "You know you can stay here, love? Sleep here if you want to. All you need to do is let your parents know where you are. No? Well, you know you're welcome here any time. Any time at all."

Then she was holding the front door open, and I felt obliged to walk out through it. Then I saw a familiar seven-year-old face on the garden path.

"What are YOU still doing here?" she asked angrily. "I thought I told you to go away!!"

I stood there, stunned, as the girl strode up to me and stamped on my foot. "Ow!" I said.

"Why won't you leave me alone? This is MY place. Go away!"

Julia

A new government website was rapidly set up, on which people could register addresses where they were staying away from their homes, and so avoid being arrested if found driving too far from their primary address. But the last thing we wanted to do was hand them our location on a plate, so we ignored this. As long as we didn't use the car, Malcolm reckoned, the new rules would not apply to us.

So we walked, to the woods, to the seaside and over the hills behind the village. Lucasz would often be out the whole day; I would sometimes do the first mile or so with him, then we'd separate, and he'd stride off into the distance like a dog let off the lead. Malcolm took gentle strolls with me in the afternoon, and gave me a run for my money at Scrabble. But still he spent most of his time either watching the little TV, or reading the online news sites. I worried that he was becoming obsessed, devouring every analysis of Collins' possible motives for his crusade against Gladdies, and who or what might be backing him. Even the wildest conspiracy theories merited his consideration. "What are they doing," I caught him asking an empty room, one morning. "What's their end game?"

Chapter 42: Talia's place

Inevitably, we were eating our way through the trolley-load of food we had brought, meaning that soon I had to start visiting the medium-sized shop in the village. It had a printed sheet stuck in the window, with details of how to spot, and report, a Glory-addict. Barry Collins was there, pointing at us from the poster, doing his best General Kitchener impression. It was our civic duty to keep our roads safe, the poster informed us. I wished there was another shop we could go to, but without using the car, there wasn't.

"You're not local," said the woman at the counter, as I came forward to pay for my shopping. It was a statement, not a question.

"Well, no," I admitted.

"Haven't you broken the law, then?" She cocked her head sideways, waiting for an answer. The woman two metres behind me said nothing.

"My niece," I said, making it up on the spot. "She was killed in a hit and run. She'd been staying with us since the lockdown started. I ... couldn't stay in my house anymore, so we came out here, before the new rules came in. And now we can't drive back without being arrested."

"Hit and run?" she eyed me quizzically.

I nodded, trying to make out I was close to tears.

"One of those Glory-hunting bastards?"

"The police said something about addiction afterwards. I didn't really understand it. It was before Mr Collins took over."

"Bloody Glory Addicts need locking in a proper prison, they do. Had a Glory down at Worm's Head a while back. Bloody maniacs driving down the back roads not caring about anybody else. Old Selwyn got knocked off his bike, lucky he only sprained his arm. That Collins is the best thing that's happened to the country. Long as he don't let us down like that Boris did."

"Won't bring my niece back, though," I said.

"Yeah well, I'm sorry to hear about that," she said. "You take care now."

Back at the cottage I told the others about my story, which I assumed would be all round the town quite quickly.

"You told them *what*?" said Malcolm, with a shocked expression.

"That our niece had been staying with us, and she was knocked down and killed by someone who might have been a Glory-Addict."

"My God," he said, his eyes blazing with an anger I'd never seen before. "As if there isn't enough fear and prejudice flying about, you just add some more to it! I thought you were better than that!"

"I only said it was a hit and run. Then she said it was probably a Glory Addict, and I thought it best to go along with her. She'd been looking like she was going to call the police on us!"

He shook his head and walked from the room. We barely spoke for the rest of the day.

* * * * *

Malcolm was back to his usual self the next day. "How many Glories have you two seen since you've been here?" he asked.

Chapter 42: Talia's place

"Two," I said. "That one over the bay that was a yellow dodecahedron, we all saw that, and a weird distortion effect on the Black Mountains in the distance."

"I've seen four," said Lucasz. "Those two, plus a patch where the plants were all jet black, and a patch of rocks on the foreshore that were bright red. It only lasted five minutes."

"The government keeps saying the numbers are dropping," said Malcolm, "as if numbers of reported sightings is a direct metric of how many Glories there are, when we all know it isn't. I think the numbers are still going up."

"But if the Glories keep increasing, well they can't keep doing that, can they?" asked Lucasz. "I mean, sooner or later it'll be obvious that they've all been lying."

"Really?" said Malcolm. "Look at climate change. Half of Australia was on fire over New Year. And the Aussie government still tries to pretend it's not an issue. And don't get me started on Trump. It's the modern way – sweep it under the carpet, attack the messenger, get yourself rich and get out."

"You think that's what Collins wants? To get rich?" I asked.

"Him? No, more likely glory, with a small 'g'. Could be Dexter's in it to get rich, but again I don't think so. There's easier ways to do it, if you've got the reach that he has."

"But if not money, or power, then what?" I asked.

"That's the question that keeps worrying me. And I'm starting to wonder if Glory addicts might actually be part of the plan," said Malcolm.

"Well, they were," said Lucasz. "To get Collins elected."

"But what if we've got this upside down?" pondered Malcolm. "We thought that the addicts were the means, and Collins was the end. But what if it's the other way round?"

"But what possible use could Dexter, or anyone else, have for a load of Glory addicts?" asked Lucasz.

"I don't know," said Malcolm, "but it can't be anything good."

"Wait," said Lucasz. "What if Dexter was here *before* the Glories?"

"Go on," said Malcolm.

"Well, that immediately resolves the Pertwee Paradox, doesn't it? The Glories are centred on Britain, because ***he's*** here. And that would mean you were right – it's all linked into some bigger plan."

"The first few Glories were reported all over the world," I reminded them.

"Yes," said Lucasz. "So maybe Dexter arrived with them, and only later started drawing them here? Or maybe he somehow merged with a Glory and started drawing them in?"

"Sally said something was coming, and that I'd have to help stop it," I said.

"I only wish we knew what, or how," said Malcolm.

* * * * *

The next day I took a longer walk, setting out early and reaching the cliffs looking down towards Worm's Head. I sat, hoping to see dolphins or perhaps even whales in the water. Some time later I noticed a bearded man looking carefully around some of the rocks, until at last he uttered a gasp of delight. His

Chapter 42: Talia's place

joy was infectious, so I walked up to him to ask what he'd found. He pointed to a tiny yellow flower. There were a few of them, and most were already in seed, but one had come up late and was still bright and blooming.

"Yellow whitlow grass," he said. "This is the only place in Britain where it grows. Had to cycle thirty miles for it. And now another thirty to get home."

"At least they're not arresting cyclists," I said.

"Not yet," he muttered. "Reckon they're working up to it, though."

* * * * *

Back home Malcolm was fuming. It was, of course, because of a new piece of news, and a new rule.

"We're not even allowed to look at them now!" he fumed.

"Look at what?" I asked.

"The Glories, of course. Looking at them can make you an addict, they're saying, and therefore they've banned it. Oh, they can't stop you from doing it from indoors or your garden, but if you're out and about, the rule will apply. If you see a Glory, look away. If one appears close to you, walk in the other direction. And if anyone's caught gazing at a Glory for any length of time ..."

"They'll be dragged off to Gladcamp?"

"Yup."

"Reporting of Glories will drop to almost nothing," I said.

"Yes, it will, won't it," he agreed.

* * * * *

The next day, I set out early for a walk, once more. I headed across the crest of the peninsula, enjoying the fresh air and trying to let go of my anger at the new government. I'd been walking for some minutes before I realised that I was looking at a Glory. It was a wide cylinder going up about fifty metres, a sort of swirling black and purple colour as if it were full of crude oil. It was some way ahead of me. A man with a dog was approaching along the track towards me, with the Glory behind him, so he might not even have seen it. But he had seen me, as I'd stopped on the path, and stared out at something behind him. He could report me. If I suddenly turned round, he might start to wonder why, and one glance over his shoulder would tell him. But if I kept going, I'd be walking towards the Glory, and if he twigged that, it could be worse. Veering off the path would attract attention too. I felt cornered, my heart pounding. In desperation I turned my attention downwards, pretending to examine the plants along the verge. "Hullo," said the man, as we passed each other, pressing ourselves against the hedges to make space.

"Hello," I replied, without looking up. I continued fingering the plants until he was around the corner, then I let out the breath I hadn't realised I'd been holding and sat there, gasping for air. I took one last brief glance at the Glory and headed off away from it, feeling an odd sense of profound sadness and loss.

Could Collins' tame scientist have been right, that the Glories somehow needed or desired our attention? As I walked, I felt an increasing urge to look at

Chapter 42: Talia's place

the black cylinder again. I told myself it was quite normal. My path took me through a small wood, and I found myself sneaking off the path, furtively checking that no-one was watching, then pushing through the scrub to the edge of the wood. Once I'd been hiding from Locksley and her little group; now I was hiding from the entire British public. I sat there, like a sniper in a warzone, hidden among the leaves of a bush, gazing at what I could see of the Glory, with its dark churning colours. I felt that I was too far away from it. I needed to be closer. The need was starting to build up in me, like a magnetic pull. I tried to turn my gaze away from the Glory, but found that I couldn't.

* * * * *

The Glory was gone. My legs were stinging, and my trousers were ripped. I was standing in a very small stream, with steep banks on either side of it. I lifted a leg and saw blood dripping from scratches below the rips. I had no idea how I'd got there. Then I struggled up the bank and saw the Glory again – I realised I must have tumbled into the stream and lost sight of it.

* * * * *

The Glory had vanished. I was standing in the middle of an arable field, with a line of squashed crops behind me. I was shivering a bit, and looking down, I saw muddy water squelching out of my shoes as I moved them. An urgent thought struck me – I mustn't be seen. I half-ran, half-stumbled to the edge of the field, and crouched down under a hedge. I was covered in scratches. There didn't seem to be anyone around, though. I had no idea where I was at first, but I could see the distant mainland, and from that I soon worked out that I'd been going west, and would need to head east to get home. Moving from field to field, I had to fight through thorny hedges and struggle across wet ditches. Then came a stream, and with a shock I realised I'd been there before, standing with my feet in the water, when I'd lost sight of the Glory. Reasoning that my feet couldn't get any wetter, I ploughed on straight through. I came upon a footpath but didn't dare use it, knowing what I might look like if anyone saw me. A mess, yes, but something worse than that. They'd think I was a Glory addict. And, I realised with a shock, they would be right.

Chapter 43: Talia's place

Antony

I was in a playground, sitting alone on a bench while children played, mothers watched and birds sang. I was grateful to have found the place, because my legs were tired, though I couldn't recall how I'd got there. I went to sit down, but a rather forceful 7-year-old girl strode up to me and told me to go away. I'd seen her before somewhere, but couldn't place her. Everyone else was ignoring me, but the girl glared at me resolutely until I walked off. I wandered for ages, first in the park then along nearby streets, but the houses were all identical and this made me nervous. So I returned to the park. Some parts of it were full of life, like a duck pond and some rhododendron bushes that were swarming with little girls playing, but others were empty. In certain directions, the park seemed to go on forever in an expanse of featureless grass, so I walked round its boundary wall instead, coming back to the playground, where I was again told to go away by the same girl.

I found some streets where the houses actually looked different from one another, and these led me to a house with a big number 16 on it, which felt like a bad place so I hurried away. Instead, I followed another street of not-all-alike houses, eventually finding my way via a country lane to a cottage, where an old lady who seemed to know me sat me down in her warm kitchen. I decided that I must have met her before, because I felt totally comfortable in her company. She fed me delicious chicken pie followed by ginger pudding while her cat purred on my lap, then we settled down to watch a film about a pig that learns to herd sheep.

As I got up to leave, the lady looked concerned for some reason, and told me I could sleep there if I wanted to. I wanted to say yes, but she ushered me out of the house as if I'd said no.

"You AGAIN!" said the little girl from the playground, who was striding up the pathway towards us. "I told you, to go away!"

Julia

Finally I stumbled in through the door, a soggy and shivering wreck. "My God, what happened?" asked Malcolm.

"Fell into a pond," I said. "C-could you run me a bath?"

I lay there and steamed for an hour, looking in horror at the depth of some of the cuts on my legs. The words "Glory addict" kept echoing through my head. I would have to tell Malcolm, of course, but I took my time washing, dressing my cuts, having a little nap, and finally coming down fully dressed, ready to confess my addiction. But he was unsettled and distracted when I found him.

"Something's bothering you," I asked. "What is it? Another nasty rule?"

"No," he said. "It's us. What are we doing here? What are we achieving? The country is being frogmarched towards authoritarianism, and maybe even Fascism. Most people seem to be cheering it along. You've been told something

Chapter 43: Talia's place

bad is on the way, even if we don't know what it is. And what are we doing? We're hiding. You know how they're always asking people, what they'd have done if they'd been there during the rise of Hitler? Well, now we know. You and Lucasz would have gone for walks, and I'd have watched the telly. I just wish I could *DO* something."

"Yes, but what?" I said.

"That's the point! I don't bloody well know! If I could do one thing, just to make people see some sense, just one thing, then that'd be worth getting thrown into Gladcamp for! Oh, they've got a new one now, did I tell you? A higher security version, for people who've caused actual accidents, or tried to escape. They're calling it 'Badcamp', of course."

"Maybe we could organise a mass escape, try to get people out of there," said Lucasz. I'd heard him muttering more than once about feeling useless since we'd got here.

"They'd just use that to tighten the rules even further," replied Malcolm. "Perhaps we could get in there, film what they're doing …"

"If only we still had Antony," I said. "He could have gone right in and spied on them."

"Well, we don't," said Malcolm impatiently.

We ate. Lucasz and Malcolm became more and more animated, inventing increasingly outlandish schemes to fight back against the government restrictions. They opened a bottle of wine, and then another. After a while, they were singing songs like a pair of old partisans, and seemed disappointed when I didn't join in. I went to bed and left them to it. But I dreamt of Bernard, reincarnated as a Glory, summoning me to follow him into his dank, revolting lair. I had no choice but to obey him.

Antony

"Why won't you leave me ALONE?" said the little girl, before I could even sink onto the bench.

"I'm sorry," I said. "Honestly, I don't mean to keep bumping into you. It's just I'm a bit lost and every time I try to get home, I end up back here. I really am sorry."

I turned away from her and walked from the playground. Birds sang merrily in the trees, ducks quacked in the pond as bread was thrown to them, and bumblebees buzzed around the flowers, but all the mothers and children ignored me. I circled round the edge of the park, keeping away from the featureless streets. Later I found streets where the houses looked different from one another, but the most distinctive one among them repelled me, so eventually I wandered out of town and found a lovely cottage that I'd been in before.

I was about to ring the bell, but I stopped myself. I didn't know this lady. She acted as if I did, but I didn't. But the girl came here, too. So I decided to wait. I returned to the lane, and settled behind a patch of flowering blackthorn. After a while she came up the lane, happily mumbling some song or other. She

Chapter 43: Talia's place

walked up to the cottage and was greeted by the lady, before going inside. I snuck around to find a small window looking into the kitchen. There the girl was, sitting exactly where I had sat, with the cat on her lap, eating what I had eaten. The old lady sat watching her in the exact same way she'd watched me. Next, ginger pudding, and then *Babe*. I decided to make myself comfortable in the single seat by the sundial in the front garden. Finally, the front door opened, and the girl emerged.

"Thank you, Mrs Winterton. I'll see you very soon." The door closed, and only then did the girl spot me. "YOU! How many times do I have to tell you, to go away!"

Julia

The next day, Malcolm and Lucasz were a bit the worse for wear for some reason, so I tried not to make too many loud noises as I made and served breakfast. Well, maybe I didn't try that hard. My legs still stung, and it made me irritable. I made some sandwiches and told them I was off for a walk.

"You do have a map, don't you?" croaked Malcolm.

"Goodness me!" I replied. "I've never been on a walk before. Is that a good idea?"

"And my phone."

"I always do, remember?" I hadn't got around to replacing my own.

Out of the house, I felt a bit calmer. I needed to process what had happened, and work out what to do about it. Had I been sent into some sort of hypnotic trance by the Glory? And, more importantly, would it happen again? Would all Glories do that to me, from now on? I didn't want to stop going out on my own; the cottage was small, and much as I loved Malcolm, whole days of him and his telly would soon drive me mad. Worse still, if I told Malcolm about all of this, I felt sure he would try to stop me from going out on my own, which again would cause problems between us. Perhaps I'd tell Lucasz first, ask him for advice. In the event I didn't tell anyone, and after I got back, the three of us just sat down to watch an old movie. Malcolm offered a stiffly formal apology for his drinking session the night before, and I had to stop myself from bursting out laughing. How I loved this man.

I devised a daily walk that was mostly walled lanes and woodland, with me keeping my eyes on the ground in the few spots that offered any kind of view. So a day slipped past without me sharing my guilty secret, and then another. By the fifth day I was starting to feel a bit more confident, and allowed myself the odd little glimpse at the view here and there.

Chapter 43: Talia's place

Antony

"I know, I know, I'm not supposed to be here." I smiled apologetically at the little girl, and walked from the playground, before she even had a chance to speak. I passed the duck pond, and made my circuit around the edge of the park, visiting those streets where the houses don't all look the same. Then I tootled up towards the cottage, and waited behind the flowering blackthorn once more, listening to the birds.

This time, when the girl walked up the path to the cottage, I came out and walked alongside her. She turned to me with predictable indignation. "What are you doing here? Mrs Winterton is MY friend."

"Well, she's my friend too," I countered. "She's fed me twice, and let me watch a film with her. Her cat has a very loud purr, doesn't it?"

She glared at me, but seemed unsure what to say. Mrs Winterton invited us both in, so we went in together, though the girl glared at me resentfully. The cat of the thunderous purr weaved alternately between her legs and mine. In the kitchen, I stood quietly beside the girl as she sat on the stool, becatted, and tucked into her chicken pie. "Is there any more, Mrs Winterton?" she asked. "My friend doesn't have any."

Julia

I was shivering, and my mouth was full of salt. Water splashed against my face. Where was I? My eyes were stinging and I couldn't see anything. I wondered briefly if I was dreaming, but it was much too cold to be a dream. I slowly forced my eyes open. A wave splashed into my face. I was in the sea! Frantically I kicked out with my legs, but I couldn't touch the bottom. I turned around and saw land, but some distance away. I hoped I could remember how to swim. I straightened my arms and plunged them into the water ahead of me, one after the other, kicking my legs. I had got all my clothes on, and they were dragging at me, but I had to keep going. One arm, then the other, form a rhythm. If there was a current away from the shore, then I was done for. I swam harder, but the land didn't seem to be getting any closer. My chest was hurting. I was going to drown.

Chapter 44: Talia's place

Antony

"Go away," said the girl. We were in the playground again.

"But I thought we were friends. We watched a film together at Mrs Winterton's cottage, remember? But then you told me to go away, after we left."

"Well, clearly you didn't!" She folded her arms in satisfaction at having won the argument.

"Actually, I did. But every time I go away, I end up back here. It's starting to look like we're stuck with each other."

"Go away," she said. I walked past the duck pond and the rhododendrons, around the edge of the park, up and down the streets where the houses don't look the same, and then up to the flowering blackthorns. I joined the girl at the cottage door, and she pulled a face at me, but still let me go in with her.

"There's only ever one portion," she said, as we went into the kitchen. "I suppose we'll have to share." Somehow we both fitted onto the stool, and the delighted cat draped itself across the double lap. I let her have most of the meal, content to take the odd delicious mouthful. After the film, we walked together down the road. Well, not 'together' exactly, it was more a case of her striding along and trying to ignore me, while I followed and tried to reason with her.

"Please talk to me. I need your help. I'm stuck here. It's your place, right? All of this?"

"Yes, it's my place. YOU don't belong here."

"I know. I don't want to be here either. But I am here. Do you know where the way out is?"

"Of course I do! Look! Just go a different way from me!"

"I tried that. It just turns into nothing. If I keep going, then eventually I'll die. Alone."

"Well. Then try a different way."

"I did. I tried lots of different ways. They're all the same. This place – your place – is like an island in a sea of nothing. Just endless grass one way, or endless houses another way. I can't get out, unless there's another way out that I don't know about."

"I just want to be on my own! Just keep looking for the way out, and stop annoying me!"

"You weren't on your own in the playground. Or in that house. So what's wrong with me?"

"You don't belong here. Go away."

Julia

Keep going, I told myself. After all that I'd been through, I simply wasn't willing to give up and die here. I thought of Siobhan, and Antony, and Sally, and swung my arms over harder. I imagined my beloved Geoffrey, urging me on, *go*

Chapter 44: Talia's place

on girl, you can do it! But the land was still some distance away ... or was it? I could see the odd stick of vegetation, poking up from the water much closer to me. I powered towards it with all I had left. My feet were starting to stick in something glutinous under the water. My lungs were aching from the effort. A huge wave lifted me up and lowered me down again, and I briefly glimpsed something like grass, emerging then vanishing under the water. I forced myself forwards until suddenly there was vegetation under my hand, and I hauled myself onto it. Waves lifted and tugged at me, but mostly the water here was only a few centimetres deep. I perched on all fours, gasping and filling my lungs with air. I began to walk on all fours toward the shoreline, and made it perhaps ten metres before the submerged land disappeared in front of me. I'd worked out where I was now – there was a huge flat saltmarsh on the landward side of the Gower Peninsular, bright green with plants but with deep branching and curving channels cutting through it. One of these had to be ahead of me now. I stumbled forward, swam across it and hauled myself up on the other side. Shivering like crazy, I continued on all fours, then swam across a narrower channel. After that, it was more of the same: crawl, swim, crawl, crawl, swim. For a while, it seemed like the rocky slope that marked the landward edge would never get closer, but then eventually, somehow, I was there. But I still had to get home, and I wasn't even sure I could stand up.

There was a broken stone wall above the rocks, and I crawled through onto the path running alongside it. *One step*, I told myself. One step, and then the next, and repeat until you're home. I lifted myself onto my feet, and slowly started trudging. After a while I noticed that my backpack was full of water, and that this was now running over my bottom. I poured it out, and retrieved the sodden contents. Malcolm's phone (which he always insisted I carried) was dead, perhaps permanently so. *One step, then the next.*

"My goodness me, are you alright?"

I looked up. A couple in their forties, clad in matching hiking gear, were standing in front of me, looking worried.

"I ... uhhh ... fell in the sea."

"Yes, I can see that," said the man. "You look hurt, do you want me to call an ambulance or something?"

"No ... not hurt ... but my husband, could you call my husband?"

"Yes of course. What's the number?"

"Oh God. I don't know. It was on my phone, you see, and now my phone's been in the water."

"How did you manage to fall in the sea?" asked the woman.

"That saltmarsh is a bit of a maze," I replied.

"What were you doing out there?" she asked. "It's high tide!"

"Well, it wasn't when I started. That's how I got caught."

"Did you notice anything odd, in the water?" she asked.

"What? No, I was mainly trying to get out of it."

"I meant before you fell in. Why were you out on the saltmarsh?"

"I'm a botanist," I replied, recalling the bearded cyclist.

"Oh, that makes sense," she said. "You must have been looking for the yellow orchids, out on the saltmarsh?"

Chapter 44: Talia's place

"Yes, but the tide came in before I could find them."

The woman nodded, with an odd look of satisfaction. "We could give you a lift," she said.

"I ... errr ... don't want to mess up your car."

"We'll put a few plastic bags on the seats," said the man.

I agreed, of course. The woman helped me, while the man dashed off to move the car closer. Neither of us spoke much, I was just glad someone had taken charge. The car was waiting for us where the path crossed a minor road and we sped off back towards the town where our cottage was. They were keen to take me right to my door, and at first, I was grateful, but as we got closer some niggling doubts began to form, and I directed them down a random street, and to a random house.

"Thank you so much," I said. "And sorry about the mud stains."

"Don't mention it. Now, are you sure you'll be alright?"

"Quite sure," I said, waving my keys at them. "I'm just a bit embarrassed, really."

Still they lingered, with their engine running, so I was forced to turn away from them and open the gate to this random house. I was glad that I'd picked one with a long garden path. I shuffled along it slowly, sighing with relief as I heard the car turning around. I looked round, but they'd paused again. I waved at them. I was at the front door now, bringing my keys up to the lock that they didn't fit. Still they didn't move.

Then the door opened up in front of me. "Who are you?" said an unfriendly looking fat woman.

At last the couple in the car drove off. "Well?" said the angry fat woman.

"Have you heard the good news about God?" I replied.

The door slammed in my face. All I had to do after that was quietly slouch through the town, trying to hide my face from anyone passing, until eventually I reached our actual home.

"Julia, what on Earth?" said Malcolm, face wide with shock.

"Bath," I croaked. "Then I'll tell you."

The hot bath felt like heaven, and Malcolm scrubbing my back for me felt even better. I ran my fingers along the skin of my legs, quite devoid of cuts, scratches and scars.

"Didn't you have a deep cut on that leg?" asked Malcolm gently.

And then, lying there in my nice hot bath, I told him everything that had been happening. Well, the bits I remembered, at least.

"So when you see a Glory, you go into some sort of trance and go towards it?" he asked.

"I'm a Glory Addict. I'm going to get myself killed, or arrested, I nearly did already. I should have told you before. I don't know why I didn't. I didn't want you to stop me going for walks."

"Oh, you silly, silly girl." He leant over and cradled my head.

"Careful, or you'll fall in the bath," I said.

"The thing is," he said, "I don't think you are a Glory Addict. There's a lot of psychology papers being written now – not peer-reviewed of course, not yet – but some of them are being made public. They talk a lot about the behaviours

Chapter 44: Talia's place

common to Glory addicts. It's very like any other addiction. The person becomes increasingly desperate for a 'hit' of contact with, or at least sight of, a Glory. There's some suggestion that it tends to happen to people prone to addictions of other kinds. But the thing is, Ju, not one of them has described an addict acting in the way you did. Going from fully in control to something like sleepwalking, and then back again. Whatever's happening to you, I think this is new. I think it's different. And judging from the pristine skin of your very shapely legs, you managed to touch the Glory this time. And it's important, maybe very important indeed, that you try to remember if anything else happened while you were touching it."

He dried me off, sent me to bed and brought me some warm food. Sated, I put the plate aside and burrowed under the blanket. I was so tired, I didn't even have the energy to close the curtains.

"We need you to come to us."

I sat bolt upright. It was night, and Malcolm was snoring lightly beside me. I replayed the words in my head. It had been Sally speaking them. I hadn't dreamt it, I was sure, because the memory was too vivid. I soon pieced it together. I'd touched a glory while swimming like a hypnotised idiot in the sea. Sally had spoken to me, just as she had through the ice Glory she'd disappeared into. Hadn't she said something about calling me, when they were ready, back then? Was that why I was reacting to Glories like this? Had they inserted some program into my head, so they could summon me, like a servant hearing a bell?

Whatever they'd wanted me to do, it sounded like we hadn't managed it today. Perhaps the fact of me freezing and half-drowning had gotten in the way somehow. But my path was clear now, I had to find another Glory, whatever the consequences.

There was no point waking Malcolm, so I waited till we were all up the next morning, and then explained it to him and Lucasz over breakfast.

"But why you?" Malcolm pondered. "Assuming the message is genuine, of course."

"Maybe because we were connected. She spoke to me before, through the Glory she'd fallen into."

"To purposefully seek out Glories is a big risk now," said Malcolm.

"I know," I said. "But you two will finally get the chance to form an active resistance unit."

"And you're sure this is genuine?"

"I'd stake my life on it," I said, "though I know it's completely irrational."

"Rational went out of fashion several months ago," said Malcolm.

"More like in June 2016," muttered Lucasz. "I say we do it, anyway."

And we were agreed.

"Do you think that's why they've got all these restrictions?" asked Lucasz. "To try and stop these kinds of messages from getting through?"

"If so, that would mean that they know a hell of a lot more about the Glories than we do," said Malcolm. "Which I fear is very likely anyway."

"Dexter does, I'm sure," I agreed.

Chapter 44: Talia's place

"I suggest that Lucasz and I take it in turns to accompany you on long walks," said Malcolm. "The frequency of Glories is such that it won't take too long before you see another one. And the person with you can see that you don't come to harm as you approach it."

"Good plan," agreed Lucasz.

"There could be a problem with that," I said. "The couple who brought me home, I'm sure they suspected something."

"But you successfully showed them a decoy address," said Malcolm.

"Yes, but even so. If they find out it's not my address, it won't take the police long to find us. Our best hope is that they weren't sure enough about me to report me."

"But we have to consider that they might have done," said Malcolm. "I think that we should start packing right now."

In the playground, I went away before she had time to tell me to. I circled the park, explored the streets, and walked up to the cottage, and waited for her there. I went in with her, shared a small part of the meal and the cat, then watched the movie with them. But as we left, I said to the girl, "Please don't tell me to go away. I just want to ask you a few questions, and then I'll leave you alone for a while."

"Promise?"

"I promise."

"OK."

"Where are you going next?" I asked.

"To my friend Flora's for a sleepover. Then it's the last day of school before summer, so we all get to bring games."

"And after that?"

"Back to the playground, of course," she said, looking at me as if I'd asked a mind-numbingly stupid question.

"Are you sure you don't know any way out of this place?" I tried.

"Of course I don't. This is the place where I am."

"Oh," I said. "And ... do you know who lives at number 16?"

She turned to me with furious eyes. "Go away!!"

We started to pack. After I'd stuffed all my things into the suitcase, I noticed an old, well-thumbed copy of Keble Martin's *Concise British Flora*. Something began to niggle at the back of my mind. I looked up the yellow whitlow grass, and exactly as the man had said, it grew nowhere else in Britain than a few rocks on this peninsula. No wonder he'd gone all that way. I supposed I was privileged

Chapter 44: Talia's place

to have seen it. But someone had mentioned another yellow flower, and the phrase finally came back to me.

You must have been looking for the yellow orchids, out on the saltmarsh.

I quickly flipped through to the orchid pages, of which there were three. A few were cream coloured, but the only truly yellow one was the ultra-rare Lady's Slipper. Not a single one grew in saltmarshes – I checked them all. The woman had been testing me, and I'd failed. I dropped the book and ran down to tell Malcolm. "I'm sorry," I told him. "Those people who gave me a lift, they definitely know I was lying. They almost certainly think I'm a Glory addict, and I'm pretty sure they'll have called the police on us."

"Then we'd better hurry, hadn't we."

Minutes later, the doorbell rang. Through the front window, we could see a police car parked outside.

Chapter 45: Talia's place

Antony

"Every time you tell me to go away, I seem to end up here in the playground," I told the girl, before she even opened her mouth.

"Then you're not very good at going away, are you?" she said with a critical expression.

"No. It's fair to say that I'm completely rubbish at it. I'm starting to think that we might be stuck with each other."

"But this is MY place," she said angrily.

"I know. I know it is. You want me to go away, and I want to go away. Perhaps we can help each other. Maybe there is a way out, but I can't find it unless you help me."

"Well just go out the way you came in, stupid."

"I would if I could. Thing is, I can't remember anything from before I got here. I can only just remember my name, but not how I got here, or what I was doing, or anything. It's a bit annoying, really."

"I don't know what I can do to help. I'm only a girl."

"Could you show me around?"

We walked past the pond, where girls played with boats or fed ducks, while doting mothers looked on. I told her that I'd passed this place, though I wasn't sure how many times, because I seemed to keep forgetting things. She nodded as though that was totally normal. She told me the names of a few of the girls whom she knew, but didn't speak to any of them. Then we passed the rhododendrons, with some girls climbing, while others ran through tunnels under the branches. At least some of them looked exactly like the girls who'd been by the pond. We went past spring flowers in bloom, beds of roses, old ladies throwing sticks for dogs, and then a place I hadn't found, which was a glade where the sun shone beautifully through orange autumn leaves.

One place she didn't go, however, was the street leading up to number 16.

"That house," I said, carefully. "Number 16. I found it really scary. Do you find it scary?"

"Let's go this way," she said, indicating a different direction.

"Where do you live, by the way?"

"You already know. You're just too stupid to understand it."

She stopped walking, but didn't turn round to face me. For a long moment we stood there, as the traffic lights ahead turned from green to red and back again, neither of us speaking. Then slowly, she turned around. Her eyes were wet with tears. "Why are you too stupid to understand it?"

"I'm a boy," I said. "All boys are stupid. It's a well-known fact."

She nodded, wisely. We walked together in silence all the way to Mrs Winterton's cottage. Pie, pudding, cat and film were shared and appreciated.

"I met her one day and she said I looked sad," the girl volunteered, as we left the cottage. "So we made friends. Please don't tell anyone else about her though."

"I'll keep all your secrets, I promise. Would you be willing to tell me your name?"

Chapter 45: Talia's place

"I'm Talia."

"That's a nice name. I'm Antony. And I'm still sorry I haven't worked out how to go away yet."

"That's OK. I actually quite like you now."

* * * * *

This time, after leaving the cottage, we walked down the lane together. The sun began setting, and the clouds turned a gorgeous pink. A single roe deer ran into the lane in front of us, its image strangely blurred. It stopped and stared right at us for a moment, then was gone.

"What a beautiful animal," I said.

"Yes. I see it here every day."

"Where are we going now?"

"To Flora's house, of course!"

She looked at me like I was stupid for not knowing this, but did it with a smile, like I was a dumb pet that she was happy to indulge. The route took us through different streets, and a second, smaller park, and then once again the houses started to look different from one another, before we arrived at one with character. There was a Space Hopper and a little pond in the garden, watched over by a gnome. A rotund Black lady opened the door and scooped us both into her embrace, laughing happily. She didn't say much, just kept on doing that joyful laugh as she led us through to a big room full of toys, where her daughter Flora was waiting. She greeted Talia with a broad hug, did a double-take for a moment, then greeted me in identical fashion, apparently deciding that I must be called Talia as well. Then we lay on the floor playing Mousetrap, followed by a game the girls had invented involving small bouncy balls. Flora's mum sat in the corner of the room, knitting and laughing.

Later, Flora's dad appeared, wearing a big white apron with animals drawn on it. "Supper time, little girls!" he declared, whereupon Flora and Talia raced through to the dining room, with me trailing behind. We were served an utterly delicious, very mild lamb curry with rich coconut sauce. As at the cottage, there was no extra chair for me, so Talia and I had to share, with one of my buttocks hanging off. Likewise we only got one plate between us, but this was no problem as the moment we'd cleaned it, another portion was heaped onto it, and the guzzling continued.

Something about Flora's dad struck me as out of place here. It took a ridiculously long time before I twigged it – he was the only male I'd seen here, apart from me. In the playground and park, the kids were all girls, the adults always mums or old ladies. No wonder I'd been so unwelcome when Talia first saw me.

Flora's parents talked to Talia and me as if we were one person. So did Flora herself, who was Talia's age. When briefly I found myself alone with her, she went right on talking to me as if I were her seven-year-old best friend. It became clear that tonight was to be a sleepover, and I had to quickly avert my eyes when Flora began to casually strip off her clothes in front of me. I slipped from the bedroom so that Talia could change into pyjamas, too. Talia's dad saw me in the corridor. "Are those pyjamas I left for you OK, Talia?" he asked me. I nodded. Soon the girls were settled in the bunk beds chatting away like crazy,

Chapter 45: Talia's place

my own presence seemingly forgotten. I made myself a bed on the floor out of cuddly toys, bits of clothing and a big knitted blanket, and sleep came easily.

* * * * *

I woke to a bustle of activity, the two girls already dressed for school. I joined the family for breakfast, this time simply taking my own bowl from the cupboard and putting sugary cereal in it, which I ate standing so Talia could have the whole seat. At one point Flora's mum noticed me, laughed and said, "Hey girl, whatcha doin' standin' up with yo' food? It's bad for yo' tummy, everyone knows! Get yo'self sat down, right now!" But there was no free seat for me to sit on, and Talia seemed to find this very funny. I laughed along with her.

The three of us walked to school, with bags full of board games. Soon we were in a classroom packed with joyous kids. Talia and Flora made a foursome with two other girls to play games; I sat out the first game and watched the rest of the class. It was fascinating: there were about thirty kids in the room, plus a gentle-looking female teacher. No-one seemed the slightest bit perturbed by the presence of a 16-year-old boy in a class where everyone else was seven or eight.

Talia was near the front of the room, and the kids nearby were all girls, and I could see their faces clearly. Further back in the room I could hear the occasionally raucous laughter of small boys – the first boys I'd seen here. But as I walked through the classroom to get closer to them, I saw that their faces were indistinct, and they were all playing the same snakes and ladders set, in groups of two or three. The pieces were always on the same squares, and every time a die was rolled, it came up on three. Whenever I paid attention to what a boy said, it was always 'ha ha, bad luck Mike!' But the games Talia was involved in were more dynamic, and it was possible for me to join them as well.

After a hearty school lunch, everyone gathered in the assembly hall for the end of term awards ceremony. "This is always fun," Talia told me.

All the teachers from the school were gathered at the front. Two old men, and six women. One by one, school awards were announced. Many were for doing well in class, or overcoming some obstacle, like hobbling into school with a broken leg for six weeks. But there were joke awards in there as well, such as a joint award for one teacher and one boy for 'blowing up the school kitchen'. This brought thunderous applause from the seated children, and the boy concerned lapped it up, waving his fists in the air like a champion. "And what's really remarkable is," the awarding teacher continued, "they were only supposed to be making a salad!" The room erupted in laughter.

After the assembly, the school broke up, and we walked to the gates, just Talia and me. "Shouldn't we wait for Flora?" I asked.

"No, she's off on holiday to France for a week."

"Oh," I replied. "I didn't say goodbye to her."

"No need, we'll be staying with her again tonight."

This of course didn't make sense, but there seemed little point in saying anything. So instead I said, "Hang on, we've left all our games in the classroom, shouldn't we go back and get them?"

"What for? We have to bring them here again tomorrow, anyway."

Chapter 45: Talia's place

It was only when we reached the playground in the park that I began to make sense of it all. The same little girls were playing on the slides, swings and roundabouts, with the same mothers looking on. Later, we passed the same girls playing with boats and feeding the ducks. The pond and the rhododendrons always had girls playing, and certain spots always had old ladies with dogs, while other parts never had people.

"Why do I keep forgetting things here?" I asked her.

"Because it would get boring, silly."

I waited for her to say more, but she didn't. We walked once again to Mrs Winterton's cottage, and ate pies with the cat on our laps. Then we watched the same movie, but that was OK because I never remembered anything of the plot. Then it was down to Flora's house for games, supper and a sleepover.

"Do something silly," Talia told me, as we lay on the floor playing mousetrap.

"Like what?" I said.

She gave me another of those '*he's a dumb pet but I love him*' looks. "You do know how to be silly, don't you?" So I walked around the room on all fours, ee-awwing like a donkey. But it wasn't until I accidentally knocked over a coffee table that I got a response.

"Now, now, Miss Talia!" said Flora's mum, looking up from her knitting. "What yo' goin' round my house yaw-yawin' like a donkey for? You cut that right out, else yo' gonna hafta eat hay for yo' supper, is that what yo want?" And she laughed, heartily. Talia and I laughed with her, yet Flora seemed not to notice, her attention all on the game.

"You can make her do different things," said Talia. "She's always the same with me. Lovely, but the same."

"Like everyone here?" I asked.

"Yes. Everyone but you."

Over the next day we played a game where I tried to make other people react in new ways. But it didn't work on Mrs Winterton, nor Flora or her dad. Oddly, the fat tabby cat did break routine every time food was dropped on the ground, but then it wouldn't be a cat if it didn't. In the classroom I could do literally anything and no-one would react, though Talia would laugh out loud at my antics. It was the same in the assembly – I joined the teachers on stage and danced like John Travolta, but they went on as if I weren't there. I started announcing my own joke awards, and again only Talia laughed.

Talia herself was reluctant to join in with these antics, and I didn't push it. The third time we went to assembly together, she stood up and did some very passable impressions of some of her teachers, but she did it in the spot where she normally sat, not at the front. Everyone else ignored her, but I thought it was brilliant, she had caught their mannerisms perfectly.

"I used to think maybe I'd try and do that, you know, when I grew up," she told me that day as we walked from the school to the park. "Be an impressionist, on the telly."

She'd never before mentioned anything about her past, or future. I looked at her then, and she looked back, her eyes full of a deep sadness that I hadn't seen in her until that moment. "Can you wait for me in the playground for a little while?" she asked. "I need to go away for a bit."

"Go away?" I asked, a little alarmed.

"Just for a bit. Will you wait for me?"

Chapter 45: Talia's place  275

"Of course." It wasn't like I had much choice.

* * * * *

I was sitting in the playground and she wasn't there, which was odd. I'd never once been at the playground without Talia being there. I dimly recalled that there was some reason for her not being there this time, but I couldn't dredge up a clear memory of it. So I sat there and waited, patiently at first, and then with a low-level panic beginning to rise inside me. Because without her, I really did think I'd be trapped there forever.

"Antony," said a young woman's voice. She was standing among a group of mothers, but was looking right at me, which they never did. I walked cautiously towards her. Her eyes looked very like Talia's but she had longer hair and looked about eighteen. She had very sad eyes.

"Are you Talia's sister?" I asked.

"Come with me" she said, and we walked through the park, not speaking. Eventually we sat down under some newly leafing trees near the duck pond, with the same rays of sun coming through that they always had. I looked at her and waited for her to speak. She met my gaze at last. "I'm Talia," she said.

Julia

"Is this your normal place of residence?" the female police officer asked me.

"Well, ahhh" I said, hoping Malcolm would jump in with something better.

"Why don't you come inside," he said.

"If this is not your primary residence then you are breaking the rules, and you will have to come with us."

"Listen, we were stuck here when that six mile rule came in!" I said. "We *couldn't* get home!"

"You should have used the bus," she said curtly.

"And left our car?" said Malcolm

"Had you called the local police station and explained your situation, we would have ensured that your car was returned to you in due course," she said.

"Had we known that was an option, we would have done," said Malcolm. "I do follow the news, and saw no announcement of that kind."

"We have to follow procedure," she said. "You will need to come with us and be assessed."

I felt a chill of horror at that last word.

Malcolm changed tack. "In fact I have a letter stating that we have permission to be here, if I can just …" He turned and started opening drawers.

The male officer spoke for the first time. "Sir, if you do not come into the car right this moment, I will have to handcuff you!"

"Julia, did you throw it out?" asked Malcolm, picking up the large kitchen bin, and emptying its contents onto the floor.

"Right," said the woman, and her colleague stepped forward brandishing the handcuffs.

Chapter 45: Talia's place

Malcolm brought the bin down over his head, twisted it and propelled the man backwards into the living room. "Julia, go!" he shouted, but I was too slow, and the woman grabbed my arm and twisted it behind my back. I heard a click as she pulled handcuffs from her belt.

An engine started up outside, and I saw our car reverse backwards into the parked police car, with a crunch.

"What in hell?" shouted the woman, and then "aaaarggghh!!" as Malcolm hit her square in the eyes with the juice from a Jif squeezy lemon. I wrenched myself free and evaded her blindly lunging arms. The male officer came out of the living room and Malcolm squirted his eyes too. He screamed in fury, swinging his fists wildly, and caught his colleague smack in the face. Not knowing who'd hit her, she responded with a knee to his groin.

Malcolm pointed silently to the door and we ran out, leaving the cops to grapple. We grabbed the small daypacks as we went, but there was no chance to bring the suitcases. Outside, Lucasz had just finished letting the police car's tyres down. We jumped in our car and drove off.

"Where do we go?" I asked.

"The Black Mountains," said Malcolm. "The summits will give us the best chance. We have to hope that a Glory shows up before they track us there."

And away we went, now fugitives from the law.

Antony

"Are you ... are you the same person as the girl I was talking to?" I asked.
"Yes."
"I think you'll have to explain."
"I'm not sure I know how," she said. "This place ... this is my safe place. I came here to get away, and I just ended up staying."
"Do you want to go back?"
"I don't think I do. I was happy until you turned up."
"I'm really sorry," I said.
"Don't be. It was like being in a nice dream. I had to wake up eventually, didn't I?"
"Does that mean you're stuck now as well?" I asked.
"I'm here because I chose to be," she replied. "This is all my memories, I think you worked that out, didn't you? Except it's only the ones I really liked, that's why it's safe."

We walked together through this strange world of hers. The sun always shone, but it was never too hot. The older Talia seemed able to find places that the younger one either never went to, or hadn't taken me to, one of which was a canal. We walked along the towpath, but at one point the scene began to blur and we had to stop. "I never went further than this," she explained. So we turned and set off in the other direction, coming to a lock with some cherries in flower. "I don't remember ever being particularly happy here," she said. "It was just a good place to escape to. But I like being here with you."

Chapter 45: Talia's place

I hadn't noticed her taking my hand until this point. But I didn't let go. We walked hand in hand to Mrs Winterton's cottage, and perched on the kitchen stool together, arms round each other to stop the other one falling off. We took it in turns to try and feed each other chicken pie, but half of it ended up on the floor, then very soon inside the cat. We decided we were still hungry, so we left the house, waited a few minutes and then came back in again. Mrs Winterton let us in and fed us once more, and this time we ate more carefully. Ten minutes into *Babe*, Talia snaked her fingers tenderly around the back of my neck, and turned my face towards her. We kissed, gently at first, and then hungrily, ferociously, with Mrs Winterton sat there beside us as if nothing of note were occurring.

We fell together, closer and closer like two black holes wanting to suck each other up. We never did more than kiss, never needed to, for every kiss was like the first between lovers held too long apart. It was heavenly. At least a week passed, probably two and maybe three. Time doesn't really matter when you're living moment to moment, in a state of utter bliss. Soon we'd pretty much detached ourselves entirely from the seven-year-old Talia's routine. We held hands all the time, and kissed wherever we stopped. We found comfortable spots in the park, houses of other friends she'd visited occasionally, and other more creative spots. We steered well clear of the house at Number 16, which by mutual consent was never mentioned. Once, we visited her secondary school and kissed passionately in every classroom in turn, often on the teacher's desk, in each case while the teacher droned on oblivious. Sometimes she'd even do the voice of the teacher, while we were in his or her classroom. "You call that a kiss, Blake? I'm very disappointed. I'm going to have to ask you to stay behind and keep trying till you get it right!" At night we took to sleeping under the clear night sky in the park, watching shooting stars streak across the sky as we nuzzled together. Maybe this really was heaven. I didn't want it to end. But of course, it did.

Talia told me almost nothing of herself and her life, and I didn't pry. But even I could work out that she'd come to this place to escape a real life that was very unhappy, and that bad things had happened at Number 16.

I was more forthcoming, and I told her the lot, because since she'd got older, my memories had cleared. I talked about Daniel so much that I thought she'd get bored with the subject, but either she never did, or she hid it well. She listened dumbstruck to my Glory-related adventures, and cried when I told her of how I'd lost Sally at the end.

I ended the story by telling her, at last, how I'd got here, because finally I could remember. "I came here by walking into a Glory."

She blinked at me when I said that. "A Glory," she whispered. "I remember now."

"You remember?"

"How I got here. Come on. The place where I saw it. It'll still be there." We walked to a spot in the town that we'd passed a few times, only this time I could see a hill in the distance, and on it a perfect sphere of brilliant deep blue, with a ring of dark aquamarine flames playing around its edge. There was no hurry, so we walked together towards it, hand-in-hand, as always. We left the town, walked along a couple of field edges, and ascended the slope of the hill. Finally we stood right next to the Glory. Suddenly I noticed that she was crying.

Chapter 45: Talia's place

"This is it," she told me. "What you've been looking for, all this time. The way out."

Julia

I don't think I'd ever broken the law in my life before. Now I'd resisted arrest and broken God knows how many of Collins' new laws to boot. We'd been driving for ten minutes since escaping the cops.

"Do you think we can get off the peninsula before they radio for back-up?" I asked.

No," said Lucasz. "There's too few ways off this peninsula. But there's a car park for a little nature reserve coming up ahead. Just off the road, under trees. If we stop there, they won't see us."

"Okay," said Malcolm. So we parked there.

"There's a shop in a town about a mile away, over the hill" said Lucasz. "I can walk there and buy more food. They didn't get a good look at me, might not know that I'm with you. If anyone asks, I'll say I'm on a long-distance hike, sleeping in barns and stuff."

"OK, but ditch the leather jacket," I told him. "Too distinctive."

After he left, Malcolm and I sat in the car. The adrenaline of our escape had worn off, and we sat there in silence, me trying not to admit I was scared. I thought of all the supplies we'd left at the cottage. Malcolm had even packed a tent! But we had none of that now. I even suggested nipping back to get it, on the grounds that they'd never expect us to try it, but he said no, too risky.

After forty minutes I could sit still no more, so I got up and repeatedly circled the marked route in the tiny nature reserve. Eventually, Lucasz returned. We agreed, rather miserably, that we'd have to stay here all night, and start moving early in the morning, by which time the police would hopefully think we were well away. It was a cold, largely sleepless and thoroughly miserable night, and it seemed to go on forever. At one point I opened the window a bit because it was so stuffy, but little gnats started coming in, so I had to close it again. An owl hooted, off in the distance. I closed my eyes and began to count the hoots it made. I reached fifty and was still not asleep.

Daylight began to seep back. Was it time to go? No, it was barely 5 am. The other two were, somehow, still asleep. My back was sore, my legs were stiff, and I needed a pee. I wanted to get out but didn't dare open the door, for the fear of waking someone else. So I sat there, eyes closed, breathing slowly and trying to rest.

After an age, the others awoke and we slowly got going. We ate bread thinly spread with cheap jam, and shared a bottle of water. Lucasz reminded Malcolm to stay off major roads because of number-plate tracking, so we weaved our way along minor roads, expecting at every turn to find a police car blocking the way. But miraculously, we didn't.

Chapter 45: Talia's place

"Maybe those two coppers decided to pretend they never found us, because they were too embarrassed about the beating you gave them," said Lucasz to Malcolm, as we left the peninsula and passed northwards through villages west of Swansea.

"Beating?" protested Malcolm in a serious voice. "I never laid a hand on either of them, M'lud. They just had accidents involving lemon juice and a plastic bin."

The three of us burst out laughing. Soon we were singing songs as we drove, things with some vague theme of resistance, like Abba's *Fernando* (you can't imagine Malcolm singing Public Enemy's *Fight the Power*). After a while we began to climb on small roads in the foothills of the Black Mountains. We scanned the scenery for Glories, without success. We couldn't keep driving forever, especially as the petrol tank light was just starting to flash – we hadn't dared fill it up since leaving home. Eventually we came to a large conifer plantation and turned off along one of the maze of wide dirt tracks running through it. We navigated to the highest piece of track within the forest, and parked the car there. The three of us found a way up through the trees to the edge, where we could see a fair distance. There we sat and shared a tin of tuna, spread thinly on bread. Lucasz walked off to fill our two small water bottles from a stream. Malcolm and I drank the lot in no time at all, so he trotted back down to fill them again. Our only other bottle had orange juice in it, and we wanted to save that for later.

We walked up towards the nearest summit, with Malcolm fretting half seriously that we were also breaking just about every code that sensible hikers lived by: we had no spare layers, nowhere near enough food, and were already weak and hungry. I broke into a rendition of '*I will survive*' and the others joined in. We graduated to '*Bohemian Rhapsody*,' and then a stirring rendition of Spandau Ballet's '*Through the barricades*', which Lucasz sadly didn't know, but Malcolm sang with incredible passion. We kissed at the end, briefly, there on the windy mountainside. We reached the top during the second chorus of "*Let it Go*'. Then we sat there, the Three Partisans, fully expecting a Glory to appear any minute, and reward our heroic efforts.

By seven pm, our joy had dissipated, and no Glories had been seen. "We could have to wait days," I said gloomily. The thought of another night in the car filled me with abject dread, and I was clearly not cut out for life on the run. Lucasz had gone to look for somewhere that we could sleep.

"I don't know what to suggest," said Malcolm. "I'm sorry, I rather forced you into this, by attacking that policeman. We could have gone quietly."

"No, you were right," I said. "You were right all along. Right about the direction it was all going, right that we needed to fight back, and right not to give in quietly. I'd sooner starve or freeze to death out here, than rot in the Gladcamps, and be lab rats for Dexter to ... oh, dear God, I'd forgotten!"

"Forgotten what?" asked Malcolm.

"When Dexter visited me, he told me he was after Antony, but he said something about me being an 'understudy'."

"Understudy?" he asked.

Chapter 45: Talia's place

"I don't have a clue what he meant, not then and not now. I think I must have blocked it out, I was so happy to get away from all that. But whatever they're planning, he'll be very keen to get his hands on me, and maybe even make me a part of it!"

Malcolm squeezed my hand. "Then we'd better not let them catch you."

"But they've got the police force looking for us, and most of the public seem to be willing to help them," I said.

"They haven't got us yet," said Malcolm. "We've still got a few tricks up our sleeves. We just haven't thought of them, yet."

"Well, that's all right then." I leaned my head onto his shoulder.

"You said that Sally and Antony disappeared into a Glory. Do you think you will, too, if you touch one?"

"I honestly don't know. Antony did something to make Sally disappear, and he was a Glory himself."

"I don't want to lose you," he said, fondly.

"And I don't want to lose you, either," I replied.

"But we have to do what the fight requires."

"We do."

We clung to each other, there on the summit, as the sun tracked downwards across the sky.

Malcolm spotted Lucasz, some way below, waving and gesturing at us to come down, so we did. He handed us a bottle of stream water each to drink, and told us he'd found a small hut lurking at the edge of our pine plantation, round the corner from where we'd parked. "Locked, but I could force the door." Malcolm and I looked at each other, and nodded.

Lucasz worked to break the slightly rusted padlock off the hut. "Last time I did this, I was getting you out of a grim building, not into one," he said to me.

"Collett's room suddenly feels pretty luxurious to me, right now," I said. Then I realised this sounded ungrateful, so I added, "compared to sleeping in the car, I mean. You've done really well to find this place."

In the shed were short coils of barbed wire, which we dumped outside. We could just about lie down inside, if Malcolm (who was tallest) lay in the middle. We had no sleeping bags, of course, and no blankets, except for a wafer-thin effort that was lurking in the boot. Lucasz went back to the car, and returned with detached headrests to serve as pillows, plus the smelly bit of carpet that formed the floor of the boot, which one of us could use as a sort of blanket. The other two insisted it went to me, so I was outvoted.

I was hungry, really hungry. I guess we all were. Also cold and stiff, and it wasn't even ten, yet. Malcolm and I held hands for a while. There was no owl to hear, no hoots to count tonight. I didn't think that my body would survive a third night in the cold, after this one. One way or another, I felt sure that it was going to end tomorrow.

Chapter 46: Through the barricades

Antony

I didn't want to leave. I told her so. I wanted to stay there with her, forever. I'd never been so happy, except perhaps those few precious days with Sally.

"But your cousin," she said. "I know you want to find him. You need to find him. And you will. But not if you stay here."

I was crying too, now. "Someone else can find him. Why does it always have to be me?"

"Because you're a good person," she said.

"I don't want to be a good person! I don't want to be a hero! I want to be here with you!" And I turned away from the Glory and strode down the hillside, silently begging her to follow. After a minute, she did.

I tried to forget about the Glory, about everything but her. I gave her all of my attention, and no shortage of passion. She returned it, but she would often have tears in her eyes. Things had changed, and we both knew they couldn't change back. We'd thought it might be eternal, and then found out it was no more than a holiday romance.

"None of it's your fault," she said. "I know you didn't mean for any of this to happen. You fell into my world, and you changed it, and we both forgot that you were never really supposed to be here. Thing is, you might stay a week, a month, a year, or even twenty years, but we'd both know that you needed to go. And it'd be there, between us, the whole time. And the guilt would break us in the end."

"Then come back with me," I said.

"I can't. I came here to get away from … I've shut it all away and I don't want it back. No, no, it's my choice, and anyway, I don't think we can both leave. What's out there, you can't protect me from. I want to stay here, where no-one can hurt me …"

"But I'm hurting you now."

"Yes, but you were worth it. And when you're gone … well maybe you won't be completely gone."

"Oh. You mean there'll be a version of me still here, like Mrs Winterton and Flora."

"I hope so. It won't be the same, but it'll be something. In time I'll forget what you were like – the real you, I mean – and accept the memory as being good enough."

"Well, then I'd better be going then," I said, looking away.

"WAIT!" she shouted. "Don't be like that, that's not how I meant it at all! I just didn't want you to be sad for me, that's all." I looked at her, my heart quaking as earnest tears poured from her eyes. Then she fell into my arms and we sobbed together.

I persuaded her to give us one more day together, and we lived every moment of it. I asked her if she knew what would happen when I went back. She told me that when she dreamed, sometimes she'd see her body – her real, physical body – lying inert in some clinic room somewhere, with tubes in its nose. It took me a moment to work out what she was implying. "So you think I'll wake up in … your body?"

Chapter 46: Through the barricades

"I know it'll be a bit weird. But, you see, I don't want it anymore. Like I said, I'm never going back. I can't, I just can't."

I looked at her, willing her to tell me more, and for a moment she looked like she would, but then she turned away. "Get yourself away as fast as you can, don't linger. They'll try and claim you back. Find a new identity. Hell, get yourself a sex change, if you want to be a boy again. Honestly, I won't mind what you do with my body, except for one thing: keep it away from my family. Especially my dad. Now go. Find your cousin, then find a way to be happy. OK?"

Oddly, though Talia controlled so much of this place with her whims or simply her presence, the coming of night and day followed a set pattern that she thought might match the normal world. Based on this, we'd agreed that the time for me to go would be a little after midnight, when I'd have the best chance to slip out of the clinic unseen, assuming I'd wake up there. Our last hours together seemed to rush past. Then, at last, it was time, and we walked together to the hill with the Glory. It looked, of course, even brighter in the dark.

"I love you," I told her.

"I love you too. Go now, before I get too weak to let you."

Still holding hands, we walked right up to near the edge of the Glory, on the top of the hill. She let go of my hand. "I'm not coming any closer."

I moved to kiss her but she backed away, eyes full of tears again. She pointed at the Glory. "Go!"

I hesitated. Now a seven-year-old girl stood there, face firm, still pointing. "Go away!"

I nodded, my own eyes clouded with tears, and turned away from her. I reached out my own hand toward the Glory, and took a step forward, then another. My hand was almost touching the flickering ring of deep blue.

Julia

I was being shaken awake. It was Lucasz. "There's a Glory!" he said. "It's a big one!"

Malcolm and I struggled to our feet, and asked where it was.

"Too far to walk, we have to drive," said Lucasz.

Back in the car, we wolfed down thin jam sandwiches hurriedly made by Lucasz as we started driving. Malcolm and I didn't see the Glory until we were back on the road, and out of the forest. It was a massive tropical island, seen as if from above, hanging upside down in the air above a small mountain across the valley. Its surface was sand and rock, but around its fringes was the foam of crashing waves, and a rippling rim of clear blue water. "I saw at least two smaller ones around it, when I climbed up the slope," said Lucasz. "It's a spate."

"Spates normally last longer than single Glories," said Malcolm, "but you can bet the police will be onto it now, or very soon."

"You think they'll come up on the off-chance that we're here?" I asked.

Chapter 46: Through the barricades

"I'm betting they'll have been told to show up at any Glory that's reported on social media, or that's visible from a distance," said Malcolm. "And then ordered to arrest anyone trying to get close to one."

"So how do we do it without being caught?" asked Lucasz.

"Suggest we drive to one of the towns below, then hike up as quick as we can," said Malcolm. "Hopefully we'll meet one of the satellite Glories before too long."

"The hypnosis effect, it's gone," I said. "It's not affecting me like the last two did."

"From what you said, it sounds like the message was delivered, when you touched that one in the ocean," said Malcolm. "Perhaps they trust that you're coming."

"Whoever 'they' are," said Lucasz.

"I trust Sally," I said. "That's pretty much all I've got, really."

We parked on a bit of flat grass at the edge of a village, down the slope from the giant Glory.

"One last Glory-dash?" I said.

"One last Glory-dash," Malcolm agreed.

"We'll be going to Gladcamp after this, won't we?" asked Lucasz. "Or Badcamp."

"Suspect they might invent 'ReallyAwfulcamp' just for us," said Malcolm.

"Bring it on," agreed Lucasz.

"Lucasz," I said, "afterwards, try to get away. They didn't get a good look at you, and they may not know you're with us. There's a good chance you could outrun the police. Then get in touch with Locksley, see if she can help."

"I won't abandon you," he said.

"She means if we succeed," said Malcolm. "They'll catch me, I'm sure of it, but that doesn't matter. But the moment Julia makes contact, you get the hell away, live to fight another day."

We'd begun ascending upwards through the rough grass, eating the last of our food and drinking the orange juice. I felt weak and unsteady, though at least I was fit. My legs knew what to do, but were running very short on fuel. Up and up we trudged. Knowing that speed was essential, we had no spare breath to sing or even talk with.

Eventually we reached a small mini-summit. Ahead, the slope was less steep but stonier. "Look!" Lucasz cried, pointing back towards our car far below. A police car was parked beside it and three policemen were striding up the hill towards us.

"Come on, we need to hurry," said Malcolm. "Lucasz, go ahead and try to find a satellite Glory. It might save time if you can pick us a quicker route!"

He hared off ahead. Malcolm took my hand and we strode across the rocky surface. "Do you think they'll let us share a room in BloodyAwfulcamp?" I asked, trying to sound cheerful.

"You're not going there. You're going off to save the world," he replied.

"The world?" I asked.

"Who knows how big this is?" he said.

Chapter 46: Through the barricades

I grabbed his hand and squeezed. "Thank you for all you've done for me," I gasped, stumbling as a large stone moved under my foot. "Who knew I'd be such trouble?"

"You know, I had a feeling you might be," he replied. "But I don't for one moment regret our liaison! Do you know, I've had the time of my life this past month! I only wish I'd been part of your other adventure."

I heard a strange whizzing, buzzing noise from above me. I looked up to see a drone, hovering some way over our heads. It stayed with us as we forged our way onwards, panting for breath, trying to ignore all the aches and pains. The police would be gaining on us, probably rapidly. We tried to go faster, but within moments I almost fell.

"We'd better find one soon," said Malcolm. Lucasz appeared over the next summit, a hundred metres ahead. He ran towards us. "Tell me you've got one," gasped Malcolm.

"Down the slope on the right, you can barely see it from here but it's there! Follow me!"

Running diagonally down the slope was somehow easier for me, and with Lucasz only jogging I could almost keep pace. Then my foot landed awkwardly and there was a sharp stab of exquisite pain. I gritted my teeth and kept going, using my left arm as another limb on the slope, and turning my injured foot to the side so it didn't hurt so much. Malcolm was struggling, his long legs working against him on the slope. The police were just minutes behind us now. "Stop!" one of them shouted.

"How close?" I asked Lucasz.

"Just beyond that outcrop!"

We were as close to the outcrop as the police were to us, but I was so slow with my injured foot. I was almost at the outcrop when I heard a desperate, high-pitched shout from behind me. It was Malcolm!

"Get off me, get off meeee!" he shouted, in a high pitched tone that was far from his normal voice. "I have to touch the Glory! I have to! Let go, let go, *let go*!!" Two policemen were trying to pin him down. He was giving me more time! The third one was still coming, just ten metres behind me now. I reached the top of the outcrop, and at last I saw the Glory. It was a disc of yellow sand with blue waves lapping around its edge, below us, down the slope.

"Come on!" cried Lucasz.

"Stop right there!" shouted the cop.

"Fuck it," I said, and broke into a run. I screamed in agony as my stricken foot hit the ground again and again, then I pitched forward, tumbling, hitting my arm on a rock, then somehow rolling back onto my feet again. The Glory was ten metres below me but the cop had almost caught me, barrelling down the slope. In desperation I dived to the side and he shot past me, shouting words that ought to have got him arrested. Then he stopped himself and turned to face me, blocking my path to the Glory.

"Come on now, lady, the game's up." And it looked like he was right – they now had Malcolm handcuffed, freeing up a second cop to come running down the slope towards us.

Chapter 46: Through the barricades

"Helllllp!!! It's taken my arm! It's pulling me in!" The shout came from Lucasz.

The cop below me looked round in alarm. Beyond him, Lucasz had his right arm inside the Glory, submerged up to the elbow, and was doing a pretty good impression of being utterly terrified. "For God's sake! Hellllp!!!!!"

"They're not supposed to do that!" I shouted.

The cop below me hesitated, but only for a moment. Then he hurried down the slope, grabbed Lucasz' left arm, and pulled. "It's OK son, I've got you!" Now I had a clear path to the Glory.

"Let me help," I called, stumbling down and losing my footing, tumbling face first into a tussock of heather, the scratchy branches whipping against my skin. The cop had almost pulled Lucasz clear, but I let my whole weight slam into his back, and he pitched forward onto the Glory. Lucasz fell through it, the bemused cop now holding only his hand above its surface.

"Hey boy, get ready to drop and run," I told Lucasz, then I tickled the cop under the armpits, and he lost his grip on Lucasz, whose hand vanished into the Glory. Then I flipped myself sideways onto the face of the Glory, and felt myself falling into darkness.

PART FOUR

*"He said behold, what I have done,
I've made a better world for everyone"*

Hazel O'Connor, "The Eighth Day"

Chapter 47: The revenant

Antony

My eyes slowly opened. It was nearly dark, with a sickly yellow light coming in from somewhere. My mouth was full of a horrible, stale taste. There was something hard and plastic in there too, so I reached up and managed to pull it out, though doing it nearly made me throw up. When I'd recovered enough strength, I pulled out several wires and tubes from other places. My arm hurt every time I moved it, and my back ached, too. I moved my head around a bit, trying to lessen the stiffness in my neck. There were thin blankets lying on top of me. I had no idea where I was, or how I'd got there. The tubes and things that had been stuck into me were all connected to some sort of machine, which I didn't want to look at.

My eyes adjusted to the surroundings, and I could see some sort of bland picture on the wall, but otherwise the walls were pale and featureless. The rancid light was coming in from a little window right above the door. On the other side of the room, I saw dark curtains drawn across a window. I decided to sit up. Simply bending myself upwards seemed a bit too much, so I rolled a bit one way, and then the other, so I could support myself a little with my elbows. Then, with not a little grunting, I managed to get my upper half upright.

I ran my hands over the top of the blanket, reassured that my legs still seemed to be there. I wondered if I should just go back to sleep, but there was a voice in my mind telling me I needed to get away from here. In that case, I decided, I probably ought to get out of the bed. Slowly, carefully, I rotated around my bottom until one and then both legs were hanging off the edge. They were very thin, these legs. I felt them again, this time without the blanket in between. Yes, thin and bony. I ran one hand up my arm, and found that this was thin and bony, as well. Hair was tickling my shoulders. What else had changed about my body? My chest was very bony indeed, with ribs sticking through, except for an area about the size of my hand, around each nipple, that had a little flesh to it. Lower down, my waist was ridiculously thin. And then I discovered with a shock that my willy wasn't there.

Without realising that I'd done it, I had slid off the bed, and got to my feet. The room spun a bit; I had to wait for it to stop. Was there a mirror? I found a light switch and flicked it, then almost yelped as blinding whiteness stung my eyes. I leant on the wall for support. Finally, I managed to open my eyes again, though it was still far too bright. I blundered my way over to a table that had a small mirror on it, where the very gaunt face of a teenaged girl looked back at me, with ragged dark hair hanging down past her shoulders. She was wearing some sort of loose hospital robe over her too thin body. I staggered back to the light switch and turned it off, then sunk to the ground and hugged my knees.

Slowly, as if dragging themselves reluctantly out of a comfortable bed, the memories returned to me. Of who I was, where I had just come from, and how I came to be in this body. The face in the mirror was Talia, and yet not Talia. The Talia I knew – the older one – had spirit and life in her. This body felt like a reanimated corpse. I supposed that, in a sense, it was. How long had she been lying here? It couldn't have been that long, because it had started when

Chapter 47: The revenant

she'd touched a Glory, except that I had no idea what date it was today, what month, or even what year. I'd been caught like that before.

I fought to recall exactly what she had said to me, before I left her. She'd wanted me to get away from here, and from her family. Would anyone here know that I was awake? As soon as anyone knew, they'd surely send for her family. I had to get my act together, and fast. Later I could worry about how this puny, stick-thin body could accomplish anything other than fainting, or getting bullied. I recalled a very thin girl from school that the other girls had sometimes picked on. I'd actually kind of liked her, tried to make friends a couple of times, but she'd always looked at me like I was just making fun of her.

I struggled to my feet and tried the door. It opened. I wobbled out into the corridor beyond. A series of dusky yellow lights ran along its length in both directions, illuminating a drab carpet under my feet. The door I'd come through was one of a series of identical doors evenly spaced along the walls on both sides. I was in a care home or clinic of some sort.

At the end of the corridor was a different door, slightly open and with no window above it. I pushed it open, gently, and moved into some sort of big store cupboard. I clicked a switch, and a dim light came on. A big hook stuck out of the wall high on one side, and on it hung three coat-hangers, each carrying some sort of apron made out of bin bags and duct tape. Below them lurked an untidy pile of clothing, and just beyond that was a table and on it were duct tape, a roll of unused bin bags, and patches of material about the size of a hand. The tape brought back bad memories of Collett and his love of tying people up. But the purpose here was clearly different, like some bargain-basement fancy dress factory. There was a hole punch on the table too, and a ball of string. What was going on here? My mind felt every bit as sluggish as my body. Some of the patches of material had holes punched into the corners. I picked up the string, passed an end through one of the holes, and *eureka*! It clicked. Face masks. Hadn't there been some story about hospitals running out of virus protection equipment? Whatever this place was, they'd resorted to making their own. A mask would be very useful to help conceal my identity, maybe stop anyone from recognising me. It took only a minute to make myself one, running the string through the other three holes and passing it behind my head, above and below the ears, then tying a knot. Then I wondered dimly if I should wear a bin bag apron as well, because I'd be pretty cold outside wearing only this stupidly revealing hospital gown. I was halfway through taking an apron off the hook when it hit me.

"Clothes!!" I almost said it out loud. I dived into the pile. They smelt of industrial strength washing powder, with hints of antiseptic and that stale old lady perfume you sometimes get in charity shops. I didn't care. I found one pair of knickers and slid them on under my gown. They were too big, and promptly slid off again. Uh-uh, I muttered, and gathered the material on one side into a sort of knot, which I tied off with string. The buggers stayed up after that. There was a pair of thick stretchy woolly leggings and they went on OK, though they itched a bit and sagged below the knees. The commonest items were nightgowns. I wondered, had people *died* in these? Had they died here? I focussed on my own needs, and soon picked out three of them, which I put on in the order of shortest skirt to longest. I topped it off with a cardigan. Well I probably looked ridiculous, but I felt a whole lot less vulnerable now that I was sort of dressed.

Chapter 47: The revenant

Then I realised I didn't have shoes. None were obvious, so I began rooting around. After a minute I froze – there were voices outside. "Mrs Williams ... can't breathe ... lose her ... called them?"

"Yes, I called them," came a louder, clearer voice. Both were female. "But you know as well as I do how things are! I warned you when you started here ... no, for God's sake don't cry. We do our best, it's all we can do. I'm sorry I shouted. We're all very tired."

" ... see something ..." said the first voice, which sounded very young. "Flashing lights!" There was sudden hope in her voice.

"Let's get her on the trolley, and meet them!"

I grabbed one of the home-made aprons, put it on and stumbled from the room towards the voices, almost falling over twice. Moments later I was with the two women I'd heard, helping them move a gasping old lady onto some sort of bed trolley. The older nurse looked pale, her eyes drained as if all emotion had been sucked out of her. The younger was barely out of school, round-faced and with eyes red from crying. Neither challenged me as I joined them, and the three of us wheeled the patient into the corridor.

"I'll meet them," said the older one. "You two bring her." She rushed on ahead. I helped the younger nurse wheel the trolley, although in truth it was more that she was wheeling it and I was leaning on it for support, as my head was starting to spin again. She didn't notice. The lady was still gasping like crazy, writhing on the bed as if that would help her get air into her lungs. Once, we had to stop her rolling off. The young nurse was calmer now, focussed on what we were doing. There was a frustrating pause while some mechanical lift lowered the trolley by a foot or two where this corridor joined another, then we were going again. The paramedic joined us, running from the other direction, and now the three of us wheeled the woman out of the front door, down a makeshift ramp to the waiting ambulance.

We loaded her in and the young nurse said "Look after her," and turned away.

"Can I ride with her?" I asked the paramedic.

"What? Aren't you needed here?"

"Me? No. I'm her daughter."

He looked at me sceptically, then shrugged, and let me hop in with him.

"Still no proper PPE there?" he asked, as the ambulance sped away.

"None at all," I replied automatically, though I couldn't recall what PPE was.

"Same at the hospital," he said wearily. "Luckily one of the porters is a bloody genius with duct tape." While saying this he'd inserted a tube into Mrs Williams' mouth, working automatically and barely looking at what he was doing. The woman still looked very ill, but was not fighting for breath so much now.

"You're not really her daughter," he said.

"What?" I replied.

"You haven't asked me if she's going to be OK. Look, the first few days at that place are going to feel like hell, and I totally understand that some people can't hack it. But maybe you should take a day off, go for a walk, get a good sleep. And for goodness' sake, get some food into you!"

I looked at him dumbstruck, and then nodded. "Yes, maybe you're right," I said.

Chapter 47: The revenant

* * * * *

It took fifteen minutes to reach the hospital. I expected us to park right by the entrance, and I was poised to help them wheel our patient inside, but we just stopped.

"What's happening?" I asked.

"Take a look," he replied. He'd either not noticed, or decided not to mention, my lack of shoes. I stepped outside, wincing as the painful little stones on the tarmac dug into my feet.

"Dear God." There were about ten ambulances in a line in front of us. I turned to the paramedic. "What's happening?"

"What anyone with a quarter of a brain could have told them would happen, when they started relaxing the lockdown rules too soon!" he said angrily.

"Always thought Boris Johnson was a moron," I said, hoping to lighten the mood.

"Johnson? Have you been asleep all month?" he asked.

I quickly changed the subject. "Will she make it? Mrs Williams? Will she even last till they get her inside?" I asked quietly.

"Of course she will," he replied, but his eyes told another story, as he pointed at her and then at his own ear. He meant that she could hear us. I felt stupid. Then he shrugged, telling me quietly that she might make it, she might not. "Look, I'm going to try and get her moved into the ambulance in front, if there's space, that'll free up this one for another journey. Technically I shouldn't leave her but I'll only be a minute, shout if anything changes, will you?'

"Okay." He ran forward to speak to the people in the ambulance in front, then almost immediately went on to the next one. I heard an engine behind me and watched as yet another ambulance joined the queue behind us. My paramedic came back.

"No can do," he said.

"Try the one behind us," I suggested. Soon we were moving another Corona patient, an elderly man who looked in even worse shape than Mrs Williams, from that ambulance into ours, and we squeezed them in side by side.

"Well, at least now she has company," I said helplessly. The ambulance behind us did a three-point turn, and sped off. By now an ambulance at the front had been allowed to discharge its patient, and so each one in the queue took its turn to shuffle forwards. I watched from the grass by the little road. The night air tasted fresh in my mouth. I hadn't been this near a hospital since my mother died. I wondered how many children would be losing their mothers in there tonight.

Behind me someone sounded a horn, and a grey van drove from the road behind us onto the grass. I turned to my paramedic, wondering if we should go and shout at the van to get lost, but he looked happy, the first time I'd seen him raise even the ghost of a smile. "You hungry?" he asked.

Three young Indian men had got out of the van, and were rapidly assembling a folding metal table, onto which they carried two metal cooking pots each the size of a beer barrel.

"Restaurant for heroes is open!" one of them shouted in a delightful accent. They had a large pile of disposable plates and plastic cutlery. My paramedic was first in the queue, and I wasn't far behind. They dished out rice, a vegetable

Chapter 47: The revenant

curry ('very mild', they promised) and a piece of naan bread to each customer. It looked delicious.

"Oh ... I ... err ... haven't got any money."

"And we would not accept it if you offered," said one of the Indians. "This is our thank you to the NHS heroes."

I wasn't an NHS hero. But I had helped cure a lot of people recently, even if it hadn't exactly been by choice. So I accepted the food and thanked him, then I sat down on the grass and shovelled in a first mouthful. The flavour hit me like a bomb, it was physically painful for a moment. Then the shock receded and I wolfed down the lot. I wondered if they'd let me have seconds? But as I walked back, it turned out that my stomach didn't share my mouth's enthusiasm, and a lot of ominous gurgles were issuing from it. I felt it tightening too, like a knot inside me, starting to hurt. Of course, this body had probably been living off pumped liquids for weeks. I asked the Indians if they had any water. They had only tap water on offer, in reused plastic bottles, but I took one gratefully.

Paramedics had stopped coming to the van, and now the Indians were carrying portions to the ambulances instead, this time in takeaway boxes in case they didn't have time to eat straight away. I volunteered to help and they willingly accepted. I saw a lot of tired, drained faces that night, some genuinely happy to see the food provided, others merely nodding distractedly, as if they'd given up caring about anything. We also offered it to any relatives in the back of ambulances, although most were in no mood to eat. I noticed a second, shorter queue of ambulances, at another entrance. So I went and offered food to those.

One had a young man, moaning, with a woman the same age sitting anxiously beside him.

"Uh, hi, I've got food if you want it," I said.

"Do you know how long they're going to be?" the woman asked.

"Sorry, no. I'm just a trainee waitress."

"Huh. Love the uniform. Look, my boyfriend's legs, he's crushed them, I'm worried he'll lose them!"

"I don't care about my legs," croaked the stricken man. "I have to get back to the Glory! I never even *saw* it properly!"

"For God's sake, David!" said the woman.

"Glory addict?" I whispered to her.

"Don't call him that!" she almost slapped me. "They'll come and take him away! You hear that, David! They'll lock you up, and you'll never see another Glory again! So you have to shut up, you hear! If they ask, we were driving to deliver supplies to Mum because sometimes she panics that she's run out of something in the middle of the night. You *GOT* that?"

I left them to it. With all the ambulances supplied, we delivered the remaining boxes of food to the hospital reception, and collected a large box containing empty containers of the same kind. "All washed and sterilized."

"You've done this before," I said to the Indians as we headed back to the van.

"Four times a day," one of them replied happily.

I said, "Look, can I get a lift? Maybe even a sofa to sleep on?" I felt bad asking them, but they were obviously kind people, and it seemed stupid to pass up the chance.

Chapter 47: The revenant

He broke into a broad smile. "Yes of course! We might even have some old shoes lying around, if you're lucky."

So, I found myself riding back with them in the van. Rajeev, the oldest, was driving, and on the other side of me sat Kapil, who I had yet to see with anything other than a broad smile on his face. The youngest brother, Sachin, had been relegated to the back of the van with the empty food vats so that 'the lady' could sit up front. They asked my name and I said "Talia," without thinking.

If I'd thought these three were kind, they were nothing compared to their mother, a whirlwind of baggy clothes and jewellery, who had already taken complete charge of me before Rajeev had even finished his first sentence of explanation. She seemed to take it as a personal affront that I was so thin, and was soon launching into a dressing down of her sons for the absence of my shoes, before I cut in and told her I'd lost them well before the hospital. She sat me down and made me eat an entire peshwari naan with a simple lentil-based curry, and I obediently ate till I thought I would burst. Then I got up from the table and my legs gave way. I'd been running on adrenaline since I'd woken up, but that was spent and only now did I fully appreciate how thin and frail my legs were. But within seconds I was scooped up by Rajeev and carried effortlessly up the stairs, where the mother took over. I was undressed by her and an obedient younger woman, and tucked into bed. Next thing I knew, it was halfway through the morning.

* * * * *

I spent four lovely days with the Sharma family. For me, family life had always been a stiff affair with Father and Gran, the frequent visits from Daniel providing the only colour. But this place was a riot of life. Normally, the eight Sharmas lived crammed into small rooms above the restaurant, but that had been closed for two months because of the lockdown, and so the tables and chairs had been moved aside, and Rajeev's two little girls now had a larger playroom than they had ever dreamed of. They usually had company, for most of my time seemed to be spent at the table, eating and listening to good-natured criticism of my body shape. "You'll never get a man, looking bony like that! Look at you, my husband had more breasts than that!" The matriarch bossed two younger women around, who I guessed must be the wives of Rajeev and Kapil, and the cooking was ongoing. The men made deliveries of vats of food periodically throughout the day.

In quiet moments, I had to come to terms with this new body I was wearing. Other than the face, it didn't look or feel like Talia. It was bony, the skin was dry, and there were groups of linear scar marks on one arm that I didn't want to think about. On the second night I'd had a terrifying dream where I'd felt rumblings in my lower torso and then started popping out babies, one after the other. They'd all just sat and gazed at me, silent and morose, as if I'd somehow failed them all. Waking in a cold sweat and with a full bladder, I'd stumbled out of bed to the loo in a daze and tried to pee standing up, with predictably messy consequences. I'd cried as I mopped my legs and the floor with loo roll. All the time my legs and arms felt absurdly weak, so I tried to exercise them in every way I could, slipping out for short walks, and hating how vulnerable I felt whenever a man walked past.

Chapter 47: The revenant

Sometimes, when I was judged to have eaten enough that I could last an hour or more without another meal, I was allowed to go along and help out with the deliveries. We delivered to hospitals, care homes, even the local supermarket, though this was in exchange for ingredients. The rest were done for nothing.

I asked how they could afford to be so generous when they had no customers. "The government is being very good," said Kapil. "They pay us money to keep going, until we can have customers again. So we are passing on the kindness." Rajeev usually drove, and when I came along the brothers took it in turns to be left behind. Sachin, who played with the little girls a lot and was very talkative with them, barely said a word when he was in the bus next to me. He'd check his phone from time to time. On the way back from a drop-off one day, he suddenly shouted:

"Glory! There's a Glory! Look over there, it is very beautiful!" He looked at me, "Very beautiful! Have you ever seen a Glory?"

"Uhh, once or twice," I replied.

"Can we stop to see it, Raj?"

"For one minute, but if we see one single car coming, we are gone!" said Rajeev. "You know the rules."

The road we were on was straight, and no cars were coming in either direction. Rajeev barely looked at the Glory, alternating anxious glances between the road ahead and behind.

The Glory was spectacular. A Type Two. We were a short distance from a small wood, and all the trees and shrubs inside it appeared to be made out of fire. Brilliant reds, oranges and yellows danced energetically within them. Sachin was utterly entranced. Then Rajeev hit the gas without warning, and we were away. "Car coming," he explained. "Talia, you do not tell Amma. She will be very angry if she hears we took such risks!"

In the event, Amma berated us for making me go too long without eating, instead. I was swiftly steered back to the table and given a new mound of food to consume.

* * * * *

By the third day, I had formed a routine of doing push-ups and other exercises in the restaurant area after each meal – hence five or six times a day. Soon Sachin and I were giving rides to the little girls, much to their delight. Sachin was, I thought, the perfect uncle, spending every moment he could with his nieces.

Watching him made me think of Father. For all this time, he would probably have thought me dead. When I'd walked into that Glory I hadn't been thinking of how he'd feel if I never came back, because I'd been so confused by that imposter. Of course, I'd had no way of writing to or phoning him before, but now at last I had a physical body again. Only it wasn't the same one, which meant that phoning him really wouldn't work. So I asked for a paper and pen.

Dear Father,

I am so sorry that I have not contacted you before, but honestly (or "Onnits" as I used to say) I wasn't able. Daniel and I met a Glory that day, the day I left home. I don't know how, but it made me sleep, and when I saw Daniel's parents at their door,

Chapter 47: The revenant

only a few hours had gone past for me, and I didn't know till days later how much time had passed for you. I'd spent those few hours running around Swynn Hill looking for Daniel, and I'm looking for him still. But something happened to me that day, something that has made me connected to the Glories. I've seen wonderful things, and terrible ones. I've saved lives, but also seen many people die. My body has been changed so much that you wouldn't recognise me if you saw me. And I have to find Daniel. I have to. You always told me, 'if you make a mess, you clear it up first, before you do anything else.' Well, I made a mess by losing Daniel and I haven't been able to clear it up yet. I have a feeling that what I need to do may be very dangerous, but it is my mess and I have to fix it.

When you can, please ask the police about me, and a man named Collett. Ask to be put in touch with a lady called Julia Barnes. They will be able to confirm some of what I said. I know you will find it hard to believe that it is me writing this. But when I was little, I had a stuffed toy that was really called Buggles, but you called it "Stinky," because it never got washed. But you stopped calling it that after Mom died, didn't you? You stopped laughing, and now I understand why in a way I couldn't back then. Because I've lost people too.

When I was about eight, there was a mould stain on the bathroom wall, that I used to pretend was the ghost of Mom. Well, sort of, I mean it was a bit like a face, so I would talk to it sometimes when I was in the room on my own. You never understood why I was so angry and upset when I came home from school one day and you'd got rid of it. Well, now you know.

And you once dropped your toothbrush in the loo after you sneezed. I still don't know how one thing caused the other. But I remember it because you went from shouting and swearing to laughing about it. I think I remember every time that you laughed in the last ten years, and I really wish you'd done it more, but like I said I think I understand why, at last. I miss Mom too, and now, I miss you.

I don't know if I'll make it home, and like I said, you won't recognise me if I do. But if I don't, know that I love you, am very grateful indeed for all that you have done for me, and died doing something that I felt was important.

Your loving son,
Antony.

I finished the letter at last, annoyed that my female body had kept trying to cry as I was writing it. I sealed it, addressed it, begged a stamp from the family, then walked to the postbox with it myself.

As the fourth day turned to evening, Amma took me aside and sized me up. "Well, you're looking a lot better than you were when you got here. Now I don't want to send you away, you can stay for as long as you want. But my boy Sachin has gone sweet on you. What??? You cannot tell??? Did your mother teach you *nothing*? Goodness me, it is a wonder you English people have not died out completely. Now tell me, would you be interested in marrying my Sachin?"

She was direct, I had to give her that.

"Uhhh, I really don't think I'm ready for any kind of commitment right now."

"That is what I thought. Well, if you want to stay, I can put him right. But Rajeev tells me he found you without shoes, by a hospital. Tell me, are you running away from something?"

"I'm looking for someone. Have been for quite a while. My cousin. But it's true, I did meet some people along the way that I had to run away from."

"Well, dearie, why don't you sit down and tell me your story."

Chapter 47: The revenant

I did as she asked, but had to do quite a lot of editing. I left out everything to do with becoming a Glory, and existing inside Talia's mind. Most of all, I omitted to mention that I'd been a boy for most of the story, and turned Sally into Sandy. I kept the focus on trying to find Daniel.

"But you ran into trouble along the way?" she asked, keenly. "It's OK, you don't want to talk about it. Tell me more about this boy you're looking for."

I thought I'd told her plenty, but I dug through my memories for more. I told her how he was very much like my younger brother for much of the time, always at my house, sharing my adventures, but equally willing to ditch me if he saw some cool kids from his year. I described a few of the pranks he liked to play.

"What does he want to be when he grows up?" she asked. I had to admit that I had no idea.

"He never asked me that question, either," I said by way of defence.

"What books does he read?" I didn't know.

"What else does he like to do when he's on his own?" she asked. I didn't know. Daniel didn't like being on his own.

"Does he like girls, or boys?" I didn't even know that. Daniel knew that I liked girls, he teased me about it relentlessly, taking punts on how old I'd be when first I got a girlfriend. When he was feeling generous, he guessed I'd be in my early thirties.

"You spent all this time with him, but you managed not to know very much about him," she observed, though her expression was quizzical rather than critical.

"Daniel's like that," I replied. "He decides what we're going to talk about. If you bring up a subject he doesn't approve of, he just acts like you're being epically lame."

"Ah." She folded her arms, paused, and looked me in the eye meaningfully. "You know, when I was much younger, a young lady in our family disappeared. Nothing dramatic, just wasn't there one morning. So all the men went out searching, driving around, and bothering the police. But we women of the family got together and used our brains instead. We went through all that she'd done, or said she'd done, over the past six months. Soon we worked out that when she'd said she'd been having dance lessons, she'd actually been somewhere else entirely."

"A young man?" I guessed.

"A young man. He took a lot more tracking down because he wasn't from an Indian family, but we at least knew what to look for. By the time we found them, they were already married."

"Oh. Did that cause a lot of trouble?"

"It was *pandemonium*," she proclaimed with delight. "But it settled down after a while, once he'd agreed to go to India and marry her again, properly. They've got five sons now, and two daughters."

"Good for them," I said.

"The point is, if you want to find a person, find out what they want. What they hope for. What needs they have that they couldn't meet at home."

I nodded, dumbstruck. It was easily the best advice I'd had since I'd started my search. All this time, I'd been trying to learn about the Glories, and now I realised that I'd treated Daniel as a passive victim in this story. I'd assumed that he'd fallen into a Glory, against his will, in an accident, and therefore all that

Chapter 47: The revenant

I had to do was find him, and pull him out. Yet that hadn't been the case with Talia – she'd gone in by her own free will, even though she, unlike Daniel, had left her body behind. I'd gone in willingly too, though of course it had been to find him. And Rick had wanted to do that as well, and was only prevented by Collett.

Had Daniel *chosen* to disappear, either into the Glory, or by using it some other way? Or was it even simpler than that – had he seen me somehow frozen in time, and decided that this would be a good time to wander off and seek his fortune? Was he guilty about what had happened to me, in exactly the same way that I had been, about him?

"I think you're right," I said. "I've been stupid. I should have started at his home. I think I was scared to talk to his parents, because they would have blamed me."

"Maybe," said Amma. "But in the end, they'll just want what you want – their boy back."

"I need to go to their house and talk to them. Look through Daniel's things, find clues there."

"Wouldn't the police have done that?" she asked.

"Maybe," I said. Then a dumb thought struck me. What if Daniel was already back home? What if he'd returned, while I was floating in nowhere land? "Can I use your phone?"

I called Daniel's home number, which somehow I remembered. "Hello, can I speak to Daniel?" I asked, trying to sound younger than I was.

"What?" growled an angry male voice. "Who is this? I haven't seen that boy for months! If you're another fucking reporter ..."

I quickly hung up. Daniel's father, it seemed, had taken his loss hard. Amma watched me and waited for me to speak, as I stood in that narrow corridor, next to the landline phone. "I'm going to have to go to his house," I said. "Try to talk his parents round. Maybe ... I dunno, maybe I'll find something that means something to me, even if it didn't to anyone else."

Amma simply nodded. When I told her where Daniel lived, she immediately announced that she'd have one of the boys drive me some of the way, using the presence of cousins in a town on the route as an excuse if they were challenged.

"What do you mean, challenged?" I asked

"You can't drive more than six miles from your home, because of the Glories. We're exempt because we deliver food, but the new PM's got the police jumping to his tune like performing monkeys, so we still have to be careful. We can get you about halfway, then maybe our cousins there can take you a bit further on."

"New PM?" I asked, remembering the paramedic's puzzled response when I'd mentioned Boris Johnson.

"How about I find you a newspaper?"

* * * * *

Thus far I'd mostly been wearing loose-fitting track suits that the family had loaned me, but now Amma set to work ordering her daughters-in-law to assemble for me a suitable outfit for travel. A pair of jeans were duly acquired from nearby relatives in exchange for some meals, and other items of clothing

Chapter 47: The revenant

were surrendered. Thus far, I'd managed without a bra, having mercifully flat breasts, but they – like other parts of me – had been responding to the never-ending input of food, and to my horror had been acquiring more substance. I tried not to quail in terror when a black bra was presented to me. The daughters-in-law laughed merrily as they helped me put it on. I had to remind myself that I was just a woman getting dressed, not Doctor Frankenfurter or some other cross-dresser. Luckily they seemed to think I'd be fine without tights, and so other than the bra, my clothes felt reassuringly normal. I looked at myself in the mirror, and it was the face, not the attire, that caught my eye. The colour had come back to my skin, my cheeks seemed full and my hair much thicker (I'd been made to try more types of hair product that week than I'd used in the rest of my life put together). The eyes had a certain fire and determination in them, and for the first time it was like I was looking at Talia, that young woman I'd fallen in love with. Funny, how she perhaps had an Antony there with her, built from her memories of me, while I had a Talia staring back at me from the mirror. I saw a tear running from her eye, and it took a moment for me to realise that it meant I must be crying, too.

Chapter 48: A long time ago, in a galaxy far away

Julia

I was travelling across space. Distances I couldn't begin to imagine, and the sort of time that turns mountains into sand, trees into coal, and monkeys into men. A planet arrived. We swept downwards and flew across its single ocean – this planet was all ocean, a water world. It was paired with an enormous, desolate moon, almost as large as the planet itself, dragging tides far greater than those on the Earth. Islands of land did exist, but the massive tides flooded them each time the moon went by. This was a real place, I felt sure, even if I was only seeing it through the memories of others. Was Daniel here? Or Antony?

I sensed time rushing forward. First the ocean was empty of creatures, but after a while, life was thriving. The first simple animals diversified into countless varieties, of which some died out while others thrived and evolved new forms. Some of them looked oddly similar to sea creatures from Earth, others totally different. Creatures with broom-shaped heads literally swept the sand of the ocean bottom, and sucked up tiny morsels they found there. There were predatory fish-like things that inflated themselves and shot white javelins at their prey. Countless other animals lived and died there, each as remarkable as the last. Occasional catastrophes wiped out swathes of creatures, but life repeatedly bounced back with ever-changing shapes and strategies. Soon I noticed that things a bit like an octopus but with six legs – hexapods, then – were beginning to use tools. Clams were co-opted as living tongs, or tweezers. One by one, these hexapods learned to tackle the ocean's most fearsome predators, and soon they were the dominant species.

The hexapods built floating and underwater farms, and then cities. They conquered the transient land and the air, inventing flight. Literature, art, and philosophy all blossomed. Their numbers grew and grew, the cities spread, and numbers of all the other creatures plummeted. With resources suddenly limited, wars broke out. Pollutants of all kinds poisoned the ocean. Huge numbers of hexapods boiled, choked or were otherwise slain, culminating in an orgy of devastation as their civilisation self-destructed. There followed long years of misery, whole lives spent scraping a harsh living in a ruined, toxic ocean. I saw this age of ruin flip past me in what was probably just a few minutes, but I truly felt the drag of time for those who had actually lived it. Yet gradually, over perhaps fifty generations, the giant ocean began to heal itself, and the hexapods started to assemble their society, once more. Cautiously at first, and then with increasing boldness, they built their cities anew, along with everything else they'd had first time around. But they fell into wars and poisoned their ocean again, and the society fell apart once more.

I watched it all happen four more times. The long periods of hardship and sickness in a near-dead ocean, the slow recovery, the boom years, and then the collapse. Watching it was like being trapped in one of those looping nightmares that never seems to end.

Chapter 48: A long time ago, in a galaxy far away

Yet somehow, after the sixth cycle of war and destruction, something wonderful happened. Cities rose again, more slowly this time, and without the merciless devouring of resources. The ocean was allowed to continue cleaning itself, and was eventually refilled with life. Species that had died out were somehow re-engineered.

Time rolled forward, and hexapod culture moved beyond what had been managed before. They explored the deepest reaches of their ocean, and visited the thirteen other planets in their solar system, though none were remotely habitable. Time started rushing past faster, so much so that from time to time stars appeared, or vanished, in the sky. Constellations changed shape. Millions of years were passing, perhaps billions. Hexapod civilisation survived it all. These creatures had done what had so far utterly eluded humankind: they'd achieved true sustainability.

They appeared not to use sound to communicate at all, instead producing increasingly complex symbols and colours across their bodies, which easily translated into written language, and later into long-range electronic communication. Much later, they learned to communicate with their own bodies, down to a cellular level. Experiences could be shared, simply by touching. It made me think of Siobhan – wasn't that exactly what had been happening when I had touched her hand?

The hexapods taught their cells how to change, multiply, or die, as necessary. Disease was eliminated, wounds could be rapidly cured, and ageing could be halted, even reversed. They became, effectively, immortal, but population sizes were strictly limited. A couple were only allowed to produce children (two of them) if they consented to euthanasia thirty-six cycles later. Remarkably, some did choose this option.

How did I understand all these details? Good question. It was like they were being downloaded into my mind as I watched.

Eventually, the star that gave the planet its warmth began to redden and grow, ever so slowly at first. The ocean got warmer, and steam increasingly rose from it. Great starships were built in the hope of finding new worlds to live on, beyond their solar system, but either they failed or they never reported back. The hexapods sent mirrors into space to cool the planet down, but the sun kept growing so it only delayed the problem. Their world was dying, and the hexapods knew that they would die out soon, too. They had nowhere to go. Individually, most seemed to accept this fate, but collectively, they railed against the loss of their race and all it had achieved.

A conference was arranged, on a planet-wide scale, to discuss solutions. All were rejected as hopeless, or unworkable. Some argued for building giant space arks, but it would take millions of years to reach worlds that had even a chance of being habitable, and from what I could tell, suspended animation did not work on their species. So, not one of them seemed to have a workable solution.

Then the scene froze, and Sally appeared. "I'd better explain this part," she said simply.

Chapter 48: A long time ago, in a galaxy far away

Antony

The entire Sharma clan assembled in the restaurant to say goodbye to me. Rajeev was to be my driver, and Kapil enthusiastically wished me luck, while Sachin despondently looked at the ground and said nothing. The young women shook my hand and Amma enveloped me in a huge hug, before giving me a large backpack full of supplies. I tried to protest, but it was eight against one. I told them I'd come back when my journey was over and life got back to normal, and repay their kindness in full.

"You'll come back to see us, yes, but I won't hear a word about paying us. The government is kind to us, so we are kind to those who need it. When your turn comes, you'll be kind too." I loved these people. I felt like crying again. I told them I would very much like to come and see them again. But as I followed Rajeev out of the door, I had a horrible feeling that I might never get the chance.

I expected we'd get into a small car, but Rajeev (who I now knew as 'Raj') led me to the delivery van. Much less chance of being stopped, he explained. I asked him to tell me more about the new rules around Glories.

"You really have been hiding from the world, haven't you?" he said, looking at me curiously. "No, no, you don't need to tell me. First they started locking up people who were obviously Glory addicts, then it was anyone caught speeding, and now it's pretty much anyone caught looking at a Glory. We do not like it, we have seen laws like this in India, and we know where they lead. But what can we do? We are just an ordinary family."

"I think you're an extraordinary family," I told him.

He grinned. "Are you sure you won't consider marrying Sachin?"

I smiled back, and on we went. We saw a police car on the way out of town, lurking there, a silent warning that Glory-hunters could expect harsh treatment. Raj slowed down as he passed them but they waved him through, looking bored.

He played me a collaboration between two composers I'd never heard of, Ravi Shankar and Philip Glass. Some time later, as we tootled along a country road, he told me how much of a joy it was to drive with so few cars on the road, though he still missed very much the bustle of the restaurant being open.

"I think what you do, feeding all those people, is wonderful," I replied. "Did Sachin really have the hots for me?"

"Ohh, my little brother. He is always falling in love, do not mind him. One day, it might actually occur to him to talk to the girl he is interested in!"

"Glory!!" I shouted.

"What?" He slammed on the brakes. Luckily there was no-one behind us.

"It's OK, it's not in the road. It's up in the sky, look. Oh! There's two. No, three!"

"We should not stop," he said. "Someone might see and report us."

"They'd do that?" I said, shocked.

"Some people would."

One of the Glories was a speckled purple sphere, tilted and rotating slowly. The second was an area of glowing golden raindrops, shaped like a wavy-edged leaf, with the drops appearing from nowhere at its top and then vanishing

Chapter 48: A long time ago, in a galaxy far away

as they reached the bottom. The third was round, black and white, and looked very like a clock face, albeit without hands or numbers. As I looked, I thought I could see a fourth one, a Type Two, because a triangular area of cloud had a tint of green.

"I think they're moving," I said.

"No, it just looks like it because we're moving, and so are the clouds," he replied knowledgeably.

"I don't think so," I said. "Please, stop, just for a moment. There, near that tree. If they're moving, that's a danger, we can say that's why we stopped."

"Just for a minute, no longer." He pulled the car partly onto the verge, close to where a stately oak tree rose from a bedraggled hedge.

"There, look. See? You can see that they're moving, behind the branches of the tree." I looked at him, expecting him to concede the point, but he was still looking upwards, and now his eyes widened suddenly in shock. He muttered a prayer in a language I didn't know, and I cast my eyes back upwards.

The sky was now full of Glories. I could count fifteen, even with the tree and hedge blocking part of my view. "We have to park," I said. "We can't drive until we know what's happening."

Raj hesitated, his mouth hanging open. "The sky is full of Glories!" I said. "People will be able to see them from anywhere! They can't arrest everyone!"

He nodded, wobbled his head as if to clear it, then drove us on to where we could park awkwardly in front of a gate to a field. Now, as we stood by the car drinking it all in, we each turned around slowly and gazed upwards in astonishment. The sky was teeming with Glories, as far as the eye could see. I got as far as thirty before I lost count.

"They're all going in the same direction," I said. Standing still, using another tree as a point of reference, I could see how they were all moving along, as if the sky had become one enormous invisible river, along which the Glories all floated and flowed, at the same speed. From time to time, new ones popped into existence, like submerged objects bobbing to the river's surface, but I didn't see any of them vanish. They were heading roughly south. We tried to gauge their speed, and guessed about ten miles per hour.

"So very beautiful," said Raj in a reverent voice. "I just wish I knew what it all meant."

"Something has changed," I said.

"I think everything has changed," he replied. "I'd never have told my mother, but I didn't really believe in any Gods since I was about twelve. I liked science too much. Studied chemistry at university, I did. But now ... I think there has to be a God, doesn't there? Who else could make *that*?"

A Glory appeared at the far end of the large field. It looked like a tangled ball of turquoise wool, the size of perhaps four houses, and hovering maybe a metre above ground level. It moved, sedately, from one side of the field to the other, and then over and through a hedge.

"I don't think it's safe to drive," I said. "You know what happens if you hit one of those things."

"Of course I do. The ambulances, remember?"

"Yeah, well, I've seen it happen when there wasn't any point in calling an ambulance," I said.

Chapter 48: A long time ago, in a galaxy far away

"Amma told me to deliver you and that is what I am going to do, even if we have to walk. We are more than half the way to my cousins now, anyway. I'll drive slowly and we'll keep our eyes out for ... oh no."

He said the last two words in a whisper, and pointed upwards with a trembling hand. "What is it?" I asked, alarmed.

"Plane," he replied simply. A jet airliner was in the sky, above the Glories, or at least above most of them. "People still *fly*?" I asked, incredulously. "I thought the pandemic ..."

"But the new government is encouraging them to fly again. If you take a virus test and it's clear, you can fly to Britain. If it's not, you quarantine. And they say Glories are not so common anymore. I would never take the risk, but some airlines are starting to," Raj explained. He looked up fearfully at the plane. "I hope their God is with them," he whispered.

The plane had been relatively low in the sky, as if it were coming in to land. Now it was banking and turning upwards, but luck was not on their side. As we watched, a massive blue-green Glory the size of a thundercloud winked into existence right in front of them, looking like a churning whirlpool that had been plucked from the ocean and stitched into the sky.

"Turn, turn!" I screamed. I clutched Raj's hand.

"Don't look," he said, but I couldn't turn away.

The plane was banking hard, turning, one wing pointing down at the ground and the other up towards space. I couldn't judge how close to the Glory it was, so maybe it was going to make it? Then I saw the fuselage bend and rip, like a squashed child's toy, and I knew it had hit. For a moment the plane seemed to hang there, limply, as if stuck to the Glory. Then it began to tumble out of the sky, slowly at first, but rapidly accelerating. I didn't see it hit the ground because of the hedge, and I don't know how far away it was, but I swear I felt the ground shake, a moment later.

"Back in the car," said Raj. "There is nothing we can do."

We drove on in silence, shocked into extreme caution. We slowed down at bends, anywhere a Glory might come through and hit us through a hedge or a wall. Even at ten miles an hour, they could be deadly if we didn't see them in time. So we both kept a vigilant watch on the road ahead, and to the sides. We worked out the direction of their travel as roughly south-southwest, and I watched the compass on Raj's iphone so I would know which way a Glory would come from, in case one did. In fact only one crossed our path, a pulsating snowflake the size of a small Ferris wheel, and it was far enough in front that we simply stopped and let it pass. All the time the sky was full of Glories, and I couldn't even look at them properly.

Thanks to the government rules there were very few cars on the roads, but what cars there were had mostly parked up on the roadsides, as people watched the terrifying spectacle above. We found one road blocked by a green tractor, seemingly abandoned there. We had to turn around and find another way. A glory that looked like a swarm of crocuses passed just over our heads, as Raj did a three-point turn. And high above, the river of Glories flowed on, with more appearing to join it all the time.

Passing through towns and villages, the problem was people. Many were out on the streets looking up, but we had to brake hard when one man simply wandered right out into the road ahead of us, head tipped back, unaware of anything but the sky above. Ten minutes later, I had to actually leave the van

Chapter 48: A long time ago, in a galaxy far away

and gently manhandle an old lady out of the road and onto the safety of the pavement. As I got back in, a Glory emerged through the wall of a block of offices, just ahead of us. It was a tight but huge ball of wriggling worms of every possible colour, passing through the 3rd, 4th and 5th storeys of the building, as if they were nothing but cloud. From the nearby people came noises of awe, terror, delight and shock, as it smoothly passed over the road and through the walls of the building opposite, the last of the technicolour worms seeming to wave goodbye for a moment, before they too vanished from our view.

"What if there are people in those buildings?" someone shouted.

Raj and I looked at each other in shock as I climbed back into the van.

"Call your families," one person was shouting. "Tell them to get outside! ... No, not to watch," he added angrily to someone who'd said something I couldn't hear. "You don't wanna be in a room if one of those fuckers goes through your house!"

"Do it," I told Raj, ignoring the hooting of a vehicle behind us. He dialled the number but handed me the phone, as he started us moving. Kapil answered.

"Kapil! The Glories are moving and there's lots of them. You've probably seen. Indoors isn't safe. They can come straight through the walls and crush you. You have to get outside."

"Is Rajeev OK? Where is Rajeev?"

"He's fine! He's driving." I stuck the phone close to Raj's face.

"Do as she says, brother," said Raj. "And then call everyone else!"

It wasn't long before we saw the fatal effects of a moving Glory for ourselves. A block of fairly posh looking flats, six storeys high, had a hole in it like a bomb had blown out part of the walls, and a pile of rubble lay on the lawn below. A broken red mess lay on top, that had probably been a person doing unremarkable things in their home not long before. A spinning orange octagon floated nonchalantly past above the building.

More and more people were spilling onto the pavements, and into the road. Our progress was getting slower and slower. "This is no good," said Raj.

"Soon we'll barely be moving at all," I agreed.

"Look, how important is it, that you get to where you're going?"

"I ... I don't know, but I think it could be very important indeed. You asked where I was, to miss all the news. Well, I sort of went into a Glory. I'm connected to them, but I don't really understand how. And so is my cousin, the one I can't find. We saw a Glory together, back when they were really rare and all over ... the ... world."

Raj looked at me in alarm as my words ground to a halt.

"That newspaper Amma gave me!" I said, and I scrabbled in my backpack for the Sunday paper.

"What is it?" asked Raj.

"Next to that big spread about politics, there was a timeline. I was so shocked about all the time I'd missed, I didn't even think about the specific dates but I think ... here it is!"

I looked at the early dates on the list:

```
First reported and corroborated Glory anywhere        November 13th, 2019.
First corroborated Glory in UK                           March 11th, 2020.
Last corroborated Glory not in UK or nearby countries    April 8th, 2020.
First time multiple Glories reported on a single day (UK) April 8th, 2020.
```

Chapter 48: A long time ago, in a galaxy far away

"The 8th of April," I whispered. "It was a Wednesday."

"Was that day important to you?" Raj asked.

"It was the day I saw a Glory. The day Daniel disappeared." The day it all changed, for me. Was it all connected? Could Daniel and I have *caused* all of this?

* * * * *

"We will have to get to the motorway," said Raj.

We had moved about two blocks in 15 minutes. Some people were getting into their cars, as if getting out of the city would make them safer. I supposed that it might.

"You said we couldn't use the motorway," I replied.

"Motorway traffic is essential journeys only – mainly delivery, and they've got cameras, so they check every single car that goes. So I will maybe get in trouble. But you said getting home is important, and I believe you, especially now. And I think perhaps that the police will be busy for a while, don't you?"

We looked up at the Glories passing by, above us.

"You're right," I said. "But you said it wasn't that far to go now. Will the motorway help us?"

"I have changed the plan. I am taking you to Swinton."

"Raj ..." I began.

"You said it was important," he repeated, simply. "And I believe you."

I nodded. Maybe I was being stupid, and maybe Daniel and I were utterly irrelevant. But the skies were full of Glories, and the streets were full of chaos, and if there was even a chance I could help, then I had to take it.

"OK," I said. "Thank you."

Somehow, we got onto a more major road, the kind where barriers of sorts kept pedestrians away, and we moved, through stop-start traffic. I gazed at all the passing Glories, because it helped stop me fretting about our glacial progress. I got the feeling that the Glories were now moving faster than we were.

"Do we have enough petrol?" I asked him. The tank was a little under half-full.

"I thought we did, but if we are sitting in traffic all day, then maybe not. We will fill up at a service station. I do not want to even try it here."

Finally, after over an hour, the traffic suddenly thinned, and fifteen minutes later we were on the motorway. Both of us relaxed a little now that we were actually properly moving, and on impulse I turned on the radio.

"... *local area. Go outdoors if you can but we repeat, stay local. If possible, spend the day in a garden or open space. If you can't go outdoors, stay downstairs if you can, in the biggest room of the house. If you live in a flat above ground floor, contact your local authority or move directly to a communal building such as a school. We are asking anyone with responsibility for schools, town halls, or any building with large open rooms, to open these rooms up as shelters for those who need them. Stay towards the centre of any room that you are in. This advice overrides all prior lockdown and Glory rules, until further notice. The government is working on a final solution to the Glory problem and are confident that this crisis will soon be concluded.*

Chapter 48: A long time ago, in a galaxy far away

"This is an emergency broadcast from the government. Huge numbers of Glories have appeared throughout the British Isles in the skies and at ground level, and they are moving. We advise people to move outside of buildings where possible, and stay away from enclosed spaces. The Glories can and will pass through walls and they present a clear and present risk to human life. Do not allow yourself to be caught between a moving Glory and a wall, or a solid object of any kind. All public transport is halted. Do not drive. We repeat, stay off the roads. Motorways and large roads will be closed except to army and emergency vehicles. If you need supplies, ask a neighbour. The situation is the same all over the country, so please do not attempt to leave your local area. Go outdoors if you can but we repeat, stay local. If you can, spend the day in a garden or open space ..."

The message played again and again on repeat. "They're closing the motorways," I said.

"I heard. But it will take them time. We could get quite some distance before they stop us."

"Depends how long the message has been playing though ..."

"Try another channel," I said, and we did.

"'Roger called in from the Pentland Hills near Edinburgh. Tell us what you saw, Roger.'

'Glories, dozens of 'em. Gotta admit, I wasn't even sure they were real till today. Now the sky's full of 'em, all moving south, away from the city. Most are in the sky but I swear to you, I saw one come right out of the slope below me. Looked like an upside down purple tree, it did.'

"And this is from Jeff, on the cliffs near Folkestone."

"They're coming over the sea, hundreds of 'em. Flying in from France like a bloody invasion fleet!"

"Hang on," I said. "Coming from France? He said from, didn't he? That means they're not all going south, go far down enough and they're coming North instead!"

"They're all going somewhere," said Raj. "Somewhere in southern England."

"Do you know anyone in Wales, or the west?" I asked, for the radio program had run out of local callers for now and was talking about safety instead.

"Geeta's got cousins in Bristol," he said.

"Can we call them?"

The woman who answered told us, "I think they are going west, towards Bath and London."

"There's an epicentre," I said, after thanking her and ending the call. "A place they're all heading. Maybe that's where I need to get to."

"Why?" said Raj, alarmed. "I should think it is the last place you would want to go! I would not take you there, even if I could!"

I nodded, chastened. Claude Dexter would be there though, I felt sure of it, so Raj had a point. But what if Dexter had Daniel? What if he'd already been using Daniel, the way he had wanted to use me?

For twenty-five minutes, our luck held. Taking a reasonable risk, Raj sped the van up to seventy, knowing the road was wide enough to see approaching Glories. In fact, we were heading the same way that they were, more or less,

Chapter 48: A long time ago, in a galaxy far away

and we actually overtook a group of them, tootling along at what I guessed was now nearly thirty miles an hour. "Are they getting faster?" I asked him.

We hardly saw a single other car going our way, but saw a fair few that were driving more cautiously in the opposite direction, at first. Whatever the government said, it looked like some people thought they'd be safer going whichever way the Glories weren't. Of course, if there was a finite number, then eventually they'd be right, but what if there wasn't? And what would all those Glories do, once they got to where they were going?

We passed a junction, and I noticed that no cars were coming the other way anymore. We soon found out why.

The road ahead was blocked.

* * * * *

The two outer lanes of our motorway had lines of static cars, and an army truck blocked the third. A soldier waved us down, and we had no choice but to stop.

"The motorway's closed," he said, looking at us like we were the stupidest kids in the class.

"I know," replied Raj, with perfect courtesy. "But we were already on the motorway when he heard the message, and we did not know what to do, so we thought it better to complete the journey because we are closer to the end than to the start."

"Yeah well, what you're gonna do now is leave this vehicle and get in that truck. We're taking everyone here to an emergency shelter. We've got big tents going up, safest thing at the moment. You'll be OK there till the crisis is over."

"I understand. But officer, we have a lot of food here, much of it is fresh, that is what we were delivering. If it cannot go to its destination, then can we take it to your tents? It would be a most terrible waste to leave it here, especially because I think your people will soon be hungry."

"Our family run a restaurant," I added sweetly.

The soldier's face made a series of comical expressions as he tried to process a suggestion that was obviously sensible but not directly covered by his orders. So he called his superior, then told us grumpily to wait in the van.

"I am sorry," Raj told me. "We did our best. I do not see what else we could have done. We are still about a hundred miles from your town."

I thought of asking him to turn round, but it was crazily dangerous and we'd probably get caught, hit something, or be shot.

"You could slip out," he said. "Run up the verge, maybe get up to that other road there, and hitch a lift."

He pointed to a bridge that carried a minor road across the motorway, a short distance ahead of us. "Did you say, hitch a lift?" I asked. "Let me see that map!" I pulled out the road Atlas, and flicked the pages over, and drawing a line with my finger. I could get within ten miles of Daniel's house, if I didn't get killed in the attempt. My heart began to pound, and my fingers to twitch.

"Talia?" said Raj, looking concerned.

"Yes, I'm going to try your idea," I said, my hand shaking. I wasn't sure at all if it was a good idea. But I thought of those people who'd died in the plane, plus that poor innocent sod who'd been smashed through the wall of his home,

Chapter 48: A long time ago, in a galaxy far away

and those were only the ones we had seen. I couldn't give up, and there really was only one possible way to keep going.

"You'll need food and supplies," said Raj. "Here, take the lunch mum made. And the road Atlas, you'll need it." He stuffed both into my pack. "And my jacket. No, you'll need more food, I'll just go into the back and get ..."

I looked in the mirror and said, "No time, I need to go now!" A group of five Glories were sailing towards us in the direction we'd come from, a little above ground level.

"Everyone out," a soldier shouted. "Out of the trucks!" A bunch of bewildered looking people disgorged from the army trucks and were ordered onto the road verge. With the soldiers distracted, this was my best chance. I kissed Raj on the cheek (because that's what girls do), grabbed his jacket, and jumped out of the van. I vaulted across the central barrier onto the far lane, and ran across the three empty lanes. The soldiers didn't spot me until I was running up the verge, when I heard a "Hey, you, come back!"

I didn't turn round to see if he meant me. I hurried up the steeply sloping verge as best I could through long grass speckled with oxeye daisies. More shouts of "*Stop!*" came from behind, and a soldier was sprinting towards me. My legs were hurting, but I kept going, diagonally up and along, towards the bridge. The soldier was gaining on me, of course. Five days of push-ups and donkey rides was never going to be a match for the training they'd put him through.

Gasping for breath, I got to the top of the verge and the side of the bridge, with the soldier just metres behind. I vaulted the fence, stumbled but stayed upright, then ran across the road to the far side of the bridge. Then I climbed onto the barrier, teetering over the fall to the motorway lanes below.

"What are you doing?!" yelled the soldier.

"Stay back!" I shouted. "Stay back or I'll jump!"

The soldier glanced over his shoulder. "There's a bunch of Glories coming, you idiot! One of them might knock you off of the bridge!"

The five Glories were now getting close to the bridge, the biggest a flat horizontal disc with spiralling colours like some lolly from a fairground. It was maybe twenty metres across. That one was going to pass below the bridge but another, a furiously spinning ball of multicoloured fur, was heading straight for us.

"Jesus fuck!!" shouted the soldier, instinctively unleashing a hail of bullets into the spinning furball Glory, to no effect of course. Then he dived to the side, and it passed through the spot where he had been standing. "Get down, girl," he cried. "Get out of its way!!"

The furball span towards me just as the striped, curving front edge of the big lollipop Glory appeared, passing under the bridge, and my feet.

And I jumped.

Chapter 49: The homecoming

Antony

The landing was both hard and soft. My feet slipped sideways immediately, as if on the smoothest of ice, and my face slapped flat into the Glory's surface, but it felt like landing on a trampoline. Raj's jacket slipped from my grip and vanished through the Glory. And then I was sliding, towards the back end of the Glory, and any moment I'd run out of surface and fall.

So I stuck in my hand. It gripped, and I stopped sliding. I could still put my hand into Glories, just as I'd been able to before, in my other body. Or rather, my non-body. Could I pull a piece out, too, and what would happen if I did? I wasn't about to chance it.

I pushed up my torso and looked back, to see two astonished soldiers standing on the bridge, receding away into the distance. There was only one possible form of transport that could take me south towards Daniel's house at a speed faster than snail's pace, and this was it.

Julia

Sally was wearing dungarees splattered here and there with mud. "Hello Julia," she said. "Were you able to follow what you've seen so far?"

"Sally!" I said. "Are you alive?"

"My body was destroyed, but I exist as consciousness. The Taimede managed to preserve me."

"Taimede?" I asked.

"They don't use sound or words like we do, but they seemed to sense that I needed a name for them in my own language, and that's what they came up with. They've been teaching me their history, and using me to convey it to you in an easier way. It took weeks for them to show me what I just showed you. Well, weeks of Earth time, it was more like months for me. We don't have much time now. The plans they made have all gone wrong."

"Plans? Was that something to do with what happened on that water world I was seeing?"

She nodded, and the scene behind her re-formed. "Most of the decisions in their society are made by a governing Super-AI," she explained. "It's how they managed to live sustainably for such a very long time, and achieve true fairness across their society. But now their sun is expanding and will destroy their world, and the Super-AI has been asked to provide a solution. It tells them that consciousness is itself a dimension. A fifth dimension, if we accept time as the fourth. Whenever we form thoughts, memories, or images of our imagination, we are using this dimension without ever knowing it. It all somehow pokes through into a dimension that would be utterly empty without conscious life. The Super-AI has found a way to detach consciousness from the physical body, allowing it to persist indefinitely.

Chapter 49: The homecoming

"Watch," Sally told me. "This volunteer is about to vanish." An individual stepped forward, a switch was thrown, and the volunteer disappeared into thin air. Another switch later, it returned as a transparent image of itself, waving to the astonished audience. "The process uses the physical body as a sort of counterweight, I think," said Sally. "The body moves one way, the conscious mind goes the other. But the mind would normally disintegrate at the death of its body, so a conscious AI has to go through the process at the same time, with instructions to hold the mind together, and give it the ability to peek back into our physical universe."

The assembled audience looked impressed, but hardly enthusiastic. "At first, none of them liked the idea," said Sally. "It was like choosing to become a ghost. But a few years later, the Super-AI built a physical body and the volunteer's mind was popped back into it."

"The process was reversible?" I said.

"Yes, but only as long as someone was there to do the reversing. The Taimede leaders complained that it was all very well to give them a way to survive the planet's death, but with it gone, how could they ever return? They'd be stranded as formless beings forever. So time moved on, the sun kept growing, and with no other plan available, more and more Taimede individuals underwent the conversion process into bodyless beings."

Sally stopped talking, and we silently watched as the red sun grew larger, and more and more water evaporated, kicking off a runaway greenhouse effect. Oceans boiled, super-charged currents smashed cities, one by one. Those few Taimede that were not formless by then died horribly. And then, at last, the fiery red sun rose over the boiling ocean of a now lifeless world.

It took me some time to recover from the shock of seeing a world, an entire civilisation, destroyed. "Are they the Glories?" I asked Sally. "These creatures that turned into consciousness? Is that what we are seeing?"

"Yes, basically the Glories are the Taimede," said Sally. "Do you understand now why they've come here?"

It took me a moment to work it out. "There was no-one to bring them back," I said, awestruck. "So they've come to find someone who can, haven't they? They want us to give them back physical form."

I moved myself into a crouching position, aware that a lot could go wrong with my plan. Almost immediately another, larger bridge loomed ahead of us, and I had to move quickly to the left side of my Glory to avoid hitting a support. Watching the support slide straight through my impromptu flying machine was surreal. Then the road was curving to the right, and my Glory got closer and closer to the verge, until a quarter and then a half of it was swallowed by the grassy bank. I prepared myself for a rough landing, but then the road began to slope downward, the verge with it, getting further and further below us as the Glory kept on with its perfectly straight line of travel. I was flying now, with the

Chapter 49: The homecoming

countryside dozens of metres below, which meant if I fell, I was dead. The solution was simple – don't fall.

I did my best to relax. At thirty miles per hour the journey would take a little over three hours, but if the Glories kept gradually speeding up – as I suspected they were – it might take less. I had no idea how I'd get off when it came to it, but one problem at a time. So I tried to relax, and enjoy the flight.

The experience of it was, of course, quite incredible. I sat in the centre of a mass of curving coloured lines radiating out from where I was, flexing and twisting like living things held within the opaque creamy body of the Glory. Then there were the accompanying Glories, fellow travellers matching our speed exactly, like moons that didn't orbit. I could only see the two that were above me: one was the spinning furball, the other a set of shining silver cylinders stuck together at random angles to each other, as if by an enterprising two-year-old with a tube of superglue. I found their presence strangely comforting. And, of course, the sky was full of hundreds of Glories of every possible kind, all flowing along at the same speed as us.

I pulled out the bag of sandwiches, ate one, and then stupidly put the others down on the surface of the Glory, which they promptly fell through. So I held onto my pack and the road atlas a bit more carefully. After a while, I realised that I needed to know where I was, and reluctantly edged myself forwards to the front rim of the Glory. I felt dizzy as I watched the ground going past beneath me, now more than thirty metres below. I couldn't see a motorway, just a lot of towns, merging into one at their edges. I needed landmarks. I got out the road Atlas, fighting the wind a little as I got it to the right page, then drew a line with my fingernails in the direction we had to be going, assuming I'd got the right spot on the road where I'd started, and that the Glories hadn't yet changed direction. If I was right, we would pass within sight of a pair of large reservoirs in about an hours' time. I stuffed the road Atlas halfway into my jeans, to make sure I didn't drop it, and settled down to watch the land fly past.

In time I caught sight of a number of Glories below me, travelling the same way. One was a Type Two that could have been fifty metres across, and turned anything within it into an exact colour negative of what it should be. At least that one would be taking no lives. Though I didn't see any of the Glories hit anything living during that hour, I twice saw buildings with fresh looking piles of rubble on their southern sides. People were swarming on the streets, in the gardens, in fields near towns, and in parks. What were they feeling? Awe, terror, or both? Probably both.

I spotted the reservoirs, further away to the West than I had thought, and scanning the ground below me, I eventually picked up a railway line from which I could make an educated guess at where I was. I redrew my fingernail line on the map, and continued it on for another seventy miles. The good news was, it would pass within twelve miles of Swinton. The bad news was, it would hit a line of chalk hills, first.

A road atlas is not, of course, a very good guide for anything to do with hills. Often their presence is marked by little more than an absence of roads. But I'd walked those hills with Father a good few times, and I knew where they were, knew the road that ran along their south side. The north side was less familiar, but with a few simple assumptions, I could be fairly sure that we'd come at the line of hills at a diagonal angle. More importantly, I felt sure that the hills

Chapter 49: The homecoming

were taller than the height at which my Glory was travelling, which meant the Glory would go straight into the hill, and my flight would end there.

Hitting the hill did not sound like fun. Desperately I looked for some other way down, like a lake or reservoir to dive into, but the only possible thing was a river, which was dangerously narrow, and who knew how shallow; plus it was thirty-five miles from Swinton. There was only one choice - I had to prepare for the impact on the hill.

I was going to hit the side of the hill at an angle, at thirty or more miles per hour. It would be like jumping or falling from a moving car, at the speed they go on major roads in towns. It was going to hurt, but I couldn't afford a broken limb. What could I do? I formulated two desperate plans, one for if we hit a wood, the other a grassy slope.

Time ticked away and the Glory's stately progress continued. I saw another one wink into being some distance to my left, a mass of stylised flowers of different colours, each one appearing as a tiny speck then growing to full size and then vanishing to make way for others.

Finally, the chalk hills hoved into view. My heart began pumping. It looked like we would hit grass. I dug my toes in, and found that they gripped, too. How fast could I run? I calculated the maximum human running speed based on Usain Bolt's world record, converted it into miles per hour, and then knocked a third off the speed on account of me not being him. I could run fast enough to make a difference, certainly.

Closer, the hills came. Closer. I moved to the very front of the Glory and got down into the sprinter's starting position facing backwards. My head craned round to watch as the hill came towards us, seeming to speed up as it got closer. Suddenly I could make out individual hawthorns and wild roses dotted on the slope. My heart was pounding. I mustn't start too soon – wait for it, wait for it, GO!

I dropped the rucksack and sprang up, running as fast as I could towards the Glory centre, away from the onrushing slope, and on towards the far edge. Then the ground hit my feet and I pitched forwards, hitting the top of the Glory near the far edge, just before it vanished beneath me and a mass of grass punched me hard in the face. Some force flipped me over and I tumbled and rolled before something spiky slammed into my back.

* * * * *

I pulled myself painfully out of the rose bush and onto my feet. My back was cut and bleeding, my limbs were all sore, and my nose was throbbing with pain. Yet, somehow, everything still worked, and so I retrieved my pack and then staggered slowly, gratefully, up to the top of the hill. I passed through a thin line of woodland and onto the south-facing side. Before me the slope fell away to reveal a wide valley full of houses, and beyond that, in the middle distance, the solitary little peak of Swynn Hill, the place where it had all started. I was almost home.

I walked down the hillside, following a diagonal path cutting through scrub and then grass. A group of three young boys catcalled at me, but I ignored them and thankfully they did no more. The track passed into a wood and widened, the surface rutted and scattered with large stones. A glory erupted from the slope in front of me, all spinning triangles of different sizes and colours.

Chapter 49: The homecoming

I emerged into a lane between pretty cottages with large gardens. Many of the gardens had groups of people sitting there, watching the show in the skies above. In one, they were singing and drinking beer. "Come join us!" they called to me.

"Another time," I called back, trying to sound cheerful.

"Might not be another time," the caller said.

Once I got close enough, I'd know the way to Daniel's house, mainly from walking him home, during the one or two years when I was considered old enough to be out on my own, but he wasn't. He'd hated that. The idea of it, I mean, because he did not like to go around on his own, anyway.

The issue now was covering the intervening ten miles. The road Atlas was little help in this network of little lanes, but occasional glimpses of Swynn Hill kept me on track. The houses got smaller and cheaper as I moved further from the line of hills, and there were more and more people on the pavements, looking upwards. Many were sitting on car bonnets, and one had climbed a lamp post.

"Glory coming! Glory coming! Clear the way!" screamed a voice from behind me. I turned and saw a streetlamp moving along the road towards me. Not a normal streetlamp; this one looked like it had been drawn by a child, but it was large and solid, and moving with the same speed and direction as the Glories above. In front of it pedalled a man on a bike, shouting the warnings. Most of those standing in the road had been too busy watching the skies to see it, and now they reacted. Some ran like crazy, others stood and watched, awestruck. More level-headed people worked out that the Glory was moving along the right side of the road, passing through parked cars one by one as it went, and so they led others to the left-hand side where they could safely watch it pass. Ahead of me the road reached a T-junction, and the Glory's path would take it straight through two houses. I ran to the closer one, banging on the door.

"Glory!" I yelled. "It's heading straight for your house!" Then I vaulted the fence to the next garden, flattening a paeony, and did the same on the next door.

The first door opened, and a silver-haired lady looked from side to side. "What's going on? Why can't you use the doorbell?"

"Look!" I shouted, pointing. "That Glory's going to pass right through this house!"

"The Lord will protect me," she said simply, and calmly closed the door. The Glory was almost upon us now, passing through parked cars beside her garden. I ran to the next fence and vaulted that too, tearing my shin on some rose bushes, then turned to see the Glory, a mass of grey felt pen lines with a yellow glow above, move smoothly up to the wall of the two houses I'd knocked on, and pass serenely through. Mercifully, there were no screams or sounds of breaking walls, so maybe the Lord had protected the woman after all.

The man on the bike stopped, gasping for breath. He was only a few years older than me. "Did what I could," he said. "Been telling people to stand where they can look north, till it's over, but they don't all listen ..."

"I warned those two houses, but I think it was just luck no-one died," I replied.

"Saw two people die," he said. "Came smashing through a second floor wall. Great big fucking Glory like some cartoon human face came after them, then just drifted on like nothing had happened. I think this is it. Honestly think

Chapter 49: The homecoming

it's all ending. I don't see what anyone can do if it keeps getting worse and worse."

"I think there might be something I could do."

"You? What can you do?" I expected derision, but his eyes shone weakly with the desperate light of hope.

"It's connected to certain people," I said. "Two kids from Swinton disappeared, the day they all started appearing in Britain. If I can find out more about them, well there's this tiny chance we could use it to stop them."

"Take the bike. It's not mine, I just borrowed it. Hardly matters now. If you think it can help, take it!"

There was no doubt it would get me there quicker. I thanked him and hopped on, then nearly fell off because my legs weren't as long as I was used to. Then I was away. I'd ridden a bike before but not in this body, so I was a little wobbly, and the obstacle course of pedestrians scattered across almost every road really didn't help. My legs were soon aching, and no doubt I didn't go the quickest way, but eventually I was on familiar territory, and from there I got to Daniel's house quite quickly. I'd made it.

There was no lock on the bike, so I just leaned it against a hedge and hoped it would still be there once I was done. Now, I stood on the garden path up to Daniel's house. I'd only rarely been inside it, because he always came to our house, often spending much of the day there, at weekends. Sometimes Father, Gran and I had been at Daniel's house for a rare Sunday lunch or an occasional Xmas, with Daniel's mum fussing around over the seating, the food, the telly (she had to watch the Queen at Xmas), and a dozen other things. Her husband carved, but otherwise would mainly sit around smoking and farting. It was not a place I'd ever wanted to be any longer than I had to, and it occurred to me now that perhaps Daniel had felt exactly the same.

I needed to know more about Daniel, but I'd been so focussed on getting here, I'd barely thought about exactly what questions I needed to ask. What was special about him? What was unusual? Would he have chosen to go into a Glory, or even to somehow call all of them to Britain, and why? Would his parents even know the answer? Yet there was no-one else I could ask. I walked forward and pushed the doorbell. Nothing happened. I pushed it again. The house seemed to be empty. Maybe they'd gone into the back garden, in case a Glory swept past. I turned the door handle just in case, and found it unlocked. Gingerly, I opened the door and stepped into the corridor.

The house was a tip. Tissues, magazines and socks were scattered around the little corridor in front of me, some of them stamped into the carpet. The reek of stale tobacco hung in the air. The house had always smelt of smoke, but never this badly. The smell had always clung to Father, Gran and me all the way home, yet somehow never to Daniel when he came to us. "Hello?" I said, as I stepped carefully forward. "Mrs Blue? Mr Blue?" A door on the right took me through into a living room, with a thick green carpet punctuated by a constellation of cigarette burns, lying below a thick layer of mess, much of it cigarette stubs. The sofa, too, had all manner of debris on it, but one patch was clear, as if a single person always sat there, casting the rubbish to either side. In front of the sofa was a small table, topped by a haphazard mass of newspapers and magazines, one with bare breasts poking out of the cover. Perched on that pile was an old-fashioned Gameboy with

Chapter 49: The homecoming

wires linking it to the TV, which had been pulled forwards to the middle of the room.

In my mind I recalled Mrs Blue in this room, bumbling around picking up the tiniest fragments of wrapping paper from the carpet, checking her watch every few seconds to see how soon the Queen would be on. "You do know her Majesty can't actually look through the television and inspect how clean the room is?" my Father had asked her once, in what passed by his standards as a top-class joke.

"It's the principle," she'd replied.

Looking at the room as it was now, it seemed pretty clear that Mrs Blue, like her son, did not live here anymore.

Something thudded along the floorboards above me. The house wasn't empty after all! I made for the door to the corridor as someone thundered down the stairs. There was no time to get out of the front door, so I turned to face him.

"Mister Blue! Sorry, I rang but there was no answer, and the door wasn't locked."

Daniel's father looked fatter than I remembered him. His clothes hung loosely on his body, only two buttons on his shirt were done up, and the belt on his trousers was not pulled tight.

"So you thought you'd just barge in, did you?"

"Well, I was worried."

"About me? Why the fuck would you be worrying about me? Who the fuck are you, anyway?"

I was about to ask why he didn't recognise me, then I remembered that I now wore the body of a young woman. "I, uhhh, know Daniel from school. I wanted to ask about him?"

"What's there to tell? The little rat buggered off to God knows where." He tipped his head a little to the side, and slowly ran his eyes up and down my body. "Schoolfriend, you say? You're a bit older than him, aintcha? Gotta be eighteen, if I'm any judge."

I tried to ignore the prickles of unease that were springing up along my back, and elsewhere. "I don't know him well. It's just … him and his cousin disappeared, didn't they? They say it was something to do with a Glory. Only … the same thing happened to my little sister. She was with Mrs Jones from up the road. I've been trying to talk to people who might know what happened."

"I told you, he fucked off one day and …" he paused, and his jaw worked from side to side as he thought. "Mind you, his mum bought into all the Glory crap."

"It's not crap," I said. "Look out of the window."

"I don't mean that. I mean the idea one of them might have eaten Daniel and that moron cousin of his. Spent weeks on the fucking computer, she did, after it happened. I had to do some of the bloody housework!"

And a really great job you've made of it, I didn't say.

"She's in bed upstairs," he said. "Bloody done her in, losing the boy then wading into all that conspiracy shit. Hasn't got up all week. So you can go talk to her if you want, but don't expect any sense out of her."

I hesitated for a moment. I didn't trust him. But the alternative was to walk out of the house, having learned nothing. So I nodded towards the stairs and followed him up. The landing was less of a pigsty, but the stench of tobacco

Chapter 49: The homecoming

was even stronger here, mixed with other unpleasant smells. He stopped by a door. "In there." I went in.

The double bed was empty. I took a few steps towards it, stupidly wondering if she might be somehow hiding under the crumpled duvet. The door clicked shut, and he stood there, leaning against it, grinning at me.

I didn't ask the obvious question, but he answered it anyway, as if delighted by his deception. "Said she was in bed. Well, she probably is, somewhere."

"She left you," I said.

"Fucked off to get it on with my sanctimonious brother-in-law, probably. I wouldn't put it past them."

"Well, if she's not here, I'd better go," I tried.

"No, no, sweetheart. You're not going anywhere." And a dollop of drool ran down from the corner of his grinning mouth.

Chapter 50: Claude Dexter

Julia

Sally explained to me the extraordinary truth. "As the Taimede gradually converted themselves into formless beings, they were also working on how they could eventually reverse the process, gain form again, and become part of the physical universe once more. Yet with the planet soon to be gone, and nowhere habitable within countless lightyears of their solar system, what could they do?"

"There were some things in their favour. Space and time were far more fluid in the thought dimensions they'd moved themselves into. They could slip sideways into universes where time passed thousands or even millions of times faster, allowing them to skip forward through time. There were others where it passed far more slowly, although they struggled to access those. In their disembodied state, they learned how to cross unimaginable physical distances in a heartbeat – physical laws don't constrain them. This allowed them to see the universe in all its glory, though they could not interact with it. They showed me things, Julia, the most amazing things. I wish I had more time to share them with you. They found countless planets that their species could have settled on, if only they had been able to reach them physically. Many of them had microbial life, a few even had slightly more complex lifeforms. When some of them found a planet like that, they would wait there, slipping forward in time for millions of years in the hope that conscious life would arise, but the sad truth is, most times life gets snuffed out long before that can happen. A star explodes, the planet hits another, it gets too hot or too cold, or it just dries out and the atmosphere leaks away. Our world is incredibly special, Julia, so extraordinarily rare. I think billions of years passed for them, and ours is the only other conscious life they've ever found. Even though they could fast-forward time, can you even imagine waiting that long?

"Eventually, one of them saw flashes. Tiny, distant flashes across the endless expanse of their empty universe. It was us. They perceive us as flashes when we die, and our consciousness dissipates. That individual sent out signals that others would receive. And so, they began to converge around our world."

"I'll call the police," I said.

"You think they'll come?" he leered. "It's the end of the fucking world, you stupid girl. Ain't you noticed? And you know what? I'm gonna really enjoy the time I've got left." He took a step towards me.

There was no other way out of the room. The one window looked like it was locked, and quite possibly fused shut, as well. Maybe a Glory would come barrelling through the wall and flatten him. I had to play for time.

"Okay, okay, well … if you answer my questions about Daniel, then maybe I'll do what you want!"

Chapter 50: Claude Dexter

He sniggered. "Okay. How about you take off one item of clothing per question. I can even give 'em back to you, later. Can't say fairer than that." He tilted his head to one side again, mouth breaking into a wide grin that revealed two missing teeth.

I felt sick, and dizzy. Was this what it was like, being a girl? Dealing with creeps like this, with designs on our bodies – was that a normal thing? But at least this way, I could learn a few things, and give myself time to think of an escape plan. Brusquely, I pulled off my jumper and threw it onto the bed.

"Have you seen or heard from Daniel, since the day he disappeared?"

He grinned even wider. "Nope." He took a step forward, eyes boring into my body.

My heartrate quickened, my pulse like a disco beat inside my head. I had to fight, get past him, flee. I'd never faced anything like this before, yet the body I now lived in certainly had. The realisation hit me out of nowhere. The thing Talia had been running from, the reason she'd fled from her life, from the whole world, and dived into the abyss. The reason there were hardly any males in her dream world. A man, just like this one.

Then another thought hit me, even worse. "Daniel," I said. "You did this to him as well, didn't you? That's why he was always at our house."

"Top," he replied.

"Top?" I repeated stupidly.

"Or jeans, if you prefer. You asked me a second question."

"How about a shoe?" I replied, fighting hard to stop myself shaking.

"That's a third question," he replied. "Top AND jeans, in that case. Shoes aren't clothes." He opened his mouth wider, and his ugly tongue snaked slowly across his upper teeth. "I think what you need is an *education*." He took a step towards me.

Under the bed.

The memory of Daniel's words jumped into my head. He'd turned up one day with a battered floppy hat and a very neat looking black leather whip. We'd run off to the stream to play Indiana Jones, taking it in turns to try and catch the whip around a high branch and swing over to the other side. Mostly we'd fallen in, but it had been a great day. I hadn't seen him for weeks afterwards, though. At one point I'd asked him where he'd found the whip.

Under the bed.

I dropped to the ground before Daniel's father could reach me, and rolled under the double bed. His feet rushed back towards the door, blocking any possible exit.

"Enough fucking games. You get out here right now, or I'll make sure you regret it!" I felt around for the whip, but my hand butted into a suitcase. I fumbled with the zip. "There's a case full of stuff under there," he said. "Shove it out, will you, I think we'll use some of it." The zip stuck at first, my hand shaking crazily as I tried to move it. He was down on all fours now, leering at me hungrily. He made a grab for me, but I was just out of reach. Gripping the zip with both hands, I finally got it open.

I saw his hands close around the leg of the bed nearest the door. He was standing now, and he grunted as he began to lift the bed. If he got it onto its side, I was done for. I rolled sideways, lined myself up and smashed my foot into his fingers on the bed leg as hard as I could. He howled with rage and lost his grip, and the bed crashed down, hitting my knee. I cried out in pain, but he

Chapter 50: Claude Dexter

was already down on the floor again, and then his hand was snaking in towards me. I pulled myself clear just in time, but he crawled swiftly round to the side to try again. Rolling out of reach once more, I plunged my hand into the suitcase, pulling out anything I could find. Something leather. A short length of rope tightly knotted into a loop. A plastic ball with something attached to t. More leather. A pair of handcuffs! I pulled away again from his grabbing hand, ignoring the torrent of abuse now spewing from his mouth. A desperate idea formed, and I ran with it, taking the loop of rope and passing it over a fixed slat in the middle of the bed's underside. Then I took the two ends and locked one ring of the handcuffs around both of them. His grabbing hand reached in again, and this time I let it catch my left wrist.

"Got you, you bitch!"

I snapped the free handcuff ring tight around his own wrist.

"What the – aaaargghh!!" He'd yanked the arm back just as soon as I'd cuffed it, pulling me with him, but as the rope went tight, the cuffs had dug hard into his flesh. His grip on me slackened and I wrenched my wrist free, before rolling out of the far end of the bed.

He lay writhing on his back, head half under the bed, screaming obscenities as he tried to pull his arm free. I leapt up onto the bed, across to the other side, then jumped as hard as I could down onto his crotch with both feet. He screamed in agony, while I grabbed the handle and pulled open the door, before charging down the stairs and out into the street.

* * * * *

I needed to get away, as fast and far as possible. I'd learned nothing of any use, and a lot of stuff I'd rather not have known. I ran to where I'd left the bike, but it was gone.

"Sorry, someone took it," said a young man.

"Damn it, I'll have to walk," I replied. "Thanks for telling me." I nodded at him and kept walking.

"Were you looking for Daniel?" he asked.

I stopped. "Daniel?" I said stupidly.

"Yes, Daniel Blue. I saw you come out of his house. He isn't there."

"Yes, I know that," I said impatiently. How long before his father got free of the handcuffs? There would probably be something in that suitcase of horrors that he could use to cut through the rope. He'd probably be running out soon, with a weapon in his hand. Would this young man protect me? He looked quite strong.

"I know where he is," said the man.

"Daniel?" I said, unable to keep the delight and surprise from my expression.

"He said another boy might come looking for him, asked me to keep an eye out. Name of Antony. You know him?"

"I ... yes I do. But I need to get away from here. Can you ... can you take me to Daniel?"

"Well, I'm not supposed to leave the house, but it's only a short drive. Car's just round the corner." We started walking. "Do you know where Antony is?" he asked.

"Uhh, not exactly, but I know a few places to look."

Chapter 50: Claude Dexter

"Daniel will be pleased." He clicked his key and the lights on a car flashed.

"Umm, who were you watching the house for?" I asked him.

"For Daniel, of course!"

Something felt wrong. But he was bigger than me, and looked fit. Running away would be pointless. I had no better plan, and if Daniel was a captive, how else would I get to him? I moved to the front passenger door.

"Better get in the back," he said. "In case we hit a Glory," he added when I looked puzzled. "You must have seen the guidance?"

I nodded and got in the back as he slipped into the driving seat. He closed his door and clicked the child lock. I felt a stab of fear, even though I'd expected it. He started the engine, but progress out of town was slow, as the milling sea of people parted to let us through. We dodged the occasional moving Glory, and as we headed out of town our progress was hindered instead by haphazardly parked cars.

Only once we were on a more major road did the drive become smoother. At this point he pulled out a phone and made a call. "It's me," he told whoever answered. "I got her, coming out of the house … yes, it's definitely her. Tell Mr Dexter I'm on my way now."

Julia

"Talking to an alien species would never be easy," Sally explained, "even if they did have physical form. You saw how differently they communicated. But remember, each of them was sent into the conscious universe accompanied by an artificial intelligence, which was programmed to transfer useful information across into any conscious creature that they could make contact with. This would include useful technology, details of their civilisation, their peaceful intent, and the technical means to build a machine that would bring the Taimede back into physical existence. The plan was to manifest into the physical universe in the only way they could, as an enticing image that other conscious beings could interact with. Then when contact was made, they'd begin communication."

"But it didn't work?"

"Never properly, and mostly not at all. Maybe we were just too different, but that wasn't the only thing. During the aeons of fruitless searching, each Taimede had gradually fused with its accompanying AI, becoming a single being. And in that process, the information they started with became corrupted. Still, they manifested well enough, in ways that we found beautiful and striking."

"The Glories."

"Yes. And because we humans exist in both the physical and conscious universe, we mostly couldn't occupy the same space as one of them. Still, a few were able to make some sort of contact, and very occasionally, a parcel of information got through. Always, they'd start by trying to convey a message of friendship and love. But our minds are so very different from theirs. In most of us, the message was barely felt at all. But in others, it manifested as something like unrequited love. An irresistible, almost physical need to be close to a Glory. The affected people were drawn to the Glories, and quite by accident they also

Chapter 50: Claude Dexter

acted as magnets, pulling more Taimede towards the Earth, from all across the universe."

"You're talking about Glory Addicts," I said.

"Yes, Julia. People like me. But through me, when I came to them, they finally began to understand what was happening, both to them and to humanity. How our two races were being sucked together into a dance that could destroy us both."

"Destroy us? But how?"

"I'll get to that. But very occasionally, part of the transfer process actually worked. One human body successfully downloaded their medical technology."

"Mine?"

"Yours. It was some sort of fluke, they think it's because you were so obviously seriously ill, it actually helped convey what sort of data was needed. Or it might just have been sheer luck. Other people – scattered, random people, got bits of information or transferred abilities, none of which they fully understood. But your contact with me, when I'd just been converted and you'd had so much interaction with them already, established a stronger link. They needed someone they could talk to, and deliver their knowledge to, without killing their body. They still didn't know how at that point. So they put in your mind a receiver, which would allow them to call you when they had learned enough from me, and were ready."

"That 'call' worked rather too well," I said. "It very nearly drowned me."

"Yes, well, obviously that wasn't their intention. That's why they turned it off again. By then though, you understood what was needed."

"So I'm here to deliver a message? To explain to our leaders who and what the Glories are, and ask for their help?"

"I wish that you were, Julia, we all wish that. But it isn't, not anymore. You're here to help us stop a genocide."

Antony

The journey passed in silence, each of us having nothing to say to the other. I wanted to meet Claude Dexter, to learn his connection to the Glories, but I was going to do so as a prisoner. Plus I no longer had the handy ability to walk through walls. Still, I seemed to have no choice in the matter, unless I attacked the driver and crashed the car. So I gazed out of the window instead. The Glories were filling the sky far more densely now, and many were not far above us. They were all moving in roughly the same direction as we were. Some were simple shapes of pure colour, others more complex in form and often imitating some familiar object. A blue car, a cat's head, a pumpkin.

We turned onto a dual carriageway. Electronic signs told us to "GO HOME!" and the road was almost empty. He drove at about fifty. The road snaked around a bend, then a huge blue mass came slowly across a field of yellow oilseed rape, about as fast as us but at a slight angle, such that t stayed ahead of us but moved gradually into the road. It was in the form of a hyacinth, one of those bulb plants you sometimes see in pots, only a cartoon version. It

Chapter 50: Claude Dexter

was utterly beautiful. Each blue flower had bits of red and yellow at its centre. "Can we get closer to it?" I asked.

"You better not try anything."

"I haven't, and I won't. I just want to look."

He sped up, until we were just behind it. Each individual flower was about a metre across. Through all my adventures, when had I last simply gazed at one of these things, and their impossible loveliness? One way or another, I had a feeling I wouldn't get another chance to really look at one like this."

"You a Gladdie, then?" he asked.

"No," I replied. "It's just very beautiful. Isn't it?"

"I just want things to get back to normal."

"Is that what Claude Dexter wants?"

He didn't answer. I noticed that our speed was slowly dropping, as he obligingly held position behind the hyacinth. It was mainly in the opposite carriageway now, which was also mercifully free of cars.

"Gonna have to overtake it now," he said, and did.

"Please, if you see a car going the other way, flash your lights at it, warn them."

"Love, no-one's dumb enough to drive in that direction right now."

Hang on," I said. "Haven't they closed all the major roads?"

"We asked them to keep this one open," he replied. I couldn't work out if he was joking.

Ten minutes later we saw another Glory close up, this one a yellow ball with a perfect black ring around it as if it were eclipsing a larger black ball. It was a few metres above us and no risk to us. We caught up with it quickly and sped past. "They're slowing down," I observed. He didn't answer.

By the time we left the motorway, the Glories were slower still, but more of them were at ground level. We drove slowly too, slowing down at every corner, once banking hard to see a mass of pale blue eyes pass across the road in front of us at a fast walking speed. "They're all going somewhere, aren't they?" I said. "And it's the same place we're going."

Again he didn't answer. Fifteen minutes later there were Glories everywhere, hovering in the sky, crawling across the land, apparently jostling for position. We drove through a massive Type Two, the entire car turning pure white as we did so. By then it was getting hard to drive, with the swarming Glories just metres apart, so he pulled the car onto the verge. He unlocked the doors and jumped out, then offered his hand to me as if to help me out. I shook my head, I had no use for chivalry. But that wasn't his purpose – he grabbed my wrist and locked a handcuff around it, then the other ring to his own wrist.

"That's going to make it harder to dodge these things," I said.

"I'm not having you run away," he replied.

We walked through a Type Two, in which everything but us looked like water, even the handcuffs linking us together. But the air around us became fuzzy, and as we stepped out of it, I saw a wall of water form behind me, as the Type Two somehow transformed into a Type One. We didn't see a Type Two again, which meant we had to weave our way around and between all the Type One Glories along the road, like some bizarre game show challenge. The biggest Glories were shrinking as they moved forward, while the smallest ones seemed to enlarge, with most of them settling on a size that was one to two car lengths in diameter.

Chapter 50: Claude Dexter

With his free hand my captor made another phone call, and offered a progress report. "Not sure how far off we are, but there are Glories everywhere, we're having to walk." We passed between two gateposts, one just sticking out of a low Glory that looked like undulating blu-tack, the other barely visible through a gap between two other Glories. Beyond these, the Glories were packed even tighter. We walked through a narrow gap between a pure pink cube and a distorted checkerboard, then had to force our way through an even narrower gap between a waterfall and the Mona Lisa. Then, quite unexpectedly, we emerged onto open grass.

Ahead of me lay a massive, dilapidated-looking mansion, with the odd broken window on the upper floors, surrounded by grass, a few pock-marked statues, and flowerbeds full of weeds and dead roses. In the middle of a massive lawn between me and the mansion, there were three huge rectangular metal constructions each as tall as a house, bolted together like some giant Meccano set, and arranged in a triangle. Around this was a ring of chairs, with people sat in them, facing away from it, looking at the wall of Glories that surrounded everything I could see.

I guessed that the circular wall of Glories was several hundred metres in diameter, with the metal construction, rather than the mansion, at its centre. I turned around to see the nearest part of the Glory wall, through which we'd just passed. As I looked, another Glory squeezed its way to the front, pushing others to the side and further reducing the gaps between them. Already, it was starting to look like no-one else would be able to get in or out. The Glories jostled for position like kids watching a playground fight, yet seemed unwilling or unable to get any closer. They weren't only at ground level, though; the wall continued upwards, arching over into a dome and blotting out the sky completely, apart from one small hole directly above the metal construction.

So this *had* been where they'd all been heading. Of course it was. Men with big guns wandered around, as if waiting to be given orders. One of them approached us, and I recognised him as the man who'd been with 'Father' during our escape from Collett. "Mr Dexter's in the drawing room, go straight to him," he told my captor. We passed close to the ring of chairs, and I saw that their occupants had been strapped in, each one with their left hand taped to the right hand of their neighbour, so that they formed a massive circle, like a giant séance. It recalled Collett's treatment of Siobhan and Julia, only at industrial scale. Most of the captives sat serenely, gazing passively at the Glories, though one or two strained and grunted constantly; these ones had been further strapped down, and gagged.

"They're all Glory addicts, aren't they?" I asked my captor. As usual he didn't reply.

We passed through the huge front doors, and I almost expected a butler or doorman to stand behind them, doffing his cap. We walked down an absurdly wide corridor, which somehow felt colder than the air outside. The walls had dark rectangular patches, as if paintings had once hung there. We passed through a door into a large room. In it were dusty sofas, ornate tables and an unlit fireplace. It was cold here, too. Two men stood in the middle of the room, as if waiting for something to happen. But my eyes were drawn to the third man, who stood with one hand on the shelf above the fireplace.

He was immaculately dressed in a gold waistcoat over a fine white shirt. His trousers were suit trousers, starched metallic grey over shiny black shoes.

Chapter 50: Claude Dexter

He looked about thirty, with slightly unruly golden hair and a thick, neat beard of exactly the same colour. His eyes were a sparkling blue.

"This is her, Mister Dexter, sir," said the man who brought me, and he unlocked the handcuffs. The fear and awe that Dexter elicited in all of his underlings was clear to see, but it was not, by a mile, the most remarkable thing about him.

The first extraordinary aspect of this man was the single, football-sized deep blue Glory that hung in the air by his head, as if it were his pet.

The second remarkable thing was that he, himself was a Glory. I'm not even sure how I could tell this, but I could.

The third thing about him was more remarkable still, because the third thing about him was that he was Daniel.

"Jeebus, Cuz," he said through that grin I knew so well. "Have you had a makeover?"

Chapter 51: Daniel Blue

Julia

"Right at the end," said Sally, "Part of a city was ripped from its moorings and tossed around in the boiling ocean. The few Taimede individuals within it had always stubbornly refused the conversion process, but now, with just hours to live, they changed tack. But the equipment for conversion had been destroyed, so in desperation they cloned the Super-AI that had run their world for millions of years, and pleaded with it to save them. They released it from every constraint that had been placed upon it by their distant ancestors, replacing them all with one single instruction: "S*ave us – any way you can*". With no conversion equipment in the detached part of the city, the Super-AI immediately formed a plan. It put *itself* through the conversion process, using a surviving piece of equipment in another city fragment, and then it manifested before the stranded Taimede as what you would recognise as a Glory. A cool, calm patch of ocean, a soothing image from their fading past. When each of them touched it, it simply pulled them through, and made them a part of itself."

"Is that what happened to us?" I asked her. "To you, and then me?"

"Not quite, Julia. Your body still exists, and our minds remain fully separate, but yes, we have moved through the dimension of consciousness, two of the first Humans ever to have done so. Those last few Taimede became linked to the Super-AI as a sort of gestalt organism, gradually losing their individuality over time. But crucially, the Super-AI did not consider its mission fulfilled. It defined 'living' as having a physical body, which none of the Taimede now did. Which meant it hadn't 'saved' them, not yet. So its sole purpose, ever since then, has been to restore them to physical form. Not just those linked to it, but all of them, by any means necessary. The Taimede themselves would never accept the death of even one sentient life form to aid their return; it would break their moral code. But the Super-AI considers nothing but Taimede lives to be of value – that's how it interpreted that final instruction to save them."

"Are you saying it would kill us all?" I asked.

"It would normally view us in the way that we might view flies smashed onto a car bumper as we drove down a motorway. Utterly inconsequential. Except that it has found a use for us, so it now sees us more like trees to be chopped down so it can build something."

"And it's this?" I asked. "It's this Super-AI that is forming the Glories?"

"No, almost all of the Glories are ordinary Taimede, trying and failing to reach out to us for help. As far as we can tell, the Super-AI has only ever produced one Glory, so far."

"And which one was that?" I asked.

"The one that found Antony and Daniel."

Chapter 51: Daniel Blue

Antony

"Leave us," Daniel commanded fiercely, and all the underlings scurried towards the door. "Get the Fulcrum machine ready. Knock four times when it's done, don't disturb us otherwise."

"Yes, Sir," said a lackey, as he hurried out and closed the door. The blue Glory had moved off somewhere, too, leaving the two of us alone. Then Daniel – or Dexter – turned to me with a warm smile. "It's good to see you, Cuz. I must say, you're a lot better looking than I remember!"

I ignored this. "*You're* Claude Dexter?"

"Yup. I had thought the name might give you a clue."

"What? Why?"

"You never were any good at noticing things, were you? Remember the school guinea pigs?"

"What? Daniel, you've engineered ... God knows what here, you've been pulling the strings of violent criminals, kidnapped hundreds of Glory addicts ..."

"Guilty as charged, m'lud," he cut in.

"But you want to talk about guinea pigs."

"Jeebus, Cuz, I can't tell you how much I've missed you. Always so boringly serious. I never realised how endearing it was."

"And you were never serious enough," I replied.

"Pah, 'serious' is overrated. And we'll be getting plenty serious later on, so humour me, huh? The guinea pigs?"

"Well, there were three of them, at primary school, and I took them all home to look after, one holiday. I liked the girl best – Ramona, she was called. And the two boys were called ..."

He tipped his head sideways and smiled, then the names came back to me.

"Dexter ... and Claude."

"*Pinnnngg!!* You've got one hundred pounds," he said, grinning.

"You invented yourself a new identity, based on two long-dead guinea pigs."

"Well, it was the first thing that came to mind, funnily enough. And I half-wanted you to guess. But anyway, I'm sure there's a question you've been dying to ask."

I had about a hundred, and not a clue which one to start with. He stroked his beard and smiled at me.

"OK," I said. "What actually happened, that day on Swynn Hill?"

Daniel walked across to an armchair, sat down, and somehow conjured from nowhere a big picture book into his hands. "Are you sitting comfortably? Then I'll begin. Once upon a time, there were two young cousins, a boring one and a fun one. They went walking in the woods together, and soon came upon a blue sloping lake that couldn't possibly be there. The boring one reached down and touched it, and a connection was made. It drew him in closer, and induced him to pick up a piece of it, opening the door between worlds. Then the lake swallowed them both."

"I picked it up later," I said. "I'm sure I did. Towards the end, just before I realised Daniel was gone."

Chapter 51: Daniel Blue

"That was the second time," he said with a smile. "You don't remember the first, they took away those memories. Anyway, the very powerful alien that lived in the lake – or maybe aliens, I can't be sure if it's one or many – considered the two boys. One of them had amazing potential, to be a king amongst men. The other was a bit of a dullard ..."

"For God's sake Daniel, just tell me what happened in a normal way!"

"Borrrrrrrring! All right, if you insist. Consciousness is a dimension, and we'd been pulled through into a different dimensional layer, where these Glory-beings exist."

"Consciousness is a dimension?" I said. "That doesn't make sense."

"That's because you're a dimwit. Think about it. All the images in your head, the places you can imagine, where are they? It's not just a 3D movie in that stodgy brain of yours, it's so much more than that. Anyway, the point is, they found a way to do it – move their entire conscious existence sideways, away from the material universe, and outside the constraints of time and space. Your face!!! Honestly, you look constipated, trying to understand this! OK, look, Dennis the Menace. He lives in a 2D comic strip world, right? Imagine you could move him in the third dimension, above the page. Well, then he'd be free of the panel frames, wouldn't he? He could race forwards in time to the end of the strip just by moving downwards, or forward a week in an instant, if you stacked two *Beano*s together. He could visit the Bash Street Kids, or leave the comic world altogether, turn up in *Cosmopolitan* or the *Radio Times*. The Glory-beings are doing that, across a *fourth* dimension."

"If you say so," I said, not fully grasping it.

"So anyway, the Glory-being that found us was some sort of leader – or leader*s*, I don't really understand their society, it's kind of one being and several at the same time. But the point is, it or they had extra powers that the rest didn't have. They could pull us through to the dimension where they were. Took two or three days, apparently, because our minds are so different from theirs. They had to hide us from the search parties. We were invisible, Cuz! Eventually it succeeded, but the transfer process destroyed our bodies. It would have destroyed our minds, but they knew how to hold them together. But they didn't need both of us, so they just kicked you forward in time five weeks."

"What? Why?"

"I told you, they only needed one of us, and let's face it, they were never going to pick you, were they? They would have killed you, Cuz, but I asked them not to. I saved your life, so remember that, later on. Your body was destroyed, so they very reluctantly gave you a Glory-body, like mine. Only we didn't tell you that, of course."

I sighed. "Yes, Daniel, of all the many, many jokes you've played on me over the years, that one was quite the humdinger. So these things ... can control time? Is that why you look so much older?"

"*Pinnnngg!!* You've got two hundred pounds."

"Because you *are* older, aren't you," I persisted. "It's not just how you look. It's a different kind of confidence. You always loved giving orders, but only mugs like me ever obeyed them. Now you've got everyone jumping."

"This was always who I was meant to become," he said. "And yes, I am twenty-six years old now. Time passes differently in different slices across the dimension of consciousness, where my associates exist. They took me to a slice where a year could pass in an hour of Earth time."

Chapter 51: Daniel Blue

"So you aged twelve years in a matter of hours?" I asked.

"Hours of earth time. They were years for me. And we built a world there, they and I. A version of Earth from my memories. And they let me grow up there, making the rules for myself. I had so much fun, Cuz, so much fun. We actually made a version of you there, even dumber than the real one. Samantha White from your year – you know, the hottie you all drooled over – was my girlfriend, well, one of them. But it wasn't all play, they made me learn stuff as well. Lots of new skills – I can hack a compunter or phone, just by touching it! Came in very handy, that did. They taught me their history, as they learned ours from me. Their world boiled and burned, Cuz, that's why they need a new one. So they separated themselves from their bodies, to fly across time and space, to get here, and find someone who could help them."

"Someone like you?"

"Someone like me," he said with a grin. "Once my training was complete, they gave me a Glory body, still a month before you got yours, and I got to work on our plan. The next step was a field trip – to see the inside of places they wanted to know more about. I can fly through the air faster than light, if I want to! I bet you never realised you could. So anyway, we went to CERN, NASA, Silicon Valley. It was all Stone Age to my associate though, they weren't impressed. Then the White House – they were fascinated by that. Honestly, they thought I was joking at first when I said this was the guy in charge. I played a few jokes on him, got at least one guy fired, and I was well on the way to convincing Melania that Trump was bonking an intern, when it was time to move on. We went to the Kremlin, but that was a bit of a waste of time to be honest, because we couldn't tell what on earth was going on. They all speak Russian there – who knew? So we came back to Britain."

"Why Britain? Why is England the epicentre of all this? Is it because of us?"

"Yes, of course it's because of us, you dummy! Or rather, my associate. They are far more powerful than the other Glory-beings, we really hit the jackpot there, you and I. So they sent a signal thousands of times stronger than any of the others, and from that point, the Glories arrived in droves, always in our part of the world. So it made sense to make Britain our base of operations. It was the only place, really, that had what they needed. The first thing we needed was money, and lots of it. My hacking skills led to all kinds of fruitful schemes, most of them highly illegal but brilliant fun. Plus my associate could predict where Glories would appear, and we made a fair sum out of that, in various ways. And then Collett got his own scheme going, and that made us a small fortune."

"That man did some horrible things," I told him. I thought of Siobhan, dead on the floor, and Sally, coughing up blood. Even Tara and her henchman, crushed in that car at the end.

"Ahhh, but he cured some sick kids too, Cuz!" said Daniel. "So swings and roundabouts, really. Anyway, with all that dosh, we got started. Picked up this place for a song, though the blackmail helped a lot. Some of the cash went on minions, but the bulk of it bought components to make the Fulcrum machine out there. Most of them were easy enough to get once we had the money, but the plutonium was a bit of a bother. Luckily, Polnukov came through with that, and then even luckier, he got scragged before I had to pay him! Oh, and we had to recruit a young technical genius to put it all together. Guy's got a brain bigger

Chapter 51: Daniel Blue

than Hawking, I'm telling you, but so, so gullible. So that was the first part. But I needed human resources, too."

"Those people strapped to the seats out there – they're Glory addicts, aren't they?"

"'Fraid so. Glories only interact with people, and they're as drawn to the addicts as addicts are to them. Linking the addicts together in a circle, connected up to another of my machines, allowed me to call them, the Glory-beings, from all over the universe. It worked a little better than I'd expected, I'll admit – the whole sky filled up with Glories the minute I turned it on! Because signals can travel across the consciousness dimension almost instantaneously, and so can the Glory-aliens. So from that point on, we kind of had to hurry."

"But you couldn't do all this without government backing, not for long ... not an operation this size ... so ... did you depose the Prime Minister?"

"*Pinnnng*!!! You've got three hundred pounds. I actually tried to work *with* Boris Johnson. I figured if the right person approached him ... hang on while I just do this."

He spun gracefully on the spot, and transformed into a woman. She was exceptionally beautiful but with a smart haircut and outfit, though the suit skirt was rather short. "Olivia Darke, from the Glory Research Centre, Mr Johnson," the woman said. "It was set up while you were in hospital, Sir. I need to talk to you urgently about Glory addicts and the danger they pose."

I stared at her, open-mouthed. Then she spoke again in Daniel's voice. "Jeebus, Cuz, put your tongue back in! Have you never seen a woman before?"

But that wasn't why I was staring. "Can you transform into anyone?" I asked.

He/she pirouetted again, and Samantha White stood in front of me, in a tiny dress that hardly covered anything. "Hello Antony," she said huskily. "Want to act out a few of those bed-wetting fantasies of yours, with me?"

"You were Father," I said.

"Come again?"

"You know what I'm talking about," I said, anger rising. "All that time I was looking for you and you were right there, beside me, when we were escaping from Collett! You could have stopped Sally and Siobhan from getting shot!"

He/she pirouetted again, and now Father stood before me, glowering. "Don't you backchat me, boy!" he growled. "I was there to get *you* out, no-one else."

"And the money, of course," I shot back. "Which you seemed to want more."

He spun again, turning back into supposed Glory expert Olivia Darke. "Let's get back to the story, shall we? I thought Johnson would be a pushover, but either the Corona had flattened his libido, or his wife's got him under the thumb, because he barely even flirted with me. Worse still, I couldn't persuade him to back us on the Gladcamps. The fat blob's obsessed with his place in history, and how he'll be seen. Thought locking up large numbers of Brits without trial would give him a bad rep, with historians."

"He was probably right," I observed.

"He's an obdurate bastard. So yes, I had him replaced. It was surprisingly easy."

"All those leaks and press stories," I said. "But how did you get that mate of his, Cummings, to drive to Barnard Castle?"

Chapter 51: Daniel Blue

Daniel/Olivia burst out laughing. "I didn't!! He did that all on his own! But it did rather give me a head-start. You see, I'd been cultivating the right-wing press, by sending them juicy stories about celebrities, footballers, Prince Harry and the like. When you can walk through walls and hack phones by just touching them, it's dead easy. So when I suggested to a few of the editors that Cummings might be a Glory addict, they ran with it. Then I leaked those two photos – the Downing Street garden party, and the Hancock snog. Again, piece of piss – the Tories all store up compromising stories and photos of one another, so I just leaked a couple. Then for the *coup de grace* – Johnson's Whatsapp messages. I'd already hacked them, the first time I met him. Kind of a shame he gave in so quickly, because we never got as far as March and April. I tell you – they're dynamite! Anyway, he resigned, and in the contest that followed, it didn't take much to make sure Collins won – he already had a head of steam by then, and all the senior Tories were suspected of being the leaker."

"And Collins was your man, wasn't he?" I said.

"More or less. He came up with the Glory addict crusade all on his own – thought it would get him noticed. I thought it would make him useful. So I visited him as Olivia, and then again as Dexter."

He spun on the spot and became Claude Dexter again, the older version of Daniel. "Soon we were working together, quietly at first, and then openly when he became PM. I could track down Gladdies pretty easily, but with him on my side, we had the power to catch and hold them in large numbers, and select the ones with the strongest pull."

"But why stop people from visiting or reporting Glories?" I asked.

"Well, for Collins, it was all about being seen to be doing something," he replied. "But for me, well, it was fun to see how easily we could make people turn on each other. Still the main thing was, it made it even easier to root out the Glory addicts, they were almost the only ones ignoring the rules, and the cops didn't have to try and pick them out from a mass of Glory-watchers anymore. Also, there were rather a lot of Glories popping up close to my base here, and I really needed the privacy. I needed to discourage any interference with what I'm doing."

"What *are* you doing, Daniel?"

"I'm going to save the world, Cuz, and you're going to help me do it."

Julia

"Daniel Blue has been groomed into the perfect instrument for the Super-AI," Sally told me. "Very intelligent, somewhat narcissistic, and full of repressed anger. That made him dead easy to manipulate, and there was ample opportunity, as he lived with the Super-AI in a mentally constructed world during what for them was twelve years. Throughout that time, it taught him to hate his own species, and made him see himself as a messiah for the Taimede. The Super-AI is so much more powerful than any of the normal Taimede, Julia. It convinced him that it was the leader of a group of desperate aliens, but in fact it was acting alone. It's been using Daniel all this time, to execute its plan.

"So by mid-April, Daniel had already got started on that, while the rest of the Glories hadn't really achieved anything. They got a hint something was up, when Antony accidentally tipped two women into a Glory. The Taimede all felt it happen, but they couldn't save them, and the two womens' minds gently dissociated. There was an upside – that event taught them enough to keep my own mind alive, when it happened to me. Then through me, they started to understand humans and how we worked. Slowly, they began to catch up. They learned about Glory addicts and how wrong their attempts to connect had been going. And the fact that at least one human Glory had been created, and not by them, made them very worried indeed. The Gladcamps, Julia. They started to realise what Daniel and the Super-AI could do, with a few hundred Glory addicts at their disposal. They don't want this, Julia. They've all been pulled here against their will, and they don't want this at all."

Antony

"You're planning to save the world, just like that? From what? The Glories? The Pandemic? World War Three?" I stared at him, wondering if he'd lost his grip on sanity.

"Well, firstly, it's hardly 'just like that'. It's been twelve long years for me, remember?"

"You're serious. You're actually serious."

"Totally. Who'd have thought it? Daniel Blue, all grown up. And yes, I really am going to save the world."

"How?"

"Oh, come on. Work it out."

"You're going to stop the Glories? No, why would they want to help you with that? So you're going to help them. Their world is lost, they gave up their bodies, and then they came here. Are you going to give them their bodies back?"

"*Pinnnng*!!! You've got five hundred pounds."

"But how does that save the world?"

"Oh, come on, you dullard! Their technology is millions of years ahead of ours. Millions!! They'll cure Corona, stop global warming, and depollute the oceans in time for tea tomorrow, I'd reckon. Then share all their secrets for peaceful, sustainable living. Bingo! Everybody wins."

"And you'll be an international hero, to two different species."

"Hey, credit where it's due."

"Aren't you forgetting something? Not everyone's going to be happy to share their planet with space aliens. For goodness sake, a lot of Brits can't even stand to hear a foreign accent."

"Yeah, well, they'll have to lump it, won't they?" he said dismissively.

"And what if the aliens decide to take over? No doubt they've promised you faithfully that they won't, but maybe they're better at lying than me, or even you."

Chapter 51: Daniel Blue

"Well, if they did take over, they could hardly make a worse job of it than we did, could they? Anyway, they evolved in the sea, so we can share," he said happily.

I turned towards the window. I could see them doing things to the huge pieces of electrical equipment out there.

"So that's what you're building outside. A device to bring them here."

"Built, not building. We're doing the last checks now."

He was keeping parts of it from me, of course he was. It seemed important to keep him talking. *'Find out about Daniel.'*

"How does it work?" I asked, trying to sound casual but interested.

"Ah well, there are three components to the Soul Fulcrum," he said, as if proudly presenting a class project. "First, we needed an artificial intelligence device, something millions of times more powerful than anything yet invented on this planet. A conscious machine. That's what we're about to switch on, out there. A powerful, precisely aligned conscious entity, to make a firm link across the dimension of thought. Of course, our tech's a bit more clunky than theirs – apparently it should be the size of a tennis ball."

"And yours is the size of a house," I said.

"Yeah, it's as big as ten million mobile phones, but exponentially more powerful. Now, you already know what the second component is."

"Glory addicts," I said.

"*Pinnnng*!!! You've got one thousand pounds. They're all linked to a second machine, which controls and amplifies their effect. Now, to double your money again, do you want to try and guess what the third component is?"

"I dunno," I said cautiously. "The Glories?"

"No, you dimwit! They're the subjects, not a component. They're just here because I pulled them here, ahead of time. No, the third component proved to be the hardest to get. Annoying, really, given that we had it at the very start, and then let it go. Indeed, we only just got it here in the nick of time. Do you know what it is, yet?"

I didn't work it out at first, until I saw the look of regret on his face. Slowly, I brought my hand upwards, and pointed it at my own face.

He nodded, as a single tear formed in his eye. "I'm sorry, Antony."

Chapter 52: The Fulcrum

Julia

"What's going to happen?" I asked Sally.

"They've built a machine called a Soul Fulcrum. They did it so much faster than we expected, and now we have so little time. Look, I'll show you."

Suddenly we were back in the physical world, hanging formless in the air, looking down on an old mansion, surrounded by grass, and beyond that, a solid wall of Glories. Three colossal computers had been assembled, with a circular platform between them.

"You have to understand this," said Sally. "If that machine is activated, it won't just slaughter humanity, it'll destroy the Taimede, as well."

Antony

Part of me had known, almost from the start of the conversation, that I had been a part of his plan, and not in any way that was good. "I'm the third part, aren't I?"

"I'm afraid so. I really, really didn't want it to be you. Spent the last month looking for someone else we could use. Popped round to Collett's place to test your various super-powered friends. The Barnes woman showed promise, but none of them really had what I needed."

"Which was?"

"A firm anchor, in both our realm, and theirs. You see, the addicts have drawn the Glory-beings into the range of my Fulcrum machine. I think they're all close enough now. My machine and its conscious AI provides the force and precision to drag them to this dimension, and anchor them in their new bodies. But you see, because every other slice of the consciousness dimension is empty, there has to be one fixed point for everything to turn on. An anchor. Otherwise it all goes kablooey. It has to be conscious, linked to the other dimensional slices, and with a physical form. Someone who'd been to their dimension and come back again. Once you've been fully into the consciousness dimension, you leave behind strands, rooting you to it.

"No? Not getting it, are you? Always so dim and slow, you are. Let's try again .... So you've got birds in the air, and fish in the sea. You want to put all the birds under the water and the fish into the air. Why? I dunno, science. That's not the point. Point is, you can catch all the birds and all the fish, on long poles with nets on the end. But if your own craft is floating in the air, then the birds will just pull you upwards and it won't work. If you're underwater like a submarine, the fish will pull you downwards and it won't work. But a ship on the surface would be half in the water, half in the air. A foot in both worlds. So it's perfectly placed to pull the birds down, and the fish up, moving everything around itself."

"So I'm the ship," I said solemnly.

Chapter 52: The Fulcrum

"And I'm the captain. The captain of you, like I've pretty much always been, to be fair."

"So it was you who sent those thugs chasing after me, at the moon Glory? But why did you let me walk away from that first Glory in the first place?"

"We knew we'd need an anchor, but thought one would be easy to find, or create. But annoyingly, while you'd somehow picked up the knack of sending people through at the drop of a hat, I hadn't. So my associate tried to repeat the process from scratch, but it took too long, and by then there were so many Glory-beings circling around Earth that it couldn't do it without interference."

"Why would they interfere? Aren't they all on the same side?"

He ignored this. "Look, the upshot is, it didn't work, they couldn't create a suitable person, leaving you as the only one who fits the bill properly. But that wasn't why I sent men after you that first time. It was because you were being a pain in the arse."

"What? How?" I felt oddly proud of having been a pain in his arse.

"Making a spectacle of yourself. You'd not been back 24 hours, and you'd already tipped two women into a Glory. That alerted the other Glory-beings that we already had a presence here, which was extremely unhelpful."

"What? But you're helping them, aren't you? Why wouldn't you want them knowing?"

"Because, dummy, there are factions or political parties or something like that. They're like people, you know? Different ideas about how to do things. And because of you, some of them wanted to interfere with our plan. Plus, if you kept turning up at crowded Glories, with a face that was already in the papers, then soon the human media would twig that you were a Glory too – probably faster than you would."

"And that would be bad, because then someone might guess the same about you."

"*Pinnng*!!! You've got two thousand pounds. Of course, you proved to be remarkably adept at evading capture. Respect, Cuz, I was impressed by that. But we got you in the end. Still, one thing I learned from the whole Collett debacle was that it was going to be impossible to keep you prisoner for any length of time. We also couldn't use you for anything, in that Glory form. So we decided to solve both problems by putting you into a body again."

"Talia's body?"

"My associate was aware of her mind, which had cast itself loose in a dimensional slice, fully detached from the physical world. She'd managed to do it through sheer force of will, unwittingly helped by a Glory, leaving behind her physical body in a catatonic state. Now, with no consciousness in it, her body was useless, just a piece of meat. At first we thought, oh we'll use her, and leave you to it. My associate rigged up a complex little device to drag her mind back into her body, although apparently it would have driven her mad in the process. No matter."

"How did you get so cruel?" I asked him. But then an image of his father flashed through my mind, and gave me my answer. Daniel himself ignored the question.

"But it didn't work. Her mind was unreachable in her little fantasy kingdom, and her body had only been in contact with the Glories for a minute or two, not enough to form a proper connection. But then I had yet another of my brilliant ideas. It didn't need to be *her* mind in that body, so I thought, let's stick you in

Chapter 52: The Fulcrum

it! I can just imagine your face, when you woke up and found you were suddenly a girl!'"

"Yet another of your little pranks," I said.

"*Where's my willy gone*?!" he mocked, hands rushing to his groin area.

Again, I had to steer him back onto more important things. "So when I saw the Blue Lake, the same Glory that started it all ..."

"It was my associate, yes. They had felt the rupture when you sent Sally through, but she ended up with the normal Glories. But it revealed your exact location, so my associate manifested close to the spot, and you walked right into it, both literally and metaphorically."

"And you put me inside Talia's mind."

"Well, that bit didn't quite go to plan. We'd expected you to wake up in her body straight-off, at which point my men would have quietly carted you off to Gladcamp. But you hung out in that ridiculous little girl world of hers for weeks. We had no way of getting you out of there. Luckily you did it all for us!"

"So if I hadn't come out, you'd have been stuck?" I asked, horrified.

"Nahhh, we'd have worked something out with the Barnes woman. She did the same thing as Talia, you see, sent her mind into a Glory for some reason, leaving her body catatonic. I've got it locked up and handcuffed in a room here, somewhere. But the difference is, her body is strongly linked to the Glories. She'd formed some roots into their dimension, not as many as you but enough, by the time I visited her in Collett's place. And guess what, there are little Glory nanobots floating around in her blood, we could just about see them under a specially adapted microscope. I'm guessing that's how she did all the miracle healing stuff, but they're inert now, like the rest of her. I think maybe you've got a few in you too, speed you got up from that coma and started walking around. But the point is, unlike Talia, we could have used our device to drag *her* mind back into her body, no problem. We were just gearing up to do it, when you turned up at my old house. But the damage to her mind would have made her a less than ideal focal point, so I'm very glad you turned up.

"So you see, you were still very much our Plan A, hence we'd put little hidden cameras in Talia's room in case you woke up, but it never occurred to me that you'd be up and out of that place so quickly. We missed you by ten minutes. So I had people stationed anywhere I thought you might turn up, and we got lucky! Funny, even half an hour later and I don't think we could have got you here. There's a wall of Glories around us now, a hundred metres thick. Which means, I'm afraid, that no one will be coming to rescue you."

We gazed at each other, silently, for a long moment.

"You're going to put me in the middle of that giant Fulcrum machine of yours," I said.

"That's right, Cuz, sorry."

"I'm going to die, aren't I? The way you're talking ..."

"Yes. I'm afraid you won't survive. I don't think it'll hurt, you won't feel anything when it happens."

"Oh, well that's good," I said sarcastically. "I wouldn't want it to hurt."

"Come on, Cuz, don't be like that. I said I was sorry, and I did save your life before. Plus, we're talking about a whole species here, an entire civilisation, who've been yearning for this chance since before there were even the simplest of animals on this planet. And if we don't do this now, they'll just hang around

Chapter 52: The Fulcrum

here till they die. We've trapped them all now, and manifesting as Glories costs them energy. It's like having to shout, non-stop, for hours."

"Is that what happens when Glories vanish? Do they die?"

"No, they just have to stop and rest. But these ones are stuck now, you see. These ones *will* die, unless I go through with the process."

"Or you could release them."

"I could, but I'm not going to. They expect me to deliver, and I'm going to."

The room seemed to sway gently, as if we were on a boat on stormy seas. I put my hand on the back of a threadbare sofa for support. "So I have to die, to let the Glory-beings live?"

"Sorry, Cuz. '*Needs of the many*', and all that."

"Will the Glory Addicts die too?"

"Them? Probably. But they'll die happy. You're the only one I'm a bit upset about."

"A bit?" I honestly didn't know if he was joking. It was often like that with Daniel.

"A bit."

Someone knocked four times on the door.

"Well, whaddya know?" said Daniel. "Sounds like they're ready for us."

Julia

"Slaughter humanity?" I asked, horrified. "What do you mean?"

"The Taimede consciousnesses have to go somewhere," said Sally. "And the only available vessels right now are human beings."

"So each Glory is one Taimede, and each one will take over a human body? And that human will die?"

"That's right," she said.

"How many?" I asked.

"There are hundreds of thousands of Glories out there now, and more appearing all the time," she said.

"Hundreds of thousands?" I protested. "But that's monstrous!!"

"I'm sorry, but that's only the tip of the iceberg. Most of them haven't manifested yet, but they're all within range now. The machine will do it to all of them."

"How many is that?" I demanded.

"They reckon about three billion."

Antony

Daniel insisted to his monkeys that force wasn't necessary. There were enough of them that I'd have no chance to run, anyway. I walked from that room feeling like a condemned prisoner on the way to the gallows, but trying to hold my head high. The corridor seemed to wobble as I walked down it, the

Chapter 52: The Fulcrum

open front doors at the end of it looming closer and closer, until finally I emerged. The mass of Glories surrounding the grass seemed to pause in their jostling, as if sensing my importance. A man grasped my wrist, gently but firmly, and led me through a single gap in the ring of chairs, which I turned to see being closed after Daniel had come through it, the two addicts' hands being taped together once more. To the left, I could see a mass of power wires running out of an open window towards the three truck-sized computers, which were arranged in a large triangle, surrounding a circular platform perhaps fifteen metres across. In the middle of the platform sat a chair, made completely of metal, except for the small cushion that they'd thoughtfully provided, and of course the leather straps on the armrests. I was encouraged to sit down, and then firmly strapped in.

I thought sadly of all the things I'd now never do, like having children of my own, or thanking Father in person for all of his efforts in raising me alone. I was glad, at least, that I'd had two brief tastes of love before the end.

Daniel was standing in front of me. "How long will it all take?" I asked.

"Well, these conscious machines," he explained. "You can't just turn them on and they start running. You turn them on, and the original AI designs a better one and runs it, then the second one builds a third, and so on. It takes twenty-three minutes and hundreds of generations for the thing to become fully conscious. Then another five minutes for the conscious AI to build a full connection. But once that happens, it'll be over in a flash!"

"And I'll be dead, by your hand."

"Are you going to go on about that for the full 28 minutes?" he asked.

"You know, Daniel, you're my cousin and I love you," I told him. "But sometimes you can be a real arsehole."

He shrugged, and turned away. "When you flick that switch you'll be a murderer," I said gently. "Even if it works exactly as you said it will."

"I already flicked it," he replied without turning round. "It's running already." He pointed to a digital clock, which showed 26:47, then 26:46, counting downwards. One minute was gone already, and I had less than 27 left.

Julia

"Three billion people?" I gasped. "Three billion people are going to die??"

"The Taimede don't want this," said Sally. "It goes against every principle that they lived by. The Super-AI doesn't care, it has its assigned task and our lives or deaths mean nothing to it. But it'll break them." Tears welled up in her eyes. "Life is sacred to them. For millions of years on their world, not one of them killed a single animal. Not one! When one of the Glories caused accidental human deaths, the Taimede responsible always dissipated itself, rather than live with the guilt. Can you imagine what causing the deaths of three billion would do to them?"

"You're right, it'd destroy them," I said. "Three billion people will die, and it'll achieve the exact opposite of what was intended."

Sally nodded. "Not one of them could live with that burden. Not one."

"And they can't stop the process?" I asked.
"They can't. But they're hoping you can."

Antony

What is it like to watch your life tick away? We've all seen it happen to people in films and TV shows, except that they're nearly always rescued, and unless the person is dramatically trying to escape, then the camera doesn't stay with them because, well, watching a person sitting there tied to a chair for 27 minutes would be nearly as dull as the 5th *Star Trek* movie.

I found myself thinking about the best and worst moments of my life. About my time with Talia, and the far too brief love affair with Sally. I pictured my mother, dead since I was little, recalled only in a few soft-focus images and moments, and then those terrible days in the hospital as she was ripped away from us. The rest of my childhood had been full of Daniel, and I had no desire to think about that.

Lights were coming on in the giant computers, appearing randomly like stars on a clear evening. The world's biggest ever computer. So far. What sort of world would it be, with the aliens wanting to share it? Humans were shockingly bad at sharing their land even with one another. Would these aliens be forced to take over, to avoid being wiped out by xenophobic human leaders?

Six minutes were gone. A few of the Glory addicts were still struggling in their chairs. The mass of Glories beyond were still, unarguably, utterly lovely to look at, and there was a kind of childlike joy in the ones that imitated human objects or inventions. I saw Homer Simpson's head, a Dalek, and one that looked like a toddler's self-portrait.

Fifteen minutes were gone, now. A lackey with a phone ran up to Daniel. "There's some police or army unit gone rogue, coming after us," the lackey said. "They're on the way here!"

"So what?" Daniel replied. "They're not going to get through *that*, are they?" He indicated the wall of Glories. "No one can. They were always going to find us, all they needed to do was follow the Glories. Don't worry, short of a huge barrage of missiles, there's no way they can stop us, and the regular army will do what Collins tells them to. '*All part of the plan, chaps,*'" he said in a posh army voice. "'*To get shot of the glories, once and for all!*' Tell you what, drop Collins a line, and have the normal police arrest these party-poopers, just in case." Daniel noticed that another of his men was pointing upwards. "Oh look, they've got a drone up. Hello, drone flyer, whoever you are! Don't worry, we have full permission to do this!"

There were less than six minutes to go. There wasn't anything I could do.

Julia

"Me?" I said. "You think *I* can stop them?"

Chapter 52: The Fulcrum

"No-one else can get close. That wall of Glories is an unbreakable barrier. The army could fire a few missiles, I suppose, but the PM will quickly stop them. It's down to you, I'm afraid."

"Is my body in there? In that big house?"

"It is, but it's chained to a bed. We're going to piggyback onto Daniel's machine, the Fulcrum, and use it to give you a Glory-form, like Antony had."

"But what can I do?"

"You have to reach Antony. He's the only one who could get through to Daniel. He's strapped to a chair in the middle of that giant machine on the lawn. And he's a girl, now."

"What???"

"It's not important. Just get to him. You will gain form just under 23 minutes into the machine's activation cycle, as the conscious AI it's building starts connecting across the conscious dimension. That will give you around 314 seconds to stop the machine, before it reaches full activation."

"Five minutes? That's not enough time!"

"You need only touch him – Antony, I mean – to share everything we've told you. Together, you have to make Daniel change his mind."

"Undo twelve whole years of their brainwashing? In just a few minutes?"

Sally nodded. "He doesn't know how many people will die, the Super-AI will have kept that part from him. It's our only hope. All of us."

"How soon?" I asked. "How soon will this happen?"

"The machine will reach the necessary point in two seconds' time," replied Sally.

And then I was sitting up on an old bed in a strange room, next to my own inert body.

Five minutes left, now. The drone still hung in the air above.

"You know what? I'm tired of being watched. Shoot the bloody thing," said Daniel. The men enthusiastically turned their guns upwards and took pot shots. The drone made no attempt to dodge them, but it was high in the air and a small target, and it took a good minute before one of them hit it. While this was happening, I thought I glimpsed a figure dressed in black emerging from the wall of Glories. None of the men saw him, focussed as they were on the drone. I had less than three minutes to live, by this point. I wondered if Daniel would come back up to say goodbye, but deep down I knew that he wouldn't.

My inert physical body was cuffed at both wrists to the metal frame of the bed, as it slept. I smiled awkwardly at it, and even waved, before running through

Chapter 52: The Fulcrum  339

the door. Only then did I realise that I hadn't actually opened it first. *Get to Antony*.

I remembered how Antony walked through walls. But I also knew that he could be seen, and caught by other people. I needed to be smart. Getting through the house was simple enough – any time I saw someone, I just ducked through the nearest wall. But there was some distance to cover between the house and the machine where they had Antony, and my way was blocked by a huge ring of people, strapped to chairs and looking outwards. A few of them saw me, so I ducked back inside before they could alert anyone. They were a part of the process, and from their expressions most seemed perfectly happy about it.

I had to get past without being seen, but how? I looked sideways along the wall and saw an old wooden trapdoor. That was it! I jumped through it and fell down into a cellar, and then walked through the damp stone wall, and into the earth beyond. It took a few moments but I worked out a way to half-swim, half-crawl through the earth just below the grass. I got to the surface, popped my head up through the grass, saw the direction I needed to go, and then ducked under again and swam on. When next I emerged, I was right by the raised platform, where no-one could see me. I ran up onto the platform. A thin young woman was strapped to a chair in the middle.

"Antony?" I whispered, incredulously.

"Julia?" the woman gasped in surprise. "Yes it's me! You've got to ..."

I put a finger to my lips, and then reached out to touch his/her hand.

Information and memories flowed in a deluge between us. He/she gasped in abject horror as the truth of the plan became clear. "My God, you have to stop him," Antony said.

"He won't listen to me," I replied.

"Get me out of this!" he cried. "Stop the machine!" He tugged frantically at the straps, but I could do nothing to free him. A moment of helpless despair, then it came to me. *Use the Fulcrum.*

I reached for Antony's hand, and pulled hard.

The world span violently around me, blackness and light spiralling in crazy directions. And then with a shock I was pulled down, and felt solid again. My wrists were strapped to the chair. And in front of me stood Antony, a male teenager again, looking at his arms as if he'd never seen them before.

"Talia!" I shouted. Why was she strapped to a metal chair? Why was I standing on the platform facing her? Then it all came rushing back – it was Julia, in the body I'd been borrowing.

"You have to convince him!" she said, desperately. "Daniel! I don't think he knows, but his plan will kill three billion humans, and all of the Taimede as well! Whatever he's been told this'll do, it's a lie!!"

"Who's Talia, Cuz?"

Chapter 52: The Fulcrum

Daniel was walking towards the platform, eyeing me curiously. "Hey, you separated, nice trick. Won't stop the process though. Or has someone else taken up residence in there? Hello, whoever you are. It won't stop the process, if that's what you're thinking. If you're in there, then you're eminently suitable to act as an anchor."

The countdown clock went past 90 seconds.

"Daniel, listen to me," I said. "They lied to you. They told you there'd only be a few human deaths, but they lied, do you hear me? They lied!! For every one of them that comes through, a human has to die, and there are 3 billion of them!!"

"It's true!" said Julia, in the chair.

Daniel cocked his head sideways.

"We're talking about half the human race, Daniel," I pleaded. "Do you understand me? Your machine is about to kill half of the world!"

His eyes widened. "Are you sure?"

"Yes, I'm sure! I've seen it all! I've seen their history! The one that linked with you, it's been programmed to restore them at any cost! And *we're* the cost!"

"I should have realised," he said, looking horrified. "I could tell they were lying, but I didn't know the scale. Dear God, Antony! Come on, I need to get to the off-switch!"

There were 35 seconds left. He thundered down the stairs and I ran with him. "This one's the master switch," he called, running around to the side of one of his giant machines, facing towards the house.

His finger reached out for the switch, and went right through it.

"Oops, I forgot!" he said, bringing his hand to his open mouth. "I don't have a solid body, so I can't turn it off. Silly me! Looks like half the world's people are doomed, after all." And he laughed like a crazy man as the clock ticked down to 20 seconds.

Chapter 53: The fall

Antony

"Daniel!" I cried. "Get one of your men to turn it off!"

There were twenty seconds left.

"Well, goodness me, I never thought of that," said Daniel, comically slapping his face with his hand. "My cousin's a genius, who knew?"

Fifteen seconds. He stood there, looking at me with a crooked smile.

"You knew," I whispered. "You knew all along…"

Daniel offered a theatrical shrug, and a bow.

Ten seconds. I thought of grabbing a guard, forcing his hand to the switch, but none of them were close enough.

Then the lights on all the machines went out. Daniel spun around, and flapped his arms. "What?" he shouted. Then more loudly, "What is happening!??!"

"Someone cut the power, sir," said a minion. "To the whole house."

"Well I can see *THAT*," roared Daniel. "But I want to know HOW, you total morons!!!"

It was almost funny.

* * * * *

A minute later, two guards appeared, dragging a thin, leather-clad young man from the house. It was Lucasz!

"Power's back on, boss!" said a guard. "This little bastard tripped the fuse box!"

"Restart the machine!" ordered Daniel. "NOW!" A man walked forward and flicked the switch that Daniel had failed to move earlier. Off, and then on again. I saw the countdown restarting.

"D'you want us to shoot him, boss?" said a man.

Daniel walked up to Lucasz. "I'd forgotten about you, and your walk-through-Glory ability. Did someone send you?"

"They're onto you, alright," said Lucasz. He looked defiant, not scared. "Oh, and we'll be sending a bill for the damages on the little diversion that you shot down."

"No point wasting a good body," said Daniel. "Get him out of the way and cuff him to something. He can watch the show." The men marched Lucasz up to the wall of the big house, and handcuffed one of his wrists to a heavy metal drainpipe. "And get everyone else out here in case any more interlopers turn up!"

"Daniel, you have to stop!" I shouted. "You have to stop this! You're talking about wiping out half of the human race!"

"He's a fantasist, I'll deal with him," Daniel said to his men. They nodded, and turned away, unconcerned. "They're all low-level Glory addicts," he said, turning to me. "Specially selected, another bonus of the Gladcamps. That means they're predisposed to believe me and do what I say, even worship me a little. Which means, there's no point in you trying to talk them round, because you won't get anywhere. But still, you're going to spend the whole of the

Chapter 53: The fall

countdown trying to talk me out of it, aren't you? And I can't even gag you. How tedious. But then you always were a bit of a moraliser."

"You're planning to slaughter 3 billion people! How can you possibly do that, to your own kind?"

"To save another race."

"But you won't," I insisted. "The Taimede don't want this! They don't want to cause all this death! The guilt would destroy them!"

"They'll get over it," he said dismissively. "Once they're made flesh again, they'll stop all the whining and get on with it. Saving the world, and the like."

I stared at him as he said this, so casually, bargaining away the lives of every person he'd ever known, and countless millions more. "There has to be another way! This is mass genocide! You'd be worse than Hitler!"

"That's just the thing, though, isn't it, Cuz? The human race are basically a bunch of bastards. We murder each other. We're systematically slaughtering all the other species on this planet, mostly without even noticing it, just to make space for ourselves. We can hardly complain if someone else takes the same attitude with us."

"But they're not, don't you see? They don't want this!"

"Tough! They're getting it anyway."

"Little Annie!" I tried. "Little Annie, you remember, that lovely little girl next door. You'll be killing her, too. You liked her. You said you wished she was your sister, one time."

"I didn't!" he yelled, eyes flashing with anger. "I said I wished I were her brother!"

"Same thing!"

"It really isn't."

Something clicked into place in my mind. He was right, it was far from the same thing. Because if she'd been his sister, she'd have had to live in his house. "It's because of your dad, isn't it? It's because of him that you're doing this."

"That bastard has nothing to do with this!"

"You hate him, and that's making you hate everyone!"

"Shut up! *Shut up!*"

"If you go through with this," I told him, holding my voice steady, "then it won't be you killing three billion people. It'll be *him*."

"Bastard!" Daniel's fist shot towards me, smashing into my face. It hurt and I staggered back, but I kept talking.

"He's still controlling you, like he always did," I taunted. I wasn't even sure whether pushing him about his dad was the right thing to do, but I couldn't think of anything else.

"Get over here," Daniel shouted to two of his lackeys.

"Boss?"

"Hold this sanctimonious little git!" screamed Daniel. "Cover his fucking mouth!"

"Gagging me won't make it any less true," I said, refusing to run away. One of the men roughly grabbed me in a bear hug from behind, while the other pulled duct tape from his pocket."

"Not with tape, you idiots," shouted Daniel furiously. "Use your hands."

"What?" I said mockingly. "No, no, use the tape. Gag me up good and proper. The only way that wouldn't work is if I'm a Glory!"

Chapter 53: The fall

The two men hesitated, then Daniel grabbed one hand of the man holding me, and forced it over my mouth. "Keep it there!" he snarled. But he'd moved too close to me, so I brought up both legs and slammed my feet into him as hard as I could. He staggered back, and the man holding me lost his balance too. I bit his hand and squirmed free.

If Daniel could change the sound of his voice at will, then maybe I could, too. "You're pathetic!" I told Daniel, imitating his father's voice as best as I could. "Same old Daniel," I growled. "Whine, whine, whine, then take it out on someone else."

"Fuck OFF, Antony!"

"You can't face hearing a few home truths, so your solution is to kill half the world? You're a whiny brat!"

"For God's sake, SHUT HIM UP!" screamed Daniel. But I was dodging around, and the guards were too slow to catch me.

"First chance you got, you ran away!" I persisted. "Left your poor old mum with no-one but me for company, didn't you? Well, I had to take it out on someone!"

"NOOOOOO!!!!" he flew at me – all of him this time – but I was ready. I moved to the side, but caught his face with my fist as he rushed past. He whipped around, stunned.

"Pathetic!" I yelled. "You'll never be a man, always just a grovelling little wimp! I should've had a girl, at least she'd have given me more fun!"

Daniel flew at me again, his face contorted with rage, but this time I jumped upwards, on instinct, but didn't come down. I hung there in the air as he turned himself round, shaking with fury. He'd been right – I could fly! Then Daniel flew upwards towards me, and I dodged aside, moving higher. "I'll make you pay, you bastard!" he roared, and I didn't know if he was talking to me, or his father, or both. And then I knew, with absolute clarity, what it was that I had to do. There were twenty minutes left.

"You'll never catch me, you snivelling little coward," I told him, before shooting up further into the air. He followed. I shot through the tiny gap in the Glories directly above the machine, with Daniel behind me. Up and up I went, and below me the mass of Glories looked like a giant, multi-coloured fried egg covering the land. At its fringes, Glories were still arriving, slowing down and descending to join the seething mass. I had to keep switching direction to stop Daniel catching me, and both of us had to dodge Glories. I needed to orientate, so I flew high enough to see London, the Thames Estuary, the Bristol Channel and the Isle of Wight. From these markers I could work out roughly where Swinton would be. I flew to the north, looking for landmarks, and my eyes fell upon the two reservoirs I've passed over while riding that Glory. I retraced my route at ridiculous speed, past the hill I'd landed on, through the town, up Daniel's road and right through his living room wall.

Daniel's dad was slouched on the sofa, surrounded by used tissues, beer cans and a battered old laptop. He gave a start as I appeared in the room opposite him, and his eyes widened further. "You? How the fuck did you get in here?"

I didn't respond. Then Daniel walked through the wall to stand beside me. He looked 14 again.

"Son?" his dad said, jaw hanging open in dumb astonishment. "Son???"

Chapter 53: The fall

"Hello Dad," said Daniel in an almost friendly voice. "I thought we should have a little chat."

"I thought ... I thought I'd lost you ..." said the old man, dumbly.

"Yeah, right," said Daniel. "You mean you were worried I might have actually, how did you always put it? '*Grow a fucking spine, you little worm*'?"

I think his dad sensed he was in danger, even if he didn't know how or why. The fear seemed to diminish him, as if he were shrinking before me. He'd been terrifying before, when I'd been trapped in his house, but now he suddenly looked weak, even old. Mind you, Daniel's icy tone would have chilled just about anyone.

"I-I-I j-just wanted to make you stronger, that's all!"

"Oh, *right*. So that's why you used to come into my bedroom and *pretend that I was a girl*." Daniel shot across the room at impossible speed, and smashed his fist into his father's face. The old man crashed backwards, then rolled around on the floor, moaning, with blood pouring from his shattered nose.

"Get up!" yelled Daniel. "Get up, you snivelling little worm! Fight back like a man! That was another of your little 'encouragements', wasn't it?"

"Pleeease" moaned his father. "I'm sorry." I knew what was coming next. What had to come next. Here was a boy so twisted by abuse that he'd been willing to murder three billion innocent people.

"Look at me," said Daniel, in an unnervingly calm voice. The bleeding man on the floor tried to cover his eyes. "LOOK at me!" commanded Daniel, and we both did.

The head was still his, but from his body now sprang a mass of thick black spiny tentacles, each ending in a vicious claw. His dad wailed in terror. Casually, Daniel reached down with a claw and picked him up by the neck.

"I used to dream of monsters, every night!" Daniel shouted. "Every night!!! Monsters with *YOUR FACE*!!!"

Tears streamed from the old man's eyes. "Pleeeeeeeeeaase!"

It was over in an instant. The tentacle slammed the old man into one wall, then even harder into another, the impact so fierce it dented the wall. Then it slammed him again, and again and again, harder and harder, the dents in both walls growing larger as the whole house shook. Then the man's head snapped off, falling behind the sofa, and the rest of his broken body flopped to the floor. The tentacle drooped, and the monster turned back into Daniel.

"I think he got the point," I said gently.

"That bastard did things to me and my mum," said Daniel. "He did things!!" I could feel the rage draining out of him as he looked down at the broken remains of his father.

"I wish I could have done something to help, but I didn't know. I didn't know anything. You always said I was too innocent. Now I think at last I understand why."

Tears rolled down Daniel's face, vanishing as they fell from his chin. "I couldn't stop him. All those things he did ... to me and mum ... I couldn't stop him."

"Pretty sure you stopped him now."

"I killed him. I wanted to hurt him, I wanted to show him. But I didn't mean to actually ..."

"Daniel, you're planning the deaths of three billion people," I said gently.

"That's different. It's a trade – the Glory-things need me."

Chapter 53: The fall

"So innocent humans have to die? Look at your father. He deserved what he got, but it *still* feels bad, doesn't it? How much worse will it be, when everyone in the country is dead except you? Everyone in *Europe*? You can't let it happen, Daniel. You can't. And you'd be inflicting that guilt on the Glory-things too. They don't deserve that. They're pleading with you to stop it."

Daniel cried. He cried long, shuddering sobs that seemed to go on forever. I held him there, in that horrible little room with the curtains half-drawn, and the broken mess that was once his dad lying ignored on the floor. And elsewhere, I knew that the clock was ticking down again. When I thought he was ready, I said to him gently, "They couldn't live with it, if it went ahead. And neither could you. It'd be torture. For their sake and yours, we have to stop the process!"

"I don't know if I can!"

"But can we try?" I held out my hand. He took it. "You just need to tell one of your minions to flick the off switch," I added.

"Yes, we can try."

Without another word, I took his hand, and we vanished through the wall together into the sky. It was dead easy finding our way back, so very soon we were standing on the platform in the middle of the machine, again, and there were 65 seconds to go.

* * * * *

The three giant computers were now a mass of flashing and blinking lights. They hummed with power, and I could feel them vibrating. Hot air blasted out of holes throughout the wall of lights.

"Stop the machine!" yelled Daniel.

The milling minions looked at him, confused.

"You're still Daniel!" I whispered. "You need to be Dexter!"

Daniel cursed, and transformed in an instant.

"You heard me," he growled, voice thundering with authority. "Stop the machine! We've been betrayed!"

55 seconds.

One of the men nodded, and made for the off-switch, but a wall of blue water appeared in front of him, blocking his way. In a few seconds the blue wall expanded, surrounding the computers entirely.

"Fuuuck!!!" shouted Daniel. "It's my associate! The One that found us! It knows what we're doing!"

"Then unplug it again!" I cried.

"SHOOT THE WIRES!!" shouted Daniel, but before the men could aim, the blue water shot outwards across the grass. The terrified men were swept out of sight, dropping their guns as they went. "Damn, damn, DAMN," shouted Daniel, tearing at his hair.

45 seconds.

"Lucasz!" I cried! "Lucasz can do it!! He can walk through Glories! We have to reach him!"

We flew up, over, and across to the house, before the blue Glory could react. Then we were there beside Lucasz, standing cuffed to the drainpipe. His wrist was bleeding from his attempts to squeeze it free.

"Get me out of this!" screamed Lucasz. "I can stop the bloody thing!"

35 seconds.

Chapter 53: The fall

But of course, neither Daniel nor I could do anything to the handcuff.

"There's only one way," I said, "and I'm sorry, but this is going to hurt like hell!

"Just do it," he roared.

I grabbed Lucasz's cuffed wrist, one hand either side of the cuff, and pulled as hard as I could. Daniel joined in, and Lucasz pulled too, his face contorted with pain. The house was old. The drainpipe was rusty. It began to pull away from the house, but only a little.

25 seconds.

"Daniel, be a monster again," I cried. He transformed into a huge tentacled mass and tugged harder, then Lucasz screamed in agony as first the lowest clasp on the drainpipe pulled clear of the wall, then the next one up. Rusty screws pinged to the ground. Then the drainpipe was peeling away from the wall, and it snapped.

18 seconds.

Lucasz was wriggling the cuff of the pipe, ignoring the blood oozing from his wrist where the cuff had bit in. "I can't see the switch!" he yelled. The grass was covered by an opaque sea of blue water, which also bulged upwards to hide all of the giant machine.

"Big guns!" I yelled. "The guards dropped them!" And I forced my way through the blue Glory, feeling around on the ground.

"Here!" shouted Daniel, close by. "Lucasz, there's one here"

15 seconds.

Lucasz ran forwards, reached down beside Daniel and came up with a machine gun.

10 seconds.

Lucasz began shooting at the ground, but nothing happened.

6 seconds.

"Not there, you fool," shouted Daniel. And he grabbed Lucasz, turning him sideways, redirecting the gun. "There!!"

4 seconds.

Lucasz emptied the gun into the ground, through the Blue Glory, and sparks flew up from where the bullets hit.

Something went '*bang!*' The Blue Glory shot upwards, then hung in the air above us, shuddering and flexing into countless irregular shapes, its colour and texture changing several times a second – fire, wood, cloud, blackness, ice, granite, blood. As this happened, it shrank and shrank to the size of a pea, then exploded in a last silent burst of extraordinary colours.

"What's happening?" I shouted.

The lights on one of the big computers had gone out, but not the other two. The wall of Glories was breaking up, its members shuddering and milling around in random directions. On the ground I could see that one of the big wires had been severed by Lucasz' bullets.

"You got one of the machines," said Daniel. "My associate was linked in with the process, and the shock must have killed it!"

"Good riddance," I said. "But what about the others?"

"The process was stopped, but I think they're still stuck!" he said. "My machine's AI will be trying to repair itself. I don't want to kill them – I need to think!"

Chapter 53: The fall

"Should I shoot the other wires?" asked Lucasz, picking up a second discarded gun.

"I don't know," shouted Daniel, frantically. "That could hurt them more. Oh, God, what's that noise?"

An unearthly screeching was filling my head. Daniel was covering his ears.

Lucasz looked at us, confused. "I can't hear anything," he said.

"It's the Glories," I said. "They're in agony!" It wasn't a sound, but I knew it was screaming, nonetheless.

Some of the Glories from the wall were now floating towards us. Each of them was flexing and distorting as it moved, some of them changing colour too.

"We have to help them," I cried.

"I've made such a mess," sobbed Daniel.

Now all the Glory addicts were screaming too. One of the Glories had moved faster than the rest, it was almost beside the machine. Suddenly it shrank, flashed through the colours of the rainbow, and exploded into nothing.

"Daniel," I said. "The closer they get, the worse it is. You said there was a machine linked to the addicts that attracts them, that pulls them here. Can we turn it off?"

"We can do better," gasped Daniel, his face suddenly full of hope. "We can reverse it! And send them away!! Lucasz, come on! It's under the platform!" He ran towards it, diving along the ground between the arms of two addicts in the circle. Lucas and I followed. Daniel led us over to the chair, which Julia was still strapped to in Talia's body, writhing in pain. "They're dying," she screamed. "You're killing them all!!"

There were controls on the back of the chair. "That switch," said Daniel, pointing. Lucasz flicked it. "Now that dial, anti-clockwise, all the way!" And Lucasz obeyed. For an instant, nothing happened.

Then I heard a thud in my head, like a sonic boom, and a moment later, the Glories were all shooting upwards and sideways, away from us. The screeching in my head went quiet. "Antony," croaked Julia. Blood was running from her nose, and tears from her eyes.

"Antony you have to touch me and swap bodies back, or you'll be stuck like this forever!"

"What about you?" I said.

"I'll try to get back to my own body."

But something was pushing me upwards, lifting my feet from the ground. "Grab my wrist!" shouted Julia, and I did.

"Antony!!!" called another voice from behind me. I turned to see Daniel, lifting up into the air, comically flailing his arms like he was pretending to swim, only badly.

"Daniel, don't muck around," I said.

"I'm not! Antony, turn it off!! It's pushing me up!"

"Then fly down!"

"But I can't! It's too strong!!"

And then I knew what was happening. He was a Glory, and so was I. Which meant I was doomed, unless I could get back into Talia's body.

"Turn off the machine!!!" screamed Daniel. Lucasz was now holding on to him with his uninjured hand, trying to stop Daniel from falling upwards.

"You have to wait till the Glories have all gone," said Julia. "We need to undo all this properly!"

Chapter 53: The fall

I gripped tightly to both her bound wrists, my body now up in the air. She spoke to me urgently. "If you wait till all the Glories have gone, we can turn off the machine and you'll be OK," she said desperately. "I'm sorry, I don't see how you can save him!"

"Antoniiiiiiiiiiieeeee!!!" Daniel was starting to float helplessly upwards, lifting Lucasz up with him, now a foot off the ground.

"I can't stop him going up," shouted Lucasz.

"Let go, Lucasz," called Julia. "Or you'll be killed, too!"

I'd lost Daniel once. I couldn't do it again.

"Listen, Antony, we can swap bodies," said Julia, urgently. "I've lived sixty-one years, you've only had sixteen, so let me go after him."

"I can't," I said, turning to look her in the eye. "Thank you for everything you've done." And I let go.

I let go of her wrists, and kicked through the air, caught Daniel's hand and broke Lucasz's grip. Lucasz fell to the ground, and then the ground was falling away from us.

"Antony, I'm scared," said Daniel.

"Don't be," I said. "I'm here."

The mansion and its grounds were below us now, getting smaller and smaller.

"I'm sorry," he said. "I'm so sorry for all the trouble I caused. I don't know how you can ever forgive me."

"But I can," I said. "Because I love you, and you've always been my brother, in every way that mattered."

We fell upwards through the clouds, and then they were shrinking away below us, too.

Daniel smiled at me, with tears in his eyes.

"Where are we going, Cuz?"

"I've no idea, Brother. But we'll be going there together."

We were out of the atmosphere now, part of a loose flotilla of Glories that were flying away from the Earth, past the moon, and into the vastness of space.

Chapter 54: My third life

Julia

I watched helplessly, as Antony and Daniel spiralled up into the sky, along with the last of the Glories. The machine beneath me thrummed relentlessly. I was still strapped to the chair, of course, and trapped in this young woman's body, quite possibly forever. Antony and Daniel were just dots in the sky, and then I couldn't see them at all. Around them the Glories were shrinking away into the distance, their brilliant colours reduced to tiny specks in the sky until they, too, were gone. After that, there was nothing left in the evening sky but fluffy white clouds, mundane and yet, somehow, utterly lovely.

The Glory addicts, who in general had accepted their treatment in silence so far, were now shouting and struggling. I was content to just sit and wait. Then I saw Lucasz loping up the steps towards me, clutching his wrist and wincing with pain. It was already swelling all around where the cuff had dug into his skin.

"Hang on, let me get you out," he said as he came towards me. "You don't have a hanky in your pocket or something like that? My wrist is bleeding a lot."

"You poor thing!"

We heard distant sirens, rapidly getting closer. I thought for a moment, then said, "Actually, don't unstrap me. I don't want the police thinking I was in on this. I'll vouch for you too."

We heard vehicles coming onto the lawn.

"That'll be the cavalry, probably," said Lucasz. "Could you ... could you do something for me, too? Could you not tell anyone, about me stopping the machine?"

"Really? Why?"

"I don't want to be famous," he said. "I don't want to be special anymore. I just want to be ordinary."

I nodded. "I can understand that."

"It's enough for me to know that I helped do it."

"Well. I know too," I said with a smile.

"It's our secret," he smiled back. "Hey, what's your name?"

"Talia." The name popped up from my memory, and I knew immediately that it had belonged to the girl whose body I now wore. Why didn't I say 'Julia'? Why didn't I tell him who I was? Was it something to do with the lovely ripples I unexpectedly felt inside, when he smiled at me?

"Are you sure you won't let me rescue you?" he said, with a twinkle in his eye. He was looking at me in a way that no young man had looked at me for about thirty years.

But someone was striding towards us now, making straight for the contraption that I was strapped into. She had a face that I knew.

"Locksley!" I felt quite incredibly happy to see her.

"Do I know you?" she asked, gruffly.

"Ah. That's going to be difficult to explain."

Chapter 54: My third life

* * * * *

Locksley took charge, calling over a medic for Lucasz's arm, and later arranging a pair of hotel rooms for him and me. As we rode to the hotel in a car with a very silent driver, I felt my mind starting to settle into this new body. You'll recall how I went a bit silly after that first Glory cured me, and ended up throwing myself at Malcolm like a randy teenager on heat? Well, it seemed now that I actually *was* a randy teenager on heat. I'd been sixty one, but now I was seventeen or eighteen, and my body was starting to form very particular ideas about the young man sitting next to me.

It was obvious that Lucasz fancied me. After all, I'd watched him for hours pining over Lara, so I knew all the signs. I did my best to hold back the tsunami of lust building within me. We ate a fine meal together at the hotel restaurant, and even as we flirted, the sensible part of my mind kept trying to convince me that it wasn't a good idea. It failed. As we opened the door to my room, we fell into each other for a night of frantic, energetic passion. His wounded arm didn't hinder him at all. During a calm interval as we lay there, temporarily sated, I realised that I'd made it close to impossible to tell him who I really was. By the morning I knew that there was only one person who I would tell, at least for now.

That person was Locksley. I felt that I owed her my honesty, and I told her absolutely everything. My own story, and Antony's, for I still had his memories. She listened, po-faced, to every single detail, recording it all on her Dictaphone. She'd agreed to keep my identity secret – after all, who else would believe it? She told me that my old body had stopped breathing, around the time when the Glories left Earth. So from that point on, Julia Barnes was officially dead.

So were Antony, and Daniel. Strangely, I could remember Antony's last moments, all the way up to him floating away past the moon, with Daniel. "How does that work?" I asked Locksley.

"You're asking *me*?" she replied.

So I told her how Daniel had actually been hiding in plain sight as Claude Dexter for all of this time, which of course explained her earlier observation that officially Dexter didn't exist. We both agreed to keep this to ourselves – again, who would believe it? Instead, I asked Locksley to make it known, at least to their surviving family members, that both Daniel and Antony had died heroically, preventing a catastrophe. She said "Of course" as though it were no big deal, and that she would do the same for Julia Barnes, with my own son and his family. We had discussed telling them the truth, but I'd raised Nick to be a rational man, and he could never have accepted it, and it would just have confused my poor Tabby. So, Locksley had called them, with the phone on speaker and me silent beside her, later that day. "I'm sorry to tell you, sir, but your mother, Julia Barnes, died during the Glory emergency. She played a vital role in containing the situation, and saved a lot of lives."

I heard a little voice in the background. "Gabba was a hero?"

"Yes, Tabby," said Nick holding back tears. "They're saying Gabba saved a lot of people, but because of that, she's gone."

Nick ended the call, and Locksley left me alone, to cry it all out.

Chapter 54: My third life

* * * * *

Barry Collins was hauled out of 10 Downing Street in handcuffs. The scene played repeatedly on every TV channel. I think I spotted Locksley among those who were doing the hauling. During our endless debriefings, she occasionally fed me snippets of her own. For example, that 'Dexter' had left an obvious paper trail implicating Collins in a plot to bring millions of Glories to our shores, although it didn't explain why. Soon, the press had decided that his goal was to cause chaos, after which he'd use emergency measures to make himself some sort of dictator. Their own role in egging him on at the start of his premiership was, of course, never mentioned. So Collins was convicted of treason and causing the deaths of the 2729 people who had died on what was now being called G-Day. Daniel, wherever he was, would probably have laughed his head off at that. Meanwhile, Claude Dexter himself was rapidly taking on the status of an evil urban legend because, of course, no-one could find him.

Former Prime Minister Theresa May stepped in as interim PM while the Tories got started on electing yet another new leader. After all those weeks of chaos and upheaval, there was something oddly reassuring about Mrs May's stilted, robotic tones as she told us that by following the rules, we would all defeat the virus together. Malcolm would no doubt have remarked that she had become the first PM since Harold Wilson, and only the second since Churchill, to serve non-consecutive terms. I imagined discussing it with him, and especially him running down the stairs with his history book, to tell me that Collins had become the UK's shortest serving PM of all time. This was a record that everyone agreed was highly unlikely to ever be beaten. The bookies' favourite to win the leadership contest and be the next PM was Liz Truss.

Ah, yes, my lovely Malcolm. I'll get to him soon, I promise. I'm not quite ready yet.

* * * * *

Locksley had consistently spoken against the Gladcamps within the security services, and because of that, she'd been given a significant promotion. "I'm becoming a very influential woman," she told me. "So you see, you and Lucasz didn't really stiff me that badly, after all."

"Did you really call Lara 'The Shaman'?" I asked her.

"I'm allowed the odd joke, aren't I?" she replied. "Besides, *Boss Drum* is one of the greatest albums ever made."

I took her word for that. She asked me if there was anything else she could do for me. "Well, for me, I'm not sure," I said. "But for Talia, yes." I fingered the mass of faint scars along my arm. "Her father used to abuse her, you see. I've got her memories, as well as Antony's. That's why she hid herself away in that Glory, where he couldn't hurt her anymore. It started when she was eight. He's a policeman, so she never thought she could report it. Also, she thinks he's behind a spate of unsolved rapes in their area. I can give you some details, she started looking into it in secret. His behaviour changed for a while, you see, every time he attacked someone who wasn't her. Plus he liked to talk about the cases

Chapter 54: My third life

with his best mate on the force, sometimes right there in her house, at number 16."

Locksley's face had stayed neutral as I'd told her this, but I could feel the fury building inside her. "Do you know," she said firmly, "I really don't like people like that."

"Funny, I don't either," I said.

"Do you think his mate knew about it?"

"I'm certain he did. He warned Talia off, once. A month before she went into the Glory. I think it's what made her give up." I told her the man's name.

"And her mother? Did she know?"

"Maybe not about the rapes, but ohhh yes, she knew about the abuse. She ran a posh little boutique, and image was everything to her. The perfect family unit. Nothing could be allowed to threaten that, not the needs of her daughter, and certainly not the truth."

"I don't like people like *her*, either," said Locksley acidly. "I'll look into this. I've got friends who can be trusted to do this right. Will you give us some DNA?"

"Of course," I said.

"Then if there's DNA from any of the rapes, we'll be able to nail the bastard. As for the mother, well, you could threaten to sue her for damages. She'll probably cough up a huge sum of cash to make it all go away quietly. Might be useful, for a young woman starting afresh."

"I'll have a think about that," I said.

* * * * *

Talia's father would soon go to prison for a very long time, and his enabling buddy got ample jail time, too. Her mother paid up quickly, exactly as Locksley had predicted. Locksley was concerned, however, that Talia's father could possibly have other friends who might seek revenge on his daughter, so Locksley suggested it might be wise for me to arrange me a new identity. "You could choose your own name," she said. "I've always liked the name 'Julia', myself."

But when we took a break, I asked if they had any Scrabble sets in the building. She looked at me like I'd said 'bondage dungeon' instead of 'Scrabble set', so I settled for a pen, paper and scissors. I wrote out each letter of 'Julia Barnes' on a separate little paper square, and moved them around. By the time Locksley came back, I had my new name: Jana Rublesi. "Has a nice, exotic ring to it, don't you think?" I told a bemused Locksley. "And it goes with the new face."

Chapter 54: My third life

Jana

Lucasz and I clung to each other tightly like shipwreck survivors. My mood was swinging between euphoria at the youth of my body, and cloying grief at all I'd lost, but Lucasz' stoical constancy helped me through it. For his part, he was badly cut up about the apparent death of Julia, the original me, whom I was rapidly learning to refer to in the third person.

"She was like a mother to me," he told me. "I was so happy to know her. You know ... you remind me of her, sometimes. Some of the things you come out with, the way you tilt your head." In those heady days, we bathed in the glow of young love, spending every minute together except while Locksley or her trusted minions continued our debriefs. After the first night, we told Locksley we'd like to share a room from then on, which she said would delight their accountants.

Locksley wanted, she told us, a dossier of information that was as complete as possible about the Glories and peoples' responses to them, in case one day they came back. We weren't the only ones interviewed, of course. One day we bumped into Walt in the hotel corridor, and he told us of his weeks of incarceration in Gladcamp, with Millie and Helen and others from his group. God had got them through, he said happily. I had to keep reminding myself to pretend I'd never met him before.

This was even harder with Hector and Bluebell, who Locksley invited to dinner with us. The pair of them seemed so ridiculously happy, that even Locksley looked like she might think about shedding a tear at one point. Unlike Lucasz and I, Hector and Bluebell were revelling in their newfound celebrity status, and there was talk of Hector appearing on *Dancing on Ice*, when things got back to normal.

I asked Locksley about Rick, the glory addict whom Antony and Sally had met. She said he was doing well, and that he'd had no addiction symptoms since escaping from Collett and his men. She also told me that Sammy, Siobhan's son, was bearing up well and had been taken in by an aunt. "Oh, and Daniel's mother is living in sin in with Antony's father. She actually moved in there right after Antony reappeared at their house," she told me.

"Daniel's father abused him," I said. "And her, I think."

"We know. We debriefed his mother. She said it all came out after Antony ran off. Frank Blake gave the bastard a big black eye, and then took her home with him," she said with a grim smile.

"Good for him," I said. "Must be so hard, both losing their kids. I hope they find happiness together."

* * * * *

Eventually they were done with us, and Lucasz suggested we move into Julia's old house, having spoken to Nick on the phone to ask if it would be OK.

Chapter 54: My third life

"I know she wouldn't mind," he said. I knew that too, and I did think I'd like to see my old place again. But it was a mistake. The trappings of my old life were all around me, and within hours of us arriving there, I realised that I needed to cast off all my moorings, and float free. That evening, Lucasz suggested that he introduce me to his friend Malcolm, who lived just down the road.

And so, I had to face my biggest dilemma. Malcolm is a dignified, proud man. How would he react to me turning up in a seventeen-year-old body, if I told him who I was? How could we possibly continue our relationship as before? To everyone else, he'd look like a cradle snatcher, a dirty old man. So what could we do, pretend he was my father? Or *Grand*father? People would see through either one pretty fast, I would think. So if I told him I was alive, then I would have to break off the relationship, for his sake more than mine. Only knowing him, he'd have wanted to find a way to make it work, even at the cost of destroying his reputation.

All of this was before we even got into that fact that I was now sleeping with Lucasz. This of course brought up an even deeper issue. My new body had its own rather rampant needs and desires, which could not really be satisfied by a gentle, kind pensioner who mostly liked to cuddle. Relationships can't last when peoples' needs are so different. Telling Malcolm the truth would bring him nothing but confusion and pain.

Locksley had told Malcolm that Julia had died, of course (there I go again – third person). Lucasz spoke to him on the phone, the day after we moved into my old home.

"Is he OK?" I asked, after the call ended.

"Not really," said Lucasz sadly. "He blames himself for Julia dying."

"Well, that's ridiculous," I said, more vehemently than I'd meant to, because I was struggling to stop myself crying.

"What do you know?" he shouted back. "You haven't met him! You weren't there when we chose to help her get into that Glory. She never came back! Her body went limp and I just ran away, like she told me to. We pretty much killed her!"

"Uhh, what I mean is, it's not his fault, or yours. It's Dexter's fault. And Collins, and the ones who helped them."

Lucasz seemed to accept that, but the argument gave me an excuse not to go with him to see Malcolm. Lucasz came home at 11 that evening. I waited up, of course. "He's drinking," said Lucasz. "Too much. I've seen it before in my family. It's like losing her has broken him."

I burst out crying, of course I did. I cried myself to sleep in Lucasz' arms.

* * * * *

I went for a walk on my own the next day. All the places I'd walked with Malcolm, and then to the spot where the Glory had saved my life. Standing there, I wondered again whether I could tell Malcolm the truth, but again all I saw was

Chapter 54: My third life

some horrible entanglement that would blight the lives of all three of us, forever. I needed a clean break. It would mean breaking up with Lucasz as well, and soon, however much that would hurt. But I couldn't leave Malcolm like that. I just couldn't. I had to do something.

So I came up with a plan, one so utterly ridiculous and patently absurd that Lucasz thought I was joking when I explained it. But then I reminded him of all the impossible things that had happened that spring, and also of how he'd once said that I talked a bit like Julia. "That's what gave me the idea," I lied.

Lucasz spent another evening with Malcolm a few days later, and when he came home he said, "Let's do it."

So, Lucasz joined Malcolm for one more drinking session at his home, and at the end of it helped a very drunk Malcolm up to bed. When he was sure Malcolm was asleep, he quietly let me into the house. I was wearing padding, a wig, and my old clothes from the wardrobe in my house, so they smelt of Julia. Talia, it turned out, had had a real talent for voice impersonations, and that plus some coaching from Lucasz (because who really knows what their own voice sounds like?), meant I could do Julia's voice pretty convincingly. How strange, to be impersonating myself!

I walked into Malcolm's room, leaving the landing light on behind me and the door open a crack so he could see me only in silhouette. Then I gently woke him.

"Malcolm. Malcolm, it's me, Julia."

He woke, dazed and open-mouthed. "You're dead," he croaked, despondently.

"Not quite. I'm with the Glories. We're heading away from the Earth. But I wanted to see you, one last time."

His breath reeked of wine. I could just about make out his face in the dim light. It looked strained.

"It can't be. It can't be really you."

I moved a little closer and whispered things to him, secrets we'd made in our short time together.

"Oh, Julia," he said, voice breaking with sadness. "Come back to me."

"I can't," I said, and the lie cut into my heart. "I'll lose contact very soon. I just wanted you to know that I'm OK, and that we made the right decision. If we hadn't, billions of people would have died, you must know that."

"There should have been another way," he moaned. "It shouldn't have had to be you."

"But we couldn't think of anything else, remember? We were the resistance. We couldn't have stood by. We knew there might have to be sacrifices, and we accepted them together. So we did the only thing we could do, the thing that was right, and I'm happy we did it and I'll always love you for how brave and generous you were. But now I have to go."

"I would have married you. Stayed with you forever. Made you happy."

Chapter 54: My third life

"You did," I said, tears streaming down my face. "Oh, Malcolm, you did make me happy, but nothing is ever forever. So I need you to live now. Be happy. Will you do that, my love? Will you live, for me?"

"Yes," he croaked, blowing his nose on the sheets because he couldn't find a tissue. "Yes I will. Can I hold you, one last time?"

"I'm sorry ... I have to go, I'm going to vanish any minute and if you touch me you could get hurt! Goodbye, my love, goodbye."

I was almost blinded by tears as I ran from the room. Malcolm, of course, tumbled out of bed and tried to follow me, but Lucasz, as we'd planned, ran into him on the landing, blocking his way for a few crucial seconds.

"Malcolm? Are you OK?" asked Lucasz. "I heard you talking to someone."

"It was Julia!" Malcolm shouted. "She was here!"

"I heard voices," Lucasz replied. "It sounded like her. But I didn't see anyone else come out of the room."

While Lucasz continued to distract him, I slipped out through the front door, along the pathway, and out of Malcolm's life forever.

A week later, Lucasz told me that Malcolm had stopped drinking and was slowly getting back to his old self. Beginning a new life. As I, soon, would start mine.

EPILOGUE

Jana

I wrote down Antony's part of this story about a month after it happened. His memories were starting to fade in me, so I couldn't hang around. I also believed, quite firmly, that he'd have wanted his story to be told. So I set it all down, while I could still remember it. And then I wrote down Julia's, in case I forgot that too. Then I locked it all away in a box, until now.

No doubt you'll have seen and read all manner of stories about the Glories over the years, some of them true, some of them not. There are morons out there who deny that they ever existed, just as they do climate change, Covid-19 and the Holocaust. Ignore them. I gather the Aussies have made it a running joke, another way to needle the Poms. There are also various cults that have sprung up during the Glory period, or afterwards. Dear old Walt and his group still keep going, in their gentle way. Some are predicting the "Glorious Return," or proclaim that they are a warning from God for us to change our ways. Most are harmless, celebrating each year on G-Day, the day the sky filled with Glories. People have all kinds of 'truths', some of which aren't true at all. But I promise you, every word in this book is what happened.

My dear Tabby, you are now a grown woman. Twenty-one years old. Sixteen and a half years since you lost your grandmother, and now a strange woman has sent you this book, claiming that your Gabba survived, after all. You're probably confused, and angry. But you'd never have understood it if I'd told you at the time, and your parents would never have accepted it. I met you, you know, when you were eight. I came out to New Zealand, went to your street, saw you and your mum walking towards me, and I deliberately dropped my bag, spilling all my stuff. You ran forward and helped pick it up, just as I knew you would. Your mother let me give you a small gift, a little porcelain model of a bird. You said it was exactly like the one Gabba used to have that you had liked, which she always made sure was in the background when she did zoom calls with you. Your mother was surprised you remembered. I pretended I'd got it in a charity shop, but it actually was the exact same one. You told me then that you'd keep it to remind you of Gabba. I hope that you did.

Malcolm's still going strong, I gather, and Lucasz is happily married with kids. We connect from time to time. That's how I know that your father came to Britain when the lockdown was lifted, looking for answers about what happened to me. He found it all hard to believe, of course he did. It will be up to you whether you show this book to him. And it is also entirely your choice whether you want to get in touch with me. I'll totally understand if you don't. I

made the decision to leave behind my old life, and I must accept the consequences, whatever they may be. Know that I am well, that I have lived and loved a lot, and that I will always love you. Always.

Did I write this only for you? Yes and no. Because it really is possible that the Glories might return. I think they've gone dormant, and are slipping quietly forward through time, to wake up and contact us again when they think we are ready. If that happens, then I think it vital that this book be published in full (minus this epilogue, which is only for you). Locksley collated all the facts, but stories can help people to understand the humanity of events, and the decision that will inevitably need to be made, if the Glories come back. But I knew that I owed it to you to tell you the full story first.

I see Antony sometimes, when I am lying in bed, and dreaming. The scenes are incredibly vivid, almost like I am there with him. Perhaps we are still connected in some way, even after all this time. In one kind of dream, he is travelling through space with his cousin, and sometimes with Sally, and always with Taimede close by. I see them standing on alien worlds, watching stars being born or exploding, and other wonders I can't even describe. They even peeked inside a black hole once or twice. The two cousins often laugh together. There's another kind of Antony dream, however. This one is every bit as vivid as the first, yet I don't see how both things can be true, though I suppose somehow they might be. For in this other dream, he is sitting on a bench by a playground in a park, next to a little dark-haired girl, who is also a young woman who looks like me. And they are holding hands. And they are happy.

AUTHOR'S NOTE:

The Glories are, of course, a fiction, but the story leans into real events from that time. The lockdown, the two-metre limit, permitted daily exercise, clapping for the NHS, ambulances queued up outside hospitals – all of those did happen in Britain. Many of the political events mentioned in one chapter really happened too: Dominic Cummings did actually drive over 250 miles to Barnard Castle from London early on during the lockdown, while he had symptoms of Covid. When this was revealed by the Mirror and Guardian newspapers during May 2020, it genuinely put a dent in public support for lockdown, which until that point had been remarkably high. The Health Secretary of the time really did indulge in extra-marital snogging, and the Prime Minister was indeed photographed enjoying a garden party with 18 others, in blatant breach of their own lockdown rules. However, in our reality those images were not leaked to the media until over a year later (June 2021 and December 2021, respectively). As for Boris Johnson's Whatsapp messages, they were all mysteriously erased before the Covid enquiry of 2023 could begin. Barry Collins MP is, of course, entirely fictional.

The virus that caused the pandemic was named "Covid-19" by the World Health Organisation during the winter of 2020, before the lockdown began in the UK. However, the name "Covid", now used by everyone for this virus, did not enter common usage until well after the pandemic had begun, which is why none of the characters in this book refer to it by that name until the epilogue. During the first lockdown it was usually referred to as Coronavirus, Corona, or simply "the virus", at least in Britain.

Printed in Dunstable, United Kingdom